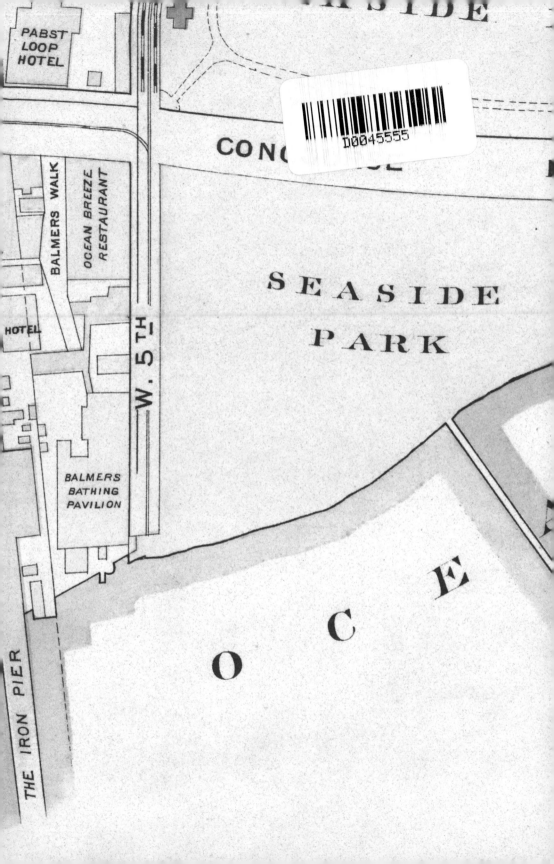

ESCAPING DREAMLAND

ESCAPING DREAMLAND

A NOVEL

CHARLIE LOVETT

BLACK STONE
PUBLISHING

Copyright © 2020 by Charlie Lovett
Published in 2020 by Blackstone Publishing
Cover and book design by Sean M. Thomas

Printed in the United States of America

First edition: 2020
ISBN 978-1-982629-40-3
Fiction / Historical / General

1 3 5 7 9 10 8 6 4 2

CIP data for this book is available
from the Library of Congress

Blackstone Publishing
31 Mistletoe Rd.
Ashland, OR 97520

www.BlackstonePublishing.com

For Bookmarks

History is happening in Manhattan,
and we just happen to be
in the greatest city in the world.
—Lin-Manuel Miranda

VE DAY, MAY 8, 1945

On those rare occasions when Magda thought of the past, she didn't recall the flames and the screams and the rows of bodies; she came here—to these mementos gathered in an old shoebox, souvenirs not of tragedy but of happiness. She was old enough now, she thought, to know that she had loved them both, but had not been *in love* with either one of them. Perhaps if she had realized that at the time, the particular happiness she had felt that golden summer would have lasted longer, but that didn't matter now. There had been many more days, and months, and years of happiness in Magda's life—sometimes enriched by the occasional glance back, but never dependent upon the contents of that box and the summer they evoked. The box contained only paper and ink, only glimpses into who she had been, who the three of them had been together. But her memory, even at this far remove, held all those long summer days of her youth, and she could return to them, and to Dreamland, whenever she liked, not with wistful regret, but with true joy.

Before Magda replaced the contents, she gently laid the two letters in the box. She doubted they would ever be opened, but their presence comforted her. While her memory held happiness, the box held secrets and hopes. By closing that lid, Magda allowed herself to go on with her life not burdened by those hopes, but secure in the knowledge that, so long as that box survived, those hopes would not be extinguished. She slid the box onto the top shelf of her closet and stepped outside to join the celebration in the streets.

I

NEW YORK CITY, UPPER WEST SIDE, 2008

It had been such a perfect day that he had nearly told her. As much as he loved Rebecca, as excited as he was to finally sell a short story to an established literary magazine, as beautiful as Central Park had looked as they took their afternoon walk, Robert's favorite part of that day had been those four hours from ten until two when he sat alone doing what he had dreamed of doing since childhood—writing. He never had any illusions that writing would be easy, especially since, in college, he had felt the pull toward literary fiction. He knew he would not sit at a computer as words streamed like clear water from a mountain spring. But the difficulty of the task, the frequent drudgery of forcing words and sentences and paragraphs out of his head and onto a blank screen, made those days when the words *did* flow effortlessly all the more glorious. On that spring day, with the window of his rented room on West End Avenue open, the cool air wafting in, and the cacophony of New York punctuating his work, Chapter Eight had appeared before him almost unbidden. It had taken months to write Chapter Seven, and Robert did not begrudge a minute of the time he had spent prying that narrative loose, banging at it, shaping it, honing it. He embraced every one of ten false starts and scores of discarded pages because each had led to a realization, an understanding of where his words needed to go. Yes, he loved the sheer, sweat-inducing work that writing demanded of him most of the time. But how much more did he love those days, so few and far between, when the starts were not false, the pages not discarded, and the words—instead of clinging to the ether until he wrenched them free—exploded onto the page almost of their own volition.

At two o'clock, when Robert felt that hardly ten minutes had passed since he had sat down to work, Rebecca had sailed into the room bearing pastrami sandwiches from Katz's and a smile that sparkled like the sun on the Hudson. They had been seeing each other for just over a year, and that smile smote him every time.

"I love having a client on the Lower East Side," she said, kissing him on the cheek and handing him a thick foil packet. "They may be a bit soggy after the ride uptown, but Katz's still has the best pastrami in town. How is your day? Because mine is great."

Nothing could make good news better like sharing it with Rebecca, and as they sat cross-legged on the floor savoring thick slabs of pastrami between dissolving slices of rye bread, Robert narrated his day—first the mail informing him that his story "Novelty and Romancement" had been accepted by *Ploughshares* and then the fountain of writing that had produced a fully formed chapter in a single sitting.

"Okay," said Rebecca, leaning back against the sofa with a groan of the gluttonous and not bothering to wipe the mustard from her face. "Your day is clearly even better than mine. Read to me."

Rebecca was Robert's most careful, and most honest, critic. It was one of the reasons he loved her. She thought deeply about his writing and reacted to it with complete candor and profound wisdom, never afraid to tell him to throw something away and start over. Robert could not easily earn her praise, so it came with weight when she did bestow it. That day she had sat with eyes closed and hands folded over her pastrami-stuffed belly as he read Chapter Eight.

When he finished, Rebecca remained silent for a long minute. Robert knew she needed time to digest his words. Finally, she opened her eyes, took a deep breath, and looked at him.

"You wrote that all today?"

"It sounds like it, doesn't it," said Robert. "I rushed it. I shouldn't have rushed it. It just . . ."

"No," said Rebecca firmly, silencing Robert's blathering. "It's beautiful."

"Really?"

"A tweak here and there, you can go over it sentence by sentence later on, but where it goes and how it gets there—Robert, this is some of your best work."

Robert felt light-headed as he looked into her eyes with a swell of pride. "You really think so?"

"All that work you did on Chapter Seven made this possible, you know."

"Do you think?"

"What is it?" said Rebecca. "You're looking at me funny."

"I just suddenly really want to kiss the mustard off your face."

"It's three o'clock in the afternoon," said Rebecca, biting her lower lip ever so slightly.

"So?"

"So," she said, pulling him toward her, "you know when your writing astounds me, it's just about the sexiest thing in the world."

⌒⌒

Afterward, Rebecca made Robert read her the chapter again, and then they walked down Seventy-Second Street and into the park, meandering through the Sheep Meadow and ending up watching children on the carousel.

"I remember when I was that age," said Rebecca, nodding at a gaggle of preteen girls climbing onto the horses. "God, you would have hated my childhood literary tastes. I couldn't get enough of Nancy Drew and the Dana Girls and Cherry Ames. You know those horrid series books? I cringe to think how many hours I spent with them when I could have been reading something good."

Robert let her words hang in the air without comment, hoping they would drift away on the music of the carousel, but just when the topic seemed about to evaporate, she added, "How about you? What did you read as a kid? Probably Dickens or George Eliot."

And there it was—the opportunity to begin a conversation he had been putting off for months, a conversation he had avoided with every woman he had ever met, a conversation that began so simply with the words, "I loved series books, too! I loved the Hardy Boys and Tom Swift and the Great Marvel books and, yes, Nancy Drew." A brave man would have dived right in. A wise man would have known the moment had come at last. But, Robert thought, he was neither of those things. He was a frightened man, a cowardly man, a man just smart enough to recognize that his own insecurities efficiently destroyed relationships.

Maybe if the day had not been so perfect—if he had received a rejection slip in the mail and had labored for hours to write a few sentences, if it had been hot and humid or cold and rainy, if Rebecca hadn't brought him Katz's pastrami and made love to him on the floor—then he might have told her. Not everything, perhaps, but at least the beginning, at least enough so that the rest could unfold over the next days and weeks. But he had neither the heart nor the courage to turn the compass of such a rare day toward things he had done his best to forget for so long.

"It took me a while to develop a taste for fine literature," said Robert. It wasn't a lie; it simply didn't delve deeply into the truth. "How about some ice cream?" He took Rebecca by the hand.

"Can we eat ice cream after all that pastrami?" she said.

"On a day like this," said Robert, "anything's possible."

That night, as Rebecca lay sleeping in the Murphy bed, Robert sat at the table—which served as both dining room and office—looking at an envelope from *Ploughshares* addressed to "Mr. Robert Parrish," a printout of Chapter Eight with a few minor edits in Rebecca's hand, and a wadded-up ball of foil that still smelled of pastrami. He saw them as items in a scrapbook, souvenirs of the sort of day that made all his work worthwhile. But niggling in the back of his head as he delayed cleaning off the table for a fresh start tomorrow, was the conversation he had avoided with Rebecca at the carousel. She had grown up on Nancy Drew and the Dana Girls. She had spent rainy afternoons with Cherry Ames. She would certainly understand his repressed love for the Hardy Boys and Tom Swift and the Tremendous Trio.

It had been a long time since he had thought about the Tremendous Trio books—they didn't come up during discussions in MFA programs or over coffee with the members of his writers' group. That Rebecca had given him a conversational opening to reminisce over the books that first made him want to write only proved how well-suited they were as a couple. But he simply couldn't bring himself to dredge up all that now, when life seemed so perfect.

Still, Robert fell asleep thinking of those adventure stories and of how they had changed his life for the better. And for the worse.

"Robbie" Parrish had been born in 1976, much too late to have bought any of the books he cherished new at a bookstore. The books themselves might not have seemed so important, if it hadn't been for the way they changed his relationship with his father. Robbie was a scrawny introvert, his father a hulking sportsman with a booming voice and a backslapping personality perfectly fitted to his career as a car salesman. Not that Robbie's father didn't make every effort to connect with his son. He took Robbie to baseball games and built endless sandcastles with him on the beach. He let Robbie pick the TV shows each evening and talked to him about *Happy Days* or *Little House on the Prairie* the next morning at breakfast. But Robbie could always sense the effort, and just as he didn't care for the baseball games, he knew his father didn't care for Robbie's favorite shows. Despite his best intentions, Robbie's father remained something of a stranger.

This was never truer than during the family's annual summer visit to Robbie's grandfather, Pop Pop, in Bloomfield, New Jersey. Pop Pop was a career army man, and even in his seventies he remained more rough and tough and loud than Robbie's father. The two men would try to include Robbie in their boisterousness, but the boy preferred to sit on the tiny front porch and read. Then one summer during this sojourn, a hurricane struck and flooded the streets of Bloomfield. When Pop Pop discovered water in the basement, he enlisted Robbie's help in moving some boxes upstairs.

Robbie set one of the boxes down on the Formica counter of Pop

Pop's kitchen and idly lifted the loose cardboard flap. Inside, he saw four neat stacks of cloth-bound books, their covers frayed and worn. He could still remember the four books on the top, the first four volumes of the Great Marvel series: *Through the Air to the North Pole*, *Under the Ocean to the South Pole*, *Five Thousand Miles Underground*, and *Through Space to Mars*. Each book had a picture on the cover—an airship, a submarine, a flying boat, and a space rocket.

"What are these?" said Robbie, carefully lifting *Through Space to Mars* from the box.

"Those are my childhood," said Pop Pop, taking the book from Robbie.

"My childhood, too, Dad," said Robbie's father, removing a book from the box to reveal another tantalizingly illustrated cover underneath. "How many hours did we spend reading these together?"

"Hundreds," said Pop Pop.

"Can I read one?" said Robbie.

"Honestly, Robbie," said his mother, who had just stepped into the room. "Can't you read a *good* book?" Robbie's mother had strong opinions about what constituted "good" reading. His usual fare of comic books and *Mad* magazine did not qualify.

"What's wrong with them?" said his father.

"They're . . ." his mother began.

"You've never read a single one of these books, have you?" said his father.

"I don't have to read them," said Robbie's mother.

"Here," said his father, handing Robbie *Through the Air to the North Pole*. "Start with this one." He leaned over and whispered into the boy's ear. "And don't listen to your mother."

At eight, Robbie would have been intrigued enough by the titles and the illustrated bindings of his grandfather's childhood books to read at least one. That his mother disapproved made them that much more desirable. But that reading these books might provide some common ground with his father, a shared conspiracy even, sent Robbie straight to his room, clutching the book like some rare treasure.

The book his father had handed him exuded a musty, slightly mildewed odor. Robbie would grow to love that smell. He would love the rough texture of cheap wood-pulp paper between his fingers and the random blotches and smudges that came with poor-quality printing.

By the end of the afternoon, he had seen teenagers Mark Sampson and Jack Darrow (along with Professor Henderson, the inventor) safely to the North Pole and had started on another book. Two days later, as the family packed to return home to Rockaway Beach, Pop Pop put a box of books in the back of the Oldsmobile station wagon. On the drive home Robbie's father peppered him with questions about the first two Great Marvel books. Even though he hadn't read the books in decades, he remembered enough to talk to Robbie about Professor Henderson and Mark and Jack all the way home. It was the best conversation Robbie had ever had with his father.

Over the next three years, all of the books Robbie and Pop Pop had rescued from the basement that rainy summer migrated to the rough shelves of Robbie's bedroom closet—not just the Great Marvel series by Roy Rockwood, but adventure series like the Dave Dashaway books about a young aviator, sports books like the Baseball Joe series, and school stories like the Rover Boys. The exploits of the boy inventor Tom Swift filled two shelves—dozens of adventures involving prescient stories of inventions like his wizard camera, his photo telephone, and his electric rifle. And of course, there were the mystery series, especially the Hardy Boys.

Robbie read every series over and over, often aloud with his father. When he read alone in his room, he would rush to talk to his father about each adventure as soon as he finished the book. Robbie's mother rolled her eyes whenever her son or husband brought up the topic of Tom Swift or the Hardy Boys, but Robbie often caught her smiling when she turned her head away. Mrs. Parrish was as happy as Robbie that he and his father had discovered a shared passion.

Pop Pop died when Robbie was eleven, leaving in the Bloomfield house a box marked "For Robbie." Inside, he discovered four short-lived series that had never made it past their first three volumes: Daring Dan Dawson, a series about a young circus daredevil who was always in the right place to perform spectacular rescues after dramatic disasters; Alice Gold, Girl Inventor, about a brilliant girl whose inventions are largely confined to the domestic sphere; Frank Fairfax, Cub Reporter, about a boy who goes to work for a newspaper and is assigned to various expeditions in search of lost civilizations; and, finally, a series involving all three of these youngsters and their adventures together—the Tremendous Trio.

"These were my favorites," said Robbie's father, surreptitiously wiping a tear from his eye. "And your grandfather's as well. We read them over and over together."

They became Robbie's favorites, too. He had not encountered the authors (Dexter Cornwall, Buck Larson, and Neptune B. Smythe) in any of the other series he had read, but their style seemed superior to the likes of Roy Rockwood and Victor Appleton. At an earlier age, Robbie might not have noticed this distinction, but the prose of Buck Larson made even the tame adventures of Alice Gold, condemned by the mores of the early 1900s to invent housecleaning machines and kitchen gadgets, exciting. Dan Dawson's adventures teetered closer to reality than any of the series he had read. Robbie's father explained that the unnamed disasters of Dan's first two books were based on real catastrophes—the 1900 Galveston hurricane and the 1906 San Francisco earthquake. Years later Robert would realize that the 1903 Iroquois Theatre fire in Chicago inspired the third volume, *Dan Dawson and the Big Fire.* The expeditions in the Frank Fairfax books mostly provided an opportunity for Frank to get into and out of trouble, but every now and then he would overhear a snippet of conversation that made Robbie sense there was a much more adult sort of danger bubbling under the surface of those escapades.

The stories became even more exciting in the Tremendous Trio books. Now disasters, daredevil stunts, inventions, and exploration all mixed together in nonstop adventures. Alice invented a barrel in which Dan could go over Niagara Falls, but Frank discovered someone had sabotaged the craft, and danger, hijinks, cleverness, a daring rescue, and a triumph over the bad guys ensued in rapid succession—that sort of thing.

Robbie had loved the Tremendous Trio, and loved sharing the stories with his father, until three children—Dan Dawson, Alice Gold, and Frank Fairfax—had ruined everything.

II

THREE CHILDREN IN NEW YORK CITY,
IN THE DAYS OF HORSES AND HANSOM CABS

Even at age four, Magda thought of herself not just as an American, but as a New Yorker, and she had never been prouder of her city.

On a cool Saturday afternoon in October of 1886, when the breeze had blown away the damp of the recent rains, her father brought his wife and daughter from their home in the "Kleindeutschland" neighborhood of the Lower East Side of Manhattan to Battery Park at the island's southern tip to see a sculpture that had been dedicated two days earlier. President Grover Cleveland had led a parade from Madison Square down Fifth Avenue, passing only a few blocks from where the Hertzenbergers lived. Magda had begged to see the parade, but her father had insisted the crowds were too dangerous. "On Saturday, my Magdalena," he had said. "On Saturday we shall go and see her."

For the rest of her life Magda would remember that Saturday as a series of images, like engravings in *Frank Leslie's Illustrated Newspaper*, but with color—the blue sky with white clouds reflecting in the water of the harbor, the fading green of the grass in the park, the dull red brick of nearby Castle Garden. As meaningful as that building had been to Magda's family, her father directed the attention of his wife and daughter elsewhere that day, out across the water to Bedloe's Island.

There stood a copper-colored woman, her arm raised to the sky and bearing a torch. Magda's father called her Liberty Enlightening the World, though most people Magda would meet over the years—as the sculpture gradually turned from brown to green—would call her simply the Statue of Liberty.

"Isn't she beautiful?" said Magda's father, and she replied with a smile and a vigorous wave at the torch-bearing lady in the distance.

A trip to the tip of Manhattan Island was something special for the Hertzenbergers, an experience Magda would not repeat for many years. But there had been another sight on the harbor that day, one her father had not expected. As they stood in the wind, Magda clutching her mother's hand, a three-masted steamship with two closely set funnels belching smoke cruised slowly past the statue. As she made a slight turn, the ship's name became visible on her port side: SS *Hammonia*.

"Wilhelmina," said Magda's father with a gasp. "It is her! It is the *Hammonia!*"

"Why, so it is," said Magda's mother, an expression of pure delight washing across her face.

"Who is she?" said Magda. "Who is the *Hammonia*?"

"My dear Magdalena," said her father, "the *Hammonia* is the ship that brought us here from Hamburg. She began our New York adventure."

⸙

At the age of eight, Thomas just wanted to play baseball in the park like any normal kid did in 1890.

Instead, imprisoned in a black woolen suit, a starched white collar that dug into his neck, and a black necktie that seemed certain to strangle him, he nearly disappeared in the miles of silk that billowed around his sisters, Florence, Emily, Eliza, and Alice, as the carriage bumped down Fourth Avenue past the Lyceum Theatre and turned onto Twenty-Third Street. At eight, Thomas De Peyster was well removed in nearly every aspect from his older sisters, who ranged in age from thirteen to eighteen, so, although there was novelty to this excursion, he took no great delight in it.

The studio was at the top of a narrow building at 115 West Twenty-Third, and the process of hoisting skirts and climbing several flights of stairs that had not been constructed to accommodate the dresses of Fifth Avenue ladies promised to take some time. Thomas managed to shoot out of the carriage as soon as it pulled up to the curb and spring up the stairs, arriving in a room smelling of turpentine. At one end of the room stood a serious man with graying hair and a clean-shaven face, his thumbs hooked in his pockets. Across from him, holding a brush and staring at a canvas propped on an easel, stood a young man with a neatly trimmed beard wearing a shirt smudged with paint—the man that Thomas, his sisters, and their mother had come to see, an artist named John Singer Sargent.

Thomas had already met Mr. Sargent when the painter had come to the family home on Fifth Avenue to pick out the dresses his sisters and mother would wear in their portrait. He had not looked into Thomas's wardrobe, only saying, "Put the boy in a black suit." Thomas blamed Mr. Sargent personally for his present discomfort, but the artist seemed not to know this, and greeted the boy heartily.

"Young Master De Peyster. A very good afternoon to you."

"Hello," groused Thomas, plopping himself down on a small divan shoved against the wall under the window.

"Do you know who this distinguished gentleman is?" said Mr. Sargent.

"Is he Oyster Burns?" asked Thomas, sitting up hopefully. Though his father refused to allow him to attend a game, calling it lower-class, Tom followed the exploits of his favorite baseball team, the Brooklyn Bridegrooms, in the newspapers. Oyster Burns had hit over .300 last season, helping the Bridegrooms to win the American Association championship and becoming Thomas's idol.

Mr. Sargent shook his head and the man posing for his portrait burst out laughing. "I'm afraid I'm not quite as distinguished as Oyster Burns," he said. "I'm just an actor." He walked across the room in two long strides and held his hand out to Thomas. "Edwin Booth at your service."

Thomas reluctantly shook the man's hand, at the same time catching Mr. Sargent's eye. "You really should try to get Oyster Burns," the boy said. "That could make you famous." On this note of wisdom, Mrs. De Peyster entered the room, trailing both a train of blue silk and a quartet of daughters.

The rest of the afternoon, and several afternoons that followed, proceeded with far less excitement than Thomas's brief fantasy of meeting Oyster Burns. While Mr. Sargent always introduced his guests to Thomas—for the boy invariably bounded up the stairs ahead of the De Peyster women, arriving before the previous visitor or sitter had departed—none of the men Thomas met provided anything like the pleasure that meeting a professional baseball player would have. Mr. Sargent seemed to take great amusement in these introductions, presenting men to Thomas with the words, "While I have not the pleasure of introducing Mr. Oyster Burns, do say hello to Mr. Henry James." Or Mr. Stanford White. Or some other mister who had some dull job such as architect or novelist or, worst of all, banker.

On the family's final trip to Mr. Sargent's studio, Thomas arrived to find the room occupied by another family—a mother, a daughter on the brink of womanhood, and a girl about his own age. She had blond hair held back in a green silk bow and a matching sash wrapped around a dress concocted out of more layers of lace than Thomas cared to imagine. Kneeling next to her mother and pretending to examine a colored engraving, she looked as miserable as Thomas felt sitting still in his razor-like white collar for two hours every afternoon.

As soon as Mr. Sargent saw Thomas, he set down his brush and said, "That will be all for this afternoon, Mrs. Vanderbilt. An excellent start, I think. Your daughters are patient sitters. Not like some young people I know." Here he shot a surreptitious smile at Thomas. Mrs. Vanderbilt, whom Mr. Sargent did not introduce—perhaps because Thomas could not possibly mistake her for Oyster Burns—immediately began gathering her skirts and her daughters and was just about to leave when Mrs. De Peyster and her retinue of female offspring came through the door. For a moment the room seemed so filled with skirts that Thomas wasn't sure he could breathe.

"Mrs. Vanderbilt, how lovely to see you," said Thomas's mother.

"And you, Mrs. De Peyster," said Mrs. Vanderbilt in a voice that belied her words. "Come, girls." Without further discussion, the Vanderbilts filed from the room and Florence, Emily, Eliza, and Alice began to place themselves in their usual arrangement.

"Did you speak to Amelia?" hissed his mother at Thomas.

"Who's Amelia?" said Thomas.

"That young girl in the green and white. Amelia Vanderbilt."

"Why would I speak to her?" said Thomas.

"Why indeed?" said Mr. Sargent. "Mr. De Peyster reserves his conversation for gentlemen named Oyster."

Mrs. De Peyster ignored Mr. Sargent. "It's just as well," she said. "This is hardly the place for a proper introduction, and perhaps we should wait until you are a little older."

"Wait for what?" said Thomas.

"Your father and I have discussed it," said his mother, "and we agree that Miss Amelia Vanderbilt would be a perfect match for you."

"Match?" said Thomas, as Mr. Sargent shooed him into his place of discomfort next to Alice.

"She means," said Eliza in a tone of great superiority, "that she wants you and Amelia to get married."

Before Thomas could react to this pronouncement with words that would certainly have appalled his mother and everyone else in the room, Mr. Sargent said in a loud voice, "Now, silent and still."

Thomas remained silent on the carriage ride home, but he pressed his nose against the window, eager to see parts of the city he did not often have a chance to observe. In the mouth of an alley, he spotted a clutch of boys about his own age, dressed in shabby clothing, playing some sort of game. He longed to know who they were, what game they were playing, what life was like outside the bubble of the De Peyster home. He tried to see their faces clearly to discern if they were as happy as they should be that none of them would ever have to marry Amelia Vanderbilt, but the carriage rattled quickly by, and within a few minutes he saw only the mansions of Fifth Avenue.

Eugene Pinkney lived for those days when he could snatch an hour or two of quiet solitude at his family's apartment on Broome Street reading a book—preferably something about science or the future.

For his tenth birthday in 1892, he had hoped for an excursion to Brentano's bookstore on Union Square and a generous allowance for making purchases. Instead, Eugene's father took him to the bakery on Houston Street where he worked six days a week in order to celebrate with the other bakers. Mrs. Pinkney joined the excursion, and while Eugene enjoyed the fuss his father's coworkers made over him, and enjoyed—even more—the freshly baked treats with which they showered him, it hardly seemed a special occasion. Eugene had stopped by the bakery at least a hundred times, and the men always made a fuss and filled him with warm rolls.

That afternoon, however, with the summer sun still beating down despite the fact that dinnertime was fast approaching, Mrs. Pinkney had led the walk back home, holding Eugene's hand and proceeding at a pace Eugene knew to be more leisurely than Mr. Pinkney would have preferred. Eugene did not often have a chance to walk along the street with both of his parents. The heat of the afternoon had broken and a soft breeze blew along Houston Street from river to river. Mr. Pinkney generally walked home via Broadway, but Eugene's mother turned down the quieter Mott Street instead.

Eugene thought nothing of the change until, near the end of the block, they came into sight of St. Patrick's Old Cathedral. The Pinkneys came from Jewish ancestors, but Eugene's parents had never taken him to a synagogue or mentioned anything about religion to him; as a result he had a certain curiosity about places of worship. Early on a Friday evening, neatly dressed men, women, and children crowded the street in front of St. Patrick's, making their way into the church for Mass. Eugene glanced across the street at the crowd and was just about to ask his parents what went on inside a Catholic church when he saw her.

The girl herself did not attract his attention. He'd never had much interest in girls. But her dress—Eugene's eyes widened at the sight of her dress. He did not know why. He had, after all, seen girls wearing white dresses in the streets nearly every day of his life. But something about the way the lowering sun caught the ripples of the fabric and cast shadows through the layer of lace made him shiver. Ribbons of silk glistened along the hem and in the bodice. She was just about his age, perhaps a little older. As they passed, Eugene turned his head to keep looking at her. The age didn't matter, he thought. The important thing was that she was just about his size.

"Glad to see you looking at a pretty girl," said his father as they reached the end of the block, but Eugene barely heard him. He was imagining, with such a fervor that he broke into a cold sweat, what it would be like to wear that dress.

III

Robert hung up the phone with a sigh. Why did they always have to ask that same question? And why couldn't he at least tell the same lie every time they did? Almost as soon as he replaced the receiver, the phone started ringing again. "It never ends," he mumbled to himself.

Robert sat at his desk in the apartment he shared with Rebecca, looking out the window onto the bare trees that lined their block of the Upper West Side of Manhattan. Rebecca would answer the phone eventually, he thought. She had answered the phone a lot over the past five months—months that followed the achievement they had both celebrated with such enthusiasm at the time: the publication in the fall of 2009 of his first novel, *Looking Forward*.

The title, chosen with help from Rebecca, alluded to Edward Bellamy's largely forgotten 1888 novel *Looking Backward*—a portrait of a socialist America in the year 2000 that had been one of the best-selling books of the nineteenth century. *Looking Forward* presented a landscape of America in 2100 that, *Publishers Weekly* wrote, "occupies a deliciously ambiguous region between dystopia and utopia and establishes Parrish as a leading visionary of our age."

But Robert didn't feel like a visionary. He felt like a man who'd had one great idea and then labored and toiled for years to turn that idea into a book.

He had reached the pinnacle of his dreams, only to realize that all roads led down. The critics had hailed him as a "bold new voice," with "something important to say," and for the past five months, journalists and critics and readers had wanted him to say something *else* important. He understood, he thought, how to write a novel, but he felt eminently unqualified to *be* a novelist—to talk to audiences at bookstores and sit on panels at festivals and answer questions about the state of the literary world.

A new idea would solve the problem, he thought. A new idea would allow him to deflect those conversations with journalists to the topic of his next novel. It would answer the questions from his agent and his editor about what he was working on. It would even give him a way to reconnect with Rebecca. It seemed like a lifetime since he had read Chapter Eight to her on that perfect spring day when they had both been so excited to discuss his work in progress. A new idea could bring that excitement back. But Robert didn't have a new idea.

The phone rang on. Those interviewers had started it, he thought. He'd been fine before they started prying and asking that question, never worded exactly the same, but always cutting to the same bone. The same question, essentially, that Rebecca had asked him at the carousel two years ago: What books inspired you to write?

"Robert, will you for the love of God answer the phone," Rebecca shouted from the living room. He pushed it across his desk and let it ring.

He hated that question, not just because he couldn't tell the truth— he couldn't tell the *New Yorker* or *The Atlantic* that his inspiration came not from Tolstoy or Fitzgerald but from the Hardy Boys and Tom Swift and the Tremendous Trio. He hated that question because of what lurked under the answer. The beast he had left undisturbed for twenty years. That damn question had woken it up.

"Does it require such a Herculean effort to pick up a telephone?" Robert turned to see Rebecca leaning in the doorway. She didn't sound angry or annoyed, just tired. Her hair hung in her face and she had a pencil tucked behind her ear.

"I thought it might be for you," said Robert.

"It's never for me."

"Just let it ring, then."

"I don't want to let it ring. What if I'd had a client out there?"

Rebecca ran her interior design business out of an office in Chelsea, but she sometimes worked at home, and the dining table was often covered with fabric samples and paint chips.

"Do you have a client?"

"Not the point," said Rebecca. "It was *New York* magazine this time."

"You didn't have to answer it."

"I did if I wanted any peace."

"I don't want to talk to *New York* magazine."

"It doesn't bother me that you won't talk to *New York* magazine. I mean if you want to go all J. D. Salinger on the literary world, that's fine by me." She stood silently for a moment, twisting a strand of hair around a finger. "But I don't understand why you won't talk to me."

Oh God, thought Robert. Here we go. He had been deflecting this conversation like an Olympic fencer for months now. "I have work to do," he said.

"What work? You don't do any work. You're thirty-four years old and all you do is sit in your office watching YouTube. I would think you were having an affair, but you never leave the apartment."

"We went out to lunch yesterday."

"We went out to lunch last week," said Rebecca. "And you barely spoke to me. You just sat there poking at your Reuben. It feels like you're hiding from me."

"I'm not hiding," said Robert.

"You are. You're just like your mother. You always say she's been hiding in Florida ever since your father died. You may be on the West Side instead of in Boca Raton, but you're still absent."

In fact, Robert's mother had called him on his cell just last week, but he wasn't about to tell Rebecca that. He had let it go to voicemail and hadn't returned the call. He never did. For so long his mother had not wanted to talk to him that when she had started calling after his book came out, he found the thought of reconciliation frightening.

After Robert got the advance on his novel and Rebecca landed a particularly lucrative client, they had moved into the top floor of a brownstone on Seventy-Fourth Street between Columbus and Amsterdam. The room the real estate agent had described, a year ago, as "great for a nursery" had become Robert's writing studio—though Rebecca was right, there had been precious little writing going on in it lately. And now . . . well, why shouldn't he talk to Rebecca? Why should he feel so alone and yet so unwilling to reach out to the one person who might break into his solitude? He thought he knew the answer, but he couldn't say it aloud. "I'm just . . . dealing with some . . . issues," he said at last.

"Okay, fine," said Rebecca. "You have some issues. We all do. But aren't we a partnership? Don't we love each other? That means we help each other with those issues. You can talk to me, Robert. I'm here for you."

"I know," he said.

"And yet you still say nothing."

"What do you want from me?" said Robert in a tone of resignation. He knew the answer and he felt a stab of pain accompany the knowledge that he could not give it to her. He had been here before—never in a relationship as promising as the one he had with Rebecca, but, in some way or other, with every girl he had ever dated. He always pushed them away.

"I want *you* from you," she said, laying a hand on his arm. "I just want you. I miss you."

"I'm right here."

"Somebody's here, but it's not Robert Parrish, at least not the Robert Parrish I fell in love with. He was a man who told me stories. When was the last time you told me a story?"

Robert didn't answer, not only because the question made him uncomfortable, but because he honestly could not remember.

"I remember lying in bed the first night we moved in together," said Rebecca, "and you told me a story about your freshman roommate getting up to go running every morning at six. It was almost the end of the semester when you discovered he was just sitting in a coffee shop for two hours and making you feel lazy."

"Not much of a story."

"That's not the point. You once said telling stories is what makes us human. And you used to tell me stories every night in bed. I've fallen asleep to your voice a thousand times. And then a few months ago you just stopped. And now I fall asleep alone to the sound of our favorite movies in my earbuds. What happened, Robert?"

He should have told her right then. She had asked a simple question, and he should have answered. He could have been brave but instead he had been a coward. It was the carousel all over again.

Even before the official publication of *Looking Forward*, the interviews began. First small newspapers and magazines, then, as it became clear the book would make a splash, more and more prestigious outlets. And every one of those journalists asked some version of that question: What books inspired you? And even while he lied and said that *A Farewell to Arms* or *The Sound and the Fury* had changed his life, the real story, the story he had spent two decades trying to suppress bubbled up inside him. That story began with the answer to the ubiquitous question. He certainly wasn't going to tell it to some book reviewer he had never met; he couldn't imagine telling it to Rebecca. Even the idea of confessing it to a therapist turned his stomach. He had tried therapy twice—once during graduate school and once just before he met Rebecca, but it had only proven how good he was at hiding the truth. When Rebecca came into his life, he felt so happy that he figured he didn't need a shrink anymore, that he could just forget the story of his past and embrace the future. This time, he told himself, the relationship would work. But now, all those journalists poking at his past and waking up the story he had tried so hard to leave slumbering had left him unable to tell any *other* story, unable to move forward.

"Maybe I ran out of stories," he said at last.

"I doubt that," said Rebecca. "You know, I watched *The Princess Bride* last night."

"What does that have to do with anything?"

"It's the first time since we met that I've watched it without you."

"Did you do the voices?" said Robert. One of their favorite activities was to put on a much-loved movie—*Princess Bride* or *Casablanca* or *North by Northwest*—and mute certain scenes, reciting the dialogue from memory.

"I wasn't going to do Inigo without you doing Westley," she said.

The first time Robert told Rebecca he loved her he hadn't used the traditional words. They had been dating about six months and were walking back to his apartment after seeing a film when Rebecca suggested they stop off for a bowl of clam chowder. He knew she loved *The Princess Bride*—they had already watched it together twice. So, he took a deep breath, took her hand in his, looked her in the eyes, and said, "As you wish." She knew exactly what he meant and answered simply, "Me too."

"It wasn't much fun watching it without you," said Rebecca.

"I was working," said Robert. He felt his face flush red with the guilt of the lie. He had been up until two solving crossword puzzles—something they had always done together. She dropped her hand from his arm and turned away. Robert knew that she knew he was lying, that something had shifted in the room.

"Remember the last time we watched that movie together?" she said. "It was right before your book came out and afterward we talked into the night about all the ways we might end up riding into the sunset. We might get married or not. We might have children or not. We had the excitement of possibilities."

"We still might get married," said Robert. "We might have kids." At the moment little terrified him more than these two prospects, but perhaps he wouldn't always feel this way. Perhaps someday he would be ready to share with his own children the stories of his childhood—those books that had once meant so much to him. If he could do it without waking the monster.

He had read so many of those books, and it had been so long ago, that he couldn't remember specific details of all the stories, but he did remember the old-fashioned language, especially the almost obsessive need by the writers never to use the word *said*. The Hardy Boys and Tom Swift never *said* anything. They shouted, ordered, cried, exclaimed (they cried and exclaimed with astonishing frequency), whispered, muttered, announced, stammered, retorted, demanded, sneered, declared, and (his favorite once he discovered its double meaning) ejaculated. By the time Robert reached twelve, he would have to stifle a laugh every time a character "ejaculated loudly."

The habitual crying and exclaiming arose from the dangerous situations in which the heroes found themselves in nearly every chapter. Tied up by bandits, balanced on runaway vehicles, attacked by wild animals, swept away by floods, thrown off cliffs, trapped in fires—the teenage heroes of his favorite books always had plenty of reason to cry and exclaim.

". . . and that's one of the reasons I thought you would make a great father—because you're such a good storyteller. Besides . . . are you even listening to me?" said Rebecca.

Cried Rebecca, he thought, but he did not answer because he could not bear to say, "No."

"Maybe I should just go to Bradley's for a while," said Rebecca. "He at least pays attention when I talk to him."

"You're always going to Bradley's," said Robert. "Maybe I'm the one who should worry about your having an affair."

"Oh, for God's sake," said Rebecca. "You know Bradley is gay."

"Yes, and I know you've never gotten over that fact. That was practically the first story *you* told *me*. 'I was in love and then he told me he was gay and broke my heart.'" Robert knew he should apologize before the words were even out of his mouth. So why didn't he? Why didn't he tell her why he was acting so distant? He felt as if he were observing himself from across the room. He had seen this movie before, had watched himself ruin a relationship because of his stupid fear of opening up, of admitting his own faults and weaknesses and history. He had regretted those train wrecks, but nothing like the way he would regret losing Rebecca. Yet still the idiot across the room kept driving toward the cliff.

"Why should you care, anyway?" she said. "You and I haven't had sex in three months." The gloves were off now, and Robert ached to rewind the conversation, to find the spot where it had gone off the rails. But he knew the problem was deeper than one conversation. And it was true—the first aspect of their intimacy to drop by the wayside as he became more and more troubled by his secrets had been their sex life. Somehow, he didn't feel right reaching for her in that way when he was holding back so much. He had missed it to begin with, had caught furtive glances of Rebecca stepping out of the shower or gazed at the curve of her shoulder as she slept. But as he slipped deeper into solitude, he no longer replayed those images in his mind. He forgot about sex as he forgot about so much else.

"We could . . ." said Robert, not even able to muster the enthusiasm to finish the sentence.

"Could what? Do it right here on the floor?"

"Well, not right now," he said, "but maybe sometime."

"You really don't get it, do you?" she said. "It's not about the sex—that's just a symptom. It's that you're not connected to me anymore, and I don't understand why. I don't understand what I did." She began to cry, and her pain cut into him like a knife. The last thing he wanted was to hurt Rebecca. She was his true love, for God's sake. Yet even as she stood there weeping and he knew he should go to her and enfold her in his arms he felt rooted to the spot. The secrets he held weighed him down. She waited for a minute, and then for another, but he knew she would not wait forever.

"I want to love you, Robert," she said at last, drawing a sleeve across her face, "but I can't if you won't let me in." She picked up her purse off the table and walked past him to the short hallway that led to the front door. Robert felt his pulse would burst his heart out of his chest as she passed him and he caught a whiff of her shampoo.

"When will you be back?" he said, as she opened the door.

"What makes you assume I'm coming back?" she said coldly.

"Jesus, Rebecca," he said, feeling sweat break out on his forehead and a lump churn in his stomach, "it's just a fight."

"It's not just a fight," said Rebecca. "I don't even know who you are anymore."

Her exit line hit him like a punch to the gut. She was right—he had stopped telling her stories and watching movies with her and reading books together. They had become roommates. And now he might lose even that. He could feel her in every detail of the apartment—not just the décor, but the neatly arranged food in the refrigerator, the copy of *Architectural Digest* that lay on the coffee table, the note in her handwriting on the message board by the front door: *Pick up dry cleaning Tuesday after 4*. He loved the way she drew her *y*'s, with the tail curled back under the previous letter. Would this ordinary note be the last place he ever saw her handwriting? Even as he stared at those words, he felt her presence receding from the apartment, from his life, as if her spirit had waited a few minutes after her departure to pass through the door. And that was when he knew. He had to tell her the only story that really mattered. It might not work; it might be too late, but it was his only chance to get her back. He had to tell her. But how?

IV

NEW YORK CITY, TRINITY CHURCHYARD,
THE NIGHT THE HORNS BLEW

Magda, Tom, and Eugene might have met on that Sunday night in lower Manhattan, but then so might tens of thousands of other New Yorkers if it hadn't been for that infernal racket.

Thomas De Peyster had not enjoyed his previous visit to lower Broadway, surrounded by the financial institutions that pumped wealth into the families of Fifth Avenue. A few weeks ago, his father had dragged him through the frenzied streets at midday to a bank that Mr. De Peyster hoped his son would one day inherit. But the noise of that outing could not compare to what now surrounded him—a raucous din such as he had never heard in this neighborhood or any other. He crossed Cedar Street, passed the eight-story Boreel Building, and found himself at the corner of Trinity Churchyard, assaulted on every side by the rattling of ratchets, the bang of blank cartridges, the shouting of voices, and especially the roar of thousands of tin horns of every size. Tiny toy horns buzzed like mosquitoes while some as long as four feet honked like foghorns. Despite the cold weather, the crowd had thickened north of Cortlandt Street, and Tom had muscled his way through to the churchyard in order to hear the chimes of Trinity Church that would welcome in 1900 with the ringing of airs ranging from "Old Hundredth" to "America" and "Yankee Doodle." He needn't have bothered, for no matter how close he came to the old church he could hear nothing but the sound of those celebrating around him. Tom didn't care. He loved the crowd, loved the noise, loved the energy and excitement with which New York was ready to greet the 1900s when they arrived in an hour or so. For five cents, he purchased his own tin horn from a street vendor and joined in the cacophony.

Though Tom had frequented the nighttime streets of lower Manhattan for years, he had never come dressed in formal evening wear before. But tonight was not about blending in; tonight all strata of New York society mixed as equals, and so Tom had come directly from the concert at Carnegie Hall without bothering to change out of his tailcoat. His parents and his last remaining unmarried sister, Alice, had attended the Grand Sunday Night Concert at the Metropolitan Opera House at Thirty-Ninth Street and Broadway. His father never missed a chance to attend the opera, claiming that regular attendance at the Metropolitan was an important part of being what he called "in society." Since Tom had distinctly mixed feelings about being *in society*, and since, to his father, he was currently a "grave disappointment," Tom had begged off the family excursion in favor of Paderewski's only New York appearance with an orchestra this season. The great pianist's solo performances of Chopin had been lovely, but Tom liked the Beethoven concerto best of all. He had slipped out before the second encore, while the audience still cheered for more, in order to make his way to Trinity Church. He loved living in a city where he could hear, in the space of two hours, a sublime performance of some of the greatest music ever composed and the roaring dissonance of ten thousand tin horns.

Every few minutes a cable car would ooze its way down Broadway, parting the crowd with the help of the Metropolitan Police, who would good-naturedly shoo away young men delighting in dodging the oncoming vehicles. Often, in the wake of the cable car, Tom would see carriages—almost certainly on excursions from his own neighborhood—with liveried coachmen and footmen picking their way through the crowd. As one of these passed him, he saw the nose of some gent flattened against the carriage window. Tom suddenly remembered his final trip home from Mr. Sargent's studio, and how he had glimpsed boys playing in an alley through the window of his family's carriage. How happy he was to be on the other side of that window now, no longer gawking at people in the street, but here among them, a part of their celebrations.

There had been some debate in the press about whether the twentieth century would arrive in a few minutes or not until 1901. Germany had welcomed that century a few hours ago; France would wait another year. Tom's father was of the opinion that, considering the amount of money he had spent to print new banking forms replacing the number *18* with *19*, it had better be a new century.

Few in the crowd seemed to realize when midnight arrived, being focused on their noisemaking and associated revelry, but Tom had positioned himself to see not just the clock on the church tower but also the doors to old Trinity herself. As 1900 came into being, a bright glow burst from the church windows, the bronze doors were flung open, and a shaft of light crossed the threshold. Tom saw the altar and the pulpit bathed in light for only a moment and then the doors swung shut and the church returned to darkness.

The revelers were not quick to disperse, but, satisfied that the new year, and perhaps even a new century, had arrived, Tom began to make his way uptown and managed to hop on a crowded cable car and ride up Broadway and Seventh Avenue to the terminus at Fifty-Ninth Street. From there he walked around the south end of the park and to the De Peyster home on Fifth Avenue. This would be the century, he thought, in which he would finally break free from it.

Magda Hertzenberger had never been in a crowd bigger than the congregation of St. Mark's Lutheran Church or the Monday-morning shoppers of Avenue B. It had taken some convincing to get her parents to allow her to join this throng. At seventeen, she didn't think she should need permission to do anything, but her father insisted that so long as she remained unmarried, she would live by their rules. Ridiculous, she thought. But when Mr. and Mrs. Fischler had invited her to join them, Mr. Hertzenberger relented, and at an hour when she would normally be fast asleep, Magda had found herself on a cable car headed downtown. They met several other members of the congregation at the cable car stop, and when they disembarked a few blocks from Trinity Church, Mr. Fischler spent fifty cents on tin horns for everyone.

They found a spot near the corner of Cedar Street and Broadway and joined in the celebration, blowing horns and laughing. Mr. Fischler tried to dance with his wife, but there was not enough space among the revelers for more than a shuffle. Magda watched for a moment, then slipped farther down Broadway with the crowd. This was, perhaps, the only night of the year when a young woman could walk down Broadway unaccompanied. She didn't care what her father thought—Magda longed to be independent, and although at the moment she couldn't even control the direction she was moving in, she had never felt as free as she did now, swept along on a tide of strangers.

How delighted she was not to be at home, looking after the twins, her unexpected two-year-old brother and sister, while her father celebrated at the beer garden with his friends and her mother attended the watchnight service at church. Mrs. Heidekamp had kindly offered to let Henry and Rosie stay over at her apartment until Magda's mother returned home from church.

The movement of the crowd slowed as the doors of the church came into view, but the noise did not abate in the slightest as the music of the church bells rang out. Magda laughed with delight—no parents to watch her, no Mrs. Fischler to chaperone her, and a crowd of happy people as far as she could see. As the light shining from the church doors signaled that a new century had dawned, Magda turned to the woman next to her and without the least sense of awkwardness or self-consciousness the two women threw their arms around each other and embraced.

"Happy New Year!" she said to the stranger.

"And to you!" said the woman, and then she disappeared in a sea of overcoats.

Alone on the cable car heading up Broadway, Magda thought about the 1900s. She knew that back at the watchnight service, her mother had prayed for an end to hunger and poverty, for cooperation among nations, for justice and kindness to triumph over hatred and evil. Everyone prayed for those things, and Magda believed that the century ahead could truly be one of peace for the world. But she also hoped the new century would bring her a new life and, although she did not know what she wanted that life to be, she whispered a prayer that *she* might be the one to guide her own path.

Magda's father thought she should go to work full-time and provide an income to help the family. She liked the idea of a job, and had worked as a shopgirl at a haberdashery on Avenue B for a few months last year, but Mrs. Hertzenberger pointed out that she could earn much more than Magda if Magda would only stay home and care for the twins. This had begun the great tug-of-war between her parents. Her father thought Magda should be out working and her mother wanted her at home to look after Henry and Rosie. Magda wasn't sure what she wanted, but she knew she did not want to be the object of her parents' disagreement, and she didn't want *them* to decide her path in life. She wanted, she thought, things that were difficult for a woman to have in 1899—independence, first and foremost. Maybe 1900 would be different.

As Magda walked the few blocks home from the cable car stop, she heard occasional shouts and the toots of horns from other revelers returning from Trinity Church, or from one of the many beer gardens in Kleindeutschland. Soon, the streets would be as quiet as usual at this early hour of a Monday morning—quieter, since New Year's Day was a holiday. Tomorrow morning her mother would want her to help with the chores and her father would start in again about finding a job, and eventually a husband, but for a few more moments Magda could stand on the street alone, the mistress of her own destiny, as a new century stretched before her.

Eugene Pinkney pulled at the collar of his shirt as he made his way east on Rector Street along the edge of Trinity Churchyard, toward Broadway.

He had decided not to venture into these crowds in his preferred evening attire and instead wore the formal evening suit purchased for him by Mr. White for excursions to Broadway theaters and fine restaurants. But Gene, as he now called himself, was never completely at ease in a starched collar. People swarmed everywhere, even—he noticed as he passed by—hanging off the massive stone monument that marked the resting place of some founding father or other. He thought it might be Hamilton.

Gene's friends in the Bowery had asked why he wanted to come here. If he wanted crowds and noise and revelry, the Bowery resorts could provide that any night. One needn't wait for the end of a century. The truth was, Gene didn't know why he felt drawn here. While there were many places, diverse places, in New York where he felt at home, a crowd on Broadway in front of a church was not one of them. Perhaps that was why he had made the trek downtown; perhaps he felt it was a rare chance to see every person in New York as an equal, to walk in a crowd of thousands without anyone forming an opinion about him.

He paused on the corner of Rectory and Broadway to buy a tin horn from a vendor. It seemed a silly thing to do—he could not possibly add any further noise to the cacophony around him. But he wanted to join in, wanted to feel a part of this crowd of people who were . . . not like him. Just inside the churchyard, he saw a group of a half dozen young men who had obviously been celebrating with the bottle for some time. If there was one thing Gene knew, it was how to talk to drunken men, though talking would clearly be difficult in the circumstances.

Squeezing his way through the crowd, he approached the men and blew his tin horn into their midst as a greeting. The men—if you could call them men, for they couldn't be much older than Gene and he was only seventeen—hooted their horns back at him in reply and welcomed him into their circle with the offer of a swig from a bottle and some considerable backslapping. One of them had almost white-blond hair onto which he had not rubbed the slightest hint of Macassar oil; consequently, it kept falling over his eyes. After another minute or so of tooting on their horns, the blond sidled up to Gene and shouted, "Are you from New York?"

Gene nodded yes, without attempting a verbal response.

"It's almost midnight," said the man, pulling out his pocket watch and dangling it an inch or two from Gene's face, as if none of them could see the clock on the tower just above them. "What do we do next?"

Gene smiled and just as the door of the church opened to let out the light of the new year, he motioned the men to make their way to the cable car. It took some fighting through the crowd to reach a car that was making its slow way up Broadway, but Gene enjoyed letting the men from the churchyard do all the work as he followed in their wake. When the car was a few blocks clear of the crowd, the blond turned to him and said, "Where are we going?"

"A place I know," said Gene with a smile. Even though midnight had passed, the celebrations at his usual haunts would be in full swing. His friends at the Bowery resorts might not recognize him in his formal evening wear—but that would be half the fun.

As the cable car picked up speed, Gene smiled at the thought of how these out-of-towners would react to what they were about to see. A wind blowing off the East River hit the car as it crossed Canal Street. Gene pulled his overcoat tightly around himself. As he watched the men joke and laugh, he wondered what the 1900s would bring, and if the world would be a different place for the likes of Eugene Pinkney by the time that century ended and the next one began.

V

NEW YORK CITY, UPPER WEST SIDE, 2010

Robert slept sporadically that night—waking frequently and instinctively reaching to the other side of the bed to feel for Rebecca. Only there was no Rebecca, and every time his hand fell into that void the ache returned and he lay staring at the ceiling unable to get back to sleep.

He hated the way he had acted, hated himself for pretending that just hating his behavior was enough. Robert knew there were plenty of men who were horrible and thoughtless and insensitive, men who hid their pasts and refused to be honest with their partners, and who didn't care about any of that. He couldn't imagine not caring. He ached about his own weaknesses every day. And then he ached about the fact that he just sat there aching instead of doing something about it like a real man.

He finally got up around dawn and drank two cups of coffee that had no more effect on him than warm water. Rebecca was both present and absent, his heart was both full and empty, and the abyss of the future yawned in front of him. He spent most of the day staring out the window at the gray sky. He tried reading a book Rebecca had recommended, but he heard her voice with the turn of every page and looked up only to be reminded again that she was gone. He stared at her number on his phone for minutes on end, wondering if it was too soon to call. But what would he say? So he started another book—an advance copy of a new novel his agent had sent. He read the first page six times before giving up and going back to staring out the window.

Robert slept no better that night, but the following morning he decided he had to do something. He couldn't just sit there and read. Or maybe sitting and reading was exactly what he needed to do, exactly the way he should start the process of growing up so that he might be worthy of Rebecca and precisely the way to prepare to tell her the story he needed to tell. Maybe, before he could move forward, he needed to go back.

An hour later, Robert stood in front of a stack of boxes he had not opened for the sixteen years since his mother moved to Florida during his freshman year at Columbia. The storage locker in which he kept them was another secret from Rebecca. No bills came to the apartment; he paid the monthly rent in cash and in person.

He managed to fit the eight cardboard boxes in the trunk and back seat of a taxi, and after eight climbs up four flights of stairs hauling books in the New York steam heat Robert stood sweaty and panting in his study despite the cold February day outside. He cleared a bookcase of the many unread books sent to him by publishers hoping for an endorsement and began to decant the contents of the boxes onto his shelves. It took nearly an hour of sorting to get the books neatly arranged in the bookcase, each series standing together, just as they had in his childhood home.

Robert felt oddly moved by the sight of those uniform rows of books. Certainly, he had known happiness many times in the years since he and his father had read those stories together, but even in his moments of greatest joy—the day Rebecca moved in, the day his book sold—reality intruded. Holding Rebecca's hand as they stepped into the apartment, talking to his agent on the phone—he was happy at those moments, but also deeply aware of the responsibilities that came with that happiness. During all the afternoons that he lay on his bed reading, or secretly stayed up late in his closet with a book and a flashlight, or best of all, lounged on the back porch listening to his father's voice narrating the adventures of the Hardy Boys or the Tremendous Trio, he had felt no such onus. That childlike, innocent, unfettered joy now peeked around the dark edges of his current situation as he ran his hand across the frayed bindings. He thought only of how his relationship with these books had begun, not how it had ended, and that memory allowed a ray of light to pierce his heart. But then he remembered there was a darkness behind that light, that he was no longer approaching these books as an innocent child, but as a man with everything to lose if he did not complete the journey those volumes mapped out for him.

Robert decided to begin at what, to him, had always been the beginning—the book his father had handed him twenty-six years ago at Pop Pop's house: *Through the Air to the North Pole; or, The Wonderful Cruise of the Electric Monarch*, the first installment in the Great Marvel series. The two teenage heroes were orphans—a handy condition for adventurers, as it prevents a meddlesome mother reminding you about bedtime just as you climb into a submarine or a space rocket. It took Roy Rockwood only a few pages to trap Jack and Mark on a runaway train and set the tenor of the book. After all, if their lives were not in serious danger at least once every few chapters, they couldn't be on a real adventure.

Robert had forgotten—or perhaps in his youthful zeal he had simply not realized—just how bad some of the writing was, but having endured a diet of serious literary fiction for the past few years, he reveled in the overblown prose. He had forgotten, too, the overt racism of some passages. Professor Henderson's assistant, Washington, was an African American whose elaborately convoluted syntax was clearly meant to be comic. As a boy Robbie had found this old-fashioned and at times even quaint—just another part of the naiveté of the world that had produced these adventures. Now he could see Washington's portrayal, and his use of words like *massa*, as blatantly offensive—a tool for indoctrinating young people into an insidious institutional racism. Robert skipped over parts of the Washington scenes as he read—censoring the text as he had never done as a child.

But if Roy Rockwood's attitude toward race showed little forward thinking, his fictional inventions and his vision of the future world were prophetic. The Great Marvel series, like the Tom Swift books and Alice

Gold's adventures, were essentially early works of science fiction. They may not have lived up to the standard set by H. G. Wells or Jules Verne, but *Through the Air to the North Pole* was published in 1906, two years before anyone actually reached the North Pole. Marveling at Rockwood's ingenuity, Robert finished the book in a little over three hours.

He was about to reach for the second of the Great Marvel books, *Under the Ocean to the South Pole; or, The Strange Cruise of the Submarine Wonder*, but the portrayal in the first volume of Washington, along with the depiction of the "Esquimaux" as human-sacrificing savages, had soured the experience of reading the first book.

He could almost hear Rebecca's voice—*How could you read trash like this?* She wouldn't say it in an accusatory or condescending tone, but in one of genuine curiosity, and behind that curiosity would be relief, because she had loved Nancy Drew and the Dana Girls maybe as much as he had loved the Great Marvel books. How could he read such trash? Why did he *need* to read such trash? That was exactly what he needed to tell her. Reading those books seemed the best way to begin to confront where they had led him all those years ago. He scanned the bookcase for his next adventure, trying to remember if any of the series were a bit more enlightened.

On the bottom shelf he saw them—three trios of books featuring Dan Dawson, Alice Gold, and Frank Fairfax, respectively—plus the trilogy in which these young adventurers joined forces as the Tremendous Trio. These had been the favorites of three generations of men in his family, and only now did it occur to him that part of the reason might have been not just the quality of the writing, but that the authors, Dexter Cornwall, Buck Larson, and Neptune B. Smythe, avoided the sort of racism found in Roy Rockwood's books. The cast of characters was hardly diverse—being all white and middle or upper class—but at least there were no black servants calling people *massa* or tribes of "savages" existing only to be shot at by the heroes.

Robert opened the front cover of *Storm from the Sea: A Daring Dan Dawson Adventure*, and saw a familiar browned sheet of letterhead which had been folded and unfolded so many times it seemed about to fall into small, rectangular pieces. He smoothed it out on the desktop and read, letting the memories flood over him.

PICKERING PUBLISHING
175 Fifth Avenue, New York
From the Desk of Dexter Cornwall

April 22, 1911

Dear Howard,

Thank you so much for your letter. I am glad you have enjoyed reading about Dan Dawson's adventures. You say that you don't think you would be brave enough to do the things that Dan does, but I am not so sure. After all, you were brave enough to write a letter to me and I can tell you, not many six-year-old children do that. I think that if you encountered a situation like the ones Dan finds himself in, you would act in much the same way. Courage, after all, is not something we know we have until we are tested. Only when an act of courage is required of you will you know whether you are truly brave. I believe you are. As for those boys at school who call you names—bravery is not fighting with a bully. Bravery is being who you are and not caring what other people think. So, Howard, if you can be brave enough to ignore those boys now, you will be brave enough for anything the future holds.

Your Friend,
Dexter

Robert stared for a long minute at the elaborate loops and whorls of that century-old signature. It reminded him that Dexter Cornwall, and all the other authors whose books he had devoured as a child, were real people. He supposed his own readers felt like this when they came to a book signing. They sought the same personal connection that Pop Pop had pursued by writing a letter to his favorite author.

Robert gently turned over the paper to read the words penciled on the back in his grandfather's handwriting, words that still raised goose bumps on his skin: *Carried with me in France, 1944–45.*

Robert remembered the first time he had seen those words. He and his father had been reading *Dan Dawson and the Big Fire* when the letter fell out from between the pages. Robbie had been impressed that his grandfather had received a personal letter from Dexter Cornwall, but at eleven he hadn't understood the note on the back. So his father had told him a story. And as much as they had bonded over their shared love of the fictional stories in those series books, this true story brought them even closer. That had been the moment Robbie had realized the power of storytelling, the moment that set him on a path to being a novelist.

☾⟋⟍⟍⟍⟍⟍

"Your Pop Pop probably could have spent the war riding a desk," Robbie's father began. "He joined the army in 1926 and he was already thirty-five when America got into the war."

At eleven, Robbie had only the vaguest idea of the politics of World War II, but he understood the difference between working at a desk and carrying a gun into a battle.

"He never talked much about the war," Robbie's father continued. "I was about your age when he came home, and I loved stories, these stories," he said, holding *Dan Dawson and the Big Fire* up, "as much as you do. But what I really wanted to hear were Dad's stories about the war. He only ever told me one. I wish I could tell it as well as he did—he could paint a picture with words, your grandfather, though he rarely did. And he never talked about the actual fighting, even though I begged him to. He was part of the Allied force that drove the last of the Germans out of France in the winter of 1945 near the city of Colmar. The day he told me about they liberated a village called Turckheim. The snow in the open fields around the village was hip-deep and they had to dig out holes to sleep in. The rations were running low, and that morning he had a Hershey's chocolate bar for breakfast. It was so cold he had to warm it up under his shirt before he could bite into it. And then I guess the fighting began, but the only thing he would tell me about that was that whenever he got scared he would think of Daring Dan Dawson and that letter from Dexter Cornwall folded up in his pocket. After the Americans took the village, the residents came out of the basements where they had been hiding to welcome them. Dad was the oldest soldier there—a married man of almost forty leading a platoon of teenagers. So, he hung back and let the boys enjoy the embraces of the young ladies of Turckheim. But then he saw something he never expected—a woman about his age stood on top of a pile of rubble, waving an American flag. This village had been overrun by Nazis for the past several years, and he couldn't imagine where she had gotten the Stars and Stripes. So, he climbed up to her and tried to ask her. She didn't speak more than a few words of English, but Dad had learned a little French. She held the flag out to him, tears streaming down her cheeks and just kept saying *merci* over and over."

"What's that mean?" said Robbie.

"It means *thank you*. Finally, Dad managed to ask her about the flag, and she told him she had made it herself in secret out of scraps of cloth, keeping it for the day the Americans finally came. That flag had given her hope that one day she would be free again."

Robbie looked up to see tears in his father's eyes and realized what stories could do. That day, a month before his twelfth birthday, he became a writer. Over and over again, he wrote the story of Pop Pop marching across France and liberating Turckheim, ripping up each version, always afraid it wasn't good enough and never quite brave enough to share his efforts with his father. The stories always ended with the woman holding the flag atop the pile of rubble.

In Robbie's versions of Pop Pop's story, none of the Allied soldiers ever got killed. But, Robert wondered if the reason Pop Pop never told his war stories was because he had lost so many friends. Was it possible that he had inherited his ability to suppress the tragedies of the past from Pop Pop? Even as Robert thought it, he realized that inheritance was no gift. His failed relationships, his estrangement from his mother, and his occasional periods of depression and isolation must all be linked to the guilt he refused to talk about. He wondered, for the first time as an adult, what had really happened on the frozen fields of France and why Pop Pop had never spoken of it.

Robert decided not to refold the letter. One more crease might spell the end for the fragile paper. He slipped it into a file folder and slid it into his lower desk drawer, wondering if a children's author named Dexter Cornwall, answering a fan letter from a little boy in 1911, could have had any idea that he would give courage to a soldier in the waning stages of World War II, thirty-four years later. And he wondered if that author, and his letter, could, in any way, give Robert the courage to confront the story he had avoided for so long. He imagined Dexter Cornwall sitting behind a wide oak desk, sipping tea from a fine set of china and looking out across a lawn to the Hudson River below his country estate. How could such a man know anything about courage?

VI

NEW YORK CITY,
ON THE DAY OF KLEINDEUTSCHLAND'S GRAND EXCURSION

Magda saw absolutely no reason why a woman's dress or skirt ought not to have pockets. She would have loved the freedom of slipping a book into a pocket and not having to carry anything.

Books almost made Magda miss the boat. Imagine, she thought, if she had—if she had spoken to Mrs. Heidekamp a little longer, or if she had not thought to cut through Tompkins Square and instead had been caught in the traffic and bustle of Avenue A. If she had stopped by to check on Mrs. Ottinger, who had missed church on Sunday on account of a chest cold, or if she had paused at the bakery at the corner of Seventh Street and Avenue B to add some strudel to her basket, then she might have arrived at the pier just in time to see the *General Slocum* pull away—loaded with the women and children of St. Mark's Lutheran Church heading to their annual summer picnic on Long Island without her. June 15, 1904, might have been a very different day for Magda. She might have heard the music of the band drifting over the sparkling water of the East River, waved at the receding steamer, its flags and banners rippling in the breeze, and then turned away, disappointed to miss the festivities, but nonetheless looking forward to a quiet day. But if she had—if she had stood on the pier waving as the boat plowed up the river and then walked slowly home, perhaps stopping in the park to read on a bench for an hour or so—would it have changed anything?

"Magdalena," cried her mother, pulling the covers off the narrow bed, "*du wirst spät sein!*"

"Speak English, Mother," said Magda. Ever since her husband's death of tuberculosis two years ago, Magda's mother had slipped back into speaking German.

"Late you are to be," said her mother. "Henry and Rosie they are . . . *bereit.*"

"*Ready,* Mother. They are *ready!* You must practice your English. We have lived in America twenty years."

"What am I to need with English?" said Mrs. Hertzenberger. "I live in Kleindeutschland. All my friends, they are German."

"You live in America," said Magda. "And how are Henry and Rosie to learn proper English if you always speak German? They are eight years old now. And they are Americans."

"You speak them English," said her mother. "But you are to hurry. The twins wish to go. They wish a spot at the rail so to see the view of city. Now they are outside with the Lunnarmans."

"The boat does not leave until nine thirty, Mother, and you know as well as I do that Pastor Haas will wait for Mrs. Fickbohn and Mrs. Kessler and *they* will certainly not be on board until nearly ten. You know what trouble they have with those broods of children."

"Do not speak such of Mrs. Fickbohn," said her mother.

"You and the twins go on to the pier," said Magda. "I will be there in time, I promise."

Magda sprang up the four steps to the doors of a narrow redbrick building near the corner of Eighth Street and Second Avenue. Even though she entered under the German words *Freie Bibliothek*, forever set in terracotta, to her this was the free library. Magda did not think of herself like her mother did—as a displaced German. She had been only two when the family stepped off the SS *Hammonia* onto the barge that ferried them to

New York City and the vast immigrant-processing center known as Castle Garden. She had no memory of life in the little town of Buxtehude where her father had worked as a shipping agent, no memory of boarding that steamship in Hamburg one spring day in 1884, no memory of the tears that glistened in her father's eyes as they came in sight of the buildings of Manhattan and he murmured to his wife, "*Willkomen in Amerika.*" She had heard the stories—stories of life in Germany, of that fourteen-day passage packed in steerage so that the family savings could be invested in their new life, of the long lines at Castle Garden under the stern eyes of the medical examiners, of finally emerging into the great rotunda and then onto the streets of lower Manhattan—but to Magda these were only stories. She had only ever known life as a New Yorker, and at twenty-two, more than anything else, she wanted to leave all remnants of her German past behind and to be an American.

"*Guten Morgen*, Magdalena," said the smiling blond woman behind the desk as Magda pushed through the door.

"Good morning, Mrs. Heidekamp," said Magda breathlessly.

"And how are your mother and little Henry and Rosie?"

"They are well, but I've no time for chatting. Today is picnic day. We steam up the river in just a few minutes and I must have a book to read."

"You are just like New York, Magdalena. Always in a hurry."

"I don't want to miss the boat."

"I'm sure Pastor Haas will wait for you. I had the day off last year for the picnic. We lay in the sun and watched the waves. I shall miss being there this time."

"Yes, yes," said Magda, "and I shall miss being there as well if I do not hurry."

"And what sort of book would you like for picnic day?"

"A book in English. Something with adventure in it."

"You never check out books in German anymore, not since your father died. What would he think?"

"He would think," said Magda firmly, "that his daughter is an American."

"An adventure book?"

"Yes, and do hurry. Mother will be ever so cross if I keep them waiting."

"You do sound American," said Mrs. Heidekamp. "Have you read H. G. Wells? Willie Müller returned this book yesterday." She slid a pale green book across the counter. On the cover was a decorative design that reminded Magda of the unopened chrysanthemums a street vendor had been selling around the corner.

"*The War of the Worlds?*" said Magda. "I'm not sure I want a book about war."

"It's not quite what you think," said Mrs. Heidekamp. "It's about immigrants."

"Oh, very well," said Magda. "I suppose it will have to do." She signed her name on the circulation log and slipped the book into her basket.

"Have a lovely day," said Mrs. Heidekamp, but Magda was already on her way out the door.

Magda walked briskly down St. Mark's Place and under the elevated railway tracks at First Avenue, where a train rattled overhead on its way uptown. At Avenue A, she dashed across the road through horse-drawn carts and a sputtering motorcar to enter the relative peace of Tompkins Square. She loved this oasis of calm in the middle of her bustling, boisterous neighborhood. She could hear children playing on the separate boys' and girls' playgrounds as she wound her way across the park. As she stepped out of Tompkins Square and into Avenue B, she reentered the din of the city. Merchants called out from their carts, all manner of vehicles jostled for position, and crowds surged along the sidewalks. The smell of fresh-baked bread mingled with the sweat of men and the dung of horses. Magda could have closed her eyes and known she stood on Avenue B—the so-called German Broadway. She lifted her skirts to avoid some—at least—of the dirt and refuse that clogged the gutters and spilled onto the street, and then picked her way carefully across the chaos. Striding down Seventh Street, she found the sidewalks soon cleared and in another few minutes she had turned down Avenue D to Third Street and was walking carefully across the cobblestones that fronted the Recreational Pier, where flags flew from the roof, and a clutch of people gathered at the rail on the upper level to watch the morning.

The sun streamed into the lower level of the pier, where a few members of the congregation still made their way toward the East River. Magda's feet clicked on the floorboards as she hurried down the length of the pier. She was fifteen minutes late but, as she had predicted, Pastor Haas and Pastor Shultz still stood at the foot of the gangplank, greeting the latecomers, including Mrs. Fickbohn and Mrs. Kessler with their crowds of children.

"*Guten Morgen*, Magda," said Pastor Hass.

"Good morning," said Magda.

"Isn't she a beauty?"

And indeed she was. The *General Slocum* idled at the end of the pier, a vision in white. Three decks high and festooned with bunting and streamers, she shone in the morning light, a diamond set in the sparkling waters. Flags and banners rippled in the breeze from her four flagpoles. The steamer measured over two hundred feet long, and every inch of her railings on every deck was crowded with women and children, eager for the journey to get underway. On her top deck, a band played, the music drifting on the gentle breeze back across the streets of the Lower East Side. Smoke drifted in wisps from her smokestack, and just behind amidships her thirty-one-foot paddle wheels rose above the top deck, ready to begin churning upstream.

"I believe you are the last one, Magda," said Pastor Schultz, as Mrs. Kessler's children tottered up the gangplank.

"I told Mother you wouldn't leave without me," said Magda, smiling.

"She's on the top deck at the rear rail with the twins," said Pastor Haas, following Magda up the gangplank onto the boat. In another minute, Magda felt the engines rumbling beneath her and watched as the shore slowly slipped away. She found her mother and the twins at the rear of the top deck, just as Pastor Haas had said.

"It's beautiful," said Rosie, clinging to her mother's dress as she pointed at the Stars and Stripes fluttering above them.

"You are late," said her mother, scowling.

"I'm here," said Magda, "and the band is playing your favorite—'A Mighty Fortress Is Our God.' You should smile."

"'*Eine Feste Burg Ist Unser Gott*,'" said her mother sternly, but Magda was right. Wilhelmina Hertzenberger could not stay angry with her oldest child. The day was too perfect. She breathed in the fresh air and hugged the twins close as the boat picked up speed. The music played, the sun sparkled, and the busy streets of Manhattan slid past them with increasing speed, promising to soon give way to the peaceful seaside of Long Island.

Magda reached into her basket and clutched the book Mrs. Heidekamp had given her. She had hoped to read on the boat trip, but the boisterous shouts and laughter of the hundreds of children were too distracting for her to concentrate. She took a deep breath of the fresh air blowing in from the sea and smiled at her mother and the twins. Later, she would wish she could have that moment back, frozen forever—the moment before everything changed.

The boat pressed up the river, passing under the construction of the new Queensboro Bridge and up the length of Blackwell's Island. From her spot at the stern rail Magda could see the occasional dockworker in Astoria waving to the passing crowd. No more than five minutes later, Magda turned to her mother to ask if she smelled smoke, but Mrs. Hertzenberger was speaking German loudly with Mrs. Kessler and did not hear her daughter. And then, the alarm sounded.

"Mother," cried Magda, shaking Mrs. Hertzenberger. "Mother, I think there is a fire."

"Not to be silly," said her mother. "It is only a . . . *ein Feuerübung.*"

A fire drill, thought Magda. She relaxed for a second, then heard the shout from the direction of the bow. "Fire! She's on fire!"

She had no time to react to this news before a mass of humanity suddenly surged toward the rear of the boat. Magda found herself pressed against the railing, and she reached to grasp Rosie's hand as her sister looked up at her.

"What is it?" said Rosie, a look of concern clouding her usually sunny face.

"Hold tight," said Magda. "Just hold me tight."

The crowd had pushed Mrs. Hertzenberger and Henry a short distance away from Magda, but they still stood next to Mrs. Kessler, who was shouting for her oldest daughter. "Frieda! Where are you, *meine* Frieda?"

Magda tried to reach out to her mother with her free hand, but the crowd pressed against her even harder as screams came from the front of the boat and the heat of what was certainly a fire suddenly enveloped her. Those around her were strangely quiet, as if holding their collective breath. Even Mrs. Kessler quieted enough so that, a minute later, as the air began to thicken with smoke, everyone could clearly hear a voice shouting—"Look! In the water! There are children in the water."

Magda looked over the port rail and beheld a horrifying sight. Three children, one badly wounded in the head, floated past the stern of the boat. They did not flail or try to swim. Just as the bodies were being pulled beneath the surface of the water, Magda, and everyone else, heard the shriek of Mrs. Kessler.

"Frieda!" she screamed. "*Meine* Frieda!" Before Magda could reach to stop her, Mrs. Kessler climbed on a seat and threw herself over the rail. In an instant she sank, sucked into the swift current. In that moment, Magda felt panic welling up within her. She could now see flames rushing back from the bow and hear the roar of the fire as it devoured the wooden decks. The passengers, so quiet just a few moments before, now screamed all around her, and many more plunged into the water to avoid the flames. As Magda watched, nearly everyone in the river was pulled under by their heavy clothes and the roiling waters. Neither she, nor anyone in her family, knew how to swim.

The flames leapt high into the air above the top deck and spread rapidly toward her as Magda, through an extreme effort, moved toward the port side to reach her mother and Henry. Henry cried, and Mrs. Hertzenberger's face had gone pale. She leaned against the rail and murmured, "*Mein Gott.*"

Just at that moment, with a loud cracking noise, a long section of the port railing gave way. Magda watched in horror as her mother fell back toward the water with dozens of others. Henry cried out and Magda grabbed his hand, pulling him back from the broken rail. She turned away, unable to bear the sight of her mother striking the water.

Magda clutched Henry and Rosie to her sides, pushing forward and away from the broken rail. Now chaos surrounded her. More and more people plunged into the water, many with their clothes in flames. The thick smoke burned her eyes and she longed to wipe her face, but she didn't dare let go of Henry and Rosie. The twins screamed in terror as the flames roared closer. Magda held her ground, not allowing the crowd to push her toward the broken rail and into the river but not moving any closer to the heat and flames. Surely the captain would beach the boat soon. Surely other boats would come to rescue the survivors. Surely the crew would battle the flames and douse the fire. She only had to keep holding on, keep her brother and sister close, and try not to think about what had happened to their mother. For a few long minutes, Magda thought they would make it. The boat steamed forward even as the fire consumed the entire front end and drove more and more passengers into the river. And then, just as she was thinking that rescue must come at any moment, there was a deafening roar and a red starry cloud of sparks and smoke shot up as the greater part of the rear structure collapsed forward into the flames. Magda could feel the twins being pulled toward the inferno as the deck in front of her fell away. She tried to pull back, but her hands were slick with sweat and Henry and Rosie slipped from her grasp. The noise of the fire was so great that she could not hear their cries; she could only watch as they disappeared into the inferno.

Magda now stood weeping on a narrow stretch of deck that had not succumbed to the collapse. She thought about diving either into the water or into the flames. Death was certain one way or another. Perhaps at least she should choose the manner of her destruction. But she could not do it. Others still huddled near her, hoping for a miracle.

The boat slowed and then jolted to a stop as it ran aground. A man to her left shouted, "Look!" He was pointing to the tallest of the ship's flag-poles, still standing above the flames. A small boy, just about Henry's age, Magda guessed, was climbing the pole, slowly moving higher to escape the deck burning beneath him. Magda held her breath as she watched. The fate of all those who had thus far survived seemed to her bound up with that of this child. He could, she told herself, be Henry. The smoke made it impossible to distinguish his features. He could be her brother.

Magda saw a small rescue craft approaching. All eyes stayed on the boy. He climbed a little higher and a little higher with each jump of the tongues of flame from below until he was almost at the top. Each time he found he had not gone far enough he would shake his yellow curls deter-minedly and work his way a few inches more. It was a brave fight. He lost it. The flagstaff began to tremble just as the rescue boat was getting around in position to get at the child. The staff fell back into the floating furnace, and the boy with it. As he disappeared below the water, Magda lost all hope. Tears streaming down her face, she turned and leapt into the water.

As the current yanked her below the surface, Magda felt a ray of comfort. Soon she would be joining her mother and the twins, and until then the cold water brought blessed relief from the heat of the fire.

Magda had closed her eyes when she jumped, but now she opened them as she felt something solid brushing against her arm. She could not make it out in the murky river, but out of instinct, she grabbed it and felt herself being pulled through the water. In a few seconds she was back above the surface and the quiet of the underwater world gave way to a cacophony of shouts, screams, splashes, and the roar of the fire behind her. She found herself, with several others, being hauled to shore clinging to a long ladder. The people who pulled them in were not burly firemen or police officers, but delicate young ladies dressed in white nurses' uniforms. Magda fell to her knees as she felt solid ground beneath her, and two pairs of arms lifted her and helped her walk a short distance away from the river.

"You rest here," said a calm voice. Magda's eyes burned and her ears rang. The world around her seemed unreal, as if she were watching the figures running back and forth to the water and listening to the shouts of the rescuers from a great distance. She could not make her mind comprehend what had happened in the past twenty minutes since that perfect moment on the deck with her mother and the twins. And as soon as she thought of the twins, the sounds around her faded to nothing and the world went black.

"Can you hear me? Miss, can you hear me?"

Magda opened her eyes and thought for a moment she was looking into the face of an angel—a figure dressed in white, a perfect woman's face framed with red hair. Then the shouts and cries of despair intruded on her consciousness and she thought perhaps she had not arrived in heaven, but somewhere else entirely.

"Where am I?" said Magda.

"North Brother Island," said the woman.

Had the fire been a dream, Magda wondered. Her mother and the twins had not died on North Brother Island; her father had died there. "But I'm not sick," she said.

"No, miss. The captain beached the boat here. I'm a nurse at the hospital. Do you think you can stand up?"

With help from the nurse, Magda rose shakily to her feet. She stood on a wide green lawn just in front of a large brick building—a building she had never seen, never wanted to see. North Brother had several such buildings. This tiny island in the East River was home to a hospital for infectious and contagious diseases.

"You work at the hospital?" said Magda weakly.

"Yes, miss. My name is Mary McCann. But you can call me Mary. I work with the tuberculosis patients."

"Did you know Herr Frederick Hertzenberger?" said Magda, gazing up at the imposing facade of the hospital. Her father had been transferred to the tuberculosis unit on North Brother Island shortly before his death two years ago. Magda still had the last letter he had written to her. In German he wrote, "When I walk on the lawn I can see where the small-pox patients are housed. How lucky we are to be among those who only cough." Three days later he was dead.

"I'm afraid not," said Mary. "There are so many, you know."

Magda shivered at the thought that the last time her father had walked outside and breathed fresh air may have been on this very lawn. Had he unknowingly gazed out at the water in which his wife and children would die?

"You're cold, miss," said Mary. "Perhaps we should walk a bit. Get your blood pumping."

Magda turned toward the water and felt her breath catch as she saw row after row of corpses laying on the lawn, their picnic clothes clinging to them. At the water's edge, men and women pulled still more bodies from the river, dragging them onto the lawn to add to the horror. A few relatively uninjured survivors staggered along these rows, stopping to wail with grief when they saw a familiar face.

"Are you German then, miss?" said Mary, clearly trying to distract Magda from the dreadful reality of what lay before them.

Magda thought of how she had wished, earlier that day, to leave behind all that was German, to be a true American. Now that wish had come true in the most dreadful way possible. Who was she now? She could not bear the thought of returning to the empty apartment on St. Mark's Place. Who knew what would even happen to the neighborhood or the church with so many of the families now devastated by tragedy? Those few who did remain would want to take Magda in, to comfort her; and that comfort would be a painful daily reminder of all she had lost. No, she thought—she did not want to walk up and down the rows of corpses until she found her family; she did not want to return to the arms of a grieving community; she did not want to attend funeral after funeral and hear words of grief pouring forth in German on every street corner. With her family gone, she saw no reason to stay in Kleindeutschland; no reason to continue as Magdalena Hertzenberger.

She turned away from the awful view of the makeshift morgue and said, in her best American accent, "No, I am not German. Mr. Hertzenberger was a family friend." She heard in her head the voice of Pastor Haas reading the lesson about Peter denying Christ three times before the crow of the cock, but she pushed that memory away. She was an American now.

"My name is Mary Stone," she said.

⌒

In the end, disappearing from her own life proved easy—although Magda had not yet had her last view of those bodies (according to the papers, the final count had been over a thousand). With a small gift from Mary McCann, Magda rented a room for the night at a residential hotel on Thirty-Fourth Street. The next day, she closed her mother's account at the German Savings Bank on Fourteenth Street and opened a new account in the name of Mary Stone at the Excelsior Bank on West Twenty-Third. Her mother's savings together with the carefully guarded life insurance money paid out on her father's death amounted to nearly a thousand dollars. The transformation of Magdalena Hertzenberger into Mary Stone required only one further, difficult step.

Late on the afternoon of June 17, just forty-eight hours after she had once again felt the firm ground of Manhattan under her feet, having been returned from North Brother Island by one of the dozens of small private boats pressed into such service, Magda entered the cavernous space of the Twenty-Sixth Street Pier, where a temporary morgue had been set up. The morgue at Bellevue had been unable to store the huge number of bodies, and so the friends and families of those who had sailed on the *General Slocum* came to Twenty-Sixth Street to identify their dead.

The sounds of grief were softer now. Weeping and sighing had replaced shrieks and cries. Magda dared not look at those bodies that were unburned, lest she recognize her mother. She stayed far clear of the rows of smaller bodies—all that was left of the children of Kleindeutschland. It took her no more than five minutes to find a corpse about her own height, with the face and hair badly burned. Glancing around to be sure no one was watching, she removed the necklace her mother had given her on her eighteenth birthday and placed it around the blackened neck of the corpse.

"Excuse me, sir," she said to a member of the coroner's staff. "I knew this woman. This was Magdalena Hertzenberger. I recognize her necklace."

The next day, from the comfort of a furnished room in a clean and respectable boardinghouse on West Twenty-Third Street, well clear of Kleindeutschland, Magdalena opened a copy of the *New York Sun* and saw her name listed among those who had died in the *General Slocum* disaster. She folded the paper and slipped it under the mattress of what was now her bed, vowing never again to think of that day.

Then Mary Stone went downstairs, stepped into the warm air of a New York summer, and began her life.

VII

Robbie and his father had rationed out the final box of Pop Pop's books to make them last, which meant that Robbie had just turned twelve when they reached the final book in the Tremendous Trio series. When they had opened the cover of *The Tremendous Trio around the World* Robbie discovered a packet of several fragile pages held together by a rusty staple.

"I remember those," said his father with a smile.

"What are they?" said Robbie.

"We have to read the book first," said his father.

Robbie had loved *The Tremendous Trio around the World,* but his father read at an excruciatingly slow pace, almost as if he wanted to delay the moment the two of them finally looked at those mysterious pages. Now, Robert picked up the packet with an echo of the excitement he had felt over twenty years ago.

"Do *you* want to read it?" Robbie had said to his father, when they had finally finished the round-the-world adventure.

"You read it," said his father, leaning back in his chair and closing his eyes. "Slowly."

Now, sitting alone in his study, Robert picked up the stapled packet of printed pages off his desk and began to read.

The Last Adventure of the Tremendous Trio

You are old enough now. Old enough to know what the world is really like; to know that not every young man is either clean-cut and well-behaved or scruffy and evil; to know that the good guys don't always win, that the dark side of human nature is darker than you thought, and that boys and girls do more than kiss on the cheek and hold hands. We think you're old enough that when you see a girl, or perhaps a boy, you feel a certain stirring, feel a haze cover your eyes and clarity disappear and urges well up inside. You are old enough to know that even made-up characters in books can't always be heroes, and that you will not always be a hero. Sometimes even the best characters do dreadful things and sometimes, in all likelihood, you will too. You are old enough to know about secrets and hidden places. And so we are going to tell you.

Are you parents watching? Make sure they are not before you read any further. This is not going to be an ordinary adventure story. This is going to be something altogether different, something we think you are ready for. But be sure no one can see you, because not everyone will agree with us—not your parents and certainly not our publisher.

This is how our publisher would like us to begin this story:

Frank looked back up the tunnel to see the Lady of the Sky hanging amidst a forest of stalactites. The airship was never intended to fly through underground caverns, but she was doing well so far. He turned to look at the two branches of the tunnel before him, knowing he needed to decide which one Dan had disappeared down. He was just leaning over to inspect the damp floor for footprints when there was a loud snap and the cave

was plunged into darkness. Frank opened his mouth
to scream, but a wet, hairy hand grabbed him by
the throat, and he could not make a sound. Frank's
last thought before fainting was that Dan didn't
know how to fly the airship. Unless he could find
Alice, he would never make it out alive.

It sounds exciting, but you've read that story before,
or something just like it. You know that Frank and Dan and
Alice will escape the cavern and bring home a fortune in
gold or diamonds. In the final chapter, Dan will kiss Alice
on the back of the hand and Alice will blush and none of
the three will say how they really feel about all this.

But have you noticed that in all those adventures
you read—whether it's the Motor Boys or the Rover Boys
or even the Tremendous Trio—the boys never actually kiss
the girls on the lips? Or that if they do, it is quick
and chaste? (If you want to know what that word means,
go look it up. As we said, you're old enough.) In this
book the boys won't just kiss the girls, they will linger.
Sometimes the girl will kiss back and sometimes she will
slap the boy so hard it will leave a red handprint. But
those kisses will always lead to something interesting—
something scarier and more dangerous than being trapped
deep beneath the surface of the earth in the clutches of
a hairy ape.

The boys and girls in those books you have been
reading are always well-washed, and well-mannered, and
kind. But not in this book. The children in this book are
dirtier and meaner and sometimes angrier and always more
real than the ones you have been reading about. After
all—are you always sweet, and clean, and kind? Of course
not. And do you sometimes act cruel, or get angry, or want
to kiss someone? Of course you do.

This is the place, in the first chapter, where the publisher would like us to tell you that you need to read the other books in the series to understand the characters in this one. There is a simple reason for this: The publisher wants you to buy the other books so he can make more money. But honestly, he has plenty of money, and besides, you may have already read all the other books about the Tremendous Trio—Dan Dawson, Alice Gold, and Frank Fairfax. If not, and even if you have, all you really need to know is this: Dan Dawson may have made some amazing rescues, saving people from floods and fires and earthquakes, but there are a lot of people he didn't rescue; a lot of people died. Dan has nightmares about that. Alice Gold doesn't just invent washing machines, and kitchen devices, and better ways to clean a house. Alice is smarter than the smartest person you have ever met—as smart as Edison or Tesla—and she has thought of all sorts of inventions. Some are what you might call "good" inventions. They feed hungry people and make boats safer or trains faster. Others are not so good—and these are the ones Alice spends most of her time thinking about. And Frank Fairfax wants to do more than write newspaper articles about other people's expeditions. Sure, he likes blazing a trail through the Amazon or stumbling upon ancient ruins, but the expedition he really wants to take is into the dark alleys of New York City. He wants to meet the people who live in the shadows—the street urchins and the orphans and especially the criminals— and he wants to write about their dirty, complicated, mysterious world.

So, find a comfortable spot where no one will discover you, and prepare yourself. This may be the last adventure of the Tremendous Trio, but it will be the first one that tells you the truth. And for goodness sake, when you are not reading

this, keep it hidden away. If your parents find it . . . well,
we wouldn't want to be around to see what happens.

                              Dexter Cornwall

                              Neptune B. Smythe

                              Buck Larson

"What happens next?" Robbie had asked his father when he reached
the end.

"No idea," said his father.

"Where is this from?"

"Pop Pop never told me," said his father. "I pestered him for the rest
of the story or even just the next chapter, but he just shook his head and
said that this was all he had."

So many questions, so many memories, so many emotions lurked in
those browning pages that now lay on Robert's desk. He and his father
had read them over and over, speculating together about what happened
next. Robbie had turned his nascent writing skills to crafting a story that
began with this chapter, but he never got far. Perhaps at twelve he had still
not been old enough to understand "secrets and hidden places" and all the
other things this "final adventure" purported to offer.

"Do you think Pop Pop tore these pages out of the book?" said Robbie
one day.

"I wish I knew," said his father. "Maybe he had the whole book someplace and thought I wasn't old enough to read it. By the time I was old
enough, I'd probably lost interest."

"I won't lose interest," said Robbie earnestly.

"You should find the book," said his father. "Someday, you should
find it."

"I will," said Robbie.

"Promise me," said his father.

"I promise," said Robbie, placing his hand on the book that lay
between them. "I swear on *The Tremendous Trio around the World*."

"What are you two up to now?" said his mother, walking into the room
and ending the conversation. But Robbie would not forget his promise.

As he carefully slid the stapled packet into another file folder, Robert thought about the vow made to his father all those years ago. As a child, he had no access to eBay or AbeBooks. Now that he did it should have been a simple matter to turn up a copy of *The Last Adventure*. But a quick search of these and other online sources revealed nothing. The occasional copy of *The Tremendous Trio at Niagara Falls* or *The Tremendous Trio and the Secrets of the Amazon* turned up, but nothing else. It was as if *The Last Adventure* never existed.

But it did exist, because he had just read the opening. And he had promised his father he would find the book, so he would. He would find *The Last Adventure of the Tremendous Trio* and he would share it with Rebecca and that would be how he would finally tell her everything that had happened, everything he had tried so hard to forget. He pulled on a coat and started downstairs, headed to the best place he could think of to start a search for a book.

Robert sat in a diminutive chair at a diminutive table in the children's area of the St. Agnes branch of the New York Public Library. Snow dusted the skylight overhead, but natural light still filled the room. Across from him was a young librarian named Elaine Corrigan, whom he had first met a year and a half ago.

"You know you can look online to see if we have a particular book in the library system," said Elaine.

"But if I did that, I wouldn't get to walk the seven blocks up Amsterdam in a snow flurry, and I wouldn't get to admire that beautiful curving staircase, and I wouldn't get to cram myself into this miniature furniture and talk to you."

It had felt good to walk in the cold. The dour mood that had been growing in him the past few months had too often kept him confined indoors. Even a walk of a few blocks had energized him.

"How's Rebecca?" said Elaine. Until recently, Robert and Rebecca had often come to the library together on Saturday afternoons—sometimes looking for something to read aloud to each other, sometimes just browsing separately. Robert thought for a moment about conforming to social convention and lying—saying Rebecca was fine and changing the subject, but Elaine had a look of concern on her face that didn't promise to let him off that easily.

"Rebecca's staying with a friend for a few days," said Robert. "I've been . . . difficult lately."

"Some people would say, 'I can't imagine that you would be difficult,'" said Elaine, "but the truth is I can imagine it very easily."

"I know, right?" said Robert. "I'm working on it, though."

"I hope things work out. You two seem good together."

Robert tried to imagine what about the way he and Rebecca searched for books in their local public library made them seem, to a relative stranger, "good together." He believed Elaine was right, but how did she know?

"We haven't had coffee in a while," said Elaine.

"You and Rebecca have coffee?" said Robert. Rebecca had never mentioned any such relationship.

"Three or four times in the last few months," said Elaine. "She said she needed someone to talk to about what she was reading."

Robert felt a pang of guilt. *The last few months* meant ever since he had started to withdraw from Rebecca. Desperate for a way to change the subject, he glanced around the room and asked, "When did this branch open?" His excursion into the books of his grandfather's childhood had made him sensitive to age, and the St. Agnes branch clearly had some years on it. The elegant three-story stone facade nestled between two less attractive brick buildings, and the interior featured hardwood floors, curved windows, and a graceful staircase that greeted every patron.

"I think 1906," said Elaine.

"This all started in 1906," said Robert. That had been the year not only of the publication of the first of the Great Marvel books, but also of the first appearance of Dan Dawson, Alice Gold, and Frank Fairfax.

"What started?"

"I wanted to talk to you about some books," said Robert.

"Okay," said Elaine, unfolding her laptop. "Which books?"

"Frank Fairfax, Cub Reporter," said Robert. "Daring Dan Dawson; Alice Gold, Girl Inventor; and the Tremendous Trio."

"Are you researching a new novel?" said Elaine.

"Not exactly," said Robert. "They were all children's series from the early twentieth century. My grandfather had a collection and I'm trying to find a missing book."

"Children's series books?" said Elaine. "You mean like Tom Swift and Nancy Drew and the Hardy Boys."

"Exactly," said Robert.

"We can look in the catalogue," said Elaine, "but if they were anything like those other series, the public library is probably not the place to look for them." She began tapping away on her laptop.

"What do you mean?" said Robert. "Why wouldn't I look in the library for books?"

"When those series came out they . . . I guess you would say the reading establishment looked down on them."

"The reading establishment?"

"It's a term I heard at a conference about children's reading. It just means teachers, librarians—the people who think they should be in charge of what kids read. At the time they thought those books were dangerous."

"Dangerous?" said Robert, thinking of what a difference those books had made in his grandfather's life, and in his own, and at the same time how truly, unexpectedly dangerous they had turned out to be.

"No copies of any of those series are in the New York Public Library system," said Elaine. "Do you know the authors' names?"

"Dexter Cornwall, Buck Larson, and Neptune B. Smythe."

"I don't have records for any of them," said Elaine after another minute of typing.

"Why?"

"Because they don't have any books in our system."

"No, I meant why did librarians think series books were dangerous?"

"There was an article a woman at the conference mentioned in her talk. I think it was . . ." Elaine continued tapping on her keyboard. "Here, read this. It's from a magazine called *The Outlook* in 1914. It's an article written by the chief librarian for the Boy Scouts." She flipped her computer around and pointed to a passage she had highlighted on the screen.

Alas! The modern penny dreadful has not been banished. Its latest appearance is in the disguise of the bound book, and sometimes so attractively bound that it takes its place on the retail bookstore shelf alongside the best juvenile publications.

In almost all of this "mile-a-minute fiction" some inflammable tale of improbable adventure is told. Boys move about in aeroplanes as easily as though on bicycles; criminals are captured by them with a facility that matches the ability of Sherlock Holmes; and when it comes to getting on in the world, the cleverness of these hustling boys is comparable only to those captains of industry and Napoleons of finance who have made millions in a minute.

Because these cheap books do not develop criminals or lead boys, except very occasionally, to seek the Wild West, parents who buy such books think they do their boys no harm. The fact is, however, that the harm done is incalculable. I wish I could label each one of these books: "Explosives! Guaranteed to Blow Your Boy's Brains Out."

One of the most valuable assets a boy has is his imagination. In proportion as this is nurtured, a boy develops initiative and resourcefulness. Storybooks of the right sort stimulate this noble faculty, while those of the viler and cheaper sort, by overstimulation, debauch and vitiate, as brain and body are debauched and destroyed by strong drink.

"Are you okay?" said Elaine. "You sort of went pale there."

The word *explosives* had hit Robert like a freight train. How could this article from 1914 come so close to describing what those books had done to his own life seventy-five years later? He swallowed hard, searching for a voice with which to answer Elaine.

"My grandfather grew up on those books," said Robert. "And so did my father and so did I. I mean, I'm not going to argue that they're great literature, but I don't think they debauched and vitiated my imagination. I became a novelist, after all."

"Different times," said Elaine with a shrug. "But it's the sort of attitude that kept a lot of those books from ending up in libraries."

"So, no help from the public library on this one," said Robert.

"If you really want to find out about this missing book, I'd start by finding out everything you can about the authors."

"But if none of those writers have books in the library, I'm not sure where to start."

"Try this," said Elaine, taking a flyer off a stack that sat on the table and flipping it over. She pulled out a pen and jotted something on the back, then handed it to Robert.

"What's this?"

"It's the name of a librarian at the Mechanics' Society library in Midtown. She's the one who gave the talk about children's series books. She might be able to help you."

"Thanks," said Robert, hoisting himself out of the chair and pulling on his coat. "I'll give this"—Robert looked at the paper—"Julia Sanberg a call."

"Good luck with your search," said Elaine. "And I hope everything works out with Rebecca."

"Me too," said Robert softly.

"You have to wonder," said Elaine, almost to herself as they walked back toward the circulation desk.

"Wonder what?" said Robert.

"What kind of person would be named Neptune B. Smythe?"

VIII

Thomas De Peyster bought his Brownie for a dollar in 1901 mostly to annoy his father, who thought that carrying such an inexpensive camera around New York with him made Thomas look crass. But then Tom found that he enjoyed capturing moments.

Now Tom looked down at the tiny image in the viewfinder of his Brownie. Although he had thrown the curtains open, the sun had not yet risen and the predawn light from the bay window did not sufficiently illuminate his subject. So, he had slowly turned up the gas to the chandelier, hoping the light would not awaken Isabella, if that really was her name. He hoped she did not object to his taking a photograph. After all, the camera couldn't see anything inappropriate. The parts of her she had revealed to him last night, the parts of a woman he had heretofore only ever imagined, were well covered by the sheets. Thomas held his breath and depressed the shutter lever. The image he recorded in black and white showed a woman's face in profile against a goosedown pillow. Her long, dark tresses cascaded across the white sheets, the fabric and the hair flowing together in way that reminded him of windswept dunes at the seaside. When he had awoken a few minutes ago, still feeling light-headed from the events of last night, he had, even in the dimness of the room, seen this exquisite pattern, and that, as much as his wish to record this monumental event in his life, had led him to pull on his clothes, retrieve his camera from the sitting room, and turn up the lights.

As soon as the shutter clicked, Isabella stirred. Thomas had no time to hide his camera or pretend he had been photographing something else— nor did he wish to do so. He wanted her to know that he found her beauty worth recording. If she was angry, he could always open the camera and ruin the picture by exposing the film to the light.

"What are you doing?" said Isabella. Her voice was thick and rich like fresh cream, and the memory of the things she had said with that voice last night threatened to arouse him, but he did his best to concentrate on the moment. If she was willing, and if the price was not too high, there would be time for him to rejoin her in bed later. He had filed his story last night and had nowhere to be until at least nine o'clock.

"Taking your picture," said Thomas. "Do you mind?"

"I've never had my picture taken before," said Isabella, sitting up in the bed and holding the sheet to her chest. "I must look a fright."

"You look beautiful," said Thomas.

Isabella smiled. Apparently, thought Thomas, even someone in her profession could appreciate a compliment. "But my hair," she said. "My hair must be awful." She ran her hands through her hair, pulling it away from her face. As she did so, the sheet slipped slowly toward the bed and Thomas saw first the plump curve of her breasts and then, for just an instant, her erect nipples. Isabella winked at him as she pulled the sheet back up and held it tightly against herself so that he could clearly see the two small bumps in the fabric. "A chilly morning," she said, and though Thomas, in his naiveté, did not understand this comment, she said it in such a conspiratorial tone that it felt as intimate as anything that had yet happened between them.

"Now, take another one," she said, lowering the sheet slightly and leaning forward to reveal the cleft between her breasts. She tilted her head up toward the light.

"Pull some of your hair over your left shoulder," said Thomas. Isabella did this with one hand, holding the sheet with the other. "Now smile the way you just did. The way you did when you told me it was a chilly morning." Isabella turned her head a few degrees and smiled at him. He could see in that smile, and in her eyes, that they absolutely would make love again. He struggled to keep the camera still as his heart raced with anticipation. Holding his breath, he pressed the shutter lever. The click echoed in the still air. It was 5:12 a.m.

Less than twelve hours earlier, Thomas had stood in the wings of San Francisco's Grand Opera House listening to a slightly pudgy Enrico Caruso sing the role of Don José in *Carmen*. Thomas and Caruso had taken the same train from New York to California—the great tenor to perform with a troupe from the Metropolitan Opera, and Thomas to write articles about Caruso before taking up his new position with the *San Francisco Examiner*. William Randolph Hearst had personally asked Thomas to make the move from New York to San Francisco. Within hours of arriving in the city, he had befriended one of the stage-hands at the opera house and secured himself a spot backstage where he could watch both the afternoon rehearsal and the evening performance. Ashton Stephens, the reviewer for the *Examiner,* would write the story of what happened onstage; Thomas's reporting would, as usual, be a bit grittier.

After the rehearsal, he had taken the short walk down Third Street to Market and into the Hearst Building where he had filed his story. It would appear in the *Examiner* the next morning alongside the review of Caruso's performance. Unlike that review, Thomas's story would also appear in the *New York Evening Journal.* Mr. Hearst bore a grudge against the Metropolitan Opera and would much rather reprint a report of conflict backstage than a rave review of the actual performance. He had asked Thomas for scandal if possible, and, barring that, at least for colorful accounts that might reflect poorly on the tenor and the opera company. Before Caruso had sung a note in front of the bejeweled, social-climbing audience, Thomas had provided just that.

CARUSO'S EXPLOSION
Special to the Examiner
April 17, 1906

The famed Italian tenor Enrico Caruso, who has chosen to sing in San Francisco rather than in his native Naples, owing to the recent eruption of Mount Vesuvius in his homeland, had something of an eruption himself today on the stage of the Grand Opera House. Caruso seems to fancy himself a Wild West gunslinger, as previously reported in these pages. Before traveling west, he purchased a six-shooter and a generous supply of ammunition and amused many of us on the train with his attempts to master the "quick draw." Today his ammunition was his powerful voice and his substantial temper as he went toe to toe with his co-star, the portly Olive Fremstad.

Madame Fremstad blamed her poor singing during this afternoon's rehearsal of Carmen at the Grand Opera House on the ineptitude of the local stagehands (who this writer can tell you are as fine a group as an impresario could hope for). Caruso came to the aid of the slandered, but exploded when Madame Fremstad suggested that if the tenor were paid less, perhaps money might be left for more talented help backstage.

"Yes," cried Caruso, "I am paid more than a thousand dollars a night." (The exact figure is $1350.) "But who would come to see this opera without me!" He insisted, in a voice that shook the scenery, that if anyone was fired, he would refuse to go on, the performance would be canceled, and he would never again appear with Madame Fremstad.

Of course, no one's livelihood had ever been in danger. Madame Fremstad would certainly have let the matter drop once she sang through the aria a second time. But Caruso insisted on making a casual remark into a moment of seething fury. His co-star seemed, later, to be unfazed by the incident. Perhaps because she did not know that, under his costume, he still carried his six-shooter. Doubtless the streets of San Francisco will not be safe while Caruso is in town!

Hearst would love this sort of gossip, and it had only required a very slight exaggeration on Thomas's part. The story had made the evening edition, and when Thomas had arrived at the stage door before the performance, he was greeted with a round of backslapping and handshaking by the stagehands whom he had defended in print. In truth, they were *not* the most efficient group one could hope for, but Thomas felt his parenthetical praise improved the story. It certainly improved his evening. While Caruso and Madame Fremstad belted their way through *Carmen*, a stream of stagehands approached Thomas, thanking him for his words, chatting with him in the wings (when perhaps they should have been attending to the scenery) and smiling at him in the oddest way. Thomas caught winks and glances between the workmen throughout the evening. He had been reporting long enough to know something was afoot.

Thomas had met Caruso three years ago, when the tenor had dined at the De Peyster residence on Fifth Avenue following his New York debut in *Rigoletto* at the Metropolitan Opera. A major benefactor of the opera company, Thomas's father had taken pleasure in introducing his twenty-one-year-old son to the singer. But the meeting had made no impression on Caruso. When he had met Thomas again on the train from New York to San Francisco, Caruso's eyes held no flicker of recognition.

Thomas remembered that performance of *Rigoletto* well, the audience growing in its appreciation of Caruso's talents with each aria. By the end of Act III, that cosmopolitan crowd had openly adored the tenor. Here in San Francisco, the adoration was close to idolatry. The audience may have been the nouveau riche heirs of Wild West gold miners, but they pretended, at least, to a sophistication that recognized the operatic brilliance of the great star. When the final notes rang from the stage, the audience surged to its feet, shouting *Bravo* until they were hoarse and bringing Caruso back for one curtain call after another. Thomas considered trying to follow the tenor when he left the theater with an entourage, bound for Zinkand's Restaurant—no doubt lured by their plates of spaghetti. But just as he was heading for the stage door, one of the stagehands stopped him, laying a hand on his shoulder.

"We wanted to thank you, sir," said the man, as several others gathered around him, "so we bought you a little present."

"That was very kind of you," said Thomas, again noting the sly smiles on the faces of the men. What sort of presents did stagehands buy for journalists, he wondered.

The men quietly parted, revealing a figure behind them in the shadows. The figure stepped forward and pulled off a hooded cloak to reveal herself. Thomas had seen plenty of prostitutes before, lurking in the dark corners of New York. More than one had approached him with offers of a discount, "if it's your first time," but Thomas had always hurried on. He had written many articles about life on the streets of New York, but he had avoided writing about those women in the shadows.

Unlike the often pockmarked and aging whores of the New York streets, who dressed in ragged fashions of years gone by, this woman wore a dress of pale blue trimmed with gold that would have been at home in the audience that could still be heard vacating the theater. She had smooth, olive skin, a cascade of dark hair, and green eyes that sparkled with life. In the eyes of the fallen women of New York, Thomas had only ever detected sadness and despair.

She stepped forward and looked him straight in the eye, reaching out her hand to gently shake his. "Hello, Tom," she said in that creamy voice he would come to know so well over the next few hours, "my name is Isabella."

And now she sat before him, posing for his camera, lowering the sheet a few more inches, and daring him to take a photograph that he would never be able to show in respectable society. Thomas centered her in his viewfinder, held his breath, placed his thumb on the shutter lever, and felt the floor fall out from beneath him.

Thomas and his camera fell backward into a chair that slid wildly across the room. Isabella, he saw, clung to the bed, which heaved up and down like the deck of an ocean liner in a storm. The invitation in her eyes had been replaced with terror, and Thomas felt that he saw, for the first time, her true self. In another second, his chair sailed back across the room, crashing into the end of the bed and almost hurling him into her arms. But as he reached for her, the room lurched sideways and he fell to the floor, landing on his back. The room roared, and Isabella screamed. Above him, the gas chandelier swung back and forth in such an arc that Thomas feared it would catch the ceiling on fire. Tables and chairs crashed into walls, and plaster fell around him. Thomas turned over and tried to crawl toward the bed, but just as he reached it, the room tilted again, sending him and much of the furniture smashing against the far wall near the open window. From outside he could hear crashes and the shrieks of men and women, even, he thought, of horses. Clutching a chair that threatened to crush him against the wall, Thomas took a breath and finally formed a cogent thought of a single word. *Earthquake.* And then it all stopped.

Thomas could still hear screams and the occasional crashing noise in the street and from the direction of the corridor came the sound of slamming doors and shouts, but the room was suddenly still. He pushed the chair away and stood on shaky legs.

"That was a bad one," said Isabella, who already seemed to have regained her composure. She had pulled a sheet from the bed and wrapped it around herself like a Roman toga.

"Does this happen a lot?" said Thomas, brushing the plaster from his clothes.

"Usually it's just a little rumble," said Isabella, crossing the room toward the bay window. "But it sounds like this one might have done some damage." Thomas stooped to retrieve his camera, pleased to see that it appeared unharmed.

"Dear God," said Isabella, staring out the window.

"What is it?" said Thomas.

But she did not respond. She only stood, speechless, at the window, leaning slightly outside to see the scene below. Thomas started toward her, dreading what he would see. But he did not make it to the window. As he walked up behind her, Isabella's head suddenly jerked forward and she collapsed into his arms, as limp and lifeless as a sack of flour. As Thomas caught her and laid her on the floor he felt a wide gash across the back of her head that had already matted her hair with blood. It was far from Thomas's first experience with a dead body, but he had never held one in his arms, never seen firsthand the death of someone he knew, someone he had, he realized as he looked down on her still perfect face, almost convinced himself he was falling in love with. For a long moment he could not move, could not grasp that In an instant she was gone. Surely, he would awake in a moment from this horrid dream to find Isabella warm and naked beside him. But she did not awaken, and the blood from her head soaked into the carpet as the sounds of despair closed in on him from every direction. Thomas had never felt so helpless, but the day was young.

He walked to the window, being careful not to lean out as Isabella had done. Outside bricks and stones fell from those buildings that were still standing—one of these, he supposed, must have hit Isabella as she leaned out to survey the street. The view that met Thomas was almost incomprehensible. The Palace Hotel—into which Mr. Hearst had booked him because Caruso was staying there—was one of the few buildings in the block not severely damaged, and many of the structures Thomas could see from his fourth-floor window had completely collapsed. The Palace was one of the largest, grandest hotels in the world with its wood paneled "rising rooms" (as they called the elevators), its central garden court, and its hundreds of elegantly furnished suites. Thomas had counted himself lucky to stay here even for a few nights. Now, as he looked out in the predawn light at the yellow cloud of dust that rose from the rubble filling the streets, he realized the Palace—built to resist any disaster—might have saved his life.

The dust floated up toward his window, and Thomas stepped away, still trying to adjust to the reality of a dead woman on the floor and a collapsing city outside. He pulled the window shut, dampening the cries of fear and agony that rose from the street. The shouts within the hotel only seemed more panicked, and Thomas knew he needed to make a plan. The Palace stood for now, but he doubted that any building in the city was safe for long, especially if aftershocks struck. He tried not to look at Isabella's pale yet still beautiful face as he hastily pulled on his shoes and gathered his notebook and camera. He turned toward the door and then stopped. He could not carry her down four flights of stairs, but he could not leave her like this. She deserved at least a little dignity. The sheet in which she had wrapped herself had become entangled in her legs when she fell, so, not wanting to disturb the body, he took another sheet off the bed and gently covered her, then lifted her onto the bed. He gazed at her outline beneath the sheet in aching disbelief for a moment, then ran from the room and joined the throng rushing down the stairs, through the garden court, and into the chaos of Market Street.

For several minutes Thomas stood motionless, watching as people poured out of the Palace and the Grand Hotel across the street. Men in nightshirts with looks of terror on their faces rushed to what they hoped was the relative safety of the open air, only to be showered with bricks and mortar when an aftershock shook the ground. Cries came from every side and the helplessness Thomas had felt in his room now froze him to the spot. He was nearly knocked over by a large man rushing out of the hotel past him. Thomas turned toward the man and saw that it was Caruso, hastily dressed and speaking in hurried Italian to a small man who was most certainly his valet. In another moment, the valet rushed back into the building. Thomas thought perhaps he should speak to Caruso, get some sort of scoop for Mr. Hearst—THE ITALIAN TENOR AND THE GREAT EARTHQUAKE. But suddenly Thomas had neither the heart nor the energy for writing stories about one wealthy man just to please the whim of another wealthy man.

Thomas made his way through the rubble to the Hearst Building, just two blocks away, but here, as elsewhere, people were coming out of the building, fearing its collapse. Even if Thomas wrote a story, he didn't know how he could file it. As day broke over the city, the sunlight filtered through the dust and Thomas began to wander. Everywhere he saw people in the streets—some dragging suitcases or trunks or carrying bags of possessions. He passed a woman picking through the remains of her house, looking for anything she might save. He saw a house whose front wall had collapsed, revealing everything from furniture to laundry to portraits hanging on the wallpapered walls. It seemed a horrible invasion of privacy that such things were on display to anyone who happened by.

He had only been in San Francisco for two days, and so did not know the geography of the city. He had no idea where he was when he heard a cry of despair coming from beneath a pile of rubble.

"Someone's in here," cried Thomas, rushing to the edge of the pile of bricks and lumber. "Help! Help me get to him."

Most of the other bystanders paid him no mind. One older man, sweeping the dust from the street with a broom as if that would make any difference, only sighed and remarked, "They've already tried. Can't get to him."

"But we must get to him," said Thomas. "We must!"

"Can't," said the man, lowering his head and returning to his sweeping. Thomas walked until he could no longer hear the man's voice, then sat down on a pile of bricks and cried.

And so the day wore on. As he walked, Thomas tried to block out the sounds of people's cries for help. He learned quickly enough that those who *could* be helped *had been* by the time he arrived. To those who still cried out, Thomas was powerless to render aid. Eventually he could cry for them no more—he could only ignore them, bury his own sense of helplessness, and do what his profession demanded of him: Observe events. Thomas had seen children frozen to death on the street; he had seen a man stabbed in the neck in broad daylight; he had seen a woman run from a burning building, flames consuming her hair and clothes; but he had never seen anything like this. A few times, he looked at the horror through his camera and snapped a photograph, but this seemed a violation of human dignity at such a time, and he quickly gave it up.

By late morning the air was filled with the acrid smell of smoke as fires raged across the city. Around midday Thomas found himself back near where he had started and watched as the fire overtook the Palace Hotel and the Hearst Building. On the third floor of the Palace, as flames leapt from the roof and smoke poured out of every opening, he saw a woman appear at a window just below his own. He could not hear her calling for help over the roar of the fire, but even at a distance he could read her lips.

He felt impotent but he forced himself to watch as she realized no help would come and finally threw herself, trailing flames from her burning clothing, to the paving stones below.

As the fire raged on, he climbed the city's hills and saw people sitting in the streets in chairs they had rescued from the ruins of their homes, watching the smoke rise over the city as if it was a sporting event. He stepped over heaps of clothing, pots and pans, luggage, furniture, and all manner of abandoned personal effects. On top of one pile of splintered wood he saw a single book in a red cloth binding. On a whim, he picked it up and slipped it into his pocket.

No matter which way Thomas walked, he found people trapped, sometimes in rubble and sometimes by fire, whom neither he, nor anyone else, could save. By late in the afternoon he felt overcome by the power-lessness that had settled on his shoulders that morning, and almost didn't notice that, after making his way through a long series of intersections clogged with wagons, horses, and pedestrians, he had arrived at the edge of a large crowd of desperate-looking refugees.

"Where are we?" he managed to mumble to a pair of men in front of him.

"The gates of hell," said one of them, in a voice that sounded as hollow as Thomas felt.

"Ferry landing," said the other. "Ferry to Oakland is the only way to get out of the city."

"For those who have something to get out to," said another.

Thomas had nothing with him but the clothes on his back, his note-book and camera, and a fifty-dollar cash advance on his salary. Clearly, he would not be taking up work at the *Examiner*, but unlike many of the newly homeless in the city now burning to the ground, he did have some-place to go. In the crowd that waited for the ferry, he wrote a story, sticking to the facts as he knew them. In short, an earthquake had destroyed much of San Francisco and fires were finishing the job. Hundreds, if not thou-sands, had died.

After waiting through much of the night, Thomas finally made it to Oakland where he wired his story to New York. He spent the following night on a bench in the train station, returning in the morning to the telegraph office to file a follow-up report about the smoke still rising over San Francisco and the refugees streaming into Oakland. When he handed the story to the telegraph operator, he received, in exchange, a telegram from Mr. Hearst in response to the story he had filed the previous day. TOO MANY FACTS, NOT ENOUGH DRAMA, was the terse response. Thomas slipped the telegram into the rescued book in his pocket. Two hours later, while San Francisco still burned, he boarded a train for New York. At the far end of the car, he spotted a rather haggard Enrico Caruso. But Thomas no longer cared about the tenor. He slid down in his seat and slept. And the nightmares began.

In his dream, Thomas was trapped in a place of darkness. He could see a pinpoint of light far overhead, and he heard a clear voice. He called for help and the voice replied in chilling words: "There is no help for you." Suddenly flames leapt up on every side of him. The heat was unbearable, and he felt burning on his skin. Again he cried out, and this time the voice echoed back, louder than before: "You are beyond help." As the flames covered him, Thomas recognized the voice as his own.

Sweat dripping from his brow, he woke in near darkness, thinking he had slept through the day, but in another moment, the train shot out of a tunnel and light flooded the compartment. Below, he saw a steep, rocky slope speckled with pines leading down to a raging river. In no mood to enjoy the spectacular view, Thomas picked up the book in his lap and turned to the title page.

Ragged Dick; or, Street Life in New York with the Boot Blacks. Despite his dour mood, Thomas nearly laughed aloud. That this should be the book he had picked from the rubble seemed both appropriate and horrifying. After all, if not for *Ragged Dick*, Thomas might never have begun his own life on the streets—a life which had led him to Mr. Hearst's employ and therefore to San Francisco.

Thomas had been twelve years old, living in luxury in a Fifth Avenue mansion, the son of a banker and a member of one of the oldest families in what had been New Amsterdam when his ancestor Isaac De Peyster had arrived in 1639. The only son in a family with four daughters, Thomas had longed for the companionship of boys his age. He was taught by a governess, dressed by a nurse, and treated like a plaything by his older sisters.

Only on his highly supervised walks through Central Park did he ever even glimpse such a thing as another boy—usually one looking as starched and miserable as himself. And then, he had discovered *Ragged Dick*.

Before that fateful day, Thomas was forever reading whatever books his sisters had cast aside—*What Katy Did* and *Elsie Dinsmore* and well-thumbed issues of *St. Nicholas* magazine which included serial stories like "Little Lord Fauntleroy." He liked the beginning of this story—the part where Cedric Errol lived with his mother in a poor neighborhood of New York. Thomas knew he was lucky to be born into wealth, but he could not squelch his curiosity about what he once heard his mother call "the other half." Though every book his sisters had abandoned seemed to Thomas to be written for girls, he still preferred this fare to the books his father continually thrust at him—mathematical treatises and biographies of prominent Union generals. "You're going to take over my business someday," his father said. "You need to learn about leadership." Thomas had no idea what he wanted to do when he grew up, but he certainly did not dream of becoming a banker.

Thomas could relate to Elsie Dinsmore, in a way. The scene from the book in which her father insisted that she play the piano and sing for his friends reminded him of how his own father liked to put him on display, trotting him out whenever he hosted a dinner party for his fellow bankers and exhibiting him like a promising Thoroughbred colt. On more than one occasion Thomas had been rousted by his governess from a sound sleep and made to dress in his Sunday best, just so he could stand before a gathering of businessmen for thirty seconds while his father presented "my son." His father did not, Thomas thought, say these words with any pride—they merely conveyed the information that the future of the De Peyster name was, after a run of four daughters, now safe in the hands of a male heir. At these times, Thomas felt like an inanimate treasure in his own house; he had heard greater delight in his father's voice when he was showing off one of his rare books or antique paintings.

Back in the "nursery," as his bedroom, being designated for the youngest child, would always be called, Thomas, now wide awake, would turn to one of his sisters' books, never quite satisfied with what he found within those pages.

On his twelfth birthday, in 1894, Thomas's mother threw him a party in a private room of Delmonico's. The guests, all of them twelve-year-old boys, all born into privilege, and all looking as bored and uncomfortable as Thomas felt in his black woolen suit, encircled a massive table. With the possible exception of Easter morning at St. Nicholas Church, Thomas had never seen so large a gathering of boys his own age. He longed to talk with them, to wrestle with them, to chase them through the park or swim with them in the lake. Instead, he and his guests were forced to sit stiffly, nibbling at one unappetizing course after another.

That night after he had opened a pile of, as he saw it, useless presents—a silver salver; a leather-bound set of books on economics; a small, dark painting by someone named Rembrandt with which he was supposed to be impressed—Thomas sat in the nursery, looking out the window into the walled back garden of the house. He wondered if any of his sisters had ever met someone like the boys he had once glimpsed from the carriage. He didn't imagine so; their lives were as contained and regimented as his own. True, they promenaded in the park on Sundays and spent summers with relatives in Newport or Hyde Park, but they did not, to Thomas, seem any freer than he felt. He had just turned away from the window when his governess stepped through the door holding a small package.

"They missed one," she said. "A birthday gift from your cousin Zebulon." She set the parcel on the table by the bed and retired from the room without further comment. Thomas had never heard of any cousin Zebulon, but he pulled the paper off the parcel and discovered the book that would change his life: *Ragged Dick*.

By the light of his gas lamp, Thomas had read *Ragged Dick*, the first and best-selling of Horatio Alger's many rags-to-riches stories in which poor boys rose to the middle class through hard work, honesty, and often some act of heroism. But to Thomas, who already dwelt well above the middle class to which Alger's heroes aspired, this was not so much a book about achieving success as a window into the world he had wondered about for so long—a world of what Alger called in his preface, "the friendless and vagrant children who are now numbered by the thousands in New York and other cities." While Alger may have seen these boys as friendless and vagrant, Thomas saw them as liberated. They lived on the streets and fraternized with one another free from governesses or nurses or sisters. And unlike the gods of Mount Olympus he studied with his tutor or the fantasy of Grimm's *Fairy Tales* his sisters used to read to him, the world of *Ragged Dick* was real—as real as the boys he had seen on that day returning from Mr. Sargent's studio—and only a short streetcar ride from the mansions of Fifth Avenue.

From the moment he read the first scene, Thomas longed to dive into that world, to meet bootblacks and pickpockets, to sleep in a box full of straw, to go to a vaudeville show at Tony Pastor's theater or drink a five-cent cup of coffee and eat a ten-cent beefsteak while wearing ragged clothes. To lonely and isolated Thomas De Peyster, it all sounded like a grand adventure.

While the world he eventually found on the streets of lower Manhattan was not exactly what he had been led to expect by Horatio Alger, Thomas well remembered the excitement of the first night he successfully escaped Fifth Avenue.

The plan had taken weeks to set into motion. He had found an old suit of his father's, out of fashion and forgotten at the back of the wardrobe, and spent time each night, when he was presumed asleep by the rest of the household, ripping the trousers, fraying the coat, and rubbing dirt and grime into the fabric. He stole a knife from the kitchen and used it to scuff the leather of an old pair of shoes. He fashioned his entire look after the frontispiece of *Ragged Dick*, an illustration showing the hero in his days as a bootblack on the streets of New York.

Once he completed the costume, except for Dick's hat, for which Thomas could find no facsimile within the confines of the De Peyster home, he mussed his hair and dirtied his face with ashes from the fireplace. He spent several nights carefully dressing and admiring himself in the looking glass, each time trying to muster the courage to attempt an escape. In the end, leaving home in the dead of night had proved a simple matter. The doors and locks on the mansion were designed to keep people out, not in. Thomas only had to slip out the servants' entrance and leave the door unlocked for his return. At five minutes past midnight on a crisp

October night, he found himself standing in the cool air of Fifth Avenue. He had no idea whether the streetcars (or the Third Avenue El, two long blocks away) ran at this time of night, so when he saw a hansom cab heading downtown, he hailed it.

The driver brought the horse to a stop, then burst out laughing. "Not usual for a bootblack to pay cab fare," he said, raising his whip to spur the horse on.

"I've got my fare," shot back Thomas, pulling a dollar bill from his pocket.

"And then some," said the driver. "All right then, in you get. Where to, young gent?"

Thomas wasn't quite sure how to answer this question.

"Where would you expect to find someone like me at this time of night?" he said.

"The Bowery it is," said the driver, and flicked his whip.

Thomas thought he had found reality during years of late-night excursions into the bowels of New York, but now, as the train sped east, he realized he had only scratched the surface of human suffering. He looked again at the book on his lap and thought about what Mr. Hearst had said—"not enough drama." Maybe he was right. Maybe what Thomas needed more than anything was to write a story filled with drama.

IX

By the time Robert was halfway home, the flurry had crescendoed into a full-fledged snowstorm. Taxis sloshed their way uptown and crosstown streets turned white. He pulled his knit hat down over his ears, turned left on Seventy-Seventh Street, and headed for the park. If walking a few blocks uptown had made him feel less depressed, then a long walk in the Ramble through the snow now blanketing Central Park would certainly be good for him. To live in the midst of millions of people, and yet to lose himself in a silent wood, carpeted in white, the sound of traffic (except for the occasional cab horn) no more than a muffled memory, was a delight he never tired of, yet he hadn't been here in months. Within minutes of entering the park he was wandering aimlessly on the Ramble's maze of footpaths, unable to see more than a few feet ahead of him through the densely falling snow.

Robert and Rebecca had met nearby at the Bethesda Fountain four years ago. He had been sitting on one side of the fountain reading William Zinsser's *On Writing Well*, and Rebecca had been on the other side, sketching *Angel of the Waters*, Emma Stebbins's 1873 statue that towered overhead. It had been a perfect New York spring day, cool and clear, the blue sky mottled with clouds and the sun glowing through a mist of pale green leaves. When an unexpected shower drove them into the beautifully tiled shelter below the upper terrace, Rebecca and Robert had collided and she had dropped her sketchpad. Robert picked it up and looked at the unfinished pencil drawing of the angel before handing it back to her.

"It's beautiful," he said.

"I'm not really an artist," said Rebecca.

"That's okay," said Robert, waving the book he had been reading. "I'm not really a writer. Not a published one, anyway."

"I just like to sketch. And I was thinking about using the angel in a logo for my business."

"What sort of business?" said Robert.

"Interior design," said Rebecca. "Designs by RGB. I'm RGB."

"Robert Parrish," said Robert, holding out his hand. "Pleased to meet you, RGB."

"Rebecca," she said, shaking his hand firmly. "So if you're not a writer . . ."

"I do write. Two hours every day no matter what. But since no one is buying what I write at the moment, I'm also a publicist at St. Martin's Press. Not exactly glamorous, but I get to work in the Flatiron Building."

"My office is in Chelsea," said Rebecca. "Not far from there."

The shower ended as suddenly as it had started and the crowd began to move out from under the terrace and into the sunlight that sparkled off the wet pavement.

"I was planning to take a walk when I finished sketching," said Rebecca.

"I was planning to take a walk when I finished reading," said Robert.

So they took a long leisurely walk around the lake and through the Ramble. Robert had never met a girl in the park, though he supposed *girl* was not exactly the right word. Rebecca looked about his age and he would be thirty soon. He always marveled that people could meet total strangers at a bar or a club or a party and simply start chatting, yet this felt natural.

They were well and truly lost in the Ramble when Rebecca said, "Since you're a writer, why don't you tell me a story? Tell me the story of the first time you came to Central Park."

And, without realizing the significance of the moment, Robert began his entire relationship with the most important person in his life with a lie. He knew if he told the true story of his first visit to Central Park it would lead to another story and another story and eventually to the one story he didn't want to tell anyone. So he invented a story about visiting the park for the first time as a teenager—wandering away from a class trip to the Met and nearly missing the bus back to Rockaway Beach. He embellished it with details about following a girl he had a crush on and wandering as far south as the Alice in Wonderland statue. He added a little boy sailing a model boat on the Conservatory Water and a homeless man sleeping under Glade Arch and finished with a mad dash chasing the bus down Fifth Avenue.

"Did it stop for you?" said Rebecca.

"Lucky for me there was a red light at Eightieth Street," said Robert. "I only had to bang on the door about a hundred times before the driver let me in."

Rebecca laughed, and when they stopped on Bow Bridge to watch the boaters gliding across the lake and Robert asked if she'd like to get a drink sometime, she said, "Yes." Robert had long thought the most romantic thing in the world would be to kiss a girl on Bow Bridge. He didn't do it that day, but it wouldn't be long before he and Rebecca stood there again with their arms around each other.

⌒

Robbie's first visit to Central Park had taken place in December of 1989. His mother liked to spend a Saturday in the city every year at Christmastime. The three Parrishes would bundle up and take the subway from Rockaway Beach to Grand Central Station. From there, they walked to Fifth Avenue and headed uptown, as Robbie's parents did their Christmas shopping. Then his mother always wanted to go to an art gallery or museum, which neither Robbie nor his father much cared for.

The year Robbie turned thirteen, when he and his father were on about their tenth reading of the Tremendous Trio books, Mrs. Parrish insisted on the Metropolitan Museum of Art.

"You enjoy the museum," said Robbie's father. "Robbie and I are going to take a walk."

"We are?" said Robbie.

"Sure," said his father. When they had stowed all their packages in the cloakroom at the museum, Robbie and his father stepped out into the crisp winter air. "Let's see if we can find Alice Gold's house," his father said.

"But how do you know where she lives?" said Robbie.

"She says so right in the first chapter of her first book. Remember— she's in the park with the bicyclist and she tells him she lives at 922 Fifth Avenue."

"Right," said Robbie.

"That's just a few blocks from here," said his father. They walked down Fifth Avenue to Seventy-Second Street, but although they found a nondescript apartment building at 923, they could find no number 922.

"Well, this is her neighborhood, anyway," said his father.

"So she walked from here to the bridge in the park?" said Robbie.

"Right," said his father. "We can do that, at least."

They entered the park at Seventy-Second Street and strolled past the Bethesda Terrace and onto the Bow Bridge. "This is the spot," said his father. "The place where the world first met Alice Gold."

"Yeah," said Robbie, "and where she almost got run down by that bicycle."

"You know," said his father, "I'll bet we could find a lot of the places in those books. It could be fun—finding where Alice Gold and the others had their adventures."

And that was how it had started—an innocent suggestion from his father for a way they could spend more time together. It seemed perfectly harmless.

Now, as he stepped out of the Ramble and onto Bow Bridge, Robert's previous visits to that spot, with his father and with Rebecca, swirled in his mind like the snow that fell around him. It had been years since he had allowed himself to think of that day with his father, but he thought often about his first encounter with Rebecca.

The memory of that spring day when he and Rebecca had barely been into their thirties, far enough into adulthood to tremble with the excitement of its promise, but not so deeply mired in it as to fear its uncertainty, seemed now like an old black-and-white photograph—crisp and clear yet recording something wholly unattainable. But Robert still believed they belonged together, just as he had believed it when he said goodbye to her that day. Somehow, he would slog through the mess of his past and win Rebecca back. But standing in the colorless, snow-covered park, he wished for even a sliver of the innocence of that golden day.

When Robert arrived home, darkness had descended and the headlights of rush hour glowed in the still-falling snow. Robert thought again about phoning Rebecca, telling her that he loved her, that the memory of their first meeting still gave him goose bumps. He could promise to give up writing (or, more accurately, give up *not* writing) and get a job doing . . . anything—bagging groceries at Zabar's if it came to that. But he didn't. He simply couldn't muster the courage. Instead, he took out his copy of *Alice Gold, Girl Inventor* by Buck Larson. He made himself a mug of instant hot cocoa and slipped into a cozy chair to read by the light of a single lamp. The snow fell silently through the haze of the streetlights. He would find out everything he could about Buck Larson and the others tomorrow; he would search for *The Last Adventure of the Tremendous Trio* tomorrow; he might even call Rebecca tomorrow. He knew he was hiding from the world, hiding from the truths he must eventually face. But he didn't care. He just wanted to read.

CHAPTER 1
ALICE SAVES THE DAY

Alice Gold stood on the curved surface of Bow Bridge in Central Park in her hometown of New York City. She knew that any minute her governess would come around the corner, angry that Alice had slipped away, but Alice didn't care. She had an idea for a new invention and she needed to watch the way the boats moved through the water beneath the bridge. She and her governess had been taking a walk down Fifth Avenue when Alice had run away while Miss Gander stopped to speak to a gentleman admirer on a street corner. By the time Miss Gander noticed Alice was missing, the twelve-year-old was halfway to the lake.

Alice loved nothing better than inventing. She read in magazines about the great inventor Thomas Edison and dreamed of one day having her own workshop as big and bustling as his. In the meantime, Alice had to satisfy herself by plying her trade as an inventor within the confines of the family mansion. Alice had already invented several improvements to devices around the house, such as the coffee percolator or the flat iron—although she had not been able to convince either the cook or the laundress to let her try out her ideas, so they remained only sketches in her workbook.

Today, she was working on an improved version of the house's flush toilets (which the upstairs maid insisted on calling water closets). She needed to understand how water flowed past a moving object, and the best examples she could think of nearby were the boats on the lake in Central Park.

Alice leaned over the edge of the rail, her toes just touching the bridge, watching one boat after another slipping beneath her. She became so lost in her thoughts that she almost didn't notice the cry from the bicyclist.

"Look out! Look out! I can't stop!"

Alice looked up to see a young man on a roadster bicycle heading straight for her. The bicycle careened onto the bridge at a frightful speed, and the young driver, who appeared to have lost both his hat and his composure, steered it away from Alice just in time to prevent a collision. At the far end of the bridge stood

a group of young schoolchildren, and Alice felt certain
that many of them would be injured as the bicyclist sped
toward them.

"Turn to the left," she shouted, seeing one way the
rider could save the children and himself, if not his
dignity.

"Now, turn! Turn!"

The young man did as Alice instructed and just missed
colliding with several of the children. The bicycle
bumped down a short embankment and flung the rider
into the lake, where he landed with a splash. As Alice
dashed to the edge of the lake, she heard several boaters
laughing. The young man stood in water up to his knees
and was soaked to the skin, but appeared unhurt.

"Thanks!" he said cheerfully to Alice.

"I thought you'd rather land in the water than on the
footpath or on the stones," said Alice.

"Right ho," said the bicyclist.

"You know, I can improve the brakes on that bicycle,"
said Alice as the young man waded toward the shore. The
bicycle lay on its side, one wheel still spinning.

"I built that bike myself," said the young man. "But
I guess I'm not very good at building brakes. What I need
is a proper inventor."

"I am an inventor," said Alice, holding out her hand to
help the young man as he reached the shore. "I'm Alice Gold."

"Alice Gold, come away from that water this instant!"
came a shouted voice from the bridge.

"My governess," whispered Alice to the bicyclist. "If
you want help with those brakes, my address is 922 Fifth
Avenue."

Alice scampered back up the hill to where Miss Gander
stood, hands on her hips and a furious expression on
her face.

"Just what do you think you are doing, young lady?"
said Mrs. Gander.

"Saving all those children and getting a new customer
for my inventing business," said Alice with a toss of her
head as she walked past Miss Gander and back across the
bridge. "Oh, and thinking about toilets," she added.

Just as he drifted off to sleep, Robert thought again about the walk
with his father in search of Alice Gold's house. He wondered if there had
ever been a 922 Fifth Avenue, and if so, whether Alice's creator, Buck
Larson, might have lived there.

X

NEW YORK CITY,
WHEN LADIES DANCED ON THE ROOF

Eugene Pinkney slipped his hand inside his jacket and felt the cool surface of the silver cigarette case that nestled in his pocket. He didn't smoke, but he had bought the case two years ago to prove to himself how far he had come from the bakery on Houston Street.

On a warm summer night in June 1906, Gene sat at his table at the rooftop theater of Madison Square Garden on Twenty-Sixth Street and wondered if Mr. White would show up. To his left the illuminated Moorish tower that Mr. White had built as part of the complex rose over Twenty-Sixth Street; in front of him chorus girls danced and sang their way through some frothy bit of entertainment called *Mamzelle Champagne*. Eugene admired the costumes and the feminine beauty of the dancers, but didn't think much of the music. Certainly he had seen better shows—among them *Floradora*, to which Mr. White had treated him on two occasions. Eugene had never been certain if Mr. White was trying to seduce him or if he had simply taken a shine to him. Nor did Eugene much care which. He enjoyed spending time with Mr. White for two reasons— the man was wealthy enough to treat Eugene to fine restaurants, the best shows, and expensive champagne; and, more important, Stanford White was the only person who had ever seen the two faces of Eugene Pinkney.

Gene's parents, who should have known him better than anyone, had seen neither side of his true self—neither the character he had displayed in the daylight on the top floor of a building on Houston Street, nor the persona he used to assume at night, at Columbia Hall on Bleecker Street. Just a few blocks separated these two buildings, which had nurtured the two parts of Gene, yet their spheres were completely disconnected, and both his artistic self and his scientific self felt as removed from his childhood home as the earth was from the moon.

Science had fascinated Gene for as long as he could remember. From the time he was ten years old, Gene made the twenty-minute walk to the Astor Library on Lafayette Street by himself at least twice a week to check out books on science. Even when his father made him begin helping with the early deliveries for the bakery and Gene rose at three o'clock every morning, he still found time for reading. Despite minimal schooling, he had learned to read quickly, and had digested the works of Jules Verne by his tenth birthday. He loved *Twenty Thousand Leagues under the Sea* and *From the Earth to the Moon*, but he wanted to know more about the science that made Captain Nemo's *Nautilus* and the Columbiad space gun work.

And so, Gene had moved on to books *about* science—specifically books about mechanics and electricity. Then, in 1895, at the age of thirteen, he read a new book, *The Mechanics' Complete Library of Modern Rules, Facts, Processes, Etc.*, compiled by Thomas Edison and George Westinghouse. Gene read the book over and over, memorizing long passages, especially the sections about electricity, dynamos, batteries, telephones, and lighting. While other boys his age read Horatio Alger and dime novels, Gene read the "Rules and Regulations for Properly Wiring and Installing Electrical Light Plants," learned the difference between voltaic and galvanic electricity, and committed to memory a chapter titled "A Few Points for Inventors Regarding Patents."

Gene's father did not approve of his "wasting his time" reading, so as Gene became more fascinated by and schooled in science, he also became more adept at hiding his books. He eventually loosened a few floorboards under his bed to create enough space to store several volumes. By then, books were not the only things Eugene Pinkney had to hide.

He was fourteen the first time he went to a fairy resort. Soon thereafter, he first kissed another boy in a dark corner of the dance floor at the Black Rabbit. At fifteen he slipped behind the curtain into one of the private booths at Columbia Hall, known to its patrons as Paresis Hall, a nickname Gene would later discover came from a term for syphilitic insanity. There he earned a dollar from a middle-class man who was slumming and looking for a thrill. By his sixteenth birthday, Gene had been a regular at Paresis Hall for nearly a year, making more money that he ever could delivering bread by waiting tables, flirting with men from uptown, and engaging in activities in the upstairs rooms which, though lucrative, would have sent his father into a rage and set his grandmother spinning in her grave.

Gene had never particularly questioned his interest in boys. He liked boys more than he liked girls, or at least in a different way. That was simply part of his being, and one of many things—his love of science, his constant reading, his distaste for manual labor—that made up the chasm separating him from his parents. To him, the fact that boys, and then young men, and even not so young men, turned his head in the streets while girls did not seemed no more "degenerate," as he would later hear people call it, than any of his other eccentricities. In fact, thanks to clubs like Paresis Hall, he found it much easier to connect with those who were like-minded on this subject than with fellow enthusiasts of electrical theory.

Paresis Hall stood on the Bowery, near Fifth Street. A rather plain building from the outside, inside it consisted of a saloon downstairs and a number of smaller rooms upstairs where private "entertainments" took place. Gene had discovered the place almost by accident. Unable to sleep one night, he had gone out for a walk and saw a young man not much older than himself standing on the corner of Bowery and Fifth. He wore trousers that flared at the ankles and cinched in tightly at the waist, emphasizing his round behind. His shirt was a frilly affair, though mostly covered by a fur-trimmed jacket that looked like something a Fifth Avenue grande dame would wear to the opera. His hair was longer than was stylish, and perfectly coiffed. His cheeks were rouged and his lips lined with artificial color. He held a cigarette in a silver holder and spoke in a high voice. Gene had never seen anyone like this man, had never heard the word *fairy*, but he felt instantly drawn to the strange figure in the shadows.

"Give a girl a light?" said the man.

"Sorry," said Gene. "I don't have one. Are you . . . ?"

"Princess Petunia," said the man, holding his hand loosely in front of Gene's face. Gene locked eyes with this odd character, and though he sensed exactly what the man wanted him to do, he hesitated. "No one's around," said Petunia. And so Gene leaned in, took Petunia's hand in his, and lightly kissed it.

"You like that?" said Petunia.

"Yes," said Gene, shivering. Excitement crashed over him like a tidal wave the moment his lips touched Petunia's soft skin.

"Come on in," said Petunia. "I'll buy you a drink."

Inside Gene found a new world, a world in which he felt not alien, but welcomed with open arms. Men filled the tables and stood two deep at the bar. Among them flitted many more boys and men like Petunia— dressed in a feminine style, wearing makeup, and using mannerisms one would expect from chorus girls. Some were even more feminine in their dress and behavior than Petunia. Most seemed to be in their late teens. All of them were, to Gene, exquisitely beautiful. By the end of the evening he had met the Duchess of Marlboro, the Queen of Sheba, Lady Lily, and a dozen others who, though certainly men, dressed to varying degrees like women and used flamboyant pseudonyms. They all treated Gene with kindness—including him in their jokes, buying him drinks, and kissing him on the cheek, always careful to rub away telltale lipstick marks afterward. He left the club just in time to turn up at the bakery at three a.m. To his father, he looked no different than usual, but Gene felt transformed.

Gene learned quickly enough the locations of the other "fairy resorts"—the Black Rabbit on Bleecker Street; the Palm Club on Chrystie Street; Little Bucks, across the street from Paresis Hall; and several more. While on some nights he would wander from one to another, he generally ended up at Paresis Hall, often chatting with Princess Petunia and the other "girls" when they weren't busy charming men, dancing, and even singing for the delight of the crowd. These friends not only didn't consider Gene abnormal because of his attraction to boys, he got the feeling they would have found him odd if he were *not* attracted to boys. Everyone at Paresis Hall liked boys. Gene had found his people.

Soon enough he started flirting with men himself—especially after he learned that he would get a percentage of every drink he sold. He would drink glass after glass of water, for which unsuspecting slummers had paid the price of gin. When he told his father he had gotten a job on the night shift of a bakery in the West Village, Mr. Pinkney asked no questions. All that mattered was that Gene brought home good money. Gene knew that money would be much better if he looked the part. So, one evening, not long after his fifteenth birthday, he went to Princess Petunia for help.

"You've come to the right girl," said Petunia. "You don't need to wear a dress. You just need flair." Petunia showed Gene how to pluck his eyebrows and how to apply rouge to his cheeks. She (Gene had learned by now that in the context of Paresis Hall, his fellow fairies preferred to be called "she") helped him shop for clothes that had, as Petunia had put it, flair, capping his outfit with a large red neck-bow and a pair of white kid gloves.

As they stood before a dusty mirror in a back room of Paresis Hall, Princess Petunia smiled as Gene gazed, awestruck, at the image before him. From an unknown source in his depths welled up the sensation that he was looking at his true self for the first time.

"Don't start crying," said Petunia, "or we'll have to put fresh powder on."

But Gene couldn't help it. He stood immobile, staring at the *real* Gene Pinkney, tears leaving wet streaks on his powdered cheeks. Petunia embraced him from behind; Gene had never been so happy.

"Now," whispered Petunia, "you need a name."

"Eugene Pinkney," said Gene dully. "It's not much."

"But it's something to work with," said Petunia with a smile.

And so Dame Pinky was born. Soon she was earning more money than any bakery would pay, and Gene opened an account at the Butchers' and Drovers' Bank on the Bowery. Petunia had told him that the oldest fairies working Paresis were twenty-one. That gave Gene six years. In that time, he could easily save enough money to be independent from his parents.

On a warm night late in the summer of 1898, Dame Pinky stood at the bar fanning herself and chatting with the Duchess of Marlboro. Business dragged, but it was early yet.

"Ooh, I wish I could look like her," cooed the Duchess, nodding toward the door.

Gene turned around and saw an unusual couple settling themselves at a table just inside the saloon. The man presented a reasonably conventional exterior—tall and broad-shouldered with striking red hair and a bushy handlebar mustache, impeccably dressed, and exuding wealth and charisma even from across the room. He was just the sort of gent Gene and his cohorts loved to see at Paresis Hall—a man swimming in both money and sexual curiosity who had decided to leave his uptown mansion or his suite at the Waldorf to go slumming in the clubs and resorts of the Bowery. He had the added qualities of handsomeness and magnetism. But on his arm hung something rarely seen in Paresis Hall.

"Is she?" said Gene.

"Yes," said the Duchess. "She's a real girl. And what a beauty."

"But I thought you . . ."

"Just because I don't want to take them to bed doesn't mean I can't admire them," said the Duchess. And Gene had to admit, the real live girl who slipped gracefully into the chair next to her towering companion deserved admiration.

She had the face of a china doll—skin so pale it was nearly white, a delicate nose and diminutive lips, and dark eyes that matched the cascade of hair falling in ringlets across one shoulder and over her white cotton dress. She wore an inscrutable expression and a superfluous fur wrap that she instantly shed onto the back of the chair. She couldn't have been a day over sixteen.

"You go," said the Duchess, nudging Gene in the ribs. "I don't trust myself around anything that beautiful."

Gene approached the couple feeling more nervous than he had since his first night at Paresis Hall. For almost two years now he had slept during the day and spent long nights working at the resort. He had not had a conversation with a beautiful girl his own age since before girls his own age had blossomed.

"May I get you a drink?" Dame Pinky said to the red-haired man, averting her eyes from the radiant young woman by his side.

"Why don't you join us," said the man, "and let someone else fetch the drinks."

This was not an unusual request at Paresis Hall. Some men simply wanted to spend a few minutes chatting with a fairy for the novelty; others would talk your ear off all evening; and some, of course, wanted to take you into the back room and . . . take you. The third scenario seemed unlikely in this case, as the man in question had a girl by his side, but Gene slid into the chair next to the redhead, trying to do so with the same grace his female companion had shown a moment ago.

"Stanford White," said the man, holding out his hand to Dame Pinky. She took the hand lightly in hers and, instead of shaking it as he clearly expected, raised it to her lips and kissed it firmly enough to leave a lipstick mark.

"Charmed, I'm sure. You can call me Dame Pinky."

The red-haired man let out a guffaw even as the young woman leaned around her companion to look more closely at Dame Pinky.

"Surely that's not your real name," said the man.

"In here it's my real name," said Dame Pinky.

"Very well," said the man. "In here my name is Stanford White, and this is Eliza Fuller. Eliza is about to star on Broadway in *The Fortune Teller*."

"Not star," said Eliza, still staring intently at Dame Pinky. "I'm in the chorus."

"Has Mother Nature ever crafted a creature more delectable than the chorus girl?" said Mr. White in a low voice.

"Wait, are you *the* Stanford White? The architect?" said Dame Pinky, forgetting for a moment her affected voice.

"The one and only," said Mr. White. "But how have you heard of me in a place like this?"

"We do have access to newspapers here on the Bowery," said Dame Pinky. "You designed the arch in Washington Square—that's just a few blocks from here. And you show up in the society pages quite a lot. You're a collector as well. Art and antiques."

"Perhaps you'd like to see some of my paintings sometime," said Mr. White.

"Perhaps."

Stanford White, it turned out, just wanted to talk. While Eliza Fuller distractedly stirred her drink with her finger, boredom sapping her face of its charm, White peppered Dame Pinky with questions and regaled her with anecdotes. He was curious about the life of a fairy, curious about how Gene (for he eventually admitted his given name) transformed into Dame Pinky, and curious about what went on in the rooms upstairs, though he claimed to have no interest in participating.

Gene found it easy to talk with Mr. White, and when the chorus girl finally fell asleep, her head on the table and the drool dripping from her mouth erasing the last of her allure, the tête-à-tête turned from idle chitchat about fairy resorts and Broadway plays to more serious topics.

"You can't stay in a place like this forever, no matter how comfortable it makes you feel," said Mr. White. "Sooner or later you have to go back to the real world."

"This isn't any less real than the world you live in," said Gene.

"Don't get me wrong," said Mr. White, "it's substantially more real than the world I live in. That's what brings me here. But I have *money* to stave off reality. What do you have?"

Gene thought for a long minute. What did he have? What would he turn to when he was too old to charm men at Paresis Hall? "Science," he said.

"Science?" said Mr. White. "That's an interesting answer."

"I know a lot about science," said Gene. "Especially electricity and mechanics. I read all the articles in the scientific journals, and I've practically memorized this book by George Westinghouse and Thomas Edison."

"You're a fan of Thomas Edison?" said Mr. White.

"Outside these walls," said Gene, "nothing makes me happier than to read about Edison and his latest inventions."

"What about Tesla?"

"Nikola Tesla?" said Gene. "Oh, he's great, too. I've read his articles on alternating current motors and on electrical discharge in vacuum tubes in

The Electrical Engineer. Did you read the speech on 'The Age of Electricity' that he gave in Buffalo after the Niagara power plant opened?"

"My boy, or if you prefer, my girl, I didn't have to read the speech. I had dinner with Mr. Tesla the next week and he told me all about it."

"You had dinner with Nikola Tesla?" said Gene, awestruck.

"He and I are dear friends," said Mr. White. "I dined with him two nights ago at my club in Gramercy Park."

"You are *friends* with Nikola Tesla?" At the Astor Library, Gene had read scores of articles by and about Tesla and his electrical experiments and inventions. Next to Edison, Tesla was the most exciting scientist in the world. His alternating current motor and his Tesla coil were revolutionizing the field of electricity, and Gene was sitting next to a man who counted Tesla among his friends. "What is he like?"

"He is focused," said Mr. White. "Even when we are dining together after he has left his laboratory for the day, I can tell his thoughts are still there. He told me once that the thrill he feels when he imagines a new creation erases everything else from his mind—food, sleep, friends, love, everything. And yet he has a kind smile and a sweet disposition. One knows one is in the company of genius, but Mr. Tesla is always modest, never condescending. You will see."

"What do you mean I will see?" said Gene, leaning forward, his pulse rushing.

"You must meet him if you are so interested in his work. His laboratory is just a few blocks from here on Houston Street."

"He works on Houston Street?"

"Near Mulberry," said Mr. White. "He's been there for almost two years now, since the fire destroyed his old lab."

"I've been walking within two blocks of Nikola Tesla's lab every day for the past two years and didn't even know it?"

"Come to think of it, he has an opening for a new assistant. It wouldn't be much more than sweeping floors at first, but if you're ready to trade in your lipstick for a chance to work with Tesla, I could put in a word for you."

A week later, Eugene Pinkney became the newest employee to climb the stairs of a seven-story building on Houston Street. Tesla's laboratory occupied the top two floors, and Gene's fellow employees consisted of a clerk and several mechanics. For the first few weeks, he rarely saw Tesla, as most of his responsibilities had to do with cleaning or organizing materials after the others had left for the day. But within a few months, Gene had demonstrated his scientific knowledge and joined the ranks of the mechanics. He would work for Tesla for the next eight years.

Dame Pinky still made occasional appearances at Paresis Hall, and a block of rouge and a lipstick brush remained among the items Gene kept hidden under the floorboards beneath his bed. Every few weeks, Stanford White would invite him to dinner at Delmonico's or to attend a Broadway show. The architect often had a young girl in tow, and Gene remembered well the night in 1901 when he met White's latest obsession, Evelyn Nesbit, a chorus girl in the smash hit *Floradora*. Evelyn's beauty was more radiant even than that of Eliza Fuller, and she did not tire with boredom or fall asleep at the dinner table. She was as magnetic as Mr. White, and if Gene had cared in the least about girls (for Evelyn was clearly still a girl, being no more than about sixteen) he would have fallen instantly in love with her.

Now, as the chorus of *Mamzelle Champagne* made their way through another insipid number, Gene sat just a few tables away from Evelyn, whom Mr. White had eventually tired of, though not before, he had told Gene, "quite a bit of imaginative lovemaking." She was now the wife of a Pittsburgh railroad heir, Harry Thaw. Gene nodded to Evelyn and they shared a look that said they agreed that this "musical bubble in two bottles," as the program described the evening's entertainment, would not run more than a week. Evelyn's husband was curiously absent from her table for much of the first "bottle," but Gene had not come to the theater to spy on Evelyn and Harry Thaw. He had, luckily, not come to be entertained. He had come to speak to Mr. White.

Tesla had become more and more driven to investigate possibilities of wireless communication, and to this end had built a laboratory, designed by Mr. White, and a massive steel tower on the north shore of Long Island at a site he called Wardenclyffe. But when Guglielmo Marconi successfully sent wireless messages via radio transmission, funding for Wardenclyffe dried up. Tesla cut expenses and began laying off workers. Gene could see that despite his years of service to the inventor, his job could not possibly last much longer. He saved Tesla the discomfort of firing him by resigning.

Mr. White had gotten Gene the job with Tesla back in 1898. Since then Gene had moved out of his parents' apartment into a place of his own—two rooms in a rooming house on Carmine Street near Washington Square, easily accessible to both Tesla's laboratory and the Bowery. As his work with Tesla became more demanding, he had visited the fairy resorts less and less often, especially after the infamous raid on the Black Rabbit in 1900. Now, those resorts had all been closed, and he hadn't seen Princess Petunia or any of the other girls in several years. Occasionally he visited one of the public baths known to cater to men who enjoyed other men, but with his transfer to Tesla's laboratory on Long Island, Gene didn't get to Manhattan often. When he had moved back from Wardenclyffe, Gene was pleased to find rooms in the same house on Carmine Street, but he feared the rent would exhaust his savings if he didn't find a job soon. Mr. White was the only person alive who had known both Dame Pinky the fairy and Eugene Pinkney the scientist. Both of those people felt far away to Gene at the moment, but Mr. White had promised to meet him here on the roof of Madison Square Garden at the end of the performance.

"We'll go have a drink and talk about your future," he had said.

Gene had never suspected those would be the last words he would hear Stanford White utter.

Because White had designed Madison Square Garden, he seemed to have access to as many tickets for this opening night performance as he wanted. He had secured Gene a table about five rows back from the stage, where he sat alone, nursing a watered-down drink. Not until *Mamzelle Champagne* was winding toward its conclusion did Mr. White appear, but he did not sit with Gene, taking instead a table slightly closer to the stage. Gene watched as a man sat down with Mr. White and the two spoke for a few minutes. Then the man walked round to the back of the stage. Gene assumed he worked for the theater. Mr. White was not the only prominent citizen in the audience, but, here at his own Madison Square Garden, he was certainly the *most* prominent, and it was not surprising that people wanted to speak with him. Gene considered moving to Mr.

White's table, but he thought it best not to disturb the architect until after the performance, so he turned his attention back to the stage. A moment or two later Gene noticed another man approaching Mr. White.

The man wore a dress coat over his evening clothes, its velvet collar turned up and pulled tightly about his neck as if it were not a warm summer evening, but a cold day in December. In contrast to Mr. White's rugged good health and lively presence, this man looked pale and drawn, almost haunted. Gene glanced over toward Evelyn to see if she had noticed the odd man approaching her former lover. Evelyn sat by herself, watching the performance in which the chorus was just launching into a song about a duel. When Gene looked back at Mr. White, the pale man had reached the table and was holding a revolver level with White's head. Gene drew in a breath to cry out a warning, but in that instant the gun cracked. He found he could not breathe as blue smoke curled from the barrel and another crack rent the air. Gene saw Mr. White's head snap backward, but most of the audience seemed to think the gunshots were part of the duel being sung about on stage. The man fired a third time and Mr. White fell to the ground, his table and chair crashing over with him.

Gene froze in his chair. He could not speak or move. He could just see Mr. White's head through the crowd that separated their two tables. Blood had already begun to pool around him, and he did not move. Gene felt in his gut that White was dead. The gunman walked calmly up the aisle, his coat brushing Gene's arm. Then the shouting began. First the people closest to Mr. White and gradually the entire audience grasped that a real murder had taken place. Although two of the dancers on stage had fainted when they realized what had happened, the rest of the performers labored on and the conductor waved frantically at the orchestra to keep playing. Gene looked behind him and saw a fireman taking the gun from the killer. The shooter looked calmly over the audience and Gene recognized him as the man who had spent only a small part of the evening sitting with Evelyn—her husband, Harry Thaw.

"He deserved it," shouted Thaw. "He ruined my wife, and now that goddamned bastard will never go out with another girl."

People were jumping to their feet, men shouting angrily and women screaming hysterically. Several women fainted away, and had to be revived or carried by their husbands. The orchestra finally staggered to a stop and the dancers rushed off the stage. A man came onstage and shouted over the pandemonium.

"Ladies and gentlemen: Owing to a very serious accident, it will be impossible to continue the performance tonight. Will you please remove yourselves from the building as quickly and quietly as the elevators can take you."

As people pressed toward the elevators that would bear them two hundred feet down to Twenty-Sixth Street, the police arrived and took charge of Harry Thaw. From the side of the theater, Evelyn rushed to her husband, flinging her arms around him and crying, "Oh, Harry!" Gene still could not move. His mind could not process what had happened. He simply sat there wondering—did Harry Thaw say Stanford White had ruined his *wife* or his *life*?

People crowded round the fallen figure of Stanford White, and Gene watched as one man took a tablecloth and draped it over the body. Clearly his instinct had been correct. Clearly Mr. White, who had done so much for Gene and who had promised to do more, lay dead. Gene had never given much thought to the consequences of Mr. White's sexual peccadilloes. Having engaged in more than his fair share of socially frowned upon sexual activity, Gene felt he was not one to judge. But White's treatment of Evelyn Nesbit, sexual and otherwise, had returned to haunt him in the person of a carefully armed Harry Thaw. There would be no more dinners at Delmonico's or evenings at the theater, no quiet chats at Mr. White's apartment among his art treasures. And there would be no job secured through Mr. White's influence. In that moment, having cut off contact with his parents, left behind his colleagues at Wardenclyffe, and long ago lost touch with his truest friends, the fairies of Paresis Hall, Eugene Pinkney felt utterly alone.

XI

The next morning Robert awoke stiff and sore. He had drifted off in front of the fire while reading *Alice Gold, Girl Inventor*. The book, with its illustration on the cloth cover of Alice facing down the out-of-control bicyclist, lay on the floor next to his chair.

It had stopped snowing, but a foot or more had accumulated. Finding nothing but a moldy half-loaf of bread in the kitchen, Robert decided to pull on his coat and boots and walk the twelve blocks up to Barney Greengrass. He hadn't had a fresh bagel covered in lox and cream cheese in ages and the famous deli offered the best in the world within walking distance of his home. Sitting at a table in the window sipping strong coffee, Robert wondered why he didn't bring Rebecca here more often. Had he started to take New York for granted? He watched pedestrians making their way up Amsterdam on freshly shoveled sidewalks while he downed a second cup of coffee, ready to continue his pursuit of the Tremendous Trio. He felt invigorated, not just by the bagel and the coffee, but by a sense of purpose—something he had been lacking lately. He needed to tell his true story to Rebecca and to do that he needed to *finish* that story. That meant keeping his promise to his father and finding the end of the Tremendous Trio's final adventure.

Robert dug into his coat pocket, retrieved the piece of paper Elaine Corrigan had given him, and looked at what she had written:

Julia Sanberg, General Society of Mechanics and Tradesmen, 20 W. 44th

Robert could not imagine why someone who worked for a society of mechanics and tradesmen would know the first thing about children's series books, but he nonetheless began tromping through the snow toward Midtown.

The General Society of Mechanics and Tradesmen occupied the first floors of a handsome building between Fifth and Sixth Avenues. In a display window outside the building, Robert read that its library was the second oldest in New York City, founded in 1820 for the education of apprentices and tradesmen. The library had moved to its current location in 1899.

Robert stepped inside, glad for the shelter from the icy wind that had whipped around him during his walk. A security guard directed him down a short flight of stairs to a pair of glass doors. He pushed his way through and drew a sudden breath. He loved this about New York—that you could walk into any one of thousands of unassuming buildings and find something within to strike awe. He stood in a three-story-high room, filled with natural light from a massive skylight. In front of him stretched a large reading room with tables and chairs surrounded by cases filled with books. Above this area towered three tiers of balconies that led to the stacks—row after row of bookcases crammed with old and tattered-looking volumes. To his left stood a circulation desk and something Robert hadn't seen in years, a beautifully crafted wooden card catalogue. Above him curved another balcony, this one with an elaborate brass railing. A dozen readers scattered themselves around the quiet space, and a young man with a neatly trimmed beard and a pair of round eyeglasses sat on a stool behind the reception desk, reading a collection of Dorothy Parker short stories. Robert descended the three steps from the entrance and approached the desk.

"Can I help you?" the man said in a friendly voice.

"I'm looking for Julia Sanberg," said Robert.

"She should be here any minute," the man said. "She texted she was running late. You can wait over there if you like." He waved Robert to an area on the far side of the desk, separated from the rest of the library by a stack of card catalogue drawers. Robert was pleased to see that the bookcases on the outer walls were filled with modern fiction—hardcover books whose dust jackets glistened in their plastic library covers. Clearly this was more than just a technical library. He laid his messenger bag on a table and scanned the shelves, noticing a copy of *Looking Forward*. But he didn't want to think about the world of contemporary fiction at the moment, so he turned to the card catalogue, pulling gently on one of the brass handles and sliding out a drawer.

As Robert flipped idly through the cards, enjoying a tactile sensation lacking from any computer, the date *1906* caught his eye. He stopped and read the card for a book titled *Eastman Johnson, Painting America*. The subject line read "Johnson, Eastman (1824–1906) Co-founder Metropolitan Museum of Art." It was ironic that Robbie and his father had abandoned his mother in the Met that December day so long ago when they went searching for Alice Gold's house, because two months later, on a Saturday afternoon, Robbie's father took him back to Manhattan and they mounted the wide steps to that massive museum. Robbie gripped a copy of *Alice Gold and the Museum Mystery* in his hand, their guidebook for the day. The book mentioned six different galleries and Robbie and his father were determined to see all of them. Robbie grinned as they pushed their way into the echoing lobby, thrilled to be spending a day in the city with his father, following in the footsteps of Alice Gold.

"I understand you were looking for me," said a voice behind him. Robert turned and saw a woman with tight black curls and thick glasses unwinding a knit scarf from around her neck. She reminded him of high school pictures he had seen of Rebecca.

"Are you Julia Sanberg?"

"That's right," said the woman, draping the scarf over a chair and slipping out of a ski jacket.

"Robert Parrish," said Robert. "Elaine Corrigan at the St. Agnes branch of the public library suggested I contact you."

"Right," said Julia, running her hands through her hair. "I had an e-mail from her yesterday, but she didn't give your name. So, Mr. Robert Parrish, how is your day today?"

He liked her already, at least in part because she didn't seem to recognize his name, or at least she was willing to engage him independently of his literary reputation.

"Better than some; worse than others," said Robert. "I had breakfast at Barney Greengrass."

"Aren't you the lucky one. I had a Kind bar on the nearly immobile Long Island Rail Road. So, how can I help you?" Julia motioned to a chair and Robert sat on one side of a small table as she sat across from him.

"Elaine said you know a lot about children's series books from the early twentieth century."

"I've done a couple of papers on the topic," said Julia. "I was a children's librarian at the public library before I came here."

"I'm trying to find out about three authors whose books I read as a child. They each did a series and then the three of them did a series together but there's a book that seems to be missing."

"Hold on a second," said Julia. "Who are these three authors?"

"Neptune B. Smythe, Buck Larson, and Dexter Cornwall," said Robert. "I mean, I suppose people know all about Victor Appleton and Franklin W. Dixon and Carolyn Keene because Tom Swift and the Hardy Boys and Nancy Drew were such blockbusters. But I couldn't find anything online about these three."

"Actually, no one knows anything about Victor Appleton or Franklin W. Dixon or Carolyn Keene," said Julia, "for the simple reason that they didn't exist."

"What do you mean they didn't exist?" said Robert. "I've read their books—dozens of them. They had to exist."

"Have you ever heard of a man called Edward Stratemeyer?" said Julia.

"No," said Robert.

"Not many people have," she said, "which is too bad, because he was one of the most successful figures in the history of publishing. He wrote, or at least outlined, hundreds of books that sold tens of millions of copies. He also made up the names Franklin Dixon and Carolyn Keene and Victor Appleton, along with Roy Rockwood and Laura Lee Hope and lots of others."

"Those people were made up?" said Robert. How could the idols of his childhood, the writers who had filled so many of his summer days, be nonexistent?

"Entirely," said Julia.

"But if they were made up then who . . ." He wanted to say, *who inspired me to become a teller of stories?* But he found he could not finish the sentence.

"Stratemeyer ran what he called a publishing syndicate that cranked out scores of children's series. He would come up with the idea for each series and outline each book. He would pay ghostwriters a flat fee to write the books from his outlines. Then he would publish them through a variety of houses. The first fifteen or so Hardy Boys books were written by a Canadian named Leslie McFarlane who got paid something like one hundred and twenty-five dollars per title."

"Those books have sold . . ."

"Millions."

The Tower Treasure by Leslie McFarlane, thought Robert—it just didn't sound right.

"And this Canadian didn't write all of the Hardy Boys?"

"No. That's why Stratemeyer invented the pseudonyms. So he could keep publishing books in a series under the same name, even if he switched authors."

"So, you think Stratemeyer invented Buck Larson, Dexter Cornwall, and Neptune B. Smythe?"

"That's where things get fuzzy," said Julia. "I know my Stratemeyer pseudonyms pretty well, and I've never heard any of those. What series did they write?"

"Daring Dan Dawson; Alice Gold, Girl Inventor; and Frank Fairfax, Cub Reporter," said Robert. "And then there was one they wrote together with all three of their main characters—the Tremendous Trio."

"Definitely not Stratemeyer titles," said Julia. "Although he might have liked the idea of the crossover series. I don't suppose you have any of the books with you?"

Robert reached into his messenger bag and pulled out his battered copy of *The Tremendous Trio at Niagara Falls*. The faded illustration on the green cloth cover showed a boy and a girl leaning over the Horseshoe Falls, looks of terror on their faces. On the rim of the falls, about to be swept over by the roaring current, was a barrel-like object. He handed the book to Julia who carefully examined the cover before turning to the title page.

"Not in very good condition," she said.

"Three generations of my family have read it about a hundred times," said Robert.

"It's not your fault. Stratemeyer didn't waste money on quality. He sold his books for fifty cents at a time when the going rate for a hardcover was about a dollar fifty. That meant he had to sell a lot of books to turn a profit, but it also meant that boys could buy Stratemeyer books with their pocket change. And millions of boys did."

"Including my grandfather," said Robert. "He had the Great Marvel series and long runs of Tom Swift, the Hardy Boys . . ."

"All Stratemeyer series," said Julia, examining Robert's book more carefully. "To sell them for fifty cents he had to manufacture books as cheaply as possible. But everything about *this* book—the wood pulp in the paper, the cloth on the binding, the quality of the printing—is even more shoddily done than your typical Stratemeyer series. No illustrations either, except the one on the front cover. Are they all issued by the same publisher?"

"Pickering Brothers," said Robert.

"Never heard of them. Maybe it was one of Stratemeyer's competitors. This is interesting," said Julia, examining the back of the title page.

"What?"

"The address: Copyright 1911, Pickering Brothers, Publishers, 175 Fifth Avenue."

"That's the Flatiron Building," said Robert. "I used to work there."

"It would have been pretty new back then. It was finished in 1902, I think."

"So, you think this Pickering Brothers outfit was something like Stratemeyer—inventing authors and using ghostwriters to fill in outlines?"

"It's possible," said Julia.

"Then how do you explain this?" said Robert, pulling out the letter his grandfather had received in 1911. "My grandfather got a letter from Dexter Cornwall."

"Your grandfather got a letter from Pickering Brothers," said Julia, glancing at the paper, "but I seriously doubt it was from anyone named Dexter Cornwall. They probably had someone at the company who answered fan mail."

Robert felt the earth below him shifting. His childhood literary idols were nothing more than a marketing ploy. The letter his grandfather had treasured in the field of battle was a fake. Yet he felt not disappointment, but curiosity. *Someone* had written the books he had loved so much as a child and shared so deeply with his father, even if from an outline penned by a man named Pickering. *Someone* had written his grandfather a letter that had kept his courage up during World War II. Just because those people were not named Dexter Cornwall, or Neptune B. Smythe, or Buck Larson, didn't mean they didn't exist. Some person or group of persons had made Robert's childhood wonderful, had connected him to his father, and had changed the lives of who knew how many other young readers. The people who created these books deserved to be recognized. And Robert would be the one to do it.

"There's one other thing," said Robert. "The beginning of a book, but only the beginning." He pulled out a second file folder, containing the opening passage of *The Last Adventure of the Tremendous Trio*. Julia looked through the pages, holding each carefully between her fingertips as she turned it over.

"And this is all you have?" she said.

"It was folded up in the back of one of the books," said Robert. "But that's all."

"Strange," said Julia.

"Elaine said that none of these books or authors were in the New York Public Library system."

"They won't be here either," said Julia. "I did a pretty thorough search for children's series books when I first came here and there's nothing."

"Because librarians considered them dangerous when they came out?" said Robert.

"It's not just that," said Julia. "It's strange how sometimes the things that are most popular take the longest to be recognized as significant by the establishment. Rare book libraries are full of Shakespeare and Jane Austen and F. Scott Fitzgerald, but they're not going to spend their money on Victor Appleton and Franklin W. Dixon, even if millions more people read them at the time than ever read Jane Austen in her lifetime."

"So, what happens? All those books just get lost?" It seemed immensely sad to Robert that the books that had introduced so many millions to the joys of reading could be simply brushed aside.

"There is a last line of defense against that," said Julia.

"What is that?"

"Private collectors. Book collectors can collect whatever they want. They have no one to answer to, except perhaps a spouse, no limitations except budget and space—though most collectors I know are good at ignoring both those restrictions. And they collect what they love."

"Are there other people out there who love children's series books?" said Robert.

"Plenty of them," said Julia. "Gradually some of those private collections are ending up in institutions where they can take their place alongside other rare and valuable children's books. Even the finest children's literature wasn't generally considered fit fodder for academic study until fifty years ago or so. It's not surprising it takes longer for the more lowbrow stuff to get a little recognition. It's happening, but slowly. Ridgefield University bought a collection of four thousand yellowbacks a few years ago, and scholars are practically wetting themselves over it."

"Yellowbacks?"

"Basically they were the nineteenth-century British version of dime novels," said Julia. "Academia is finally realizing that popular books may not be literary, but they had a huge impact on the culture and on people's lives."

"Are there any rare book libraries that have good collections of children's series?"

"There are a few," said Julia, "but if you really want to see a nice collection, you should contact Sherwood Whitmore."

"Who's that?"

"He has one of the biggest collections of Stratemeyer books in the world. I visited him when I was working on my papers, and his collection is amazing."

"And he makes it available to the public?"

"Not to the public, exactly, but he loves showing off to people who appreciate the genre."

"Where does he live?" Robert didn't relish the idea of dropping a thousand dollars on last-minute plane fare to Chicago or Los Angeles, but to find the missing book, he would consider it.

"East Eighty-Seventh," said Julia.

"What, here in New York?"

"Forty blocks away," said Julia.

"That's fantastic," said Robert with a laugh.

"You'll like Sherwood," said Julia, scribbling down an address and a phone number. "Be sure to give him my regards."

Somehow discovering the anonymity of the creators of the Tremendous Trio only added purpose to Robert's attempt to fulfill his promise to his father, to cast out the demons of his past, and to make himself into the kind of man that Rebecca might be able to love. If, by learning everything he could about Pickering and his ghost writers, he could not only recover the final episode of the Tremendous Trio, but also bring recognition to writers who had brought joy to his childhood, he might not only close the book on the story of his own past, but perhaps bring some of that same joy to the present generation. Most important, this entire journey was feeling more and more like a story; Rebecca had loved the storyteller in Robert and if he could get that back, maybe she would love him again. He punched Sherwood Whitmore's number into his phone, then stepped back into the cold of Forty-Fourth Street and started uptown, waiting for an answer.

XII

THE FLATIRON BUILDING,
IN THE DAYS OF STREETCARS AND SHIRTWAISTS

Magda carefully slid the letter out of the envelope on the top of a pile on her desk. In addition to typing correspondence, proofreading manuscripts, and making the rounds of the bookstores on Twenty-Third Street to make sure that Pickering titles were prominently displayed, one of her responsibilities at Pickering Brothers, Publishers—where she had been working for the past six months—was answering the fan mail. There was rarely as much mail as the publisher would have liked, but there was always some. With the promise of a quiet afternoon, she began to read the first of several letters to authors who did not exist. The letter, addressed to Cornelius Donovan, care of Pickering Brothers, Publishers, 175 Fifth Avenue, New York City, was written in a childish hand on a piece of business stationery bearing the letterhead of Herman Chlebowsky, tailor, of Perth Amboy, New Jersey. At least, thought Magda, some of Pickering's books had made it across the Hudson River. Most of the fan mail came from inside the city.

July 11, 1906

Dear Mr. Cornelius Donovan,

My name is George Chlebowsky and the books you rite called <u>Drew Stetson, Boy of the Seas</u> are my favorite books in the hole world. I like the one where he sales around Africa and the one where he sales to Antarticle, but my favorite is where he sales to Alaska and camps in the wilderness. The seen when he fights the bare is the best. I like that you have wild animals in your books. I live in Perth Amboy and the only wild animal I ever see is the dog that lives across the street when he sees a cat. Can you please tell me how a boy like me can become a saler? I wood like to go to Alaska and Antarticle, but not Africa because it is to hot. If you will please rite back to George Chlebowsky, 985 Sutton St., Perth Amboy, New Jersey.

Your Friend,

George

Magda loved answering letters like these. Most of them came from young boys, and she imagined each of them like her own brother, Henry—bright and curious, with a fresh-washed face and eager eyes. Her secretarial training made her want to correct the errors of spelling and grammar, but she simply laid the letter on the desk and loaded a sheet of letterhead into her old Hammond typewriter. Like everything else in the Pickering offices—which managed to look shabby, cluttered, and dusty despite occupying rooms in a skyscraper only four years old—it had been purchased secondhand by her parsimonious superior. In secretarial school, Magda had learned to type on the QWERTY keyboard of the Remington, so the unconventional curved layout of the nearly twenty-year-old Hammond had taken some getting used to, but now she found she could type faster than she had in school.

PICKERING PUBLISHING
175 Fifth Avenue, New York
From the Desk of Cornelius Donovan

July 13, 1906

Dear George,

Thank you so much for your letter. I have just returned from an expedition to southernmost Patagonia to collect

material for my new book, Drew Stetson around South America,
so it was nice to find some mail awaiting me. I am very
pleased that you like my books about Drew Stetson. The
character of Drew is based on a fine young man like yourself
who accompanies me on all my journeys. If we hadn't had him
with us on our latest expedition, I shudder to think what
might have happened.

   It is too bad you do not have any wild animals where
you live, as they are quite exciting to encounter. In my
new book you will meet a creature called an anaconda,
and you may find yourself pleased there are not many of
those in Perth Amboy.

   I am glad that you wish to become a sailor like Drew
Stetson. Perhaps you will have a chance to meet the real
Drew someday and he can talk to you about how to get
started in that line. In the meantime, I can tell you
this—study hard in school and learn lots of geography.
It is also helpful to read lots of books about faraway
places. Drew once told me that he learned a lot from
reading the Wild West Boys.

   I hope to see you one day when I am out sailing the
seas.

                         Your friend,
                         Cornelius Donovan

   Her letters generally had the same conceit—that the authors were real
people who participated in the same sort of activities as portrayed in their
books, that the young boys who featured as the heroes of those books were
also real, and that the readers' aspirations to emulate those heroes could
be fulfilled by working hard and buying plenty more Pickering books. She
never specifically instructed fans to buy books, but she had become skilled
at weaving that message into the letters. Of course, Cornelius Donovan
was as fictional as Drew Stetson. His was just one of many pseudonyms
that Pickering Brothers used. The publisher wrote most of the Drew

Stetson series himself, although lately he had gotten busy with sales and accounting and had handed off the most recent volume to a ghostwriter with only a few chapters written.

She was just pulling the letter out of the typewriter when the door to the hallway, a door with a frosted glass window bearing the words *Pickering Brothers, Publishers* in black and gold letters, swung open. This was an unusual enough event that Magda took off her reading glasses and watched with curiosity as a tall figure strode into the office.

"Good morning," said the man.

"It's five past twelve," said Magda.

"Well, good afternoon, then. My name is Neptune B. Smythe, and I'm here to see Mr. Pickering."

"Which one? This is Pickering Brothers."

"Is there more than one?"

"No, but he thought Pickering Brothers sounded more impressive than Pickering and Company."

"If there is only one, then that's the one I'll see."

"Do you have an appointment?"

"Not exactly."

"So, no, then."

"But I'm sure he'll want to see me."

"And what makes you sure?"

"I have this—"

"There are two reasons Mr. Pickering won't see you," said Magda, interrupting. "The first is that there is no Mr. Pickering. His real name is Lipscomb. Mr. Julius Lipscomb."

"That's all right," said the man with a grin. "There is no Neptune B. Smythe. My real name is Thomas De Peyster."

"Imagine that," said Magda, smiling. "And Neptune B. Smythe is such a realistic-sounding name."

"It is a real name. I stole it off of a plumbing wagon."

"Well then," said Magda, "we must be sure to contact you if we have any trouble with the pipes."

"But you can call me Tom."

"It seems unlikely that I shall have much occasion to call you anything."

"What's the other reason he won't see me? Mr. Lipscomb, I mean."

"He's not in," said Magda. "He makes sales calls on Friday afternoons."

"And, as you so astutely pointed out, it is the afternoon."

Magda perused the young man. His blue eyes sparkled in the midday sun that shone through the window. He had taken off his hat and not a strand of his blond hair was out of place. He wore a gray four-button double-breasted suit and carried a silver-handled walking stick. She didn't often see uptown gents in the offices of Pickering Brothers, Publishers, but Mr. Thomas De Peyster, alias Mr. Neptune B. Smythe, seemed exactly that. Magda had little time for flirts and even less time for flirts from Fifth Avenue. And yet, this man seemed somehow uncomfortable in the latest fashions, and he held his walking stick not with the casual arrogance of the elite, but almost with distaste. Magda sensed that he was something other than—or perhaps more than—what he seemed. That intrigued her.

"May I ask what you wished to speak to Mr. Pickering . . . that is, what is your visit regarding?"

Tom slipped into a chair next to Magda's desk and, as out of place as he looked in his suit, he seemed completely at ease leaning his elbows on the furniture and looking her over. She could feel his eyes scanning every inch of her.

"I have a manuscript—a story, the beginning of a series like the ones Pickering publishes. You see, I've been working for Mr. William Randolph Hearst at the *Journal* for quite a while—newspaper reporter. You've prob-ably read my work. But a few months back I was in . . . well never mind where I was, the important thing is I got this idea for a story. I mean, a series of stories. You remember Horatio Alger? *Ragged Dick* and all that. Well it's like that—boy hero, lots of adventures. So, I go down to Putnam's all the time and I see these series books for kids flying off the shelf—not just Alger but Roy Rockwood and the Motor Boys, the Bobbsey Twins and the Great Marvel books. So, I figure, if all those books are selling, then why not Frank Fairfax, Cub Reporter."

"So you decided to pitch your idea to Mr. Pickering."

"No, I decided to pitch my idea to Edward Stratemeyer. He's the top man in the business, which I found out on account of my reporting skills."

"They must be remarkable," said Magda.

"Oh, they are," said Tom, who either failed to understand or chose to ignore her sarcasm.

"And what did the top man in the business have to say about your cub reporter idea?"

"Hated it," said Tom with a smile. "Hated the premise but mostly hated the idea of anyone besides himself coming up with a character."

"Because he develops all the series himself," said Magda.

"Exactly. Writes outlines and then sends them out to—what do you call them?"

"Ghostwriters."

"Right. Ghostwriters. Well, Neptune B. Smythe is no ghostwriter. So, I took my idea to someone else."

"And then someone else and someone else."

"Right."

"Until you finally reached the bottom of the publishing barrel that is Pickering Brothers."

"And here I am."

"You seem awfully cheerful for someone who has been rejected by every publisher in town."

"Did you know that *The War of the Worlds* was rejected before it was published?" said Tom. "I did an interview with H. G. Wells when he was in New York last spring and he said one publisher called it 'an endless nightmare.' But it's done pretty well. So, no, I'm not bothered by rejection."

"You've read *The War of the Worlds*?" said Magda quietly, losing a bit of her confidence as she tried to suppress the memory of the day she first encountered that book. The library copy had been lost when she fell into the water, and it had been another year before Magda bought a copy of the book at Putnam's, read it, and mailed it anonymously to the Freie Bibliothek.

"Sure," said Tom. "But I'm here to talk about my book. It's about this boy who gets a job as a reporter—he's twelve or thirteen in the first book. And he's always saving people because he always ends up in the middle of these big disasters. You know—earthquakes, floods, fires, that sort of thing."

At the mention of the word *fire*, Magda felt the blood drain from her face. She immediately saw an image of that little boy—a child who she had told herself a thousand times was *not* her brother, Henry—falling into the flames as the flagpole he had climbed collapsed beneath him.

"Are you all right?" said Tom. "You look pale."

Magda did not respond, but only swallowed hard as she tried to banish the picture from her memory. She had managed to think of that day less and less often over the past two years, but it had a way of creeping into her consciousness at the most inconvenient moments.

"Lunch," said Tom. "You need lunch. Where are my manners? Let me take you to lunch and I can tell you all about Frank Fairfax, Cub Reporter, and you can tell me if you think Mr. Pickering—I mean, Mr. Lipscomb—will like it."

"I couldn't possibly accept such an invitation, Mr. De Peyster," said Magda.

"I'm not talking Delmonico's," said Tom. "I know the suit is nice, but it's all for show. There's a Childs right around the corner. Nothing scandalous about lunch at Childs."

He was right—the whole point of places like Childs was that a single man and a single woman could eat there without raising eyebrows. Magda often ate alone at the counter at Childs on Twenty-Third Street, and as it was a Friday, she could order the fishcakes. She did need to eat, and as long as Thomas De Peyster didn't pay for her meal there could be no harm in listening to his tales while she had her lunch.

"Let me get my coat," she said.

"Excellent," said Tom. "By the way, I didn't get your name."

"I didn't give it," said Magda. "It's Mary. Mary Stone."

"That sounds as made-up as Neptune B. Smythe."

"It most certainly does not," said Magda with false indignity. In a way she had not felt since she lost her family, Magda believed she could trust this man—even though she had only known him for a few minutes. She leaned toward him and whispered, "In confidence, though, *Mary Stone* is made up. You can call me Magda."

As they walked down Twenty-Third Street, Magda felt comfortable chatting with Tom about books and reading. They had both read and been shocked by *The Jungle*—Tom carefully dropped into the conversation the fact that he had met Upton Sinclair at a cocktail party. Sensing that Tom's own relationship with both the upper and lower classes was more complicated than he admitted, she recommended *The House of Mirth* by Edith Wharton, about a society woman's slow loss of standing.

Magda liked the intrigue of Tom's contradictions. If he went to cocktail parties with a socialist like Upton Sinclair and also carried a silver walking stick, did he really live on a reporter's income and dream of nothing more than writing adventure stories for boys? He seemed like one of those Russian nesting dolls. Magda had been clever enough to realize that fact, and perhaps to remove the first doll—but there were many layers still between her and the truth about Thomas De Peyster.

Childs was only a block and a half from the Flatiron Building and Magda felt suddenly ravenous as soon as they stepped through the door. The walls and floors were covered in white tile, and white-clad waitresses busied themselves with the lunchtime rush. From the wall on the right extended a series of marble-topped tables, each with twelve café chairs. Most were already filled with diners, both ladies and gentlemen, the latter group having placed their hats on a convenient ledge about six feet up the wall. Magda and Tom found a table in the back where only one other diner sat and ensconced themselves at the other end from the young man who hunched over a bowl of chicken soup.

After they placed their orders they sat in self-conscious silence until the waitress arrived with their food. Tom then resumed the conversation as if it had never stopped.

"My problem with *The War of the Worlds*," he said between bites of his oyster sandwich, "is that I wanted to know more about the Martians. What are their lives like? What sort of culture do they have? Were the invaders just members of the army? And if so, what does everyone else do? I wanted to understand them and their motivations."

"You're missing the entire point of the book," said Magda, surprised to find herself animatedly arguing with a man she had met less than an hour ago. "It's not about the Martians, it's about us, the humans. It's about how we deal with disaster, how we react when death is all but inevitable." Her entire experience of the book had been inextricably linked to her own encounter with disaster and death on the *General Slocum*. Wells, she thought, did a wonderful job of portraying how despair, hope, and abject terror can intermingle.

"You say that as if you have some experience with the subject."

Magda blanched as she tried to think how to reply, but as she struggled for the words to hide her past, the young man at the far end of the table came to her rescue.

"I beg your pardon," he said in a soft voice, "but I couldn't help hearing you talking about *The War of the Worlds*."

"That's right," said Tom jovially. "Would you like to join us?"

The man picked up his bowl and moved to the seat next to Tom and across from Magda. Everything about him seemed as soft as his voice, thought Magda. His brown hair was too long to be fashionable and reminded her of pictures of Oscar Wilde. He had delicate features, eyebrows that looked almost as if they had been carefully plucked, and pale cheeks. Although he looked like a boy, his eyes gleamed with the maturity of a man and the rest of the room seemed to fade away into a silent mist as he spoke. Magda could not take her eyes off him.

"The trouble with *The War of the Worlds*," the young man said, "along with most of what you might call science fiction published these days, is that there is too much fiction and not enough science. Real science, I mean. Wells writes that the Martians arrive and that they use their death rays, but he never explains how. He doesn't base any of what happens on actual scientific principles—things an advanced civilization could eventually achieve."

"And are you a scientist?" said Tom, with a slight tone of condescension.

"I'm unemployed at the moment," said the man. "But I suppose you could say I'm a scientist. I spent the last eight years working for Tesla."

"Nikola Tesla?" said Tom, clearly impressed.

"That's right. I was on the staff at Wardenclyffe out on Long Island, but . . . well the money ran out and most of us are looking for work else-where."

"How could you have spent eight years working for one of the most famous inventors in the world?" said Magda. "You can't be more than seventeen."

"I'm twenty-four," said the man.

"So am I," said Tom.

"Me too," said Magda, without thinking.

"I'm Gene, by the way," said the man. "Eugene Pinkney."

"Pleased to meet you, Gene," said Tom, holding out a hand. "Tom De Peyster."

Gene shook Tom's hand lightly, looking intently into the other man's eyes. This gave Magda the chance to stare at Gene again—for some reason she desperately wanted to do this. Looking at the soft curves of his cheeks and the shadows of his hair on his forehead made her feel off balance. She liked that.

"I'm Magda," she said, dropping her eyes to the table when Gene finally turned his attention to her. "Magda Hertzenberger."

"You never told me your whole name," said Tom.

"I've never told anyone," said Magda, looking back up at Gene. "No one except Thomas De Peyster and Eugene Pinkney."

XIII

Sherwood Whitmore's voicemail explained he was out of town and would return Sunday evening. Robert did not leave a message, preferring to speak to the collector directly. Back home, he laid out his clues: twelve hardcover books, three from each of the presumably nonexistent authors and three from the Tremendous Trio crossover series; the letter to his grandfather from Dexter Cornwall; the opening of *The Last Adventure of the Tremendous Trio*; Sherwood Whitmore's phone number; and the piece of paper on which Elaine Corrigan had written Julia Sanberg's name and place of employment.

Looking over the evidence, he thought about a creative writing teacher in college who said, "Every good story begins with a question." There were plenty of questions here—even ignoring the question of "How can a bunch of old books create a relationship between a boy and his father that didn't exist before?" That question's answer had led down a dark path indeed. But before him were questions that might bring light to that darkness: Who were the people who stood behind the names Buck Larson and Dexter Cornwall and Neptune B. Smythe? Who had written the letter to his grandfather? And what was the final adventure of the Tremendous Trio?

Robert absentmindedly turned over the piece of paper Elaine had given him and read the notice on the other side:

VOLUNTEERS WANTED

ADULTS NEEDED TO READ FOR CHILDREN'S STORY HOUR

WEDNESDAYS AND SATURDAYS AT 10:00 A.M.

CHOOSE A FAVORITE STORY TO SHARE WITH CHILDREN

CONTACT ELAINE CORRIGAN

ST. AGNES BRANCH LIBRARY

Robert slid into his desk chair and stared at the notice. Again and again he had put Rebecca off whenever she had raised the topic of children. The thought of being responsible for a child was so enmeshed in his own relationship with his father that he couldn't begin to untangle it. Avoiding the subject was an easier way out. But he had never considered sitting in front of a group of children that were not his own and reading a story. The idea intrigued him. More than that, it resurrected Rebecca's words on the morning of their last fight: ". . . I thought you would make a great father because you were such a good storyteller." Yes, Robert could tell a story to Rebecca or to an adult lover of literature, but could he tell stories to children? He felt his heart quicken with the excitement of that possibility. "Choose a favorite story," the flyer said. Had any child today even heard of the Tremendous Trio? He could see if children of 2010 would react with the same excitement and pleasure to their adventures as he had. If they did, his love of these books might not seem so irrelevant. And that love might become separated from the story of his past.

⟳

"I don't think we've ever had a bestselling author read at children's story time," said Elaine Corrigan over the phone.

"I could be the first," said Robert.

"We have an opening tomorrow morning. Our scheduled reader is stuck in Connecticut. If you're available on such short notice . . ."

"I'll do it," said Robert. "How long do I get?"

"There's no set time," said Elaine. "Most people usually read for about forty-five minutes, but you don't have to go that long. Or you can take as much as an hour."

"And the kids," said Robert, feeling more keyed up by the minute, "how old are the kids?"

"On Saturdays they usually range from about five to twelve."

"Perfect," he said.

Robert quickly calculated the length of the Tremendous Trio book at about forty-five thousand words. As he obviously could not read a thousand words per minute, he couldn't read an entire volume. Would they let him come more than once so he could read the book in installments? Even if they did, he didn't imagine he could hold the children's attention over more than three sessions. He timed himself reading about a hundred and fifty words a minute at a brisk pace. That meant nine thousand words an hour. He would try editing one of the Tremendous Trio books down from forty-five thousand to twenty-seven thousand words. If the children liked it, he could read the whole book over three visits. He'd be sure to end each of the first two installments of the story with a juicy cliff-hanger.

This meant some pretty serious editing. Robert dropped his copy of *The Tremendous Trio around the World* off at the copy shop on Amsterdam with instructions to photocopy every page, then killed an hour in the café across the street, eating a croissant and trying not to think about how Rebecca might not come back, that all this digging up of his past might be pointless. By midday he sat at his desk with a stack of photocopies and a red pen.

As he read through the book, he realized his task was more complicated than he had expected. He suspected that kids from the smartphone generation might have little patience with sentences like: *The flying machine pitched and yawed, but Dan clung to the underside of the armature, taking umbrage with Alice's assessment that it was only the drag co-efficient of the young daredevil that interfered with the equilibrium of her craft.* After a few chapters, it became clear to Robert that making this thrilling adventure of three teenagers who invented, tested, and built an airplane, then flew it around the world, exciting to twenty-first century children for whom the idea of air travel was as ordinary as walking down the street, would take more than just judicious cutting. With the marked-up photocopy spread out on his desk, Robert opened a new Word file and began to type.

Many paragraphs he lifted verbatim from the original, but others required at least some adjustment in language and tone. He also needed to create a historical context, to help his listeners understand that the story took place just a few years after the first airplane flight, a time when the Wright brothers were still kings of the sky. He needed to streamline the language, not writing down to children but rewording some of the archaic vocabulary and usage. And, he needed to cut eighteen thousand words. That meant eliminating several ports of call on the round-the-world journey.

At one o'clock in the afternoon, this all seemed an exhilarating literary challenge. By eight thirty that night, when Robert stopped to eat some Chinese delivery, it seemed a foolish undertaking. At midnight, it seemed impossible, and Robert wondered why he didn't just read some Dr. Seuss books and be done with it. At seven a.m., bleary-eyed and exhausted, feeling like he had competed in some sort of writing marathon, Robert hit *print*. Despite his doubts of a few hours before, he felt a satisfaction unlike any he had known since the publication of *Looking Forward*. True, the revised and abridged version of *The Tremendous Trio around the World* was not likely to win any literary prizes, but it might engage the attention of a few children for three hours. Even if the kids hated it and wandered away before he had finished reading the first chapter, Robert had, for the first time since the publication of his novel, completed a piece of writing. It might not be wholly his own, but he liked to think that Buck Larson and Neptune B. Smythe and Dexter Cornwall—even if they did not exist— would approve. As the printer hummed away, he dragged upstairs to bed, hoping that a couple hours' sleep would be enough to energize him for the morning ahead.

Robert need not have worried. Where a morning nap and three cups of coffee failed, the sight of three-dozen expectant faces looking up at him from their seats on the floor of the St. Agnes Library succeeded. Parents hovered around the edge of the group of children, but he barely noticed them. To Robert, only those children waiting for him, ready to fall backward into his arms, mattered. He opened the folder on his lap and began.

Alice Gold gasped in awe as she stood on the shore and watched Wilbur Wright, inventor of the aeroplane, circle his flying machine around the Statue of Liberty and over the giant passenger ship *Lusitania* in New York Harbor before landing on Governors Island. She turned to the two muscular young men at her side. "Dan Dawson, Frank Fairfax," she said, "I'm going to build one of those and we're going to fly it."

"I've never seen them sit still for a whole hour," said Elaine afterward. As Robert had read, the children had scooted closer to him, parents had stopped their whisperings, and some of the adult patrons of the library had joined the crowd that listened. Robert began to feed off the crowd, instilling the exciting moments with drama, lowering his voice at the scary parts, and turning what began as a reading into a performance. When it was over the children applauded for a full minute and mobbed him asking where they could find a copy of the book and what happened next to Alice, Dan, and Frank.

"Was that from one of those books you were telling me about?" said Elaine.

"Sort of," said Robert. "I edited it from the original."

"Well, the kids loved it. People were swamping the desk wanting to check out anything about the Tremendous Trio."

Robert blushed with pleasure. He couldn't wait to tell Rebecca about the looks on the children's faces.

"If it's okay, I'll call you the next time we have an opening in the schedule and maybe you can read some more."

"I'd like that," said Robert.

As he pulled on his coat and stowed the manuscript in his bag, Robert thought about how much he had loved the energy of the morning—so different from the staid events he had done promoting *Looking Forward*. What would his public say if he redefined himself as a children's author? The Tremendous Trio books were old enough to be out of copyright, so there would be no legal issues with rewriting them. And it might mean that instead of sitting on panels at book festivals he would get to visit schools and libraries and read aloud to groups of children as excited and eager-eyed as those who had come to St. Agnes this morning.

Outside the library, where sun gleamed off the heaps of snow that lined the street, Robert felt suddenly ravenous. Zabar's was right around the corner and he decided to swing by and pick up some food. Thirty minutes later, laden with breads and cheeses, pastrami and smoked fish, and a box full of rugelach, he headed home. He was halfway through a pastrami sandwich on rye bread when his phone buzzed. Without even looking, Robert hit *answer*.

"Is that you?" said a woman's voice.

"This is Robert," he said, trying to quickly swallow a bit of sandwich so he could be understood.

"It's Rebecca."

"Oh God, Rebecca . . . how are you?"

"How am I?" said Rebecca. "I walk out and tell you I might not come back and you don't even try to call me for three days and all you've got for me is *How am I?*"

"I'm sorry," said Robert. "I . . . well to be honest, I was afraid to call. And I got . . . distracted."

"*Got* distracted?" shouted Rebecca, loudly enough that Robert held the phone slightly away from his ear. "Robert, you've been nothing *but* distracted for months. Don't you understand that?"

"I do," said Robert. He could feel her pain and anger radiating through the phone. He wanted to take that pain away—the pain he had caused. And maybe he could. Maybe if he followed the path those books laid out for him, a path into his own broken past, he could be the person she wanted him to be. But her voice on the phone seemed to obscure that path. It made him feel sick, especially when he knew that her anger was his fault.

"Are you still there?" said Rebecca impatiently.

"Yes," said Robert gently. "I was just . . . thinking."

"Well, can you think out loud, because I can read you pretty well in person, but I'm not there in person, in case you hadn't noticed."

Rebecca was silent for a moment. He could hear her breathing, waiting, but he didn't have the courage to begin the conversation he knew they needed to have.

"How's Bradley?" he said.

"Jesus, Robert, do you really care how Bradley is?" Tears crept into her voice.

"Not particularly," said Robert. "It's just that I'm so afraid of saying the wrong thing, of losing you because I didn't handle this conversation right, that I'm reverting to small talk as a defense mechanism."

"I think we're past small talk," said Rebecca.

"I'm sorry," said Robert, "I just . . ." Robert fumbled for the words to guide this conversation in a more comfortable direction. None came.

"Just what, Robert? Just what?"

"I don't know," said Robert, deflated. "I miss you."

"Do you really? From what I've heard you've been having quite the time with me out of the way."

"What do you . . ." Robert felt panic surging up in his gullet.

"I called my friend Elaine Corrigan at the library today. We have coffee sometimes, and I thought she might want to meet up."

"And she told you about story time," said Robert.

"I find it awfully convenient, Robert, that the moment I'm out of the house, the moment you don't have to face any realistic possibility that you might actually be in an adult relationship that could lead to parenthood, you're out telling stories to children."

"It wasn't like that at all," said Robert. "It was wonderful. And the first thing I thought afterward is that I wanted to tell you about it."

"And yet I'm the one calling you," said Rebecca. "Elaine thinks you're a shit for driving me away." After another silence, she added, in a softer voice, "And she said you were great with the children."

"I don't know about that," said Robert. "But she's right about me being a shit."

"At least there's something we can agree on," said Rebecca. The softness was gone again. "So, what are we going to do here, Robert? I want to come home, but I want to come home to the Robert I knew before . . . before all this. You don't have to hide or pretend with me. I just want my Robert back."

"I'm sort of working on that," said Robert.

"Sort of working on it? God, Robert, this isn't a second-grade homework assignment. It's like you've turned back into a child, and I can't wait forever for you to grow back up."

"What if I told you there's something I need to do before we try . . . to get together. And that I have a plan for doing it, that I'm actually taking some action for a change. Then how long would you wait?"

"Bradley says I've waited long enough already, and so does Elaine."

"What do *you* say?" said Robert.

"You seriously want me to give you a deadline?"

"Yes," said Robert, suddenly feeling in control of the conversation for the first time. He worked well under pressure. Maybe if he had a deadline, he could face down his past, keep the promise he had made to his father, and come out the other side ready to tell Rebecca everything.

"A week," said Rebecca. "I'll give you a week. But then that's it. This is my life, too, Robert, and I'm not going to keep it on hold."

"Okay," said Robert. "A week."

"I'm not kidding," said Rebecca. "There are no extensions on this paper."

"I know," said Robert. "A week—that's next Saturday at . . ." He glanced at his watch. "Noon. We'll meet and we'll talk and you can decide if you want to . . . to take this any further." Robert felt his own tears welling up as he brushed up against the possibility that Rebecca would decide to leave him altogether.

"Where do we meet?" said Rebecca. "On top of the Empire State Building?"

"I'll meet you on the Empire State Building or on the Brooklyn Bridge, or wherever you say."

"The Ramble," said Rebecca, sounding calm for the first time in the conversation.

"As you wish," said Robert.

He spoke the words softly and with his heart beating as rapidly as it had the very first time he had said them to her. And he hung up before she had to decide whether to reply.

XIV

NEW YORK CITY, WHEN EVERYBODY LOVED THE CIRCUS

After the *Slocum* disaster, Magda had determined to put her German life behind her and be as American as Teddy Roosevelt. She had gone to work as a salesgirl at Putnam's bookstore on Twenty-Third Street, just three blocks away from her new rooming house. She enjoyed working in a bookstore, surrounded by the objects she loved above all others. But Magda had no interest in spending the rest of her life as a shopgirl, barely making enough money to pay for her two-dollar-a-week room without dipping into the family savings. By the end of 1904, she had enrolled in night classes at Grace Institute on West Sixtieth Street, studying stenography, bookkeeping, and typewriting. In the spring of 1905, to celebrate her completion of these courses, she decided to do the most American thing she could think of. She went to the Barnum and Bailey Circus at Madison Square Garden. And that's what had given her the idea.

Magda remembered that day as clearly as if it had happened only hours ago. The smell of sweat, animals, and sawdust tickled her nostrils. She could picture the disturbing sights as she followed the crowd through the sideshow filled with its "freaks" like the three-legged child and the lion-faced boy. And then the feel of the hard, wooden seat and the tingle of anticipation as the murmuring crowd awaited the "Greatest Show on Earth."

Magda had felt gloriously assaulted by the awe of everything from the grand entry of the Angel of Peace accompanied by the *oompah* of the band and rows of horses and chariots, to the lines of acrobats turning somersaults over the backs of elephants; a seal juggling a billiard cue; a man climbing a flight of stairs on a bicycle; a pair of clowns engaged in a comic boxing match; performing dogs, elephants, ponies, and a host of other animals; and the roaring thrill of Mademoiselle de Tiers flying upside down through the air in an automobile as she performed her famous "Dip of Death."

With its three rings of simultaneous entertainment, the circus felt like a fantastical version of New York itself—everything happening at once, with never a moment to catch one's breath. Nor, she thought, did she have any desire to do so. Magda overheard the little boy next to her say to his father, "They don't give a feller a chance. They ought to do these one at a time."

"That would take all night," said the father.

"That wouldn't bother me any," said the boy with delight.

But as much as she enjoyed the near chaos of the three-ring show, demanding that her focus constantly shift from act to act, one performance caught and held her attention for its entire duration. The Florenz Troupe, a family of Italian acrobats, climbed on one another, tossed one another through the air, and put their bodies through contortions and configurations Magda could not even have imagined, much less emulated. She found them entrancing, and especially so the youngest, a girl of no more than twelve or thirteen who sailed through the air over and over again, hurled by one adult and caught by another, with the grace and mystery of a fairy sprite. And then, just as she had climbed to the top of an impossibly high tower built of her family members and plummeted to the ground, arrested from certain doom at the last second by the strength of the largest man in the troupe, Magda heard the little boy beside her say in unselfconscious awe, "She's beautiful."

The father burst out laughing and Magda, clapping furiously for the Florenz family, could not resist leaning across the little boy to ask what the man found so funny.

His son now thoroughly distracted by a herd of elephants parading into the center ring, the man winked at Magda and replied, "It's not a girl. That's a little boy dressed in a girl's clothes."

Magda watched the Florenz Troupe jog out of the arena, and at that moment the idea struck her. She had seen, in the past year of working at Putnam's, how adventure stories and series of books with recurring characters sold by the thousands. She tried to stay familiar with the interests of her customers, so she had read several of these books. They had much in common with the circus, she thought—full of constant action, flitting from one peril to the next, and always featuring at least one young hero, usually a boy of twelve or thirteen. What if, she thought, that hero was a circus acrobat?

She had read in the previous day's paper that Barnum and Bailey's circus was about to embark on its first transcontinental tour to the West Coast. Think of the adventures a young acrobat could encounter traveling across the great North American continent—not just the dangers of the circus ring, but the storms of the great plains, the crossing of the Rockies, the outlaws of the Wild West, and then California with its prospectors and its immigrants from the mysterious Far East. What could be more American than a young boy in the circus, crossing this great land and having adventures all along the way?

As soon as the show ended and she could extricate herself from the crowd, Magda dashed across Madison Square and rushed down Twenty-Third Street. Back in her room, she sat in the ladder-back chair by the window—she had no desk and the small table across from the bed held a washbasin and her hairbrushes. On her lap she placed a sheaf of papers covered on one side with typewriting exercises. She took a pencil from the drawer of her tiny bedside table and wrote at the top of the page: *Ideas for Children's Series—Circus.*

Two months later, Magda had a detailed outline of the first book and a cast of characters, including her hero, a thirteen-year-old boy named Dan Dawson, the precocious star of an acrobatic family. More important, she had secured a new job, performing secretarial and bookkeeping work for Pickering Brothers, Publishers. She had seen Pickering books on the shelf at Putnam's ever since she started working there, and while Drew Stetson and the Wild West Boys didn't sell as well as the Rover Boys and the Bobbsey Twins, when she read in the classifieds that Pickering Brothers needed a secretary she jumped at the opportunity. Mr. Lipscomb had hired her not just because of her talents with a steno pad and a typewriter, but because she had actually read, and appreciated, Pickering books. Someone who had worked in a bookstore, and had direct contact with Pickering customers, he had said, would understand those readers and what they wanted.

For over a year now, Magda's writing had been largely confined to answering fan letters and typing Mr. Lipscomb's correspondence. She worked long hours at the office, and sometimes even took her work home, writing drafts of letters in shorthand to be typed the following day. But now and then, especially on Sunday afternoons, she found time to work on *Dan Dawson, Circus Star*.

She had not admitted her dream of getting published to Tom De Peyster and Gene Pinkney as they talked at Childs—not even when, after Gene kept complaining about the phony science in current fiction, Tom suggested he try his own hand at a children's series.

"I'm a scientist," said Gene. "Why would I write stories for kids?"

"Who better?" said Tom. "You could make the hero a young inventor, and you could get the technology right. If you think H. G. Wells messes up the science, you should read the Great Marvel series."

"I've never really given much thought to writing," said Gene.

"Read the books," said Tom with a laugh. "I'm not sure Roy Rockwood has given much thought to writing."

Magda agreed that the quality of writing in most children's series books was not going to land them in the literary pantheon. "But I suppose your book is an exception," she said to Tom.

"Hardly," said Tom. "I'm no literary luminary. I'm just a journalist . . . a . . ."

"I think the word you're looking for is *hack*," said Gene, lifting his glass of milk toward Magda.

"Exactly," said Tom. "Which puts me on equal footing with Roy Rockwood."

"And then some," said Magda.

"So, do you think Mr. Lipscomb will meet with me?" said Tom.

"Come to the office on Tuesday morning," said Magda. "I'm sure we can fit you in."

With an experienced journalist like Tom De Peyster coming to the office on Tuesday to pitch *Frank Fairfax, Cub Reporter*, to Mr. Lipscomb, Magda determined to do on Monday what she had wanted to do for weeks—ever since she finished a draft of *Dan Dawson, Circus Star—Danger under the Big Top*. She had stayed late in the office night after night to type her manuscript, and now it nestled in the bottom drawer of her desk, waiting for her to muster the courage to show it to her employer. Tom De Peyster would have an easy enough time impressing Mr. Lipscomb. The publisher would love Tom—an experienced writer who knew powerful people like William Randolph Hearst and Upton Sinclair. More important, Tom had one attribute Magda would always lack. Tom was a man. Mr. Lipscomb had very specific ideas about the appropriate spheres for men and women. As long as Magda sat at her desk and typed letters, Mr. Lipscomb would be perfectly happy; but to get him to make her one of Pickering Brothers' authors would take more than a little convincing.

Every Monday morning, Magda met Mr. Lipscomb in his office at ten o'clock to review the schedule for the week. The first time she saw Mr. Lipscomb, when she had come for her job interview, she had expected a captain of industry—an imposing figure the likes of a Carnegie or a Rockefeller. Instead, she discovered a small bespectacled man in a rumpled cardigan sweater and worn corduroy pants. Instead of chomping on a cigar, he chewed an endless succession of sticks of Wrigley's gum; instead of sitting in a swiveling leather chair behind a massive mahogany desk, he perched atop a three-legged stool that seemed ready to topple over at any moment and that rose from within a square of cheap pine tables, all barely visible under piles of magazines, manuscripts, newspapers, book jackets, and a thousand other bits of paper. He spoke not in a booming, bass voice but in a volume just above a whisper and in a register well above a tenor with the occasional hint of a Cockney accent. She had both feared him and wanted to take him home and make him soup.

Now she knew him well. An English immigrant, he rarely revealed anything about his personal life in their professional interactions, but she had gradually pieced together his story. Spending most of his early years on the streets of East London, he had escaped first into the pages of discarded copies of Samuel Beeton's *The Boy's Own Magazine,* with its tales of manly adventures, and then, as a young man, to New York, where he worked his way up through the ranks of the publishing industry in a manner inspired by the tales of Horatio Alger, eventually founding his own company. Though he would don a formal suit in order to rub elbows with New York's elite at Vanderbilt parties or the Metropolitan Opera in the evening, during the business day he cared nothing for his personal appearance. He didn't even seem that concerned with making money. Now in his late fifties, he just wanted to write and publish adventure stories like the ones that had rescued him from the misery of his childhood. Magda hoped she could play on this central desire as she pushed open his door at five minutes to ten.

"Good morning, Mr. Lipscomb," she said softly. Lipscomb, as usual, had a pair of reading spectacles perched on his nose, a manuscript in one hand, and a red pen in the other.

"Ten o'clock! Ten o'clock!" came a harsh voice from behind him. Mr. Lipscomb's pet mynah bird, Portia, was a regular fixture in the office, and had a habit of interjecting herself into the conversation.

"You are wrong, Portia dear," said Mr. Lipscomb, without lifting his eyes from the manuscript to where the bird perched atop a pile of books. "It is not ten o'clock; it is nine fifty-five, and so I must ask, why am I being disturbed by Miss Stone?"

"I just wanted to ask you a question before we went over the appointments," said Magda.

"Ask then," said Mr. Lipscomb. "You've already interrupted my work."

"I just wondered what you would say if I told you I had written a manuscript."

"I'd say don't be ridiculous, Miss Stone. Books are written by men, not women. Especially Pickering books."

"But what about Edith Wharton?" said Magda. "She's written books."

"I've no idea whom you are speaking of, Miss Stone," said Mr. Lipscomb, finally laying down his spectacles and looking at Magda as if she were a schoolgirl. "Besides, if I say man is not meant to commit murder and you say, 'What about Harry Thaw, he killed Stanford White,' that doesn't change the validity of my assertion, does it?"

"But you said you wanted to start selling books to girls," said Magda. "In the letter that you sent to the ghostwriters last week."

"I'm sure men are perfectly capable of writing books for girls, Miss Stone."

"So, you would never accept a manuscript written by a woman?"

"Of course not."

"But how would you know?" said Magda. "If you got a manuscript in the mail, how would you know it was written by a woman?"

"First of all, Miss Stone," said Mr. Lipscomb, sounding more exasperated with each passing second, "I would know. I would know by the inferior quality just as I would know if I was living in a house built by a woman or riding in a streetcar driven by a woman." Magda had a sudden vision of Mademoiselle de Tiers sailing her automobile through the air at the Barnum and Bailey Circus. *If women are such poor drivers*, she wanted to say, *how do you explain that?* But she knew the point would carry no weight with Mr. Lipscomb.

"And secondly," Mr. Lipscomb continued, "I would know because if there is one thing I believe in here at Pickering Brothers, it is personal contact. I would never publish a book without meeting the author or the ghostwriter face-to-face—looking him in the eyes and shaking his hand. I can tell an honest man, Miss Stone, just as surely as I can tell if a book has been written by an honest man or a dishonest woman."

What a pig, thought Magda. But she was already beginning to form an idea.

ᘓᗞ

Tom De Peyster was the most beautiful man Eugene Pinkney had ever seen. Perhaps not objectively—his shoulders were not as broad nor his chin as strong as they might be. But his eyes gleamed with worldliness and pathos and passion unlike any Eugene had seen before, and he had seen a lot of eyes. Gene did not believe in love at first sight. But if he did, he would already be in love with Tom—or at least with his eyes. But Eugene knew that being in love with Tom, though perhaps inevitable, was hopeless. For he did not detect in Tom's eyes that glint that said *I am like you, I share your secret.*

Nonetheless, Gene could not resist the idea of spending more time around Tom. If that meant trying his hand at writing an adventure book for children with some real science in it, why not? Gene had built up a substantial savings over the past eight years; he could afford to take some time off and write a book. It had been years since he had read Jules Verne; he read every new H. G. Wells book as soon as it appeared in the library. But he had never read any of the series books Tom and Magda had mentioned. Gene discovered one reason for this gap in his reading was that the Astor Library didn't carry any of these titles. A few dollars spent at Putnam's and Dutton's on Twenty-Third Street remedied this problem, and Gene was soon ensconced in his room with a stack of books, rolling his eyes every time he came across any hint of "science." A previously undiscovered lighter-than-air gas; an unexplained "etherium" motor that powers a rocket to Mars; breathable atmosphere on the moon—none of these things made any sense scientifically. Yet, the salesmen at Putnam's and at Dutton's said these books sold more copies than H. G. Wells or Jules Verne.

He skimmed through all the volumes, then set them aside and pulled out a sheet of paper and a pencil. He needed a hero, obviously—perhaps someone who worked for a famous scientist, but also pursued his own experiments and inventions. The main characters in all these series adventures were young boys. Gene thought back to his days at Paresis Hall and how he had loved blurring the line between male and female. He had never felt more honest than when he dwelt in that neverland between boy and girl. Could he do the same thing in a book? The salesmen at the bookstores had said that boys came in every week to buy the new books in the many adventure series. But what about girls? Could Gene create a girl heroine? He wrote at the top of the paper, *Alice Gold, Inventor.*

But what would Alice do? What would she invent? And more important, how did it feel to actually be a girl? Gene had hovered in the

shadows between boy and girl, but as an only child who had spent the
past ten years in the all-male clubs of Paresis Hall and the Tesla laborato-
ries, he had never really known a girl. What did girls feel? How did they
think? He needed someone to give him a tour of the mind and heart of
a girl. And then he realized he already had someone—Magda. The trio
had agreed to eat at Childs again on Wednesday. That would give him a
chance to ask Magda if she would help him create a realistic girl. And to
look in Tom's eyes again.

Tom had felt his facade dropping as he had talked to Magda. Or at least
one of his facades. He had lost track of how many masks he wore, of where
the real Tom hid behind them all. He had presented himself at Pickering
Brothers as a wealthy gentleman, hoping to impress the publisher with his
debonair, moneyed demeanor. And Tom did still live with his family on
Fifth Avenue. But he never felt that Thomas De Peyster of Fifth Avenue
was the real Tom. He had told Magda truthfully that he worked as a
journalist, but his journalism, from the earliest days when he wandered
the streets of Manhattan dressed as a bootblack and looking for stories,
had always involved pretense. He thought back over the past few years of
working for Mr. Hearst, years in which he was as likely to be wearing a
white tie and interviewing an opera star as to be sitting on a street corner
in rags collecting stories about Silent Charlie Murphy or Big Tim Sullivan.
Until he met Magda, he had almost always felt the need to hide the real
Tom De Peyster.

Tom had shown his true self one time that he could remember. On
that horrible morning just a few months ago in San Francisco, as he
watched Isabella sleeping, he had felt that no walls existed between them.
Though he did not know her, had only just met her, though she clearly
played the role she was paid to play, Tom had still felt genuine for a few
moments. He had felt authentic after the earthquake, too, but that had
been different. Then his facade had been forcibly stripped off by death and
destruction and horror. But he remembered those few moments before

the earth began to shake when he did not feel like a reporter pretending to be someone in order to get a story, or like a wealthy man trying to act the part, but simply like a normal young man, infatuated with a girl.

Sitting at Childs with Magda, he had started to feel that way again. Though he still wore the fashionable suit and the silver walking stick leaned against the wall next to his chair, Tom felt himself becoming someone less interested in discovering other people's secrets than in sharing his own. Magda, with the knowing smile that crept across her face when she chided him and the intense intelligence in her eyes, seemed to see right through his pretense. It unbalanced him, at first. He was so used to wearing a mask he had almost forgotten it until Magda peeked behind it. Perhaps he had fallen for Isabella only because she had gone to bed with him; he'd never had time to discover the truth of those feelings. But maybe he was the type who tumbled into love with any woman who could pierce his armor. Whatever the reason, Tom couldn't get Magda out of his thoughts.

Now he prepared to see her again, waiting for the elevator that would bear him to the seventh floor and the offices of Pickering Brothers, Publishers. His meeting with Mr. Lipscomb, his chances of shaking off the shackles of Mr. Hearst and becoming a different kind of writer, all that was simply business and business never made him nervous. Knowing he would see Magda again, that she would see through whatever part he played—that was something else altogether.

XV

NEW YORK CITY, UPPER WEST SIDE, 2010

After lunch, still shaken by his conversation with Rebecca and keenly aware of his deadline, Robert decided to read every article he could find about Edward Stratemeyer and his publishing syndicate. He discovered that when Stratemeyer launched a new series, he issued the first three volumes simultaneously. If these "breeder" sets sold well, the series would continue; if not, Stratemeyer would cancel it and move on. A Stratemeyer title could go from an idea in the publisher's head to a hardbound book sitting on the shelves of a bookstore in just forty days. Robert thought back over the road to publication *Looking Forward* had taken—two years of writing, rewriting, and submitting to agents and, even after a publisher bought it, another year of editing, design work, and waiting for a slot on the summer list. That Stratemeyer could move a book from initial conception to the hands of readers in less than six weeks seemed a remarkable achievement. And he did this hundreds of times, without the benefit of digital technology.

Turning to researching the Tremendous Trio authors, Robert had a brief moment of excitement when he found the name Neptune B. Smythe in several documents from the early twentieth century, but it turned out they all referred to a plumber working in New York City. Robert thought it unlikely that the plumber moonlighted as a children's author, but the name, including the middle initial, seemed an awfully big coincidence.

In a series of digitized New York City directories, he found, beginning in 1902, entries for Pickering Brothers, Publishers, at 175 Fifth Avenue in what was then called the Fuller Building, soon to be known to locals as the Flatiron Building. The last entry for Pickering was in 1912.

None of this information did Robert much good. Frustrated and exhausted from lack of sleep, he turned in early. His dream followed the plot of *The Tremendous Trio at Niagara Falls*, but, unlike in the book, Alice Gold's specially designed breathing apparatus didn't work, Frank failed to recover the barrel, and Dan Dawson disappeared under the roiling water and did not resurface.

On Sunday Robert set out to read as many Pickering books as he could get through, hoping he might find clues within the texts to the identities of the authors. As he began comparing volumes, the first thing Robert realized was that Pickering had not always employed the "breeder" system used by Stratemeyer. The first Dan Dawson book bore the notice "Copyright 1906, by Pickering Brothers, Publishers." Frank Fairfax and Alice Gold also began in 1906. The second volume in all three series was dated 1907 and the third 1908. The Tremendous Trio books, on the other hand, were all dated 1911. Was it coincidence that the three series had proceeded on exactly the same schedule, or had the authors worked together before the crossover series began? Or had Dexter, Buck, and Neptune all been the same person?

Robert skimmed the first book in each series, moving from volume to volume one chapter at a time. Almost immediately, he noticed something he had taken for granted as a child, but that now seemed important. Each of the heroes had a significant link to New York City.

Alice Gold lived in that mansion on Fifth Avenue. Frank Fairfax worked for a newspaper baron whose cigar-chomping, make-no-excuses attitude gave him more than a passing resemblance to the popular image of William Randolph Hearst. Although the book made no mention of Frank's hometown, his father was a founding member of the Explorers Club—hence Frank's presence on various expeditions to mythical lands. The Explorers Club had been founded in 1904 on West Sixty-Seventh Street. And then there was Dan Dawson, the circus acrobat. In the second chapter of *Storm from the Sea*, a flashback told how Dan joined the circus, performing for the first time before the crowd at Madison Square Garden.

That chapter had been the inspiration for another of the excursions Robbie and his father took—this time to the new Madison Square Garden at Penn Station to see Ringling Bros, and Barnum and Bailey Circus.

"It may not be the same Madison Square Garden where Dan Dawson performed," said his father as he and Robbie took their seats, "but it's basically the same circus. Barnum and Bailey and the Ringling Brothers both go back to before Dan was born."

Robbie had marveled at elephants dancing and tigers jumping through flaming hoops. He had laughed at clowns and gasped at stilt walkers. But his favorite—and his father's favorite, he had said afterward—had been the acrobats. Watching those figures high on the trapeze or walking the tight rope, Robbie was able to imagine Dan Dawson doing the same act nearly a hundred years ago. On the train on the way home, Robbie's father had produced their much-loved copy of *Storm from the Sea*, and read to Robbie until the boy fell asleep, dreaming of flying through the air.

"Dan, you go on in two minutes," shouted the ringmaster.

"Don't worry," said Dan from his perch atop the elephant. "I'll be there."

Dan Dawson was not the youngest performer in Anderson's Circus. Sophie Anderson, the owner's daughter, was only twelve—a year younger than Dan—but all she did was get shot out of the human cannon, and anyone who could hold still could do that. Dan, on the other hand, was adept at both walking the high wire and doing stunts on the flying trapeze. Among the adult members of the circus, he was also known for arriving at his position at the last possible moment, often spending his time loitering in the elephant's cage with Bessie, on whom he now sat.

"I can get from Bessie's back to the top of the trapeze ladder in thirty seconds," thought the lad. "I don't see why Mr. Anderson needs to shout."

Dan was right—even after stroking Bessie and feeding her a few peanuts, he still managed to arrive at the top of the trapeze ladder with nearly ten seconds to spare. In another instant, he was flying through the air, tossed from one acrobat to another while the crowd below gasped in amazement.

Dan was never afraid soaring high above the crowd. He had performed the act hundreds of times. To the crowd below, it may have looked dangerous. To Dan, however, walking on tightropes and flying on trapezes was fun and exciting, but perfectly safe. But little did Dan know, as the wind outside fluttered the flag surmounting the big top, that before the band played to announce the next afternoon's performance, a storm would arrive, and Dan, and all the rest of the circus, would be in a greater danger than they ever imagined.

Robert had thought of those words, that book, that magical afternoon with his father, years later when he and Rebecca had gone up to Randall's Island to see the latest big-top extravaganza by Cirque du Soleil. He enjoyed the show, but not in the same way as he had Ringling Brothers. That circus had been cacophonous and confusing and dirty and felt as if the history of all those years since Dan Dawson's time clung to every performer. Cirque du Soleil had been clean and slick and all just a little too perfect.

Now, as he reread the reference to Madison Square Garden in the Dan Dawson book, Robert wondered if the connections between the Pickering books and New York City had any significance. The Tremendous Trio, too, appeared in New York—most dramatically in the scene Robert had read to the children the previous day—when they witnessed Wilbur Wright flying around the Statue of Liberty—a real event, Robert discovered, that had taken place in 1909. Did Pickering write the books himself from his office in the Flatiron Building? Or did he write outlines and, as a New Yorker, set parts of the books in a city he knew well? Or did he hire ghostwriters who lived in New York?

The sky had grown dark, and the streetlights glowed against the snow as Robert stood and stretched. Time slipped by quickly when he was lost in the worlds of Alice and Dan and Frank, and time was something he did not possess in generous supply. He gazed out the window at the beauty of the city for a moment, then picked up his phone to call Sherwood Whitmore, hoping the collector might be home by now and might be able to shed some light on the fate of the Tremendous Trio.

XVI

"You look the part," said Magda, brushing a bit of lint off Tom's coat. He was dressed once again in imitation of a successful businessman. Magda had told him that money impressed Mr. Lipscomb and to come for his meeting looking as wealthy as possible. She had watched in the past as Lipscomb changed his entire attitude in the presence of the outer signs of affluence. He could suddenly become subservient and agreeable instead of his usual cantankerous self.

"Now go in there like you own the place, like you're doing him a favor."

Tom had shivered under his coat at Magda's touch but now squared his shoulders and gripped his walking stick. He knew well enough how to play a part—he did that every day. True, he was more accustomed to pretending to be poor than to flaunting his wealth, but he trusted Magda to know what would work best for Lipscomb.

"And flatter him," whispered Magda, as she knocked on Lipscomb's door.

"Your eleven o'clock appointment is here, Mr. Lipscomb."

Without waiting to be invited, Tom strode in with an air of authority he had observed in Mr. Hearst. "Julius Lipscomb, we meet at last."

"Do I know . . ." said Mr. Lipscomb.

"I've heard about your operation here. Word does get around in the publishing world."

"And you would be?" said Lipscomb, glancing at his appointment book.

"Thomas De Peyster," said Tom, presenting his card. "I'm an associate of William Randolph Hearst. More than an associate, really, but I'm not here to talk about Mr. Hearst. I'm sure, being a publisher, you know him well." Tom was absolutely certain that Mr. Hearst had never heard of Pickering Brothers, much less met Mr. Lipscomb.

"Actually," said Mr. Lipscomb, but Tom could see the little man was flustered and he pressed his advantage.

"I came to you, Mr. Lipscomb, because I believe you deserve an opportunity. I believe we need to stand up to that scoundrel Edward Stratemeyer and his plan to run his competitors out of business." Lipscomb blanched and slipped back onto his stool. Tom could see he had hit a nerve. He had no reason to believe Stratemeyer was trying to run anyone out of business, but clearly Lipscomb was a small enough fish that he feared the appetite of the shark around the corner.

"You need new properties, Mr. Lipscomb, and I'm here to give you one." He produced a neat stack of manuscript leaves from inside his coat and slapped it down on the only corner of one of Lipscomb's tables not already covered by books, magazines, or papers.

"*Frank Fairfax, Cub Reporter.* A book that will get reviewed in every one of Mr. Hearst's papers." Again, Tom had no means of ensuring this, but he reasoned he probably had a better chance of getting the book a mention in at least the *New York Evening Journal* than most other aspiring authors.

Lipscomb reached forward and picked up the manuscript. Tom remained towering over the publisher, but he had nothing more to say, having reached the end of his script. This pause in his monologue gave Lipscomb a chance to seize control of the conversation for the first time. A wealthy man making threats and promises was an uncommon sight in his office; someone bringing him a manuscript was business as usual.

"Give me an hour," said Lipscomb quietly as he pulled on his spectacles. "I'll leave word with my secretary if I wish to see you after looking at this." He turned his attention to the manuscript and Tom knew the interview had ended. He backed out of the office and quietly closed the door.

"How did it go?" said Magda.

"You might have told me about the bird," said Tom. "It was rather nerve-racking to try to maintain my composure with that thing staring at me from behind your employer."

"And the manuscript?"

"Mr. Lipscomb took my manuscript and told me to come back in an hour. I don't suppose I could interest you in a cup of coffee at Childs?"

"I have work to do, Mr. De Peyster. Besides, I don't think it would be proper to go out with you without Mr. Pinkney as a chaperone. I'll see you in an hour."

"You'll see me *for* an hour," said Tom, sitting in the chair by her desk. "I can wait."

And he did. Magda did her best to attend to business, which this morning consisted of retyping a manuscript that had been heavily edited by Mr. Lipscomb. Every few minutes, Tom would stand up and stroll to the window, staring down at the bustle of Fifth Avenue seven stories below. Without pausing her typing, she could sense when he stole glances at her. She liked Tom, she thought, and could even imagine his becoming something she hadn't had since she left Kleindeutschland—a friend. But she didn't need him surreptitiously eyeing her while she tried to work. She was a little relieved when, at exactly eleven o'clock, Mr. Lipscomb opened his office door.

"Has Mr. De Peyster returned?"

"Oh yes," said Magda, "he's just arrived."

In his second interview with Mr. Lipscomb, Tom hardly got a chance to speak. As soon as Lipscomb started in, Tom realized that the publisher viewed him now not as an impressive, well-connected gentleman, but as a manuscript, a commodity. This time, Lipscomb was all business.

"I like the name," he said. "Frank Fairfax sounds like a reporter. Names are important. But forget about saving people from disasters."

"But the whole point . . ."

"I don't care about the point," said Lipscomb. "I care about what I need. I need exploration. Stratemeyer has boys going to the North Pole and the bottom of the ocean and the surface of the moon. The Explorers Club opened over a year ago and the closest thing I have to an explorer is Drew Stetson. But I've got something Stratemeyer doesn't have. I've got imagination. Do you have imagination, Mr. De Peyster?"

"Yes, sir," said Tom, who suddenly felt like an eight-year-old being chided by his governess for some infraction of her rules.

"Here's what I want you to do. Keep your hero a reporter, I like that, but make his father a member of the Explorers Club—that gives him connections. Then have his editor send him along on expeditions. But here's where we'll get Stratemeyer. Your hero won't go to the moon or the South Pole; he'll discover places of legend. Here's your first title: *Frank Fairfax and the Search for El Dorado.* If that one sells you can do Atlantis next. If I do the outline and you write it, you get a hundred and twenty-five dollars; if you do the whole thing without my outline, it's one fifty, but if I don't like it, it's zero."

"I think I can write it without the outline," said Tom. "If I—"

"And follow the rules—no kissing, no smoking, no drinking, and nothing mamby-pamby or wishy-washy. Every third chapter ends in peril, nobody gets killed, and the hero has impeccable morals. Got it?"

"Yes sir, I—"

"I'll need it by the end of September." Mr. Lipscomb turned away from Tom and picked up a paper which he began reading, clearly signaling that the interview was over. Tom wasn't sure what to think. His carefully prepared manuscript had been torn to shreds. His idea that he would end the nightmares that began after the earthquake by writing a series of stories in which the hero saved people from disasters had been squelched. On the other hand, Mr. Lipscomb had offered him a hundred and fifty dollars to write a book. Everything he had ever written before had ended up wrapping fish or keeping vagrants warm on a winter's night. His words in newspapers were ephemeral. But a book, a hardcover book, even one written in two months for a children's series, might last. He turned to leave, and as he opened the door to the outer office, Lipscomb called after him.

"Keep the pseudonym," he said. "I like Neptune B. Smythe."

"So, what's the problem?" said Gene. The trio sat again at the back table at Childs, where they had spent the last hour in conversation. Tom had shared the exciting news that Mr. Lipscomb wanted him to write a book about a boy explorer who discovers El Dorado. Buoyed by his enthusiasm, Magda had admitted her own desire to write a series for Mr. Lipscomb. She was so used to keeping secrets that she thought she would struggle to tell Tom and Gene about *Dan Dawson, Circus Star*, but in fact it had felt entirely natural. She didn't understand why talking to them was so easy, but it was. She went on to relate the story of her interview with Mr. Lipscomb on the subject of women writing books.

"The problem is he won't consider a manuscript without meeting the author face-to-face," she said. "And I may not look like Evelyn Nesbit, but I think it's pretty clear I'm a female."

"Crystal clear," said Tom. Magda felt a blush rising in her cheek. Tom had been paying her altogether too much attention during dinner and the cups of coffee that followed.

"Yes," said Gene, leaning forward, "you look like a woman now, fair enough. But that problem is easily overcome."

"It's not a problem," said Tom, smiling.

"What do you mean? Have some man pretend to be me?" Magda had her own idea about how to deal with Lipscomb, but she wanted to hear what Gene had to say.

"What if Lipscomb asks about details of her book?" said Tom. "It needs to be her."

"And it will be," said Gene, "but Lipscomb will think she's a man."

"Exactly what I was thinking," said Magda, smiling at Gene. He could read her mind, she thought. Ever since she had met him, she had felt a connection, and his ability to understand just what she was thinking only strengthened it. She wondered if he could feel it, too.

"How?" said Tom. "Magda looks less like a man than anyone I know."

"Trust me, if there is one among the three of us who can make someone look like a member of the opposite sex, it's me."

"That's a very specific claim," said Tom.

"And I'm willing to share my talents with my friends," said Gene cryptically, hoping Tom would not follow his journalist's instinct to dig deeper into this particular subject.

"Is that what we are?" said Magda, boldly laying her had on top of Gene's. "Friends?" She hoped he would say something wildly romantic like, *Oh, we're so much more than that*, but this time Gene did not read her mind.

He gently extricated his hand from beneath Magda's, all the while looking at Tom. "Yes," he said. "We're friends. Aren't we, Tom?"

"Absolutely," said Tom.

"It's been a long time since I've had friends," said Magda.

"I used to have friends," said Gene, "but then things changed."

"What changed?" said Tom.

"I lost one of my last friends quite recently," said Gene, deftly avoiding the subject of Paresis Hall and Princess Petunia and the other girls. Magda had mentioned Evelyn Nesbit, so why not regale them with a story that involved her.

"I remember an evening we spent together a few years ago. He took me along to dine about once a month or so, just to check on me and sometimes to show off his latest conquest. We often dined at Café Martin, since it was close to his apartment, and sometimes he took me to the Players Club in Gramercy Park, where we sat at his usual table under a portrait of Edwin Booth, but that night we ate in a private dining room at Delmonico's."

"You've eaten at Delmonico's?" said Magda in awe. That an orphan from Kleindeutschland should be sharing a table with a gentleman who had dined at the grandest restaurant in New York seemed to Magda to define America perfectly.

"I'll take you there sometime," said Tom, winking at Magda.

"Earlier in the evening, my friend had invited me to meet him at Madison Square Garden for a boxing match," said Gene. He had never paid much attention to sports before or after that night, but Gene remembered how those perfect bodies had gleamed with sweat. He had never seen such musculature except on the Greek statues at the Metropolitan Museum, and those did not move. But these men moved—oh, how they moved. He wished he could see

Tom move like that. "We sat in a box," said Gene, "slightly removed from the roaring crowd, yet close enough to feel their energy. I have never followed boxing, and couldn't even name the fighters, but there was a raw excitement to the whole experience. After the bout, my friend took me round to the dressing room where he chatted briefly with the victor. Knowing nothing of the sport, I could think of no more to say beyond 'Congratulations.'" Gene had been utterly tongue-tied not because of his ignorance of the nuances of boxing, but because of the presence of the most perfectly sculpted male specimen he had ever seen. The champion had removed his gloves and shoes, and wore nothing but a pair of shorts around which his muscles bulged. Gene felt his breath coming in shallow gasps and feared he might show visible signs of arousal as he ran his eyes up and down the athlete's figure. He knew this was why Stanford White had brought him to the dressing room. "I thought you'd like a little treat," he had said to Gene as they strolled up Broadway after escaping the crowds outside Madison Square Garden.

"Who was this friend?" said Magda.

"Shh," said Tom. "A good storyteller saves a surprise for the end."

"Our next stop was the Casino Theatre, where we ducked through the stage door and met one of the chorus girls from *Floradora*, who was waiting for my friend backstage. The detour to the dressing room at the Garden had delayed us and she had waited nearly half an hour and was none too pleased, but when my friend explained that we had a table waiting at Delmonico's, she softened. It was only a few blocks to the restaurant, and it was a lovely spring evening, so we decided to walk.

"Delmonico's is not the sort of place where a married man can dine with an eighteen-year-old chorus girl, but my friend had reserved a private dining room and besides, rules never seemed to apply to him. The maître d' showed us upstairs to our room where several other guests awaited us. I had thought we would have a quiet dinner for three, but it soon became apparent that the chorus girl and I would be shunted to the side while my host and his influential friends had one of their late-night round tables. Among those already seated were my own employer, Mr. Tesla, along with Mr. Clemens, whom I had met once before, though he did not remember me, and whom the larger world knows as Mr. Mark Twain."

Magda had read most of Mark Twain's books. Reading Twain was part of being an American, a librarian had once told her. This time she did not interrupt Gene, but she gazed at him with increasing infatuation. She had never seen herself as the sort of person who would fall in love with a man just because he had important friends, but of course her attraction to Gene had begun before she knew of these connections. Nonetheless, she could not deny that the fact that he had met Mark Twain made Gene even more captivating. She did not consider that she had had no such reaction to the news that Tom knew Upton Sinclair and William Randolph Hearst.

"Now, it may sound exciting to have dinner in a private room in a fine restaurant, and I'll grant you the food was exquisite. I can't recall every course, but I remember lamb cutlets, terrapin, and roast duckling, heaps of vegetables, and meringues and ice creams for dessert with preserved cherries and pineapple. But though I was well known to my friend, and of course to Mr. Tesla—although I did not work directly with him at that time, I saw him in the lab nearly every day—they did not include me in their conversation. I listened for a while, and enjoyed hearing the bon mots of Mr. Clemens which I knew would turn up in his writing sooner or later. But eventually I noticed that I was not the only member of the party excluded from the intellectual bantering. The chorus girl sat between me and my friend, looking exhausted and miserable, though perfectly able to devour several plates of food.

"She was, by then, something of a celebrity, and I had seen postcards of her for sale at newsstands on Broadway. We had met several times before in the company of my friend, but had never spoken more than a few words. On that night, I addressed her first with some kind comments about *Floradora*, to which my friend had taken me some weeks prior. She responded demurely, but then launched into an anecdote about one of the chorus girls who had been dismissed owing to her having gotten in a family way, and soon we found ourselves chatting away like old friends. I don't recall what we spoke of, but I do remember that the evening suddenly went from dull to pleasant. I think of that night often—how one can find enjoyment in the most unexpected places. The room was filled with prom-inent men, yet I'll venture that the two of us enjoyed talking over nothing in particular more than those men enjoyed solving the problems of the world." Gene also recalled, though he did not say, that this had been one of the only evenings in his life that he had spent in the company of a girl.

"You promised us a surprise ending," said Tom. "That's a pleasant ending, but I'm not sure I'd call it a surprise."

"I never promised a surprise ending," said Gene, smiling at Tom. "You did."

"But who was the friend?" demanded Magda. "And who was the girl?"

"As it happens, there is a surprise ending," said Gene, his eyes clouding over. "A rather shocking surprise to me and to the rest of New York. I remained on good terms with my friend, though I never met Mr. Clemens again. The girl I saw several more times, and then her relationship with my friend ended and I did not see her for some years, until just less than three weeks ago. The twenty-fifth of June." Gene paused and felt a catch in his throat.

"Is that the end?" said Magda. "It's not a very good ending for someone who wants to write adventure books."

"My goodness," said Tom, "June twenty-fifth. That *is* a surprise ending. Though I should have deduced it before."

"Deduced what?" said Magda in frustration.

"The identity of Gene's friend and the chorus girl," said Tom. "Unless I am mistaken you saw the girl again at the rooftop theater at Madison Square Garden, the same building where the story began."

"Correct," said Gene. "On a night the horror of which I shall not soon forget."

"I still don't understand," said Magda.

"Perhaps you don't read the papers," said Tom. "And if that is the case, I take offense as a journalist." He smiled at Magda as he said this. "But I doubt you can have missed this story. Gene's friend was Stanford White and his chorus girl companion was Evelyn Nesbit."

"*The* Stanford White," said Magda, "the one who was murdered?"

"Murdered right in front of me," said Gene, his voice shaking. "The most frightening experience of my life, and one that left me without friends, until I found you two."

"Is it true what they say in the papers?" said Magda.

"Why, Magda," said Tom in mock seriousness, "we journalists would never print anything but the truth."

"It's not for me to say," said Gene. He had read some of the horrible things the papers had printed about Mr. White, and he could certainly believe that the architect had behaved shamefully toward more than one underage girl. "He treated me well; he got me a job; and we planned to meet that night because I needed another one. Now, I've rambled on for much too long. I'm sure we should all be going." He pushed back his chair and stood up. "Magda, I will meet you in front of the Flatiron Building tomorrow evening at six o'clock."

"What for?" said Magda, her heart leaping. Might she be able to entertain Gene with as much charm as Evelyn Nesbit had apparently shown?

"To show you how to turn yourself into a man."

XVII

NEW YORK CITY, UPPER EAST SIDE, 2010

Sherwood Whitmore lived in a penthouse apartment on East Eighty-Seventh Street, between Park and Lexington. To reach his building, Robert had walked across Central Park, skirting the bottom of the reservoir where Rebecca liked to run. The paths were slushy with melting snow, and the park was nearly empty of people. Rebecca had taken up running when they moved into the new apartment and loved to do laps on the cinder track that wound more than a mile and a half around the reservoir. On sunny mornings, Robert would walk with her to the South Gate House, where he would sit reading on a bench while she ran, passing him every fifteen minutes or so. He could always sense her approach, and always looked up in time to see her smile and wave, holding up two or three or four fingers to let him know how many more laps she had planned. They hadn't done that for several months and, as he walked within sight of what had been his usual bench, Robert suddenly missed that routine with a pain that stabbed his chest like a cardiac needle. It shocked him, this physical reaction to the absence of a once ordinary event.

By the time Robert stepped onto Fifth Avenue at Eighty-Fifth Street the pain had eased slightly, and he understood he did not miss sitting on a bench watching Rebecca run; he missed Rebecca herself. He felt tears welling up as he turned uptown. How could he have let his own fears, his own haunting past, interfere with the one relationship he truly cared about?

Robert stopped on the corner of Fifth and Eighty-Sixth and tried to catch his breath, wiping a sleeve across his face. Should he give up this ridiculous quest, forget about the deadline, and call her, tell her everything right now? He pulled out his phone and stared at the dark screen. He had asked for a week, he thought. He should take it. He should try to finish what he had started and prepare himself for the story he must tell Rebecca. As he crossed Fifth Avenue, he promised that if she came back, he would never take her for granted again. Maybe he would even run with her.

Now, Robert stepped from the lobby of marble and polished brass into the elevator that would take him to meet a retired investment banker obsessed with children's series books. He liked meeting new people. It had become a way to cope over the years. New acquaintances never delved too deep. They expected superficial conversation, and Robert felt comfortable providing just that.

The elevator opened into a wide reception room, with French doors leading onto a balcony at the far end. Every inch of wall space was lined with glass-fronted bookcases. Within each gleamed the plastic-covered dust jackets of hundreds, if not thousands, of volumes.

"You'll forgive me if I don't get up," said a man who sat in a Queen Anne chair at a wide oak library table. "I'm not as spry as when I started this collection. I'm Sherwood Whitmore."

Robert tore his eyes away from the bookcases and strode across the room to greet his host. He guessed that Sherwood was somewhere between eighty and a hundred years old—his body looked shrunken and only a few wisps of hair sprouted from his spotted scalp. He wore a pair of tailored trousers, a starched and ironed button-down shirt, and highly polished leather slippers. A pair of reading glasses perched on his nose, and a pen and a book of sudoku puzzles lay on the table in front of him. He held out a hand as Robert approached.

"Robert Parrish," said Robert. "It's very nice to meet you."

"I always enjoy having a visitor," said Sherwood, taking off his glasses. "Especially one who shares my peculiar passion."

"This is amazing," said Robert, turning his attention to the rows and rows of books. Some titles he recognized, but others were completely new to him—series like Tommy Tiptop, Ralph of the Railroad, Boys of Pluck, and many others.

"I am rather proud of them," said Sherwood.

"I didn't know they were all issued in dust jackets," said Robert. "May I?"

"Please," said Sherwood. "There is no point in having these things if we don't ever have the pleasure of looking at them."

Robert opened the door to one of the cases and pulled out a pristine copy of *Under the Ocean to the South Pole*, one of the Great Marvel books. The bright, gaudy dust jacket showed the two heroes in the control room of Professor Henderson's ship, the Submarine Wonder, being pitched off their feet by some unseen crisis.

"Beautiful," said Robert.

"Not a first edition, unfortunately, but the earliest copy I've been able to find in a dust jacket."

"You must have been collecting for a long time," said Robert, carefully returning the book to the shelf.

"I bought my first Stratemeyer book in 1933," said Sherwood. "The Hardy Boys in *Footprints under the Window*."

"I read my grandfather's copy of that when I was nine," said Robert.

"I was eight," said Sherwood, "and an immediate addict."

"If you bought it in 1933, it must have just been published."

"That's right. It was the heyday for children's series. I bought a new book every five weeks."

"Why every five weeks?" said Robert, sitting in a chair across from Sherwood.

"I got an allowance of ten cents a week," said Sherwood. "That meant in five weeks I could save up fifty cents, which was all it took. Can you imagine? Fifty cents for a hardcover book of twenty-five chapters with illustrations, all wrapped up in a colorful dust jacket."

"That must have been exciting," said Robert. "To take your fifty cents to the bookstore and come home with Frank and Joe Hardy."

"We lived in New Jersey, but when I had saved up my fifty cents I would demand a trip to Brentano's on Fifth Avenue. What a glorious book-store, with its wrought iron railings and two-story main level. Mr. Brentano would greet us at the front door, and I would dash up to the mezzanine where they kept the children's books, where I had to make that deliciously painful decision about which book to buy. Would I choose the X Bar X Boys, or Don Sturdy, or Roy Stover? I wasn't sexist, either; I sometimes picked Nancy Drew or the Dana Girls. And of course, if there was a new Hardy Boys or Tom Swift I couldn't resist. I would take my choice up to the counter, cradling it like a puppy and counting out my five dimes. Then the clerk would wrap the book in brown paper, and I would insist on holding it all the way home. I wouldn't let myself peek inside that wrapper until I got back to my room. Then I would peel back the brown paper until I got just a glimpse of the dust jacket—maybe Bomba's curly hair or Nancy's white dress or Teddy Manly on a horse—but that first peek would satisfy me for a while. After all, I had to make that book last for five weeks."

"I wouldn't have been able to wait," said Robert.

"I never held out long," said Sherwood. "I'd usually read the book through by the second or third day. I always took off the dust jacket when I read and replaced it before I shelved the book on a bookcase my father had built for me. I remember looking at that shelf at the end of the first year. I had bought eight books with my own money and received four more as Christmas and birthday gifts. Twelve books. That's when I started to think of myself as a collector."

"How many do you have now?" said Robert.

"Four thousand two hundred and seventy-three," said Sherwood.

"Wow," said Robert. "All children's series books?"

"All Stratemeyer books and all published before World War II. You have to set some boundaries as a book collector."

"I had no idea he published that many titles," said Robert. "I'd read it was several hundred, but four thousand?"

"They're not all unique titles," said Sherwood. "I started out trying to find one copy of each title, then upgraded to getting each title in a dust jacket, then each in a first edition, and then I started in on later printings, changes in the dust jacket designs, and so on. It's a funny thing about book collecting—no matter how tightly you define your collection, it keeps expanding."

"Do you still read them?" said Robert.

"Mostly to my great-grandchildren," said Sherwood, "though occasionally I pull one down if I'm feeling nostalgic."

"What do you read when you're not feeling nostalgic?"

"I've read your book," said Sherwood, with a sly smile. He had not previously given any indication that he recognized the name Robert Parrish. "I try to keep up with contemporary fiction and I read a lot of biographies—especially political figures. And of course, the *Times* and the *New Yorker.*"

"So you surround yourself with all these children's books, but you read *Looking Forward* and the *New York Times*?"

"By the time you're my age, perhaps you'll have learned that childhood is something you should never forget or leave behind, but that doesn't mean you should dwell in it. There is a great chasm between a man who always has a child*like* part of his spirit and one who is eternally child*ish*."

"But you've devoted your life to children's books," said Robert.

"I've devoted some of my spare time to preserving a piece of childhood culture. These books are worth collecting, but that doesn't make them great literature. Food that is perfectly suitable for the mind of a child will not nourish that of a man. And I have done a few other things in my life—raise a family, build a business, and the war of course."

"You fought in World War II?" Robert asked.

"US Army Air Corps," said Sherwood. "I think it must have been all those flying stories—Ted Scott, Slim Tyler, the Sky Flyers. I enlisted as soon as I could. I flew transport missions and then flew a C-47 full of paratroopers over Normandy on D-Day."

"My grandfather fought in Alsace," said Robert. "He carried a letter with him from Dexter Cornwall."

"Who's that?" said Sherwood.

"That's what I wanted to talk to you about. I'm researching three writers of children's series books—only they didn't write for Stratemeyer. They were all published by a company called Pickering Brothers. Dexter

Cornwall, Buck Larson, and Neptune B. Smythe. I wondered if you knew anything about them—or about Pickering."

"Probably pseudonyms," said Sherwood.

"That's what I thought, too. But you know the identities of a lot of the writers behind the Stratemeyer pseudonyms, right?"

"Most," said Sherwood, "but not all. What books did they write?"

"Daring Dan Dawson, Alice Gold, Frank Fairfax, and the Tremendous Trio," said Robert.

"I vaguely remember the Tremendous Trio," said Sherwood. "When I started collecting seriously in the 1950s, I didn't even know about Stratemeyer. I just collected anything that looked like the sort of series books I had loved as a child. Eventually I focused on Stratemeyer and got rid of anything he didn't produce. Everything else is long gone."

"But Stratemeyer wasn't the only one publishing children's series?"

"Oh heavens, no—just the most successful and the one who carried on the longest. The family controlled the syndicate until 1987, when they sold it to Simon and Schuster. But there were scores of others, probably publishing hundreds of series. When did your Pickering Brothers books come out?"

"The ones I have are from 1906 to 1911."

"Let's see, around then outside of Stratemeyer you have adventure travel series like the Four Boys—I especially liked *Four Boys in the Yellowstone*. Then you have school series like Raymond Benson and Jack Lorimer, and pretty soon after that you get the Pony Rider Boys and the Auto Boys and the Border Boys and the Submarine Boys. By 1912 you have the Aeroplane Boys, the Inventor series, the Big Game series, the Boy Scout series."

"That's a lot of books."

"Of course a lot of them came and went like summer flowers—now long forgotten even by collectors like me."

"Can I show you something?" said Robert, pulling a file folder from his messenger bag.

"By all means," said Sherwood.

Robert laid the folder on top of the sudoku book and opened it as Sherwood put on his reading glasses. "This was in the back of one of my grandfather's books. It's the first few pages of a Tremendous Trio story, but I can't find the rest of it. It's like the book never existed."

Sherwood leaned over and read, carefully turning over each fragile page. When he finished, he sat back in his chair and looked at Robert over his glasses. "That's some opening. But it's possible the book never *did* exist," he said. "Certainly these pages are not from a book."

"What do you mean?" said Robert.

"Look at the page numbers. This is the first page of the story, but the page number is thirty-six. These are from a pulp magazine."

"What's that?" said Robert.

"Open up that case to the left of the fireplace and look on the bottom shelf."

Robert did as he was told, squatting down to examine a row of paper-covered magazines, each in a glassine envelope.

"Bring a couple over here," said Sherwood. Robert pulled out two of the magazines at random and took them to his host.

"These aren't really part of my collection, but my brother gave them to me, so they have sentimental value. When I was upstairs on the mezzanine of Brentano's, my little brother was in the basement, where his fifty cents would buy five pulps. His favorites were *Amazing Stories* and *Adventure*. Each issue had five or six stories; some of them were serials that continued from month to month."

"So you think my Tremendous Trio story came from one of these magazines?"

"Probably this Pickering fellow published pulps as well as books and he used them to promote his series."

"But if the books are hard to find, won't the pulps be even harder?"

"There are plenty of them out there," said Sherwood. "But if you don't know what title you're looking for, it's a needle in haystack."

"How did people find out who really wrote the Stratemeyer books?" said Robert. "I mean, the actual authors behind the pseudonyms."

"Collectors and researchers have been working on Stratemeyer for a long time," said Sherwood, "but the best source of information is the archive of the syndicate itself. It's at the New York Public Library—hundreds of boxes of correspondence and manuscripts going all the way back to 1905. You might talk to the archivist there—woman by the name of Susan something. Afraid my memory's not what it used to be. Susan . . . or Sarah. Dark hair, tall girl. Anyway, maybe she's heard of your friend Pickering."

"Thanks," said Robert. "I'll do that. Shall I put those pulps back on the shelf for you?"

"I need something to read to my great-grandson when he comes to visit this afternoon," said Sherwood, "so you can leave them here."

"Does he like your collection?"

"Loves it," said Sherwood. "He's ten, and it drives him crazy that I won't let him take books home with him."

"What will happen to all these books when . . ."

"When I die?" said Sherwood. "They'll join the syndicate archives at the New York Public Library. They have a lot of the books in the archive, but there are some missing, and a lot of theirs are lacking the dust jackets. Finally there will be a complete collection of Stratemeyer titles in a library in this city. I'm sorry I can't help you more with your project."

"You've been a great help," said Robert. "Knowing this story is from a magazine and not a book—that's fantastic." He looked around the room once more, amazed by what surrounded him. "Your collection is magnificent."

"Thank you," said Sherwood. "It's nice to find someone who appreciates it. You must come back sometime and browse."

"I'd like that," said Robert.

"Now, believe it or not," said Sherwood, lifting himself slowly from his chair, "I have a trainer coming in a few minutes, so I need to change into my exercise attire."

Robert smiled. "Of course," he said. "You've been very kind. I hope we can meet again soon."

"I hope so, too," said Sherwood.

Before Robert even made it back to the park, he had the New York Public Library on the phone, trying to find an archivist named Susan or Sarah who was in charge of the Stratemeyer collection.

XVIII

NEW YORK CITY, WHEN GEORGE M. COHAN WAS A STAR

"I did what Tom suggested," said Gene as he and Magda walked west on Twenty-Third Street the next day. The summer had grown hot and even though evening had arrived, the air felt stifling, but Magda did not notice. She was alone with Gene; that was all that mattered. She knew she should be scandalized by what he had suggested when they met in front of the Flatiron Building, but she didn't care. After all, who would know? Magda had no father to be outraged, no mother to be ashamed, no sister to be tainted by association, no brother to be roused to defend her virtue. As long as Mr. Lipscomb never found out—he would stand for no moral turpitude among his employees *or* his ghostwriters.

"And what did Tom suggest?" shouted Magda, as the Sixth Avenue elevated train rumbled overhead, sending a cascade of ash down on them.

"That I write a book for your employer using real science."

"You wrote a book since last Friday?"

"Not a book," said Gene, "but a proposal."

"Give a lady a hand," said Magda, holding out her gloved hand as they mounted the steps leading up to the El platform. She lifted her skirts with one hand as Gene took the other. She was perfectly capable of climbing the stairs to the platform without assistance. She had, after all, been doing so for years. But she sighed inwardly as Gene took her hand. He seemed oblivious to the notion that holding her hand could be a sign not just of chivalry, but of affection. Just because she had felt herself falling for Gene almost as soon as they met didn't mean he would reciprocate immediately. Still, they were on their way to his lodgings, a single woman and a single man. Whatever the official purpose of the visit, Gene must have some feelings for her to take such a risk.

Five minutes later they were crammed into a crowded, airless train car, rattling downtown. Magda caught glimpses of domestic scenes as they raced past windows. She was glad her room did not look out onto the El, although she could hear the Ninth Avenue trains, just a block away, through her open window. They got off at Bleecker Street and walked the few blocks to Gene's rooming house.

"Will your landlady allow you to take a woman to your rooms?" said Magda teasingly.

Gene laughed. "You might be surprised at what my landlady allows," he said. "As far as she is concerned, my rooms are my own home and who I bring to them is my own business, as long as I pay my rent. It's one of the reasons I chose her rooming house."

What happened in Gene's rooms was both less intimate and more intimate than Magda had hoped. Certainly, she had never taken her clothes off in the home of a man before, nor had she expected that such an unveiling would be so uneventful.

The rooms occupied part of the third floor of a four-story house, tucked between a butcher shop and a café in the middle of a block of Carmine Street. The staircase was poorly lit, but when Gene opened the door to his rooms for Magda she found a cheerful, clean, and neat sitting room, flooded with early evening light from the large window looking onto the street.

"Some of the lodgers only have one room," said Gene, "but I have a royal suite."

"How long have you been here?" said Magda, turning to take in the room. There was a settee under the window, two armchairs sitting in one corner, bracketing a small case full of books, and a wooden chair and table standing against the far wall, covered with neat stacks of papers and precisely sharpened pencils. Draperies in a floral pattern of blue and pink flanked the window, and a well-worn rug covered much of the floor.

"I first moved here a couple of years after I started with Mr. Tesla," said Gene, "nearly six years ago. His lab was not far from here, and the location worked for . . . other places I liked to visit. While I was working at Wardenclyffe I lived on Long Island, but lucky for me Mrs. Garner, the landlady, had these rooms available when I came back—even nicer than the ones I had before. And, as I said, she doesn't ask questions."

The landlady had greeted Gene as he came in the street door—she seemed surprised to see him with a young woman, but to Magda had only said, "How lovely to see you," before returning to her dusting.

What Gene did not tell Magda was that his landlady had not been surprised to see Gene take a companion up to his rooms. He had done that on a regular basis for six years—though perhaps less often in recent years than when he first moved in. But in all those years, Gene had never escorted a woman into the house. Mrs. Garner had raised an eyebrow not because she was scandalized to see a man taking a woman up to his rooms, but because she was shocked to see Gene Pinkney in the company of a female.

He had been busy since last night's dinner, making stops at a tailor on Bleecker Street and a pharmacy on Houston before taking the train uptown to a theatrical supply company on Forty-Second Street. He walked back downtown, stopping at Macy's on Thirty-Fourth Street before taking the El back downtown from Thirty-Third. Now a pile of parcels lay on his bed in the next room, waiting for Magda.

In his years of haunting the nightspots of the Bowery, Gene had often come into contact with women dressed as men. He had met one such woman at a private event in 1901, shortly after the death of Murray Hall, a politician and bondsman who had been revealed as a woman only at the time of her death. Hall had lived with a wife, and had, for more than twenty years, drunk and played cards with the men of Tammany Hall, with whom she was, as one paper described it, a "hail-fellow-well-met." Gene loved that Hall had successfully duped the powers of New York for so many years. When he happened to find himself in a conversation with a "man" of similar talents, known to him only as Terence, he asked how the deception was accomplished. Terence, for whom Hall had quickly become an idol, had given Gene a somewhat drunken lecture on the process, and Gene had thought no more about it until Magda's account of her frustrating conversation with Mr. Lipscomb.

Magda trembled as Gene opened the door to his bedroom. That single gesture was more forbidden than anything she had ever experienced with a man. The narrow bed below a tiny window seemed alive with potential. A wardrobe in the corner was the only other piece of furniture in the room. While the sitting room had felt homey and hospitable, this room had all the charm of a monastic cell.

Gene seemed oblivious to the unspoken meaning of a man ushering a woman into his bedroom. Rather than gazing adoringly at her beauty as she stepped across the threshold, he eagerly began to tear the paper off one of the parcels on the bed.

"Now," he said, "this is the trickiest part, other than the hair." He held out a large roll of bandaging. "After you . . . you undress, you'll have to wind this around your . . . you know . . . your torso. It will . . . well, it will flatten out . . . things. And here are some pins to fasten it."

Magda had never heard Gene stumble over his words like this. His face had turned a deep red. If he wasn't going to throw her down on the bed and rob her of her virtue, she thought, then at least she would have a little fun with his embarrassment. She took the bandaging from him and began to unroll it.

"So, this gets wrapped around my breasts," she said nonchalantly. "And will you help me out with that part?" She put the bandaging onto the bed and began to unbutton her shirtwaist.

"No," said Gene loudly, turning away from her. "No, I think . . . that is I believe . . . you should do that part on your own."

"Calm down," said Magda playfully. "I'm not going to undress in front of you. And by the way, my breasts aren't so terribly horrifying."

"It's just that, as a gentleman . . ."

"Yes, yes, you are a gentleman, Gene. I can tell by the way you invited me into your bedroom and asked me to undress. Now tell me what else to put on besides this roll of gauze and then you can take your gentlemanly leave of me."

Magda wished he would take no such leave. She knew the rules of society, but by coming to Gene's rooms, she had broken those already. She hadn't really expected he would behave in an improper manner, but she had thought, with a woman about to undress in his bedroom, Gene would at least flirt a little. She wanted Mr. Lipscomb to act like a gentleman and he acted like an ass; she wanted Gene to act like a cad and he acted like a gentleman.

"Here is a suit of clothes," said Gene in a businesslike tone. He seemed to have regained some of his composure as he unwrapped another of the packages. "I chose double breasted because I thought it would do a better job of hiding . . ."

"My double breasts?" said Magda.

"Your figure," said Gene. "I got the smallest one I could find, but we still may need to take in the trousers, and you'll probably need pads in the shoulders."

"Because of my tiny waist and my womanly shoulders?" said Magda.

"Well, yes, just because you're . . . you know . . ."

"A woman," said Magda.

"And in this package is a shirt and tie and a pair of socks, and these are your shoes—I think they're small enough. I wasn't sure about . . ."

"Underthings?" said Magda.

"Yes, well . . ."

"Don't worry," she said, "I can manage." She leaned forward and gave him a light kiss on the cheek. "Now run along, or you might see something."

Wrapping herself in bandaging to make her breasts disappear was neither easy nor comfortable. By the third unsuccessful try, Magda began to wish she had a mother, or an ungentlemanly gentleman, to help her. She had never given much thought to the fact that her breasts were a bit smaller than those of many of the fashionable women of New York, but now she was thankful for that. Even so, the flesh had a way of squeezing out at the wrong place just when she thought she had herself properly wrapped. Magda finally managed to successfully bind herself by pulling the bandages so tightly they dug painfully into her flesh. Compared to this, she thought, a corset was the height of comfort. By the time she had put on the rest of the clothes—barring the tie, which she had no idea how to knot—she had managed to contrive to move a little less stiffly in the binding, but she still couldn't take a deep breath, so tightly constricted was her rib cage.

With the outfit nearly complete, she opened Gene's wardrobe and found a mirror on the back of the door. Aside from her overly long trousers, from the neck down she looked like just the sort of person Mr. Lipscomb would want as a writer.

"It's a start," said Gene, as he knelt in front of her and began marking the length of her trousers with a piece of chalk.

"So, you're an electrical genius *and* a tailor?" said Magda.

"I can hem a pair of trousers," said Gene. Years of adjusting clothes for his nights at Paresis Hall had made him adept at sewing. "How's the waist?"

"It's a bit cinched in," said Magda. "But only a bit. I guess my figure is not as ladylike as I thought." This, of course, was Gene's cue to say, *Why, no, your figure is most ladylike,* but instead he simply stood up and began adjusting her jacket.

"Just be sure you keep the jacket buttoned, and no one will see your waist. Now, the hair," he said. Magda wore her long hair piled atop her head in the style of a Gibson girl. "I'm afraid that's where my expertise is lacking. But you'll have a high collar in the back, and I've got you a silk scarf. It's not quite the thing for a daytime suit, but it will have to do. See if you can get your hair pulled back tightly and hidden away under your collar as much as possible. Here's some Macassar oil and a few combs—I wasn't sure exactly what kind to get you, so you have some options. In the meantime, I'll hem your other trousers."

"My other trousers?" said Magda.

"I have a little surprise for you."

A half hour later Magda stood once again before the mirror, this time with Gene standing beside her. Her hair was slicked back with oil and, from the front, looked like that of a gentleman who had not quite mastered the art of personal grooming. She wore the "little surprise," a full evening suit with a cutaway jacket and white bow tie, which Gene had knotted for her. Above her upper lip was a small mustache, fashioned by Gene with material from the theatrical supply company and attached with a pungent-smelling glue. A pair of similarly attached sideburns completed her ensemble.

"You look very handsome," said Gene, who also wore an evening suit.

"Tom wanted me to take a picture. He loaned me his camera." Gene disappeared into the bedroom and appeared a moment later with Tom's Brownie camera. Magda had asked Tom about the camera when he arrived at Childs with it hanging around his neck.

"I'm strictly an amateur when it comes to photography," he had said, "but I enjoy it. It sometimes allows me to . . . to capture a moment." Tom had sounded wistful and Magda had not pressed him further on the subject.

Now, Gene posed Magda in front of the fireplace, where the light from the window illuminated her face.

"If you take a picture of me," said Magda, "then I get to take a picture of you."

"Fair enough," said Gene, "but hold still."

After both pictures had been taken, Gene quickly returned the camera to his bedroom. "Now, we'd better be going," he said, "or we'll be late."

"Late for what?" said Magda.

"We need to be sure this will work," said Gene. "So, I've arranged a night on the town."

"How do you know I don't have plans with some other gentleman?" said Magda.

"Do you?" said Gene.

"Where are we going?" said Magda.

Twenty minutes later, they sat in the gentlemen's smoking lounge at the New Amsterdam Theatre on Forty-Second Street. Gene had hailed an electric taxicab on Sixth Avenue and they had been whisked uptown in style.

"I'll bet you understand how this thing works," said Magda.

"It's very simple," said Gene, and for the rest of the ride he had explained the principles that propelled them onto Broadway and into the recently renamed Times Square in words that Magda understood no better than if he had been speaking Cherokee. On a summer's evening the smoking lounge was hot and stuffy, but none of the gentlemen gathered there gave Magda a second look. Shortly before eight thirty, she and Gene climbed up to the Aerial Gardens, a rooftop theater that was far more elaborate than the one Gene had so recently attended atop Madison Square Garden. Magda had never visited a Broadway theater, and to enter through a garden terrace ten stories above Forty-First Street into an elegant auditorium fairly took her breath away. They found their seats and settled in to watch a musical play called *The Governor's Son*, in which a young man named George M. Cohan sang and danced his way through the evening.

"Mr. White took me to see Cohan in *Little Johnny Jones* a couple of years ago," Gene told Magda. "When he sang 'Give My Regards to Broadway,' and the audience went mad with delight, Mr. White told me, 'Mark my words—that boy is going to be a star.'" Throughout the performance, and during the intermission when they stood in the garden sipping champagne and looking out over the traffic below, no one gave the slightest indication that they thought Magda was anything other than a man.

After the play, they strolled over to Fifth Avenue and, to Magda's delight and surprise, Gene pulled her under an awning at Forty-Fourth Street and into the lush interior of Delmonico's restaurant. Never had she seen such elegant paneling, such meticulously carved ceilings, and such an endless array of silver, crystal, and fine china. A smiling maître d' greeted them at the door.

"Mr. Pinkney, so good to see you. Mr. Tesla is not with us this evening."

"I shall be dining with my friend." Gene hesitated for just a moment. Magda realized that, though they had perfectly disguised her, they had failed to give her a name.

"Mr. Stone," said Magda in as deep a voice as she could manage. "Marcus Stone of the Philadelphia Stones."

"Of course, Mr. Stone. Welcome to New York. A friend of Mr. Pinkney's is a friend of Delmonico's."

For years Magda had dreamed that a young man might one day take her to a Broadway musical and dinner at Delmonico's. Now, as they sat down at a table in the far corner of the main dining room, she smiled at Gene. Surely he had not planned an evening as romantic as this simply to test her disguise. He must feel at least some of the affection for her that she felt for him. She trembled to imagine how the evening might end—a kiss goodnight . . . or more? In her wildest fantasy, Gene brought her blessed relief by unwrapping the awful binding that still restricted her breathing.

As they ate, Gene told her about a few of the many times he had come here with Mr. White, often meeting Mr. Tesla. Gene spoke with genuine affection for the two men, one of whom was now dead and the other fallen on economic hard times.

Gene told her, too, about his idea for a children's series that would include what he called "real science."

"It's about a girl inventor who lives here in New York," he said.

"Why a girl?" said Magda.

"I did a round of the bookstores," he said, "and all the series books I found had boys as heroes. But girls read, too, right? And I felt I really wanted to create a girl."

"Do you think you can write a girl character? I mean you've never been . . ."

"If you can be a boy," said Gene, "I don't see why I can't be a girl. And besides, I thought I might find a real live girl to help." He winked at her and she melted a little more.

After the waiter cleared away the dishes from their dessert of brandied pears, Magda leaned across the table.

"Can I ask you something impolite?" she said quietly.

"Certainly," said Gene.

"How can you afford this? You're unemployed and living in rented rooms in Greenwich Village. How can you afford to take a girl, even if she's a boy, to the theater and Delmonico's and for a ride in an electric taxicab?"

"I'm frugal most of the time," said Gene. "Mr. Tesla paid me well and I had other sources of income before that. I've saved my money, and for the last several years anytime I came someplace like this, Mr. White footed the bill. Besides, it's not like we're going to do this every night. I just wanted to be sure you could be a man."

Magda's heart sank at the nonchalance of this last remark. She could tell from his tone that there would be no goodnight kiss. And there wasn't. But, as Magda lay in bed in the early hours of the next morning, unable to sleep, her heart paid no attention to her head. She had gone to the theatre and dined at Delmonico's with Eugene Pinkney. Never had a girl been so swept off her feet. Forget the gentleman's suit hanging in her wardrobe. Forget the bottle of Macassar oil and the artificial facial hair on the table by her bed. Forget the fact that she hadn't been able to breathe properly all night. Gene had taken her out for a night on the town. True, she had been Mr. Marcus Stone of Philadelphia, but maybe the next time Gene went to the theater, he would have Magdalena Hertzenberger on his arm.

XIX

When he discovered that Angela Robbins, whose name was neither Susan nor Sarah but who did curate the collection that contained the Stratemeyer papers, was at a conference in Chicago and wouldn't be back until Wednesday morning, Robert had returned home and started researching pulp magazines. He soon discovered that something called the Gotham Pulp Collectors Club met at the Muhlenberg branch of the New York Public Library on West Twenty-Third on the third Saturday of every month. A quick call to the Muhlenberg put him in touch with one of the members of the club, Tony Esposito, whom the librarian called "king of the pulps."

"He's got a stupendous collection—something like ten thousand magazines. Plus, he's a human database. He can tell you practically every story in every magazine."

Tony Esposito ran an IT business out of his apartment in a modern building overlooking the High Line, a section of disused elevated train track that had been converted into a linear park. He worked at home, and would be happy for Robert to stop in any time, he said. "I'm always ready to take a break from work to talk about pulps," he said.

Tony Esposito greeted Robert at the door wearing a *Star Wars* T-shirt and a pair of cargo shorts. His dark hair was mussed, and Robert got the distinct impression he had been in bed as recently as five minutes earlier.

In the living room, with its floor-to-ceiling windows on one side, stood a fifteen-foot-high wall of built-in sleek white bookcases with locking glass doors and a rolling ladder. The room was furnished with a desk, chairs, and a table of polished chrome and pale maple along with several leather armchairs. Rebecca would have loved it. Robert felt the pang of her absence as he stepped into a room she could have designed.

Every shelf in the towering bookcases brimmed with pulp magazines in glassine bags. In the center of the wall stood a custom-built glass display case with its own lighting.

"These are the real gems," said Tony. "*Amazing Stories* number one, *Weird Tales* number one, *The Shadow* number one, and *Astounding Science Fiction* number one. Originally that was forty cents worth of stories; now they're worth about twenty-five grand. Not exactly comic book prices, but still."

Robert stared at the cover of the first issue of *Amazing Stories* from April 1926. A Saturn-like planet hung in the background of an image of ice-skating men dressed in furs. Above them, atop mountains of snow and ice, perched two sailing ships, from which men were rappelling down. In bold orange type the cover advertised stories by H. G. Wells, Jules Verne, and Edgar Allan Poe.

"How many pulps do you have?" said Robert, stepping back to take in the expanse of the wall.

"About twelve thousand. I'm getting new ones in all the time. I just keep the good stuff here at home—five thousand or so. The rest are in a storage unit."

"Rumor has it you know every story in every magazine."

"I don't know about that," said Tony. "But I read as many as I have time for, and I have a pretty good memory."

"Have you ever heard of the Tremendous Trio?"

"Doesn't ring a bell."

"I'm trying to track down the pulp that this story came from," said Robert, pulling out the pages of *The Last Adventure of the Tremendous Trio*. "I think it was published around 1911."

"Any idea of the publisher?"

"Probably a company called Pickering Brothers."

"Pickering. That sounds familiar," said Tony crossing to the desk on which stood a keyboard and computer screen. He tapped away for a minute.

"I wonder if it could be this. *Tales of Excitement for Boys and Girls*, volume one, number one, published by Pickering Brothers, New York, April 1912. I've got a copy in my storage unit. I don't have the contents listed in my database, but it's the only thing I have by that publisher and the date seems to fit."

"That has to be it!" said Robert. At last he had found something useful. "What about volume one, number two or number three? Do you have those?" Could the remaining chapters of the Tremendous Trio's last adventures be sitting in a storage unit right here in Manhattan?

"Nope," said Tony. "Looks like they only published one issue."

"Are you sure?" said Robert with a tinge of desperation in his voice. "Maybe you just don't have it in your collection. You said you were getting new things in all the time."

"If there is a second issue, it's not in any of the major collections, either private or public. I've got them all in my database."

Robert sighed with exasperation. It didn't seem right that Dexter Cornwall and Buck Larson and Neptune B. Smythe could tease the world with those opening paragraphs and then never write the book.

"If you give me your address, I'll have my assistant dig that issue out of the storage unit and messenger it to you. Might not be able to get it until tomorrow morning, though."

"That would be great," said Robert.

"All I ask is that you handle it carefully. These pulps are pretty fragile."

"Of course," said Robert.

Outside, the day had grown warm and the sidewalks were nearly dry. On a whim, Robert decided to take the twenty-minute walk to Washington Square Park. He entered the square from the north, passing under the triumphal arch erected there in 1892. He walked a few yards into the park, then turned and looked up.

He hadn't stood in front of the Washington Square Arch since he and his father had sought it out. It was one of many places he had subconsciously avoided his entire adult life. Now he remembered his father's puzzled expression as they gazed upward at the marble structure gleaming in the light of a summer's day.

"It's pretty," Robbie had said.

"But why?" said his father.

"Why is it pretty?"

"No, why are we here?"

"Because," said Robbie, "Alice Gold's second book begins here."

"Yes," said his father, finally dropping his eyes from the arch and looking at his son. "But why? Why does Alice's second book begin here? She lives on Fifth Avenue up near Seventy-Second Street; her governess is always scolding her for wandering even a block or two from home. Why does she suddenly show up under the Washington Square Arch in the first chapter of book two? Nothing happens here. She just looks at the arch and goes home."

"She saves that little girl from getting run over by the streetcar," said Robbie.

"Yes, but she's practically home when that happens. Why did she have to start here?" Robbie's father shook his head. "It's like the author . . ."

"Buck Larson," said Robbie enthusiastically.

"Right, as if Buck Larson, I don't know, had some connection with this arch and wanted to put it into the book, even if it didn't make sense."

"Anyway, it's pretty," said Robbie.

It was pretty, thought Robert. He had missed that for all the years he had been avoiding it. As he set off toward the subway, he wondered what else he had missed.

XX

CENTRAL PARK,
AT A TIME WHEN PROMENADING WAS EVERYTHING

That Saturday afternoon, Magda, Gene, and Tom sat on a bench in Central Park watching the ladies and gentlemen promenade up and down the Mall. Magda had tried to sit next to Gene, but he and Tom seemed to be conspiring against her and she found herself on one end of the bench with Tom in the middle and Gene on the far end. The men both seemed pleased with this arrangement, and Magda resigned herself to a pleasant afternoon with friends rather than a continuation of her imagined romance with Gene. They had set Monday as the day for "Marcus Stone" to meet with Mr. Lipscomb. Magda had explained to her employer that she would not be able to come in until after lunch on that day, so that she could meet the ship on which her sister was returning from a trip to Europe.

"Miss Stone," Mr. Lipscomb had said. "Am I to have no secretary in the office every time you have a sister returning from Europe?"

"I assure you, Mr. Lipscomb," she had said, "I only have the one sister and she does not intend to travel abroad frequently. Your only appointment in the morning is with a Mr. Marcus Stone of Philadelphia, Pennsylvania. He has a manuscript to show you."

"Your brother?"

"No relation," Magda had said. She had decided to keep her improvised alias. If she had the good luck to convince Mr. Lipscomb to publish her book, it would be an easy matter to deposit a check made out to Marcus Stone into the account of Mary Stone. And as Magda herself would be making out the check, she could make the one name look quite like the other.

"I see from the photograph Gene took that you make a handsome gentleman," said Tom. "Though I can't say I'm surprised. It would be hard to make you anything other than handsome."

The summer heat had broken slightly and a cool breeze wafted through the park. Magda carried a parasol, but the trees of the Mall provided enough shade for her to leave it folded by her side.

"It was just lucky that Magda came up with a name as quickly as she did at Delmonico's. I did a good job dressing her, but I completely forgot to name her."

"Marcus Stone. Not bad," said Tom. "But I'm not sure I like it as a pen name."

"Oh, I won't sign the adventures of Dan Dawson with that name. My book will be written by Dexter Cornwall."

"So, Magda Hertzenberger, alias Mary Stone, alias Marcus Stone, will sign her book Dexter Cornwall. With all those layers of secrecy, I'm surprised there's not a series of books written about you," said Tom.

"Dexter Cornwall," said Gene. "I like that. I'm Buck Larson, pleased to meet you." He reached across Tom and held a hand out to Magda who shook it firmly as if she really were Dexter Cornwall in a business meeting.

"Dexter Cornwall, Buck Larson, and Neptune B. Smythe," said Tom. "Soon to be the gods and goddess of children's books."

"Mr. De Peyster," said a young woman promenading by. She wore a magnificent purple summer frock of hand-embroidered batiste and lace, with a matching parasol and hat, from which protruded two peacock feathers. She dipped her chin ever so slightly toward Tom as she passed. She walked on the arm of a man dressed equally finely, but who stared forward, oblivious to the fact that his companion had spotted an acquaintance.

"Miss Vanderbilt," said Tom.

"Who was that?" said Magda, after the woman had passed.

"Just a friend of the family," said Tom.

"Miss Vanderbilt? A friend of the family? And this after Gene takes me to a Broadway theater and dinner at Delmonico's. Am I the only one of the three of us who isn't chummy with every millionaire in New York City?"

"I wouldn't say I know every one," said Tom, "but I know quite a few. That particular Miss Vanderbilt who just greeted me is the younger sister of another Miss Vanderbilt who lived down the street from me when I was growing up. My mother would have liked us to end up married, but I had other ideas. As did Amelia Vanderbilt's mother."

"So you grew up on . . . ?" said Magda.

"I grew up on Fifth Avenue, not far from here, in a house smaller than a Vanderbilt or Rockefeller mansion, but bigger than any family needs. By the time I was twelve, I had grown tired of starched collars and tailored suits, and I discovered Horatio Alger. So, I dressed in rags and started sneaking out at night looking for the world of *Ragged Dick*. Once every couple of weeks, I would put on a tattered outfit and wander around the Bowery or someplace else a long way from Fifth Avenue."

"That must have been eye-opening," said Gene, who had spent plenty of time on the Bowery.

"It was," said Tom. "I met bootblacks and newsboys, learned how to throw dice and recognize—you'll have to pardon me, Magda, but—how to recognize women of easy virtue. Some nights were terrifying. I saw a man knife another man in the street in a fight over a bar debt. He just left him there, bleeding to death, and there was nothing I could do to help. But I loved talking with the boys on the streets, learning about their lives and the clever ways they managed to survive.

"I had plenty of money—it was easy enough to filch a dollar or two from my father without his knowing—so I could stand my friends to a steak and a mug of coffee or treat them to a vaudeville show at Tony Pastor's. I told them my name was Tommy Poster, and they used to call me Tony Pastor in jest. For years I would slip out of the house and spend time with Tiny Tim, a newsboy who hawked his wares at Twenty-Third and Sixth. Not far from your place, Magda. He liked to drink coffee late at night before the papers hit the streets and he was always happy to see me, knowing I would buy him a few cups. Or I'd listen to the stories of Johnny Nolan, a bootblack who took his name from Horatio Alger. This

Johnny loved vaudeville, and I took him to Tony Pastor's or the Liberty more times than I can count.

"I did my best to steer clear of gangs like the Eastmans, but sometimes I found myself in a scuffle. Usually I'd have a friend nearby to help me out. I gave a lot of boys money to buy shoes or overcoats in the winter, and they never forgot a favor like that when I was in trouble.

"Mostly I just talked to boys—sat on piles of straw at the ends of alleys and traded stories until they fell asleep and I wandered back home, feeling guilty about the gulf that yawned between us. And then I started writing about them. Not anything I would show anyone else, just accounts of their lives. I wrote down the stories they told me and hid the papers under my mattress. I eventually burned them in the fireplace, afraid the housekeeper would find them and take them to my father. I wish I still had them."

Tom stopped for a moment, and Magda thought she saw his eyes glisten, but perhaps it was just the summer sun filtering down through the leaves.

"My parents didn't find out about my nocturnal excursions until one day in 1899. By then I was seventeen. My father wanted me to go to Princeton within a year or two, so I was in his study reading one of his books of Herodotus, or Plato, or one of that crowd, when a friend of his came storming in. I'd never paid that much attention to my father's associates or the men with whom he socialized. I had become more and more interested in the other end of society's spectrum. But I knew this man, and if I hadn't, I would have guessed his identity as soon as he started talking. It was William Randolph Hearst, and he was in a fury because the newsboys of New York had gone on strike against his paper the *New York Evening Journal* as well as Joseph Pulitzer's the *New York World*. I had been trying to think of a way to come clean to my father about my secret explorations of the city before he sent me off to college—which I dreaded, having no interest in study, no interest in becoming a banker, and no interest in giving up my friends on the street. Mr. Hearst's tirade against the newsboys suddenly presented me with a golden opportunity—I could tell my father about my nights in lower Manhattan, and at the same time present a reasonable alternative to college.

"I told Mr. Hearst that I knew some of those newsboys. I had even met Kid Blink, the self-proclaimed leader of the strikers. I said I had no intention of playing informer, but as he had his hands full trying to resolve the strike, perhaps he would like a reporter on the ground with a firsthand knowledge of the world of those newsboys and even some close personal friends among their ranks. If he hired me, I could write honest stories about the strike and when it ended, I could use my contacts to write anything else Mr. Hearst might want about the world of New York's streets late at night.

"Well, my father was aghast, I could tell, but he wasn't about to dress me down in front of William Randolph Hearst. Mr. Hearst, on the other hand, was fascinated. He began asking me questions, as my father sat there steaming. No, I hadn't been out on the street since the strike had started a couple of days ago. Yes, I knew plenty of newsboys and yes, a lot of them survived solely on the money they made selling his papers. Yes, I had experience writing, but no, I could not show him samples of my work. Yes, I read his paper every day—this was a bit of an exaggeration—and was familiar with the style of writing he demanded from his reporters. And finally, yes, I would be willing to go to work for him on a trial basis, to write stories about the strike and perhaps profiles of some of the newsboys, which he may or may not publish, in order to show him my abilities. If, once he settled the strike—though as I recall he used the word *broke*—he decided my work was worthy, he would take me on full time.

"Then came the moment of truth, when Mr. Hearst turned to my father and said, 'With your permission, I'd like to give the boy a chance.' My father was in a tight spot and he knew it. The last thing he wanted was for me to forego Princeton to wander the streets of New York writing newspaper stories. But he also wanted to do everything he could to ingratiate himself, and attach himself, to Mr. Hearst, a powerful man deeply involved in some of Father's business interests. In the end he had no choice but to agree, and so here I am, seven years later, still writing for Mr. Hearst."

"What happened with the strike?" said Magda. In 1899, she had lived in a household in which any newspaper available was printed in German, so she knew nothing of the striking newsboys.

"Mr. Hearst says they reached a compromise, but the boys always said they won. The first thing I did after that conversation with Hearst and my father was to go to the rally on Frankfort Street. I met up with Tiny Tim and walked up Broadway with the boys as they carried their placards. I listened to what they said and took notes. I remember Kid Blink speaking to the crowd in his distinctive way."

Tom stood and took on the pose of an orator, affecting a voice Magda and Gene had never heard. "Dey can't beat us! Me nobul men is all loyal and wid such as dese to oppose der nefarious schemes, how can de blokes hope to win?" Magda burst out laughing at this performance.

"Did Hearst publish any of your stories about the newsies?" said Gene.

"No," said Tom, "but he did read them, and maybe they helped him understand the boys a little better."

"So why children's books?" said Gene. "When you already have a successful career as a journalist."

"That's a story for another day," said Tom, loath to discuss his experiences in San Francisco. "I've gone on long enough."

With the other promenaders, they strolled the length of the Mall and descended to Bethesda Terrace and its magnificent fountain, surmounted by the statue of an angel. On such a beautiful summer's day, people thronged round the fountain to feel the coolness radiate off the waters.

"Did you know," said Gene, as they stood watching the crowd, "that the angel was made by a woman?"

"I wonder what Mr. Lipscomb would have to say about that?" said Magda.

Gene had it on good authority, though he did not share this information with the others, that Emma Stebbins, the sculptor, had spent much of her adult life living with a female lover. He had always felt a connection to that angel, as if it were watching over people like Gene and Princess Petunia and so many other men and women he had met in his nights at Paresis Hall—men and women who, like him, had to spend most of their lives pretending to be something they were not.

A sudden gust of wind blew spray across the terrace and, amidst little cries of mock terror, the crowd on the south side of the fountain moved away, leaving a wide-open spot along the pool just below the gaze of the angel.

"We need a photograph," said Tom, whose Brownie camera hung around his neck. "A portrait of three writers on the brink of greatness." A young man was standing nearby with his own Brownie, taking a photograph of the fountain, and Tom quickly imposed on him to take a picture using Tom's camera. They stood at the edge of the pool, looking serious as the angel gazed down on them and keeping still as the young man pushed the shutter lever.

"That seemed a bit stiff," said Tom. "Let's do one more, only this time, let's show the world Dexter Cornwall, Buck Larson, and Neptune B. Smythe." Gene inclined his head to one side and placed a finger at his temple, in the way he imagined a young inventor would when pondering a new idea. Tom held out a palm and pretended to write on it with an imaginary pen, in the style of his invented cub reporter. Magda held one arm over her head and one in front of her, a pose she had seen acrobats take at the circus before beginning a trick. Once again, the young man pressed the lever.

XXI

When *Tales of Excitement for Boys and Girls* arrived by messenger, Robert knew, even before he read the familiar chapter on pages thirty-six to forty-two, that he had found the source of the opening of *The Last Adventure*. Beneath the title on the front cover a banner proclaimed, FEATURING THE LONG-AWAITED RETURN OF THE TREMENDOUS TRIO. Robert guessed that the gaudily colored illustration on the cover showed Dan Dawson, Alice Gold, and Frank Fairfax—but the picture seemed unconnected to either the first chapter of *The Last Adventure* or to any other story in the magazine. It showed three youngsters sitting in the back of a fancy automobile, waving to crowds who stood on the sidewalk and leaned from the windows of office buildings (including the Flatiron Building). In the background, a driver struggled to control a runaway horse pulling a wagonload of vegetables, but neither the children nor the crowd seemed to notice this.

Of the twelve stories in the magazine, six were complete in themselves and six purported to be the first installments of various serials. In a "Note from the Editor," on the first page, Mr. Herbert Pickering described the stories thus: "All of them are stories of vigorous adventure drawn true to life, which gives them the thrill that all really good fiction should have." The claim that these outlandish stories were "drawn from true life" may have been the biggest lie Robert had ever seen in print.

He read through every story, but found none of the sort of subversive writing that characterized the first installment of the Tremendous Trio story. The rest of the content was poorly written and, despite the claims of the editor, dull. No wonder, he thought, the periodical had apparently folded after a single issue.

As he set the magazine on his desk, he had a sudden flash of memory, a cinematically clear picture of a spring day when he was twelve years old, walking on Rockaway Beach with his father, pausing their conversation whenever a jet roared overhead on the way to JFK a couple of miles away. He could feel the sand under his feet and hear the surf lapping the beach, and he could also feel that delicious sense of childhood excitement that came from living a fifteen-minute walk from the beach. Every time Robert stood on that strip of sand looking southeast across the water, he thought about the fact that the first piece of land in his line of sight was Brazil— where the Tremendous Trio had had their adventure in the Amazon. On the day that presented itself so vividly in his memory, Robert and his father had been strolling the beach, kicking the sand, and idly speculating on the fate of Dan Dawson, Alice Gold, and Frank Fairfax.

"Maybe they sail across the ocean," said Robbie.

"Maybe they go into outer space," said his father.

"Or to the center of the earth," said Robbie.

"There's only one problem," said his father.

"What's that?"

"Other adventure books had already sent people all those places long before the Tremendous Trio was written. That opening chapter makes it sound like this adventure will be something completely new."

"Maybe it's not about where they go," said Robbie softly. "Maybe it's about who they are."

That comment rang in his ears as Robert returned his attention to the magazine in front of him. Advertisements mostly aimed at boys cluttered the final two pages. Readers could earn a hunting rifle or printing press or pocket watch by selling jewelry or sticking plasters or "popular articles." They could become expert magicians or save their chewing gum wrappers to earn a stickpin or toothbrush or combination knife.

Besides the cover illustration, the only hint about the future of the Tremendous Trio came on the inside back cover where an advertisement proclaimed, "In Next Month's Issue of *Tales of Excitement* . . ." This was followed by a short teaser for the next installment in each of the serial stories. About halfway down this list, Robert read, "The Tremendous Trio set out on their grandest adventure yet, but they each are carrying secrets that will shock and surprise their fellow travelers." It wasn't much to go on, and it raised more questions than it answered. How could this adventure be grander than a flight around the world? What secrets did they carry? Maybe he had been right that day at the beach—maybe the story was more about identity than adventure.

Robert thought how much Rebecca would love this puzzle. The two of them constantly solved conversational conundrums by looking up information online. Often, when whatever bit of TV they had chosen for the evening failed to stimulate them, they would each end up surfing Wikipedia and trivia sites, trying to surprise one another with obscure bits of information. "Did you know tug-of-war used to be an Olympic sport?" "Did you know the word *Idaho* was made up by a lobbyist?" They would work the *New York Times* crossword simultaneously, and on Fridays and Saturdays would offer each other help to finish the toughest puzzles.

It was all silly and pointless and Robert suddenly missed it terribly. He didn't want to wait until Saturday to see Rebecca, no matter what he had said. It had been a stupid idea. Why should he hold her at arm's length until he finished this journey? Why not let her travel with him? He carefully closed *Tales of Excitement*, picked up his phone, and called her.

"Hi, this is Rebecca," said the message. Her voice was calm and measured. Robert could tell she had rehearsed this recording. "Leave a message and I'll call you back. If this is Robert, I'll talk to you on Saturday like we agreed." Then, nothing.

So, he would have to wait until Saturday.

A few minutes later, Robert still sat staring into space, willing the time to pass faster when the phone rang.

"Mr. Parrish?"

"Yes."

"This is Elaine, at the St. Agnes Library. We've had a cancellation by our reader on Saturday morning, and wondered if you would like to do story time again. Maybe read some more of the book you were sharing last week?"

Robert certainly wanted to read more of the story to the children at the library. But could he read to a group of eager children knowing he was little more than an hour away from meeting Rebecca? Last week, the children had clamored for more when he had announced that story time was over. He remembered the look of excitement and anticipation in their eyes as he read, the way they sat upright or grabbed a neighbor's arm when something scary happened, the collective holding of breath when one or all of the Tremendous Trio faced danger. He had loved that and had imagined Rebecca would sit beside him the next time to share in that experience. But he could not resist saying yes to Elaine. Story time ended at eleven. That would give him an hour to get to the Ramble.

Robert sat back in his chair and dared to imagine their reunion—Rebecca's curls sparkling in the sunlight, her smile as she looked up to see him. But before his mental movie had reached the point where either one of them spoke a word, the projector sputtered to a stop as a painful thought struck him—what if she didn't come?

XXII

Magda had finally stopped her hands from shaking as she sat in a chair in Mr. Lipscomb's office in the guise of Marcus Stone of Philadelphia. They had been talking for ten minutes now, and Mr. Lipscomb gave no hint that he recognized either Magda or her gender. She began to relax.

Mr. Stone's manuscript, *Danger under the Big Top*, had arrived in the post two days earlier, or so Magda had told Mr. Lipscomb.

"It's the first in a series called Dan Dawson, Circus Star," said Magda.

Lipscomb had read a few chapters and then asked Magda to set up a meeting with Mr. Stone, who had, she told her employer, been happy to take an early train up from Philadelphia.

"He needs to do more than just have adventures under the big top," said Mr. Lipscomb, chomping on his gum.

"Oh, he does," said Mr. Stone. "He travels around the country and—"

"That's not enough," said Lipscomb. "I had a manuscript in here the other day about a boy who saved people from disasters. What if your circus daredevil did something like that?"

Magda recognized the description of Tom's proposal and saw an opening. She knew that Lipscomb had forced Tom to give up the idea of having his reporter rescue people, so why shouldn't she use it in her book?

"A brilliant idea," said Mr. Stone. "He's an acrobat with the circus but wherever he travels he ends up in some sort of disaster—fires, floods, that kind of thing. And he uses his acrobatic skill to save people. He could climb burning buildings or swim across raging rivers." Magda hoped Tom would be pleased she had found a way to keep his idea alive.

"Excellent, excellent," said Lipscomb, leaning forward in his chair. "Now you're talking like a writer of children's series. Make the first volume about a storm. Something like what happened in Galveston back in 1900. How soon could you get me a manuscript?"

"How soon do you need it?"

"I want to launch three new series for Christmas," said Lipscomb. "That means a clean manuscript by the first of October."

"That shouldn't be a problem," said Mr. Stone.

When Magda came in later that day, Mr. Lipscomb asked her to please draw up a contract for Mr. Marcus Stone. She had sent a contract to Tom a few days earlier. It only remained to get Gene into the Pickering stable.

Magda now knew that Lipscomb wanted one more new series for Christmas. She had proposals from six different writers tucked away in her desk, hidden from him until she had a chance to make her own pitch. She did not feel particularly guilty about withholding these submissions, as none of them were as good as the ideas she, Tom, and Gene had. Most were, in fact, rehashes of series that Pickering was already publishing (or had already canceled due to low sales figures). On top of the pile lay what Gene had given her when he took her home after dinner at Delmonico's— his proposal for a series called Alice Gold, Girl Inventor.

"Mr. Lipscomb," Magda said the next day as the editor pulled on his coat to leave the office. "Did you still want one more new series for Christmas? Maybe something Stratemeyer doesn't have?" She knew exactly how to pique Mr. Lipscomb's interest. There was nothing he wanted more than that which Edward Stratemeyer did not have.

"That's right," he said.

"This one came in today, and I think it's worth a look. It's about an inventor who travels to different cities across the country solving problems."

"Stratemeyer has inventors in the Great Marvel series," said Mr. Lipscomb, reaching for the door.

"Yes, but this inventor is a girl." Lipscomb stopped and turned back to Magda.

"A girl?"

"Fifty percent of children are girls," said Magda, "and we publish almost nothing for them."

"Yes, but an inventor? Do you really think a girl can be an inventor?" Magda seethed inside. She wanted to shout at him—*Do you really think an airship could travel to the center of the earth? Do you really think a fifteen-year-old could pilot a submarine? Do you really think an acrobat would make any difference during the Galveston hurricane?* Of course a girl could be an inventor. And a girl could be an author or a publisher. A girl could rope a steer or ride a runaway train or sail through a typhoon or any of the other things the heroes of Pickering books did. A girl could sculpt an angel for a fountain. A girl could even watch her family drown and burn in a horrible tragedy caused by men, and get a job to support herself, and fool an idiot of a publisher into thinking she was a man and into publishing her book.

But she said none of this.

"Fifty percent of potential customers, Mr. Lipscomb. And look at the new series Stratemeyer has out this year: Boys of Pluck, Boy Hunters, Boys of Business. You could have the field practically to yourself." She did not mention that Stratemeyer's Bobbsey Twins series had been selling well among girls.

"But this Alice Gold series, it's not written by a woman?"

You filthy, smug, misogynistic rat, Magda wanted to say. But she cared about Gene and she cared about keeping her job, so she played Lipscomb's game.

"Why of course not, sir. It wouldn't be proper for a woman to write books."

"Exactly so, exactly, so," said Lipscomb.

"The author is a man named Eugene Pinkney, but he's using the pseudonym Buck Larson."

"Buck Larson," said Mr. Lipscomb thoughtfully. "I like that. Sounds manly."

"I'm sure Mr. Pinkney is quite manly," said Magda, feeling a blush creep into her cheeks. Lately, she had been thinking altogether too much about Gene's manliness.

"She can't go traipsing about," said Mr. Lipscomb. "This Alice Gold character. She needs to stay at home, invent things for the modern household."

"It's dizzying to watch your mind at work," said Magda.

"Have this Mr. Pinkney come and see me," said Mr. Lipscomb.

"I'll set up an appointment tomorrow," she said.

⟡

Two days later the three of them sat at Childs eating an early supper.

"I guess now we have to write the books," said Tom.

"Easy for you two," said Gene. "You've both already written one. You just have to change it around. I'm starting from scratch."

"More than change it around," said Tom. "No daring rescues, new type of adventure. The only thing that's the same is that my character is a reporter."

"And thanks to Tom," said Magda, "my circus acrobat is the one who has to contend with all the disasters."

"I really wanted to write about those," said Tom wistfully. He did not say that his desire to invent fictional rescues stemmed from his frustration at being unable to effect real ones in San Francisco.

"You can help me," said Magda.

"I'd like that," said Tom, resting his hand tentatively on Magda's shoulder.

"And you can both help me," said Gene.

"We'll all help each other," said Tom.

"So, tell us about your meeting with Lipscomb," said Magda, turning toward Gene. "Was he as much of a pig as when I talked to him about Alice Gold?"

"He's pretty horrible," said Gene. "He insists that Alice stay at home and invent things like a vacuum duster or an electrical dishwashing machine. Hard to imagine how *that* is going to lead to exciting adventures. Then, after going on and on about how glad he is I'm a man, because by God, Julius Lipscomb would never pay a woman to write a book, he asks me, since I'm writing a female character, if I know what it's like to be a girl."

"What did you say?" said Magda.

"I said I have a pretty good idea," said Gene.

"You helped me become a boy," said Magda, "so, like you said the other night, I can help you become a girl."

Tom opened his mouth to speak, but Gene cut him off. "It's the first of August. That gives us about eight weeks. If we're going to work together, we need a place and a time we can meet every day."

"There's a new library that opened in February just a block from here."

"Sure, the Muhlenberg," said Tom. "I did a story on all the new libraries in the city funded by Mr. Carnegie, and that was one of them."

"It's a block from my house, close to the Sixth Avenue El, so it's easy for Gene to get home," said Magda.

"And I can take the same train uptown," said Tom. "How late is it open?"

"Nine o'clock most nights," said Magda. "And they're open a few hours on Sunday afternoon. There's a spot at the back on the second floor that's usually quiet in the evenings." She had spent many an evening in the past few months at the Muhlenberg branch of the New York Public Library sitting on the second floor reading—sometimes new novels, sometimes classics. Occasionally she even delved into their collection of children's books, to compare them to Mr. Lipscomb's output.

"Perfect," said Tom. "I'm writing for the evening paper, so I have to file my stories by three. I can meet any time after that."

"I usually leave work around six," said Magda.

"I'm unemployed at the moment," said Gene. "So I'm flexible."

"Okay," said Tom, "we meet at Childs for some dinner at six-fifteen, we're at the library no later than seven, and we work for two hours. Sundays we work in the afternoon. Saturdays we take a break." And with that pronouncement, Tom ushered in the most glorious two months of Magda's life.

Although officially each of them had their own book to work on, in reality they all contributed to all of the stories. Tom wrote most of the rescue scenes for Magda; Gene dealt with any sections that involved mechanics or science; and Magda helped Gene understand the inner life of girls. In doing this last, Magda took the opportunity for a little subtle flirting, but apparently she was too subtle, as Gene never responded.

"When a girl likes a boy," Magda whispered to Gene one evening, "she'll find excuses to touch him, like this." She laid a hand gently on Gene's arm.

"Good to know," said Gene, turning to record this fact in his notebook. Magda sighed and went on with her work. Tom kicked her gently under the table and smiled when she looked up at him.

Gene soon decided to push Alice Gold at least a little bit out of the domestic sphere, no matter what Lipscomb said. Together, they came up with a scene in which Alice, during an outing in Central Park, rescues a young bicyclist from crashing. Alice then invents an improved braking system to prevent such accidents in the future. Magda tried to convince Gene that he needn't go into quite so much detail about the design of the brakes, but eventually gave up when she realized that Gene, in addition to writing a book about Alice, was designing all her inventions in ways that would actually work.

"I just wish she could invent something more exciting than bicycle brakes or house-cleaning machines," said Gene. "I want her to build a flying machine."

"Didn't the Wright brothers already do that?" said Magda.

"Yes, but their longest flight has been what, about twenty-five miles? I want Alice to fly around the world."

"Maybe have her invent the dishwashing machine first," said Magda, "and work your way up."

On most nights they each gave an update at Childs on progress they had made, exchanging ideas as they wolfed down sandwiches and soup or plates of corned beef hash. Then they would work at a table in the library, sliding pages back and forth, rewriting one another's chapters and trying to make these three books better in every way than the Rover Boys and Dave Porter and the Great Marvel series, and the other factory-produced children's series that had preceded them.

Magda concentrated on her work, but not so hard that she didn't steal the occasional glance at Gene, sitting erect at the table, holding a pencil as delicately as a great master might wield a paintbrush. Even if he didn't respond to her flirting, she still entertained the fantasy that their night on the town had felt as romantic to him as it did to her. And so, she glanced. She glanced at the curls in his hair and wondered how her fingers might glide through them. She glanced at the curve of his cheek, and wondered how it would feel pressed against her lips. She glanced at his slim fingers and wondered what it would be like to have them intertwined with her own. Gene never saw her stealing these furtive looks, though Tom often did. He would only smile ruefully at her and shake his head before returning to his work. It never occurred to Magda that the reason Tom so often caught her was that he was glancing at her.

As much as she loved those evenings of work and camaraderie, Saturdays were even better. They took it in turns to plan excursions, and Tom always happily paid for the others. Gene chose afternoons at the theater—they heard Maude Raymond sing in *The Social Whirl* at the Casino and saw a David Belasco play called *The Girl of the Golden West*. Magda loved the trip Tom organized to Tony Pastor's vaudeville house where the bill was headed by an act called "The Big Show, A Story of Circus Life," which featured a variety of circus acts. Magda took copious notes when she got home that evening and used several of the acts in her Dan Dawson book.

Tom's favorite act at Tony Pastor's was DeWolf Hopper reciting the poem "Casey at the Bat." Tom had, he said, heard Hopper's famous rendition many times before and even owned a Victor record of the performance, but he still laughed until tears rolled down his cheeks. Gene preferred the performance of "Eltinge," a woman who sang and danced and looked for all the world like a Gibson girl until the end of the act when she pulled off her wig to reveal that "she" was actually a man named Julian.

Tom also loved baseball, so one Saturday the trio rode the Ninth Avenue El up to 155th Street to the Polo Grounds to watch the New York Giants take on the Pittsburgh Pirates. Magda had never seen a baseball game and Tom patiently explained every play to her. The game had lasted eleven innings and ended when Cy Seymour hit a home run to break the tie and win it for the home team. Though Magda and her companions stood where they were, applauding vigorously, much of the crowd swarmed the field to celebrate the victory. Magda felt exhilarated.

When it was her turn to pick the Saturday excursion, Magda opted for more sedate activities. She had never visited either the Metropolitan Museum of Art on the east side of Central Park or the Museum of Natural History on the west side, and so they went to both. Magda always showed an interest in whatever captured Gene's attention—such as the sculptures of Greek men in the Metropolitan—but Tom, not Gene, always held the door for her, or offered a hand when they climbed a set of wide marble stairs.

⌒

Early in September, with the three books well on their way to completion, Gene arrived late to Childs. He walked gingerly and held his left arm across his midsection. Magda might not have noticed this, had it not been for the deep purple bruise below his left eye, his badly swollen lip, and a cut on his right cheek.

"What happened?" said Magda, leaping up to help him to a seat.

"Are you all right?" said Tom as Gene slid into a chair, wincing slightly.

"It's nothing, I'll be fine," he said.

Magda longed to throw her arms around him, to protect him or comfort him or heal him in some way, but he clearly wanted no such attention. Still, she could not resist asking one more time.

"You're really not going to tell us . . ."

"I got into a little scrap, that's all," said Gene. Forcing a smile, he added, "You should see the other guy."

⌒

Gene had no intention of telling Magda, who was clearly infatuated with him, and for whom he cared deeply, the real story. He could imagine telling Tom—beautiful, muscular, perfect Tom—someday if the moment was right, but here in Childs he would never describe what happened last night in honest terms; he would only call it "a scrap." Gene still had the same desires he had had when he'd frequented the fairy resorts. But those resorts were all closed now, so sometimes he would haunt certain street corners, showing a bit of his fairy attire—a red tie perhaps, just enough to make the message clear to those who understood. And sometimes he would meet a man and take him home and his landlady would turn a blind eye and the man would leave an hour or two later. And often the man behaved like a gentleman, kind and sensitive and as longing for connection in a world in which he felt like an outcast as Gene was. But there were times the man was neither kind nor sensitive. On occasion the man saw a fairy as less than nobody—less even than human. A fairy could not only be used and cast aside but, if it made the man feel better, if it made the man feel like more of a man, a fairy could be roughed up a little—or a lot. A fairy's rooms could be ransacked; his valuables, such as they were, stolen. A fairy could be left weeping and bleeding on the bed the man had so recently used for his own base enjoyment and the man could walk away, knowing the police would never bother coming to the defense of the fairy. It had happened to Gene three or four times over the years. It had happened last night. And it wasn't the bruises and cuts that hurt the most—they, after all, would heal. Gene felt the worst pain in his heart, where such encounters permanently etched the knowledge of man's talent for cruelty. He would never forget the delight that the man—Gene would not name him as that would only make him more human—had taken in beating him. He had grinned with glee—not when he climaxed with his face twisted in shame but when he brought blood to Gene's face. Gene hoped Tom and Magda would never know this, but there was nothing so immeasurable as the capacity for malice and brutality in men. And Gene was doomed to love them.

⌒⌒

They finished early. On Friday, September 21, Magda presented the three typescripts to Mr. Lipscomb. Tom had bought her a new Remington typewriter to keep in her room as well as a small table to place it on, and she had typed all three books over the past week. They had taken no Saturday excursion the week before and spent no evenings at the Muhlenberg Library.

Magda had done nothing but type during every free moment that week. She knew the books not only outshone anything Pickering Brothers had ever published, but also anything Stratemeyer had issued. Tom, of course, had been writing since childhood and knew how to tell a story. Gene, it turned out, had a lovely way with words. And Magda had learned from her years of reading the difference between a delicately wrought sentence that danced across the page and one that slogged through the mud. The latter clogged the pages of the typical Pickering book, but not the three volumes she presented to Mr. Lipscomb that Friday afternoon: *Storm from the Sea, A Daring Dan Dawson Adventure; Alice Gold, Girl Inventor;* and *Frank Fairfax and the Search for El Dorado.* The books still contained everything Lipscomb demanded—nonstop adventures, frequent cliff-hangers, and moral rectitude—but they had the added benefit of being well written.

"When will we hear back from him?" said Tom, as they sat eating pie at Childs. Gene's injuries had healed quickly, though the cut to his cheek had left a small white scar. "Do you think he'll want us to make changes?"

"You've got nothing to worry about," said Magda. "For three reasons. First, he doesn't care if the writing is good or bad, as long as you follow the Pickering rules, which we have, so you'll be fine. Second, he's a hasty editor. He'll put red marks all over a typescript, but they're mostly to do with commas and verb tense. As far as story goes, he likes to give his instructions up front and trust his ghostwriters will do exactly as he asks."

"And the third reason?" said Gene.

"The third reason is that he wants these books ready for the Christmas market. He's already advertised them in the trade magazines. That means they need to be in the stores by early November at the latest. He doesn't have time for rewrites."

"So, we're through?" said Tom.

"Nothing left to do but cash the checks and start planning the next books in the series," said Magda.

"Tomorrow's Saturday," said Gene. "I think we should celebrate."

"How?" said Magda.

"It's the last weekend of the season at Coney Island," said Tom. "Let's go to Dreamland."

XXIII

At ten o'clock on Wednesday morning Robert mounted the steps between two stone lions, Patience and Fortitude. He wondered why his father had never taken him to this library, or any library, in search of *The Last Adventure of the Tremendous Trio*. Robbie had cherished the mystery of the missing book as shared with his father, but he had never considered that his father made no attempts to locate the volume. He now wondered if it was precisely the fact that the mystery had brought Robbie and his father closer together as they speculated about the fate of the three adventurers, that had prevented his father from trying to find the book. And perhaps Robbie's father wanted his son to have the chance to keep his promise and find the book himself. Robert felt, pressing through the revolving doors and climbing the wide marble staircase, that he was seeing the entire mystery from his father's point of view for the first time. To him, this had not been a puzzle to be solved, but a point of contact between himself and his son.

Unlike the massive main reading rooms of the library, in which Robert had spent many happy hours, the elegantly paneled reading room of the Berg Collection occupied a fairly small space. An attendant sat at a desk by the door and two other desks stood empty. At the two reading tables, each large enough for four researchers, no one sat in any of the other seats. On one side of the room, to Robert's great delight, stood a card catalogue, surmounted by busts of literary figures. Glass-fronted bookcases full of treasures were built into the paneling. Silence suffused the room as if it had taken up residence there a century ago and planned to stay forever.

Although there was no one to disturb, Angela, the librarian who had ushered him in, and Joseph, the attendant at the desk, spoke in hushed tones as they explained to Robert how to handle the materials. On one of the reading tables stood two large boxes containing the personal and business correspondence of Edward Stratemeyer from 1905 to 1915. Angela had told Robert she had never heard of Pickering Brothers or the Tremendous Trio.

"But you might try looking through the Stratemeyer correspondence files," she said. "He might have conducted business with Pickering at some point or maybe used one of the same ghostwriters."

Robert eased into an armless leather chair, opened the first box, and pulled out the first file, marked "January 1905." The first books by Neptune B. Smythe, Dexter Cornwall, and Buck Larson were published in 1906. Robert reasoned that the writers might have worked for Stratemeyer before that, so he decided to start at the beginning of the archive. He opened the file onto the large rectangle of green baize that lay on the table in front of him. The wide brass light mounted down the center of the table illuminated the pages in the dimness of the reading room.

Most letters he could tell at a glance had no connections to either Pickering or his authors. But he could not resist stopping his search once in a while to read a letter from Howard Garis (who had assumed the pen name Roy Rockwood) or one from a young reader who wanted to say thank you for the Rover Boys series to Arthur Winfield (Stratemeyer himself). Robert wondered if his own grandfather's fan letter to Dexter Cornwall sat in an archive like this one somewhere. He dispensed with 1905 in about two hours with nothing to show for it but the excitement of reading original letters to and from some of the authors he and his father loved.

At this rate, it would take him twenty hours to get through a decade of correspondence. As he began the 1906 files, he proceeded more quickly, avoiding the distraction of fascinating, yet irrelevant, letters. He needn't have worried; in the first file for 1906, he found what he was looking for,

a letter typed on the letterhead of the *New York Evening Journal* and dated
January 12, 1906.

Dear Mr. Stratemeyer,

    I am writing with an idea for a children's series that
I think you will want to publish. I am an experienced
writer, having been a reporter for the newspapers of Mr.
William Randolph Hearst for some years. Mr. Hearst would,
I'm sure, be happy to vouch for my character.

    The hero of my story is a young boy named Frank
Fairfax who goes to work as a cub reporter. Having
started my work as a reporter at age seventeen, I have a
good understanding of that world. Frank travels around
the country writing stories and having adventures. Each
book builds to a scene in which Frank is confronted with
a disaster—a fire, flood, shipwreck, or something similar.
Frank uses his cleverness to save people from death and
danger, thus becoming a true hero.

    I think boys would find the adventures exciting and
would also enjoy a look at how a real boy can earn
a living in the newspaper business. I have had many
experiences in my years working for Mr. Hearst that could
be incorporated into my stories.

    I would be happy to deliver to you, either by post or
in person, the typescript of the first adventure in the
series, which I have already completed.

    I look forward to hearing from you.

                    Sincerely,

                    Thomas De Peyster

Robert wasn't sure whether Thomas De Peyster was Neptune B.
Smythe, who wrote stories about a cub reporter called Frank Fairfax, or
Dexter Cornwall, who wrote about a different character making fabu-
lous rescues. Frank Fairfax, the cub reporter, did not rescue people from

disasters; he went on expeditions to mythical places. On the other hand, Dan Dawson, who did rescue people, worked not as a reporter but as a circus acrobat. Somehow the ideas in Thomas De Peyster's letter had ended up spread across two series. Possibly Thomas De Peyster was both Neptune B. Smythe *and* Dexter Cornwall. Whatever the case, Robert had his first useful clue in identifying the authors of the Tremendous Trio.

With permission from Joseph, Robert took a photograph of the letter with his phone. The next sheet in the file was a carbon copy of Edward Stratemeyer's response:

```
Dear Mr. De Peyster,
     Thank you for your letter. I am not seeking new work
at this time.
                              Edward Stratemeyer
```

Robert grimaced, recalling many similar rejection notes received early in his own career. He wanted to reach across the years and tell De Peyster that the rejections would hurt less over time. He wondered if Thomas had someone like Rebecca to take the sting out of those moments. Only a few months before *Looking Forward* had found an agent, Robert had sat at the table in the kitchen, staring gloomily at his laptop.

"What's the matter?" said Rebecca, breezing into his apartment and shaking the rain off her jacket and all over the floor.

"Another rejection from another agent," said Robert. "We regret that your work is not a fit with the Nelson Agency. We wish you the best of luck in your endeavors."

"Great! With this weather, it will be nice to have an excuse to celebrate," she said, leaning down to give him a soft kiss on the cheek.

"Celebrate? Jesus, Rebecca, this is my career. My life. You want to celebrate the fact that I've been rejected yet again?"

"No, silly," said Rebecca, slipping an arm around him. "You're forgetting what I told you. Every rejection brings you one step closer to acceptance."

Rebecca's mantra to her friends in the creative world—designers, actors, writers—was that each rejection was a necessary step on the road to success. Robert was not wholly convinced, but going out for a celebratory dinner with Rebecca sounded better than sitting at home sulking, so he accepted her embrace and had a lovely evening.

"Sometimes," she whispered to him in bed that night, "you have to allow yourself to be happy." Robert had shivered at the memory of hearing similar words from a therapist he had seen a few years earlier.

"I'm not sure what's weighing on you," the therapist had said. "Maybe after a few more sessions, you'll be ready to tell me. But I do know that you need to give yourself permission to be happy." Robert had never gone back to that therapist.

Robert found no more clues in the 1906 or 1907 files, and at three o'clock decided to stop reading and see what he could find out about Thomas De Peyster. A quick check by Joseph revealed no books published under that name in the New York Public Library collections, nor did there seem to be anything online about an early twentieth-century journalist named De Peyster.

"Did you try the New-York Historical Society?" said Angela, when Robert and Joseph had told her about Thomas De Peyster.

"I hadn't thought of that," said Joseph. "Good idea."

"The Historical Society?" said Robert. "Do you think because he was a journalist, they might—"

"Bingo," said Joseph from behind his computer screen.

"What?" said Robert.

"I'm in their catalogue and listen to this—'Album assembled by Thomas De Peyster, circa 1906.'"

"That's got to be him," said Robert excitedly. "What's it mean, 'album'?"

"Probably a scrapbook or photo album," said Angela. "Might be worth checking out."

"And this album is at the New-York Historical Society?" said Robert.

"Yep," said Joseph.

"That's three blocks from where I live," said Robert. "I've been all over the city trying to find out about this guy, and there's something about him a five-minute walk from my apartment?"

"That's the thing about New York," said Angela. "She will eventually give up her secrets, but only to those who are persistent in their pursuit."

"Thank you," said Robert, excitement edging into his voice as he shook Joseph's hand vigorously. "Thank you very much."

On the way back down to the street, he took the stairs two at a time.

XXIV

CONEY ISLAND,
ON A SATURDAY WHEN THE WORLD WAS INNOCENT

Tom and Gene arranged to meet Magda outside her rooming house at nine thirty Saturday morning. Tom had had another fight with his mother the night before on the subject of his future prospects. He had thought that marrying off her four daughters to wealthy husbands would be enough for her, but apparently not. Because of the time Tom had spent with Magda and Gene—about whom he had told his parents nothing—he had missed, according to his mother, several opportunities to court wealthy young women. Tom's protest that all the women his mother would find desirable were out of the city for the summer held no credence for Mrs. De Peyster. Tom, she said, did not take the necessity of a good match seriously and, as a result, was a disappointment to both her and to his father. But here, Tom thought, she was not entirely correct. He did take the necessity of a good match seriously—but his definition of a good match was not aligned with his mother's. The fight had ended with his mother in tears and Tom more determined than ever to move out of his parents' house.

❧

Magda had been waiting for them on her stoop, dressed in her best summer dress. Soon they were rattling southward on the Ninth Avenue El, the

morning sun filling the car with hazy light. They rode the train to its terminus at Battery Place on the southern tip of Manhattan, and when they exited
the station Magda found herself back at the site of her earliest memory,
gazing on the setting of a story her father had told her over and over, a
building she had passed through at age two and not set eyes on since that
day when she and her parents had come to see the Statue of Liberty. It was
now the New York Aquarium, but the huge round brick building with an
American flag rippling in the breeze above its cupola had once been Castle
Garden, the center in which immigrants arriving in New York had been
processed for almost fifty years. For the past two years Magda had succeeded
in pushing thoughts of her family deep down inside herself, locking them
away in a place below her heart where they could not harm her. But the
sight of Castle Garden, the knowledge that her American life began just a
stone's throw away, ignited an explosion of memories from her gut. Magda
staggered for several steps, thinking she might fall as she heard her father's
voice, as clearly as if he, and not Tom, had caught her elbow and steadied
her. In the time it took her to walk two steps, Magda heard her father's entire
narrative, from boarding the ship in Hamburg, to the hours spent in Castle
Garden and how, at the end, when that massive building had disgorged
them onto the streets of lower Manhattan, a passing man had tipped his hat
to the Hertzenberger family and said, "Welcome to New York."

They skirted the edge of Battery Park, walking closer and closer to
that building her father would remember until the day he died on North
Brother Island. Magda thought for a moment that this had all been a
trick, that Tom and Gene somehow knew her secrets and had brought
her here to confront her past. She watched the crowds walking the paths
of Battery Park and milling around the entrance to the aquarium waiting
for opening time. When Magda finally looked away from the aquarium
building, she saw a woman holding a small girl in her arms walking briskly
toward them. Though she knew that woman could not possess the face
of her mother, that the child could not be two-year-old Magda freshly
arrived in America, she started as if she had seen a ghost.

"Is something wrong?" said Tom. The sound of his voice transformed
the woman into just another New Yorker out for a walk on Saturday

morning. Magda found herself once again not in 1884 with her parents alive and the twins as yet unborn, but in 1906 on a perfect September day.

"I just . . . remembered something," said Magda.

"Well, let's go make some new memories," said Tom. "Come on, the steamboat is waiting."

"Steamboat?" said Magda, coming to a stop.

"The Iron Steamboat to Coney Island," said Tom, pointing to a sign overhead. Magda realized they had been walking toward a pier at the end of which stood a horrifyingly familiar sight—a white-painted steamboat, its three decks crowded with festive people. In the center of the boat, a huge paddlewheel rose above the top deck. Banners fluttered from its flagpoles, and, but for the words *Iron Steamboat Company* painted across its midsection, it might have been the *General Slocum*.

"Don't you like boats?" said Gene, as Magda stood rooted to the spot.

"It's perfectly safe," said Tom. "The boat has an iron hull. Look at the sign: 'They cannot burn. They cannot sink.'"

Without realizing it, Magda began to cry. The faces in her mind of a happy couple newly arrived with their two-year-old daughter in a land of opportunity were now replaced with Henry and Rosie plunging into the fire. She began to back away, pulling Tom and Gene with her until she collapsed onto a park bench.

"Magda, what is it?" said Tom, sitting next to her and taking her by the hand. "What's wrong?"

"Give her a minute," said Gene softly. He sat on the other side of Magda as the Saturday morning crowds streamed toward the ferryboat, paying no attention to the sobbing woman on the bench.

Magda saw it all as clearly as a film in the nickelodeons in Herald Square. The flags in the breeze, the sun sparkling on the water, the smiles on the faces of the twins. And then the wisps of smoke, the crowd rushing to the back of the boat, the joy turning to fear and then terror, the unbearable intensity of the fire, the unbearable darkness of the water. When the film had run its course, when the water had taken her mother and the fire had taken Rosie and Henry, her crying subsided, her breathing returned to normal, and she looked up into the concerned faces of Tom and Gene.

"I'm sorry," she said. "Sorry I never told you."

"Never told us what?" said Tom.

"About the last time I was on a boat," said Magda, reaching for Gene's hand. "I need . . . I need to tell you."

And so, with a steady voice and gripping the hands of her two best friends, Magda told them what had happened on June 15, 1904. She told them about a day as beautiful and full of promise as the one that stretched before them now, about the shining white steamboat in the sun, about the band playing on the deck, and about her mother plunging into the dark waters and the twins falling into the fire. She told them of the boy climbing the flagpole and of how the nurses pulled her from the water. She did not tell them how she had gotten her own name onto the list of the dead, how she had avoided all the funerals, or how she had left her neighborhood, her heritage, and even her identity behind after that day. She still kept *some* secrets.

Gene had read about the *Slocum* disaster in the papers; Tom had actually gone to the mass funeral for unidentified victims, reporting on the event and interviewing some of the survivors.

"We don't have to go to Coney Island," said Tom, when Magda fell silent.

"No," said Magda, forcing a smile. "I want to go." And she did. As black as the past had been, the future held a day of glorious adventure and she wanted that more than anything. It had felt good to finally share her story with Gene and Tom. She felt no less sad, but a great deal less burdened, and more herself than she had since the tragedy. She had not realized what a knot her secret had tied inside her.

"We could take the train," said Tom, "or a streetcar."

Magda rose and looked across to the pier. The ten-fifteen ferry had sailed while she told her story, and passengers were streaming onto an identical boat that would sail at eleven fifteen. "They cannot burn; they cannot sink," she said calmly, walking toward the steamer.

Tom and Gene quickly followed, and soon Magda found herself again at a stern railing on the top deck of an excursion steamer, the wind whipping loose strands of her hair and the sounds of excitement surrounding her.

"Are you all right?" said Tom.

"I think so," said Magda firmly. She knew exactly why the Iron Steamboat Company had chosen the motto *They cannot burn; They cannot sink.* It meant—*This is not the* Slocum. *That will not happen here.* And of course, it didn't. As they made their way past the Statue of Liberty, Magda heard once again the voice of her father, saying "Isn't she beautiful," as clearly as if he had been there at the railing beside her. They sailed the length of New York Harbor, through the Narrows, and around the end of Long Island until the piers of Coney Island hove into sight. She could see the beaches already packed with bathers and hear laughs of delight drifting across the water. She could hear, too, the exhilarated cries coming from the attractions of Dreamland, Coney's biggest amusement park. To the left, Dreamland's magnificent pier and ballroom jutted out over the ocean, and behind it rose the blazing white radiance of Beacon Tower. That Magda would, before the day ended, let out her own shrieks of excitement and even ascend to the top of that tower sent a thrill of anticipation through Magda as the boat slowed to dock at the end of Iron Pier.

A few minutes later they stood in the Hippodrome, the main courtyard of Dreamland, surrounded by dazzling white buildings and thousands of people. In front of them, horses thundered past in the midst of a Roman chariot race; a dozen "airplane boats" twirled from a tower high overhead to the delight of their occupants; the sounds of roaring lions came from one end of the courtyard and that of squealing passengers "shooting the chutes" from the other. Soaring above it all was the glittering white facade of Beacon Tower, with its views out to the sea.

"Welcome to Dreamland," said Tom.

"Have you been here before?" said Gene.

"Last summer," said Tom. "I wrote an article about the Lilliputian Village, but I only saw a few other attractions."

"I want to see everything," said Magda.

The day proved more wonderful than Magda had dreamed. She felt like a butterfly emerging from the dark, confining space of its chrysalis. Her secrets had been shared, her fears conquered, and she was ready for the most spectacular, the most frightening, and the most thrilling experiences Dreamland had to offer. By her side, through it all, stood her friends, and on that day she thought of them as just that, forgetting in the magnificent spectacle of Dreamland her unrequited love for Gene, and simply laughing and screaming and gasping with the boys.

At Bostock's Animal Arena they saw every kind of wild animal act—from tightrope-walking elephants to Bengal tigers, polar bears, lions, jaguars, leopards, and more.

"I could put an animal act in my next circus book," said Magda.

"No research today," said Tom, as they watched Captain Jack Bonavita and his thirty lions. Bonavita exercised full control over his lions with only one arm, having lost the other following an attack by one of his charges two seasons ago. Magda was especially taken with Black Prince, a Barbary lion with a dark mane and intense eyes.

"He's magnificent," she whispered to Gene.

Magda liked the rides best of all. At "Hell Gate," they first watched as a boat full of passengers was swept round and round a fifty-foot-wide whirlpool, before being sucked below the surface amid screams of terror and delight. The idea that being pulled under the water could be transformed from the horror she had experienced two years ago into an entertainment thrilled Magda, and soon the three of them were seated in a boat, slowly spiraling around the whirlpool, describing a smaller and smaller circle, building up more and more speed, until they plunged into darkness. Magda grabbed Gene to her left, grasping him tightly in her arms as they seemed to fall; she felt Tom's hand gripping her arm hard enough to leave a bruise.

"The whole point of the rides at Coney Island," she had heard a young lady say on the ferryboat, "is that you get to grab hold of the men."

"And they get to grab hold of you," giggled her companion.

They all released their grips as the boat steadied, and they sailed through a dim tunnel on the walls of which were illuminated scenes supposed to be of the center of the earth.

"I shall decline to comment on the scientific accuracy of these depictions," said Gene with a laugh.

A few moments later, the boat gathered speed again and, with an explosion, shot upward. This time, the three held both their breath and one another's hands until the boat surfaced back into the sunshine, on the edge of the great whirlpool.

"Shoot the Chutes" provided more opportunity for clinging to one another. The ride began by standing on a "moving stairway," which took them on a pier out across the surf and three hundred feet into the ocean, at the same time carrying them up and up to the top of the ride. There, they boarded a boat, perched atop a steep track. As the boat teetered at the precipice and they linked arms, pulling one another close, Tom shouted, "Who are we?" to which they all replied, as the boat plunged downward, "We are the gods and goddess of children's books!" The boat seemed to fly through the air, then hurtled under a bridge and splashed into the lagoon at the center of the courtyard, skimming across the surface before finally coming to a stop at the water's edge. Magda did not stop laughing until they were back on solid ground.

"I'm going to buy us some postcards," said Gene as they walked across the courtyard on slightly wobbly legs. "I think we might want to remember today." He left Magda and Tom underneath the airplane boats while he joined the line for a vendor selling colored views of the various attractions.

"Isn't it wonderful?" said Magda, gazing overhead at the boats that spun high above them. "It's so lovely to have a day that is just about today. No worries from the past, no thoughts of the future. Just today." She twirled round and round, face turned to the glorious sky, skirts flying up around her and let out a laugh. Tom laughed at her joy and when she came to a stop, weaving back and forth from dizziness, he held her elbow to steady her.

"It's nice to see you so happy," he said.

"How could you not be happy in a place like this," said Magda. "It's magical."

"No thought of the future, eh?" said Tom.

"Not one. I have planned my future as far as looking at the postcards Gene brings us."

"But surely you sometimes think of the future. Marriage, children, all those things."

"I suppose," said Magda.

"Do you think it might be for you? Marriage, I mean. You're as independent a woman as I've ever known, so I just wondered—could you ever imagine yourself married?"

"I don't give it much thought," said Magda, and the statement was *mostly* true. She would like to imagine what it would be like to be married to Gene, but he had given her no real cause to entertain such fantasies, so she did her best to avoid them. "I suppose I might get married if the right man comes along."

"Maybe he already has," said Tom as softly as the sounds of Dreamland would allow.

Was it possible, thought Magda, that Tom knew something she didn't? Had Gene made some sort of confession to Tom? With a racing heart she answered, "True, maybe he has."

"Postcards for all," said Gene, bursting into the conversation and handing a trio of cards to Magda and another set to Tom. One showed the Shoot the Chutes attraction they had just ridden, one Beacon Tower, and the third illustrated a giant angel towering over Surf Avenue.

"What is this one?" said Magda, holding up the angel.

"That's the entrance to the creation panorama," said Gene.

"Oh, let's go, let's go," said Magda. "I have to see it. The biggest angel I've ever seen was . . ." she had been about to say *was in Holy Redeemer Catholic Church in Kleindeutschland* but she stopped herself. "Was not nearly as big as that," she said.

A few minutes later they stood on Surf Avenue, gazing up at a thirty-foot-tall, bare-breasted angel, holding up the cavernous arch that led into the creation attraction with her spread wings. They had to cross the street to take it all in, and they walked up Surf Avenue a short way so that the angel, who looked down and to her right, gazed directly at them. Magda held her hands up next to her eyes, blocking out the view of Zeller's Pharmacy and its signs advertising cigars and ice cream, and suddenly felt herself embraced by this heavenly vision. Though she had promised not to dwell on the past today, she couldn't help thinking that this angel was the spirit of her mother and of Henry and Rosie, embracing her from above, upholding her, protecting her. She wiped away a tear and grabbed Gene and Tom by the hands.

"Let's go in," she said.

They sat in the darkness, still holding hands, and experienced the biblical story of creation in brilliant illusions. Magda would have been happy sitting there, feeling Gene's slightly sweaty hand in hers, for hours—even though the beauty of the creation story was followed by the much more frightening "end of the world."

Back in the sunshine, they watched acrobats in a ring at the end of the lagoon while eating popcorn and peanuts. They even met the Broadway actress Marie Dressler, hired as a celebrity overseer of the boys who sold the salty snacks and posed while Tom took her picture. Magda laughed to see how Tom fawned over the buxom star, saying, with deadpan seriousness, how much he had enjoyed her performance last season as Matilda Grabfelder in *Twiddle Twaddle*.

Magda had previously seen all of the same acrobatic feats featured at Dreamland in Barnum and Bailey Circus at Madison Square Garden, but they took on a new sense of danger and beauty when performed outdoors. Against a blue sky and with Beacon Tower rising above them, she saw tightrope walkers and trapeze artists in a new light.

"I can see you're thinking of putting Dan Dawson on an outdoor tightrope," said Gene.

"Tom told me I'm not allowed to do research today," said Magda, who had been thinking exactly that.

"Tom is wise," said Gene.

After the circus acts, they rode a boat through the "Canals of Venice," marveling at the Italianate architecture that greeted them at every turn, then descended the steps to the beach, where their attempts to walk in the sand were impeded by a solid wall of humanity, many of them wet, all of them seemingly delighted.

When Magda mentioned she felt hot, Tom immediately led them to the "Coasting through Switzerland" ride, where they boarded a train that zipped them along through Swiss scenery and up to the top of the "Alps," where a blast of cold air made Magda laugh with glee during the entire dizzying descent.

They left the precincts of Dreamland only once the entire day, because Tom insisted that they lunch next door at Feltman's, which was famous for a dish it had "invented" a few decades ago—a sausage served on a roll that locals called a *hot dog*. It seemed like standard German fare to Magda, but she said nothing. Today, more than ever, she felt American, and if that meant calling a sausage a hot dog, then that's what she would do.

Tom went to fetch beers as they sat over the detritus of their sausages. Gene looked more relaxed that Magda had ever seen him—almost as if every time she had seen him before, he had been hiding something, or holding back slightly.

"You can really be yourself out here," he said, leaning back with his hands behind his head. "Look at everybody—so free. Not like in New York."

"What do you mean?" said Magda.

"You've seen it," said Gene. "Men holding girls and girls holding men and people shouting when they're happy and looking at . . . whatever they want to look at." Gene had his eyes locked on Tom's muscular shoulders as he shoved his way toward the counter.

"I don't know what you mean," said Magda in a teasing voice, sitting up primly in her chair.

"You certainly do," said Gene with a laugh. "Shoot the Chutes and Hell Gate—those are just excuses for people to grab hold of each other. I saw you clutching on to Tom."

"I never clutched Tom," said Magda with mock indignity. Anyhow, it was true, Tom might have clutched her, but she had grabbed hold of Gene.

"I'm sure you clutched somebody," said Gene absently. He had lost track of Tom in the crowd, but still stared toward the counter, waiting for that beautiful face to reemerge from the crowd. "What was Tom talking to you about when I came back with the postcards? He seemed awfully serious for a day like today."

Magda thought for a moment about saying that Tom had suggested she and Gene would make a nice couple, but even Dreamland hadn't given her that much courage. "Oh, some nonsense about whether I'd ever thought about getting married. Not the sort of discussion for a day at Dreamland."

"And what did you tell him?"

"I told him I might think about it, if I ever found the right man."

"I'm not sure I'm the marrying type," said Gene, a smile breaking across his face as he spotted Tom returning with three frothy mugs of beer, "but I understand what you mean about finding the right man."

After Feltman's, Tom wanted to go to the "Fighting the Flames" attraction. He had seen the show the previous season and, despite his stricture against research for any possible future books, he thought its depiction of a hotel on fire and the ensuing rescues might prove useful if Magda ended up writing another Dan Dawson book. As they sipped their beers, he had told them all about the show.

"It starts out with all these little street dramas," said Tom. "A horse cart almost gets run over by a trolley, a street fight gets broken up by police, and then comes a parade of firefighters led by a fife and drum corps. Then it gets exciting. Smoke and flames start pouring from the windows of a six-story building, and horses race in pulling all sorts of firefighting equipment. The best part is all the people escaping from the flames. Some get rescued by firemen on ladders, but some jump from five or six stories up into this huge net where they bounce around before they climb down to the ground. It's very acrobatic."

"Sounds exciting," said Gene.

"It is," said Tom. "And I was thinking that maybe the next Dan Dawson book could have a fire rescue."

"If there is another Dan Dawson book," said Magda.

"I suppose that depends on the first one selling lots of copies," said Gene.

"Exactly," said Magda.

"Of course there will be another book," said Tom. "I don't know about me and Gene, but Magda's got the goods. That Lipscomb troll is going to love Dan Dawson." The others laughed and they clinked their glasses together and for about the hundredth time in the past few hours it seemed the day could not get any better.

Tom led them back across Dreamland to Fighting the Flames, but when they arrived at the massive white facade that fronted the arena, the lettering that stretched across the entire structure did not read FIGHTING THE FLAMES, but SAN FRANCISCO EARTHQUAKE.

"That changed fast," said Gene. "The earthquake was only a few months ago."

Tom's face blanched and he staggered backward. He did not say that he had been in San Francisco—that was still *his* secret. He did not say that with the earthquake had come havoc that made the most realistic amusement park show seem like little more than an insult. He did not say that even Dan Dawson with his strength and acrobatic skill would have felt helpless against the mass of death and destruction in San Francisco that day. All he could see in that moment, as he looked at those horrible words, was Isabella lying dead on the floor, her life snapped out as easily as turning off a light switch.

"Is everything all right?" said Gene, slipping an arm around Tom. "You look like . . ."

"Like you've seen a ghost," said Magda.

"Just a little light-headed," said Tom. "Must have been the beer." As quickly as it had come, the vision faded and Tom felt the blood flowing back into his cheeks. He took a deep breath and stepped toward the entrance. "Shall we go in?"

Inside they sat on wooden bleachers and watched a show that rapidly depicted the whole history of San Francisco. In the first scene, white men arrived in a wagon train at the beautiful natural bay and fought the natives, defeating them with superior weaponry. There followed a scene of a mining camp and its accompanying gamblers and criminals, culminating in the lynching of one of these evil men by a group of vigilantes.

Tom struggled to watch impassively as the next scenes unfolded, trying not to show the pain he felt. The first depicted a typical evening on Market Street in April—well-dressed men and women strolled to the theater (many of them, as Tom well knew, off to see Caruso), and gaiety filled the air. Tom searched the crowd for Isabella, caught up for a moment in the fantasy that the earthquake had not yet happened. Darkness fell, and when the light returned, the earthquake struck. As the whole arena seemed to shake, buildings toppled and fires blazed. The audience cried out in terror, and only Tom seemed to realize what a pale reflection of the true horror this sideshow was.

Yet he watched intently, as if he was recording the whole scene on a reel of moving picture film. Tom wanted to replace his memory of the actual events with this frothy bit of amusement. He wanted to turn the most horrible moments of his life into something as insignificant as a carnival entertainment.

As the smoke cleared in the arena before them, a final scene appeared, under the sign SAN FRANCISCO, 1909. Before them stood a gleaming city of white—all spires and towers, parks and boulevards, with the sea sparkling in the background. It was as if Dreamland itself had been transported across the continent and taken root by San Francisco Bay.

They sat breathless for a minute or two as the crowd filed out around them.

"It seems to me there is only one place for Dan Dawson to go on his next adventure," said Gene.

"San Francisco," said Magda. "Tom, you could write the rescue scenes. Think of all the opportunities for Dan to help out."

Tom was torn. On the one hand, he wanted to forget San Francisco, to put the earthquake and all its associated anguish behind him. However, if Dan Dawson could do the things that Tom could not, if he could save a man entombed in his cellar under a collapsed house, or a woman trapped by fire in the upper floor of a hotel; if Dan Dawson could save Isabella, might that somehow atone for Tom's own shortcomings? Wasn't the very reason Tom set out to write a children's book about a character who rescued people to expunge the helplessness he had felt on that horrible day? And besides, he would welcome any opportunity to spend more time with Magda.

"I might be able to help a little," he said softly.

"I don't know why I didn't think of it before," said Magda. "*Dan Dawson and the Great Earthquake*. Mr. Lipscomb will love it."

"Yes," said Tom, rising from his seat on slightly shaky legs. "I suppose he will."

As dusk approached, the lights of Dreamland came on—every roofline and turret, every tower and arch and statue, every bridge and colonnade lined

with gossamer threads of incandescent lights, their glow gradually intensi-
fying as darkness fell. Magda felt she stood at the center of a great galaxy,
cradled in the vastness by the twinkling stars. She knew that to Gene all
this was just a scientific achievement, but to her it was transcendent, and
she stood for a long time on the boardwalk, soaking in the lights, while the
others urged her to come along and ride the Leap Frog Railway.

They boarded a rather squat-looking open-sided railway car that took
them at a moderate pace on a pier out into the ocean. From the far end of
the pier an identical car traveled toward them on the same track. Collision
seemed inevitable until the oncoming car rolled onto tracks affixed to
their car, and "leap frogged" over the top. At the end of the pier their car
reversed direction, and this time it was their turn to go over the top of the
approaching railway car. Like everything else at Dreamland, the ride was
accompanied by a soundtrack of shrieks and screams that purported to be
of fear, but actually expressed unalloyed delight.

Evening had fully arrived by the time they finished their ride—though
the bulbs of Dreamland refused to admit that fact.

"Have we done everything?" asked Magda, as they stood at the foot of
Beacon Tower, gazing across the lagoon where the lights reflected in the water.

"Not everything," said Tom.

Tom shared a knowing glance with Gene. "Wouldn't you like to see a
better view than this?" he said to Magda.

"What could possibly be better?" said Magda.

"The view from there," said Tom, pointing to the top of the tower.

"I'm not sure I have enough energy left to climb a tower that tall,"
said Magda.

"The only energy needed is electrical energy," said Gene. "We go up
in an elevator."

"I think I might need to stop off at the ladies' side of the bathing
pavilion first," said Magda, blushing.

"Certainly, certainly," said Tom, taking her by the elbow and guid-
ing her through the crowd. In another moment, Magda had disappeared
inside the pavilion and Tom and Gene stood together by the entrance.
Tom jammed his hands in his pockets and turned to look out toward

the sea. The two men had rarely been together without Magda, and an awkward silence fell between them.

"We got lucky with the weather," said Gene at last.

"Yes," said Tom. "Lucky."

After another silence, Gene tried again. "That Shoot the Chutes is something else."

"Listen," said Tom, turning toward Gene. "I'm sorry. I really am."

"Sorry for what?" said Gene.

"Sorry that I can never feel about you the way you feel about me," said Tom.

"What are you talking about?" said Gene, a defensive tone creeping into his voice.

"I see the way you look at me," said Tom. "And I know things."

"What things do you know?" said Gene.

"I'm sorry, okay. But you need to tell Magda."

"Tell her what?" said Gene.

"You know what. She's in love with you, for God's sake, not that you would know it."

"Of course I know it," said Gene, stepping back from Tom and crossing his arms.

"Well then, tell her, will you? Don't make me do it. Tell her that you are the way you are."

"You want me out of the way, don't you?" said Gene. "So you can swoop in and have her all to yourself."

"Christ, why do you even want to be *in* the way?" said Tom. "You don't even like girls."

"I like Magda."

"Not the way I do. I want to marry her. I'm going to ask her tonight."

"And why should you ask her instead of me?"

"Because you can't . . . you can't be with her the way I can. You like . . . you like boys the way I like Magda."

"What makes you say that?"

"Are you denying it?" said Tom.

"I said, what makes you say that I like boys?" said Gene, raising his voice.

"Because I saw you, okay," hissed Tom, taking a step closer to Gene. "I followed you and I saw you. I saw you kissing a man and taking men up to your room." The conversation was not going the way Tom had hoped. Gene was supposed to tell Magda about his proclivities and then gallantly stand aside.

"You followed me?" shouted Gene.

"Keep your voice down," said Tom.

"What gives you the right to follow me?" said Gene.

"Protecting Magda gives me the right," said Tom angrily.

"So now I'm dangerous? You violate my privacy, you betray our friendship, and I'm the one who's dangerous?"

Tom felt a sweat breaking out on his face. He had somehow taken what was supposed to have been a civilized conversation between friends and turned it into accusations and argument. He had thought only of saving Magda's feelings when he had followed Gene to confirm his suspicions, but Gene was right, it had been a betrayal of his trust. "I'm not saying you're dangerous," said Tom calmly. "I'm just saying you need to tell Magda before you hurt her any worse."

"How many times?"

"Just once, for God's sake. You only need to tell her once."

"No," said Gene, stepping uncomfortably close to Tom and staring him in the eyes. "How many times did you follow me? You said you saw me with *men*; not a man, but men. And I don't invite men up to my room that often, so how many times did you follow me?"

"A few," said Tom, meeting Gene's steely stare.

"How many?" said Gene.

"Eight times," said Tom, turning to look out across the crowd. People streamed by them as if nothing dramatic was happening at all, as if they had no idea that a friendship was disintegrating in the middle of Dreamland. "I followed you eight times and twice I saw you with men. I wanted to make sure the first time wasn't just an experiment."

"Keep away from me," said Gene, turning his back on Tom and striding across the courtyard.

"Gene, wait," said Tom, rushing after him and placing a hand on his shoulder. Gene stopped and spun around.

"Don't you touch me," he said, fighting back tears. "Don't you dare touch me, and don't you come near me. I trusted you. I opened myself up to you, and this is how you repay me?"

"You lied to me," said Tom. "But worse, you lied to her."

"I never lied to anybody."

"You let her think you could love her."

"I do love her," said Gene.

"Not like I do," said Tom. "Never like I do."

"That's true," said Gene. "Because I would never stoop to deceiving a friend just to be sure her heart gets broken. So I guess you win, Tom. Congratulations."

"You could never love her back . . . not the way she loves you."

"Probably not," said Gene. "But that was my decision to make, not yours. Goodbye, Tom. Tell Magda I'm sorry I had to leave."

"But aren't you going to tell her about . . ."

"You tell her," spat Gene. "Tell her everything you know. Print it in the newspaper for all I care. I'm done with you." He turned and strode off, disappearing in the crowd.

Tom couldn't breathe for a moment. He tried to understand where the conversation had gone wrong, what he could have done to keep his friend. The last thing he wanted was to alienate Gene. He only wanted him to be honest with Magda so that Magda could answer Tom's proposal without any misconceptions about Gene. Tom thought by telling Gene what he knew that he'd be unburdening him of his darkest secret. But he had let his emotions take over and had handled the situation with an utter lack of grace. Now he stood, alone in the crowd, crushed by the sense that he had lost his best friend. Darkness deepened beyond the borders of Dreamland and the revelers seemed to be raising their voices and their level of excitement, but all Tom could hear, echoing in his ears, was Gene's voice, full of hurt and anger, saying goodbye. And Gene had loved him; Tom knew that. As painful as this moment was for Tom, it must have been heartbreaking for Gene.

"It took forever to get to the front of the line," said Magda. "Where's Gene?"

"He had to go," said Tom.

"What do you mean?" said Magda. "Isn't he going to come to the top of the tower with us?"

"He didn't feel well," said Tom. "He decided to go . . . to go back."

ᥡ

It didn't take Gene long, wandering on the Bowery of Coney Island, to find what he was looking for—a dive with a tinny piano playing in the background, cheap liquor flowing from the bar, and a clientele as far removed from the happy revelers at Dreamland—who thought holding hands or grabbing a girl round the waist was the greatest of illicit thrills— as he was removed from Tom. Tom who could never be his; Tom who, even now, was probably celebrating his engagement to sweet Magda. The provocatively dressed women who gyrated on a makeshift stage near the back held no interest for Gene, but he knew that racy burlesque shows were not the only things that had been chased off Manhattan and taken up residence on Coney Island. Even without the tools of his former trade, his effeminate clothes and makeup, Gene knew how to signal, to anyone interested, by his stance and demeanor, just what he had to offer. He bought a glass of caustic gin at the bar, downed it in a single gulp, and lurked in a dark corner, far from the stage. Within a few minutes a burly Italian approached him. Gene and his fellow fairies called men like this *trade*—men who might even be married and who certainly did not iden- tify themselves as *fairies*, but who, under the right circumstances, enjoyed the occasional encounter with another man. Twenty minutes later, Gene and the nameless Italian were naked on a hard bed of the cheapest hotel room in Coney Island. There were rules when trade took a fairy to a hotel room—trade were men, masculine men, and they took the man's role in bed. But Gene didn't mind. He didn't mind the first time or the second time or the third time. As he lay there, submitting to the sweaty, panting, pounding of a man he would never see again, he wept—not from pain or shame, but for the loss of Tom. He had never truly loved a man before and he feared he would never love a man again—that the rest of his life would be meaningless encounters in cheap hotel rooms with men who wanted to use him like an object and then creep away, pretending nothing had ever happened, leaving him with a tear-stained pillow and a hollow heart.

Magda had only ever ridden in the elevators in the Flatiron Building— slow, bouncy, hydraulic-powered chambers. As the electric elevator of Beacon Tower made its smooth, rapid way to the top, she felt as if her stomach had been left behind. When the doors opened onto the observation platform, it took a moment for her legs to feel steady again. Then, she walked to the railing and looked out.

Below her the lights of Coney Island glittered in the clear night air, a million bulbs lining the buildings of Dreamland that cast a light more bright and magical than any imagined fairyland. In the distance Magda could see the dim glow of Manhattan, and on the water a ferryboat full of revelers had just pulled away from the pier. The city looked perfect from here—there were no orphans or thugs, no hunger or hatred, no disease or fire or tragedy. And even though she knew all those things still existed down there, Magda loved New York at that moment in a way that filled her with joy. She loved this dazzling, fairy-tale city. Anything could happen here. And, while *anything* included a thousand people killed in a burning steamer or a man murdered in a rooftop theater, it also meant a girl from Germany could be independent, American, and free—even write a book.

"It's so beautiful," she said softly.

"It is," said Tom. They turned to look out of the west side of the viewing area, across Long Island, perhaps toward where Gene and Nikola Tesla had hoped their future lay, at Wardenclyffe. Tom slipped his hand into the small of her back, and Magda leaned back slightly to press against him.

Tom took a deep breath. He had botched his conversation with Gene; he didn't want to do the same with Magda. He needed to handle the situation carefully, but he wanted to tell her how he felt, and he couldn't imagine a more perfect spot, a more perfect moment.

"I love you," he whispered.

"That's sweet," said Magda. "Friends should love one another."

"Not as a friend," said Tom. "I mean I love you, really love you."

"What are you saying?" said Magda, sounding genuinely puzzled. "We're friends, Tom, good friends." She took a deep breath and readied her confession. If Tom truly cared for her, he would know what she should do. "And as your friend, I have something I want to tell you. I'm in love with Gene."

"But Gene can never love you," said Tom. "Not the way you want him to."

"Gene does love me," said Magda, feeling a chill in the air. The hand in her back suddenly felt not comforting but menacing. Why had Gene really left? She knew him well enough to know he hadn't been feeling ill.

"As a friend, yes," said Tom. "But Gene can never love you the way I do."

"What do you mean?" said Magda, pulling away from Tom and wrapping her arms around herself.

"Let's just say that Gene is never going to be a family man."

"No," said Magda, "let's not just say that. Say what you mean."

"Gene doesn't like . . . well, he doesn't like girls in . . . in that way."

"What way, Tom? If you have something you think you need to tell me, then do it. Or you could always just mind your own business."

"It is my business," said Tom, laying a hand on her arm. "Because I love you."

Until a few moments ago, no man had ever said those words to Magda, but they seemed cold and empty to her at this moment. She didn't want to hear them from Tom but from Gene. "What does that have to do with Gene?" she said.

"You love him. He can never love you. I thought maybe you would consider me as a substitute."

"He *can* love me," said Magda, pulling away from Tom and turning to look again at the view over Dreamland. "He does love me," she added in a whisper.

"Magda," said Tom, stepping to the railing next to her. "Have you ever heard of fairies?"

"Little creatures who live in the garden?" said Magda. "What in the world . . ."

"Not those fairies," said Tom. "Men who dress as women and who . . . who love other men. Physically."

"Why would . . . I don't understand."

"Gene isn't attracted to women. He doesn't want to . . . to go to bed with women. He goes to bed with men."

"But that doesn't make any . . ."

"Why do you think he dressed you as a man the one time he took you out?"

"That was for business," said Magda, feeling more confused by the moment.

"God, Magda, please understand. Gene is not the right man for you. Gene likes men. He's attracted to men, not women."

"Why are you being like this?" said Magda, feeling tears welling up in her eyes. "Why would you tell horrible lies about Gene?"

"They're not lies," said Tom calmly.

"They are," said Magda, raising her voice. "They are lies and I wish you would just stop."

"You have to trust me about this, Magda. I know."

"You don't know anything," said Magda, turning away from him. "And you certainly don't know Gene."

"I know, Magda," said Tom, grabbing her by the arm and pulling her back toward him. "I know!"

"How, Tom? How could you even pretend to know a thing like that?"

"I know because I followed him," said Tom, dropping her arm.

Magda stood speechless for a moment, almost unable to breathe. "You did what?" she said at last.

"I followed him and I saw him kissing a man and taking a man up to his room—a stranger."

"You followed him?"

"I'm a reporter, Magda, it's what I do."

"What you do is betray the trust and privacy of your best friends?"

"Listen, Magda," said Tom more calmly, "we're getting off the subject here. Forget about Gene. I love you, and I brought you up here to this beautiful place to ask you if you'll marry me."

"Marry you?" said Magda in shock, taking a step away from Tom. "How could you possibly think I would marry you? I can hardly stand to look at you right now." She felt that the beautiful sparkling world that lay below them had been pulled out from beneath her feet and that she was falling through the vortex of Hell Gate—not the ride with its manufactured terror, but the real swirling waters that had consumed her mother. She couldn't believe what Tom said about Gene, and yet she had seen the way Gene fawned on Tom while ignoring her. The only time he had ever treated her like an object of affection was when she had been dressed as a man. Still, how could Tom act like this? How could he turn on Gene and spy on him? How could he use Gene's secrets against him, against her?

"Where is Gene, really?" said Magda.

"He left," said Tom softly. "I told him that I followed him and we got into a fight and he left."

"I don't blame him," said Magda. "I think it's time for me to leave, too." She turned and walked through the shadows toward the elevator doors, hoping that Tom would stay away from her, stay at the railing and look out over the shattered dream of Dreamland, thinking hard about how he had thrown away two wonderful friendships. But she heard his footsteps behind her and felt his hand on her shoulder.

"Magda, please. Can't we talk?"

"We have talked," said Magda, whirling around. Now she felt flint-hard anger exploding inside of her. This day had been perfect, this summer had been perfect, and now Tom had ruined it all. Everything was tainted with his betrayal. "I don't want to talk to you anymore. I don't want to see you anymore." She felt hot tears in her eyes as she turned and violently pressed the button that would summon the elevator operator.

"At least let me take you home," said Tom. "You can't go by yourself."

"You have no idea what I can do by myself," said Magda, not turning to look at him. "You have no idea what I've done by myself. I don't need any man and I certainly don't need you."

At that moment, the elevator arrived and the door opened to reveal the smiling man who had brought them to the top of the tower a few minutes earlier. A pair of giggling couples tumbled out onto the viewing platform, loudly marveling at the lights below. Magda let them pass and then stepped into the cubicle.

"He'll take the next one," said Magda to the operator, nodding toward Tom.

As the doors began to close, Tom tried to catch Magda's eye, but she would not look up at him. He had never felt more broken and empty. She was right; in his high-handed pursuit of the woman he loved, he had ruined everything, and lost her in the bargain. As she disappeared behind the elevator doors, he muttered softly through his tears, "Goodbye, Magda."

XXV

By the time Robert returned to the Upper West Side, the New-York Historical Society was closed for the day. He stood in front of the Beaux Arts building on Central Park West gazing up at the familiar facade. Rush-hour pedestrians streamed past him as he stood rooted to the sidewalk, remembering an exhibition he and Rebecca had seen there a couple of years ago.

The Late Gilded Age in New York had told the story of daily life in the city between 1900 and World War I, a time when Thomas De Peyster had been writing children's books and working for William Randolph Hearst. While Rebecca pored over pictures of interior décor in Fifth Avenue mansions, Robert preferred the relics of life away from the millionaires. He read a menu from Delmonico's restaurant, trying to decide what he would have ordered. He studied the map of the elevated train system, imagining what Sixth and Ninth Avenues must have looked like with the sun blocked out by train tracks. He read framed front pages of newspapers recording the great events of the day—from the 1900 election of Teddy Roosevelt to the Chicago Cubs' 1908 World Series Championship.

Robert had become so lost in the exhibit that he didn't notice Rebecca had left the gallery. He found her waiting patiently on a bench near the coat check. He could still see her there, sitting quietly, not a hint of perturbation or impatience on her face as she smiled when he came into view.

"Sorry," Robert said, "I didn't mean . . ."

"It's okay," said Rebecca, bouncing up and taking his hand. "I don't mind waiting for you."

Now Robert understood that she had always been waiting for him. Not just because he plodded his way through museum exhibits and took forever to find his keys, but because she had moved into adulthood, into a world where marriage and children were reasonable next steps in life, while he had remained tethered to his past, unable to move forward and unwilling to look back. He did not blame her in the slightest for deciding she didn't want to wait any longer.

❧

A gust of wind reminded him that evening had arrived, and he shoved his hands into his coat pockets, put his head down, and began the walk home. Waiting at the light at Seventy-Fourth and Columbus, he took out his phone and tried to decide whether to call Rebecca. He knew she wouldn't answer, but maybe she had left another message. He waited until he was inside the warmth of the apartment, then made the call.

"Hi, this is Rebecca, leave a message." Nothing else. She didn't need to say anything else. Robert knew that tone of voice and understood the message as well as if she had spoken for an hour. *I'm really angry with you, Robert. I might love you and care for you, but that doesn't necessarily mean I can live with you, build a life with you. And this whole idea of a deadline is ridiculous. To be honest, I'm not sure if I'm going to show up on Saturday or not. Maybe Bradley and Elaine are right. Maybe I've already waited long enough. Maybe I should just move on.*

The voice scared Robert. He could hear in it the real possibility that he would never see her again. Or if he did, it would be years from now at some cocktail party when he was the rumpled, eccentric, bachelor has-been writer and she was the elegant mother of three with her work featured in the Style section of the *Times*. This time he left a message. "It's me. I just wanted to say I still love you. I'm doing story time at the library again on Saturday, but I'll leave at eleven and be waiting for you just like we agreed. And maybe we can take a walk in the park, because I have a story to tell you." It was the first time he had verbalized his need to tell Rebecca his buried secrets.

With nothing else to do, rather than waste his time watching comedy clips on YouTube and not laughing at them, which he had done a lot of over the past few months, Robert logged into a digital newspaper archive and began reading stories from William Randolph Hearst's *New York Evening Journal* published in 1906. Though the articles had no bylines, Robert liked to think Thomas De Peyster had written some of them. He chose, at random, the first week of October and was surprised to find several stories that seemed almost drawn from the pages of children's adventure books like the Tremendous Trio.

On October 2, the paper published an article about Lieutenant Frank P. Lahm, an American who had won a long-distance balloon race beginning in Paris. He had traveled 415 miles, across the English Channel and much of the length of England, to land on the edge of the North Sea in Yorkshire.

Two days later came an article about Colonel Max Fleischman and his wife, newlyweds from Cincinnati who had spent four months exploring the far north, prevented only by pack ice from arriving at King William Island, Canada. Their party included at least one other married couple, who seemed to enjoy hunting and dressing in leather and sheepskin. After four months in the Arctic, they had returned in order to watch an automobile race. Colonel Fleischman had brought a polar bear cub back with him as a pet.

October 5 brought the tale of another couple exploring the icy north—Stephen Tasker and his "young bride," who had traveled by dogsled farther north in Labrador than any "white man" ever had before. They had left some months ago and had been presumed dead until Tasker's mother received a telegram attesting to their safety. When warned before the expedition that she could face death at every turn, Mrs. Tasker said only that she wished to accompany her husband.

The next day, Louis Wagner, a Frenchman, won the third annual running of the Vanderbilt Cup, the Long Island automobile race that had brought the Fleischmans and their friends back from the Arctic. He finished the 297-mile race in just over 290 minutes. Over 250,000 New Yorkers traveled out from the city to line the twenty-seven-mile course and fill the grandstands at the finish line. Robert could imagine Tom Swift or the Motor Boys or even the Tremendous Trio competing in a race like this.

All of these stories—of amateur exploration in the Arctic when man had not yet reached the North Pole, of balloon and car races when such competitions were new and novel—had taken place in the span of a single randomly chosen week in October 1906. Robert began to see not just the Tremendous Trio, but all the early twentieth-century adventure series, in a broader context. Yes, he had been delighted by these adventures as a boy, but at the time they had been written, real adventures were splashed across the front pages almost every day. Explorers would reach both the North and South Poles for the first time during the years that Dexter Cornwall and Buck Larson and Neptune B. Smythe were writing. Powered flight had begun just a few years earlier. The Explorers Club had been founded in 1904. When the Tremendous Trio books were published, radio and motion pictures were exciting new technologies.

If a young married couple could take a dogsled across Labrador, reaching places no non-native had ever gone; if an American balloonist could land on the front page and a Frenchman driving at sixty miles an hour could draw a quarter of a million people to the side of a dusty road on Long Island—then why couldn't a teenage boy pilot a submarine or fly an airplane; why couldn't a circus acrobat save a group of children in a hurricane; why couldn't the Tremendous Trio fly round the world or navigate over Niagara Falls or explore the darkest reaches of the Amazon?

Those series books, which had seemed so outrageously fanciful when Robert first encountered them, suddenly seemed much more real, and the most realistic of them all were the Tremendous Trio books. In those three volumes, Dexter and Buck and Neptune seemed to take pains to avoid the outrageous, to present science and discovery as they might reasonably be, and yet, even within those strictures, they offered amazing adventures.

Those articles about amateur Arctic exploration reminded Robert of

Through the Air to the North Pole. It had been the book in which he had first found, as he got older, the clunky prose that characterized those series books beginning to wear thin. Or maybe he just didn't want to hang out with his father instead of with his friends. On his fourteenth birthday his father had appeared in his room, waving Pop Pop's copy of *Through the Air to the North Pole.*

"How about a few chapters for old times' sake," he said.

"It's so awful, Dad," said Robbie.

"You didn't used to think so."

"Yeah, well, I didn't used to have friends and actual, you know, stuff to do."

"What stuff do you have to do on your birthday that doesn't leave time for a chapter or two with your old man?"

"I'm playing Dungeons and Dragons," said Robbie. "And I'm already late." And with that, he had shouldered past his father, knocking *Through the Air to the North Pole* from his hand onto the floor.

That moment had, more than any other perhaps, led to everything that followed. Robert wanted to reach across time and shake his teenage self by the shoulders and tell him not to be such an ass. Spend twenty minutes with your father reading a book and you might be able to avoid everything. But that instinct, to reach out to his former self, made him wonder: Was he punishing himself for a crime committed by someone else? Was thirty-four-year-old Robert Parrish the same person as fourteen-year-old Robbie? Was it time he returned his mother's phone calls and talked openly about the past and allowed himself to be happy?

Robert thought how much his father would have enjoyed reading these old newspaper articles that seemed ripped from the pages of the Great Marvel series. He snapped off his computer at two a.m. and fell asleep wondering how he might incorporate into his modern retellings of the Tremendous Trio that ever-present sense of possibility that pervaded the world of 1906.

XXVI

CARNEGIE HALL,
THE DAY CAMILLE SAINT-SAËNS PLAYED BEETHOVEN

After Dreamland, Magda was not surprised to discover that Tom had left town. She had not seen him since that day. She heard from him in mid-November, when an envelope postmarked "Chicago" and addressed to Mary Stone arrived on her desk at Pickering Brothers. She recognized Tom's handwriting, and inside found a ticket to a Sunday afternoon concert at Carnegie Hall with an unsigned note reading, *I sent the other ticket to Gene.* Magda liked the idea of seeing Gene, especially at a concert, where little conversation would be necessary. She missed him, and though she knew it might be hard for him to see her, she didn't want all that had happened at Dreamland, and all of Gene's unspoken secrets, to ruin their friendship. She had, as the weeks passed, become resigned to the truth of what Tom had told her, however cruelly—that Gene would never love her in the way a husband loves a wife. But, even with that knowledge hovering in the air between them, she thought she could bear to see him. Magda hoped they could find a way to be friends that wouldn't feel awkward. The concert was in honor of Camille Saint-Saëns, the featured soloist that afternoon. Tom probably bought the tickets weeks ago, before Dreamland, when he pictured November as an altogether different month.

Magda took the Sixth Avenue El up to Fifty-Eighth Street and walked around the corner to Carnegie Hall. Without Tom or Gene by her side, she felt out of place among the stunningly dressed men and women who streamed into the elegant auditorium. She had worn her finest dress, but she imagined many of the people who surrounded her had servants who dressed better than she did. This was Tom's world, she thought. No matter how far she had come from Kleindeutschland, she could not imagine ever fitting in here.

Magda's seat was near the center of the first balcony, allowing her a perfect view not only of the stage but of the cream of New York sitting below and around her. She arrived almost a half hour early and sat quietly as the seats filled. Her heart raced every time she saw a gentleman's shoes appear at the top of the balcony stairs. But every time those shoes belonged to a gentleman who was not Gene. The lights dimmed and the orchestra tuned their instruments as Magda slumped into her seat, resigned to the fact that, just because she felt ready to see Gene and to pretend that everything was fine, didn't mean he felt the same way. Then, as the first notes of music rang out in the crowded hall, she felt someone slip into the empty seat beside her.

"Sorry I'm late," whispered Gene.

Magda felt a weight lift from her shoulders and relaxed into the music. At intermission, Gene excused himself to go to the gentlemen's lounge, but Magda didn't care. She could understand if he didn't want to talk to her yet. She was just happy to have him sitting beside her in the dark as the music washed over them.

But after the concert, as the crowds poured out onto Fifty-Seventh Street, they did talk, if only briefly.

"Have you heard anything from Tom?" said Gene.

"Just the ticket," said Magda.

"He wrote me a note. Not much—just to say he took a newspaper job in Chicago. And to say he was sorry."

"It was a horrible thing he did," said Magda.

"I just hate you had to find out that way," said Gene. "I should have told you."

"You would have told me," said Magda. "Eventually. He didn't need to do that."

"Don't stay angry with him forever," said Gene. "It will only hurt you."

"Are you still angry with him?" said Magda.

Gene smiled ruefully, but did not answer.

"Suppose we talk about something else," said Magda, as they emerged onto the sidewalk and into a cold wind.

"I'd love to," said Gene, "but I really should get going. I've got a job now, with United Electric. Crazy hours." Gene leaned forward and gave Magda a light kiss on the cheek. He had never kissed her before. "We'll get together again soon." And with that he turned and disappeared in a sea of black coats. Magda stood for a moment, letting the crowd swirl around her like the waters of a violent stream, then allowed herself to be swept along toward the El station. As she watched the lights flash by the windows of the train, she felt a chink in the armor of her anger at Tom. He, after all, had orchestrated her reunion with Gene.

On the first Saturday in December, Magda and Gene stood on the sidewalk outside Putnam's on Twenty-Third Street. She had dropped him a note suggesting that they meet there. She knew Gene would want to see what stood on the shelves inside.

"How did they turn out?" said Gene.

"Beautifully," said Magda. Her job dealt strictly with Mr. Lipscomb's immediate needs and the handling of incoming and outgoing correspondence from his office, but in the case of these three books, she had sneaked upstairs and had long conversations with Max Stein, the man creating the artwork for the cloth covers and for the dust jackets. Max worked for a magazine based in the same building, and Mr. Lipscomb hired him on a contract basis whenever he needed an illustration. With no instructions from Mr. Lipscomb other than to read the books and paint the pictures, Max happily took guidance from Magda, assuming her instructions came from Lipscomb. The publisher had not been thrilled with some of the choices Max had made, but he was too parsimonious to ask the artist to paint new versions, so Magda had gotten her way and the results were, she thought, perfect.

Magda had not seen the finished books until she had found them at Putnam's a few days earlier. For the past two weeks she had stopped there every day after work, checking the shelves just in case. Now she and Gene went inside and made their way to the children's section where a case of series books greeted them, most, they knew, published through the syndicate of Edward Stratemeyer. But sprinkled among the Great Marvel adventures and Rover Boys and other Stratemeyer series, they caught sight of the occasional Pickering title. Magda carefully scanned the display and pulled out three books, sparkling in their freshly printed dust jackets.

"We did it," said Gene softly, as Magda laid the books on a table. He picked up *Alice Gold, Girl Inventor* and smiled. "She looks just as I imagined."

Alice, to Mr. Lipscomb's disgruntlement, was not depicted on the cover holding a parasol and wearing a flouncy white dress, but holding a wrench and clad in a pair of greasy blue coveralls. Her hair was pulled back and a tiny bead of sweat glistened on her forehead as she leaned over a collection of gears, rods, and other mysterious metal items.

If Alice Gold looked somewhat like a boy on the jacket of her book, Dan Dawson looked ever so slightly like a girl on the jacket for *Storm from the Sea*. Magda had been inspired by the Florenz acrobats she had seen the previous year at Madison Square Garden, and especially by the little boy who dressed as a girl. While Mr. Lipscomb would not allow her to include this detail in the text of her book (for he did, in the end, read through the three typescripts she presented him), she did manage to tip a hat to the little Florenz boy in the illustration of Dan Dawson on the dust jacket. The picture showed him stepping onto a high trapeze, the colorful stripes of the big top behind him and the tiny figures of the amazed audience members far below. Dan's hair was just a little longer than one might expect for a boy of his age, and his costume had an element that could easily be mistaken for a skirt. He had the soft, feminine features of a boy several years younger than himself, or of a girl, or, Magda thought as she looked proudly at the picture, of Gene.

"Is that Tom's face?" said Gene, pointing to the cover of *Frank Fairfax and the Search for El Dorado*.

"I thought I did a good job of telling the artist what he looked like," said Magda. "I just closed my eyes and remembered the summer." Describing Tom's face to Max Stein while remembering the happiest days of that summer had, Magda thought, been a step toward forgiving Tom. She still had many steps to go.

"Would you like to get some coffee?" said Magda.

"Magda," said Gene, turning to her. "You know what Tom told you?"

"It's okay," said Magda. "You don't have to explain."

"I just want you to understand," said Gene. "It's who I am. And I'm sorry I wasn't honest with you about that, but it doesn't mean I don't care for you, it just means that I can't . . ."

"I know," said Magda.

"Why don't we walk," said Gene. "I like to stroll the Ladies' Mile at Christmas to see all the window displays."

"Sounds lovely," said Magda.

"But first, I'm going to buy a copy of this book," said Gene, holding up *Alice Gold*. "Do you have one yet?"

"I bought one of each a few days ago."

"Well, give your *Alice Gold* to a friend. I want to give you one signed by the author. And I want you to sign your book for me."

"How literary," said Magda.

Gene took two copies of *Alice Gold* and one of *Dan Dawson* to the counter and joined the line for the cashier. The stores were crowded with Christmas shoppers, and he had to wait a few minutes. Magda looked back at the shelves. Putnam's had only a few copies of each of the Pickering titles in stock. Mr. Lipscomb had been having a harder and harder time competing for shelf space in the big stores with all the Stratemeyer books.

"Here you are," said Gene, handing Magda a book wrapped in brown paper. "No peeking until Christmas."

"I'll never be able to guess what it is."

"I had to borrow a pen from the cashier. Here, you can sign *Dan Dawson* for me."

Magda took the book from Gene and laid it on a display table, opening to the blank first page. She had never signed a book before—it seemed like the sort of thing that Mark Twain or H. G. Wells would do. That she was raising a pen to put her autograph in a book she had written suddenly made the act of creation much more real to her. This simple act validated her work in a deeper way than depositing the check from Pickering Brothers in her bank account ever could. Before she had even made a single stroke she felt a deep sense of pride. She wrote, *For Gene, who is more like Dan Dawson than he will ever know. Fondly, Magda.* She had thought about putting *with love*, but she didn't want Gene to feel uncomfortable.

"I'm really an author now," she said, handing the book to Gene.

"You are," he said.

The Ladies' Mile shopping district ran from roughly Twenty-Fourth Street to Fourteenth Street along Sixth, Fifth, Madison, and Park Avenues. Here most of the major department stores and high-end specialty retailers had built their grand emporia in the late nineteenth century. Though some, like Macy's and B. Altman, had now moved farther uptown, this was still the center of the city's upscale retail business, and every store had a fancy window display designed to lure in Christmas shoppers. Magda and Gene strolled down Sixth Avenue, stopping to look at these windows. O'Neill Adams, which took up two blocks between Twenty-Second and Twentieth streets featured everything from jewelry to silk umbrellas, sewing machines, furniture, and lace curtains in their displays. Both Cammeyer and Franzin & Appenheim invited customers to visit Santa Claus while shopping for shoes. At Simpson Crawford Dry Goods, Gene insisted on going in, passing under the imposing granite columns and the Beaux Arts facade that glowered at its lesser neighbors.

"Have you ever been in here?" said Gene.

"Never," said Magda, who wasn't sure she could afford anything in the store.

They walked through the soaring atrium, with its cast-iron railings on level after level of balconies finally giving way to statues of classical figures just below the skylight. Gene led Magda to the foot of a staircase that was like only one other she had ever seen in her life.

"Moving stairs in a department store," she marveled, as he took her hand and helped her step on.

"Just like Shoot the Chutes at Dreamland," said Gene. "The mechanics are actually fairly simple." As they rode up and then down, Gene explained how the moving stairs worked. Magda nodded, and smiled, and stared wide-eyed at the vast array of expensive goods and the carriage trade who came to buy them.

Despite the crowds and the rattle of the El trains overhead, Magda and Gene managed to chat as they strolled downtown. He told her about how United Electric used alternating current, and how Mr. Tesla had written a letter attesting to his abilities. She spoke of Mr. Lipscomb's hope for the Christmas season, that the new books would finally put Pickering Brothers on the map. "Surprisingly, he actually understands that our books are better than what Stratemeyer produces," she said. "He just doesn't know if that will translate into sales."

"And when will he decide if he wants more?" said Gene.

"More of Dan and Alice and Frank? Probably after he sees the sales figures for the holiday season. Will you have time to write another book if you're working now?"

"I think so," said Gene. "I can always work in the evenings. I've . . . curtailed my social life."

"Because Tom is gone?"

"And other reasons," said Gene. He did not know if Magda noticed the thin layer of powder he wore on his face—not because he wished to draw the attention of men interested in such things, but because he wanted to cover up the bruises. A month ago, he had suffered another beating, this one severe enough to break two ribs and leave his face swollen and blackened. At work he had told a story about being struck by an automobile on Broadway—hurled against the paving stones and fearing for his life. He *had* feared for his life, but not because of an automobile. After that night, he had sworn to himself—no more. No more men in his rooms, no more taking the streetcar to Coney Island to seek out the seediest of the seedy night clubs, no more trying to forget Tom in the grip of men who used him and cast him violently aside. He would concentrate on his work, on science, and, if Mr. Lipscomb wanted, he would write another book. But as far as his other desires, he would pretend they did not exist. He would force that part of his life into the darkest recesses of his being and leave it there.

They reached Siegel's at the corner of Fourteenth Street, and Magda gasped when she saw the window display.

"You knew about this, didn't you?" she said with delight. "That's why you walked me here."

"I read about it in their newspaper advertisement," said Gene, "but I hadn't seen it until now. It's most impressive."

Laid out in front of them, across four huge windows, was a vast model of Coney Island, shown as it appeared, according to the sign hanging above it, "in the good old summertime." Here were bathers crowding the beach, the roller coasters and thrill rides and sideshows of Steeplechase Park and Luna Park, and, glistening white in a window all of its own, Dreamland.

"I wasn't sure I should show you," said Gene. "If the memories are happy or painful."

"Both," said Magda quietly, as she gazed at the miniature buildings, the perfect re-creation of her own memory of that day. The elaborate architecture of Dreamland had been copied to perfection—at a cost of five thousand dollars, bragged a sign in the display. Beacon Tower reigned high above the boardwalk, the water of the lagoon glistening below it. The model rendered every attraction in exquisite detail, all crowded with the tiniest revelers one could hope to see. Magda stood for a long time, reliving the events of that day, doing her best to forget how it had ended. She felt certain that she would forever remember the summer that had led to Dreamland as the happiest time of her life.

Gene laid a hand gently on her shoulder—a gesture that once would have given her a thrill but which she now understood was only a sign of friendship and support. "I just thought you might want to see it," he said.

"Thank you," said Magda, reaching up and taking his hand in hers just long enough to give it a squeeze. "Thank you so much."

When Magda returned home that night, she decided she could not wait until Christmas, so she ripped the brown paper off of the copy of *Alice Gold, Girl Inventor* that Gene had given her, and opened the front cover to read his inscription.

To Dexter Cornwall from Buck Larson,
in memory of a summer day. Christmas 1906.

Magda clasped the book to her chest and wept at last.

XXVII

NEW-YORK HISTORICAL SOCIETY, 2010

Access to the De Peyster album in the New-York Historical Society library was by appointment only and Robert didn't have an appointment. A polite man sitting behind a broad desk explained that the reading room had limited space and that the next available appointment was next Thursday. Frustrated, Robert left the library with the assurance that the man behind the desk would call him if a researcher happened to cancel an appointment.

He felt too nervous to go home. He didn't want to read more newspaper articles or vainly search for clues about the authors of the Tremendous Trio in the text of the books. He wanted answers. He wanted to discover, if not the complete biographies of Dexter Cornwall and Buck Larson and Neptune B. Smythe, at least *something* about them. He didn't expect to stumble upon an unpublished manuscript of *The Last Adventure of the Tremendous Trio*, but he wanted a few more clues—hints, at least, about how the story might play out. He didn't need to answer every question, but he wanted to answer some. And he was starting to formulate a plan about how he might use those answers and where the unanswered questions could lead him. After months of inaction, this crisis—Rebecca threatening to leave for good—had finally goaded him into action; and this chase after the silly mysteries of his childhood had taken on importance not only because it had given him some purpose, but also because it offered a doorway into what he needed to confront if he was going to win Rebecca back.

With nothing else to do, he walked laps around the neo-Romanesque brownstone monster that was the American Museum of Natural History. This museum had been here in 1906, he thought, as he marched up to Eighty-First Street, across to Columbus, and then back down to Seventy-Seventh. The original Victorian building was all but invisible now behind the additions of the past century, but this institution had inspired, and even sponsored, the explorers of that age. From here expeditions went forth to the four corners of the earth—and to the poles at its top and bottom.

Robert and Rebecca had never visited the Museum of Natural History. Rebecca had little interest in dead animals and Robert had scrupulously avoided the museum since his visit there with his father a few weeks after their spat on Robbie's fourteenth birthday. He had reluctantly agreed to the excursion only because his friend Kevin, who organized the Dungeons and Dragons group, was laid up with the flu.

"It's raining out," Robbie heard his mother say from the next room when his father told her the plan. "Why don't you just stay here and read?"

"He doesn't want to read anymore," said his father. "He's a teenager."

Robbie had heard this before. It was so annoying. Of course he was a teenager. He still read the Tremendous Trio books; he just didn't want to do it with his father anymore. Now he read them secretly, when his parents had gone to sleep. Reading stories out loud was for little kids.

"I thought we could find all the animals that the Tremendous Trio see in the Amazon," said Robbie's father fifteen minutes into the awkward silence of the train ride.

Robbie thought the descriptions of various frightening beasts were the most boring parts of the book, like the endless catalogue of fauna in *Twenty Thousand Leagues under the Sea*, but he answered his father only with a wordless grunt.

Robbie sulked his way through the day. "There's nobody here but little kids," he complained every time he saw someone that looked even a few months younger than himself. When others got between him and the display cases he would carp, "It's so crowded I can't see anything." When they found themselves alone in a room, his mantra became, "This stuff is so boring."

$$\sim$$

Most fathers would have given up, thought Robert, but not his. He had the stubborn streak inherited from Pop Pop and didn't rise to the bait of Robbie trying to pick a fight. He ignored the complaining and instead of arguing decided to up the ante, planning more and more exciting excursions in an attempt to hold on to his son's affection. If he had just shown some interest in that damn museum, thought Robert as he trudged past the grand facade on Central Park West, maybe everything would have turned out fine.

On Robert's fifth lap around the museum, as he was weighing whether to stop and join the line at the Shake Shack, his phone rang. There had been a cancellation. Five minutes later Robert was back in the Historical Society library. He filled out the request form for the album, and Ralph, the man at the desk, showed him to the one empty seat in the library's reading room.

The same Ionic columns he had seen outside surrounded the space, but while the gray granite columns on the front of the building felt cold and out of place, these cream-colored columns fit right into the grand neoclassical hall. A skylight fifty feet overhead let the cold winter light mix with the warm glow from brass lamps and hanging fixtures, all of it gleaming off polished oak tables. Two huge stained-glass windows were set into the east wall. It felt like the library of some grand college in Oxford or Cambridge.

After a few minutes, a librarian brought Robert an oblong black volume bound in cloth and stamped in gold on the front cover with the word *Photographs*.

"Please handle the pages by the corners, and don't touch the photographs," said the librarian. "And take notes only in pencil." Robert had come prepared for this last rule and had already set a notebook and pencil on the table. A buff-colored card with a description of the item lay on top of the volume. Robert copied out the words: *Album of photographs and memorabilia, most associated with New York City, collected and signed by Thomas De Peyster, ca. 1906. Gift of Sarah Thomas, 1977.*

Robert could hardly believe he was looking at something that had belonged to Dexter Cornwall or Neptune B. Smythe, or possibly both. His fingers trembled as he set the card aside and gently opened the volume. On the inside of the front cover was the name "Thomas De Peyster" in an elegant hand. Robert didn't know exactly what he had expected inside the album—perhaps a portrait labeled *Neptune B. Smythe* or a plot summary of *The Last Adventure of the Tremendous Trio*. What he hadn't expected was a menu from Childs restaurant, with the date July 13, 1906, written at the bottom. Determined to give his full attention to every item in the album, Robert dutifully read the menu. There seemed nothing significant about corned beef hash or graham crackers and milk. The menu had been pasted onto the paper album page but had come loose at the bottom and on most of two sides. As carefully as he could, so as not to hasten its complete detachment, Robert turned the page.

The next page held two black-and-white photographs, each just over two inches square. They showed two different men, dressed in formal attire, posed in front of the same fireplace. Beneath the photos a caption read: "Gene and 'Mr. Marcus Stone of Philadelphia.'" Both the men in the picture had rather soft features, but neither held a copy of a Dan Dawson or Frank Fairfax book. Robert moved on.

The next several pages held a variety of uninteresting memorabilia: a ticket stub from a baseball game between the New York Giants and the Pittsburgh Pirates together with a baseball card for a player named Cy Seymour; programs from the plays *The Social Whirl* and *The Girl of the Golden West*; a postcard of the actress Evelyn Nesbit; and postcards and photographs of several New York landmarks, including the Flatiron Building, the old Madison Square Garden on Twenty-Sixth Street, and the Metropolitan Museum of Art. Most of these items were captioned with dates in the summer of 1906. Robert dutifully took notes on everything, becoming more and more convinced that he had arrived at another dead end.

With waning enthusiasm, he turned a page about halfway through the album. He almost couldn't process the perfection of what he saw. Hands trembling with excitement, Robert laid down his pencil, leaned back slightly in his chair, and gazed in amazement at the page. Before him lay the Rosetta stone of the Tremendous Trio mystery.

He had a sudden and almost painful desire to share this moment with Rebecca, but of course he had kept secret all that had led him to this point, so even if she was at home waiting for him, this spectacular discovery would mean nothing to her. He wished he had shared all this with her years ago: his fascination with series books, the mystery of the Tremendous Trio, even the disastrous roller-coaster ride of his relationship with his father. As Robert stared at the page in front of him, memories of his happiest moments flooded back—all experiences made happier because of Rebecca. The acceptance of his novel, the glowing reviews—these events hadn't seemed real until he shared them with her. He ached that, because of his own guardedness, he had no way of letting her share the thrill of what lay before him.

Two similar photographs showed a woman and two men posed in front of the Bethesda Fountain in Central Park. In the top photograph they posed seriously, with stern looks on their faces. The woman held a parasol and one of the men had his hand in his coat, Napoleon-style. In the second picture, they stood in strange poses, the woman with one arm over her head. They all smiled broadly. Clearly, they were friends, with senses of humor. Below the first image, a caption read: "Eugene Pinkney, Magda Hertzenberger, Thomas De Peyster." The second photo was captioned "Buck Larson, Dexter Cornwall, Neptune B. Smythe." At the bottom of the page, in much larger script, were the words, "The Gods and Goddess of Children's Books."

XXVIII

The first indication of his approach was the whistling of tugboats, soon joined by other craft tooting and snorting. The sound moved toward Magda like a wave, and soon another noise melded with it—a sound like a gasoline-powered automobile, but deeper, a staccato so rapid that its individual percussions were nearly undetectable. And then she saw him. He wore a gray business suit with a vest and a simple cap on his head, looking for all the world like a man who might be striding down Broadway on the way to an office on a crisp autumn morning. Except he wasn't striding down Broadway; he was hanging in the air more than two hundred feet above the Hudson River. Magda waved madly and cried out with excitement as Wilbur Wright flew his aeroplane straight up the river, gaining altitude as he passed by the end of Twenty-Third Street where she stood in a crowd near the river's edge. She could feel the wind blowing stiffly downstream, yet Wright seemed to travel faster than any automobile or train. The crowd, which had been struck breathless at the first sight of the flying machine, cheered wildly as Wright rounded the bulge of Manhattan and disappeared up the river.

The papers for the morning of October 4, 1909, had said the aviator would attempt a flight from Governor's Island up the Hudson to Grant's Tomb and back, a distance of some twenty miles. Now the crowd waited to see if he would return safely, each wondering how quickly an aeroplane could make a trip that would take more than an hour by elevated train.

Wright's appearance in the New York skies was part of the Hudson-Fulton Celebration, a two-week commemoration of the three hundredth anniversary of Henry Hudson's arrival in New York Harbor and the centenary of Robert Fulton's steamboat. Surprisingly, Mr. Lipscomb had allowed Magda to take the morning off to watch the flight. More than a million other New Yorkers had made similar plans. A week earlier she had watched a massive fireworks display from Riverside Park, and two nights ago she had seen the Carnival Parade, marveling at the display of floats on the theme of "Music, Literature, and Art."

As she watched the floats in that parade depicting folklore and fairy tales, Magda could not help imagining what a float in honor of Dan Dawson, Alice Gold, and Frank Fairfax might look like. Three years had passed since those heroes had made their debut, and while no one could argue that they had made any great mark on American culture, Magda knew from the fan mail she answered that the exploits of Dan, Alice, and Frank had entertained and even inspired at least a few children. Mr. Lipscomb had, with only slight reluctance and under constant prodding from Magda, commissioned a new book in each series in 1907 and 1908, but had taken a hiatus from those series in 1909.

Magda had finally written to Tom in Chicago the summer after Dreamland. She had still felt bitter toward him, betrayed by the way he had cast a shadow over their summer together, but she needed his help. She was surprised to find that her need for his advice tempered her anger, and though she did not exactly write him in a spirit of friendship, she did feel herself softening as she read his reply. Tom had said he might help her with the rescue scenes in *Dan Dawson and the Great Earthquake*, her second book, and she had written asking for that assistance. Tom had answered Magda's request with the suggestion that she mail him any sections of the book dealing with the earthquake itself for him to look over. He returned each section with additions and emendations, and Magda had been impressed with his ideas about how to depict the earthquake and its aftermath. With each returned chapter, he included a short note—*Hope you are doing well, I think of you often. Say hello to "Mr.*

Pickering" for me—and with each note, Magda felt her bitterness eroding. The note included in the final packet read, *I know your book will do well. You were always the best writer of the three of us. I hope someday you can forgive me for Dreamland. I doubt I'll ever forgive myself.*

When Magda again needed Tom's help on her third book, *Dan Dawson and the Big Fire*, which was loosely based on the fire at the Iroquois Theatre in Chicago in 1903, he copied out a stack of articles about the fire from the newspaper archive and included a note reading, *Hope we meet again someday. There are no goddesses in Chicago.* While she would never forget Dreamland and what Tom had done, Magda came to realize that Gene was right, she was only hurting herself by staying angry with Tom. Though she wasn't sure she completely forgave him, she found that as she read his note she could once again think of him with fondness.

Tom mailed his own books about Frank Fairfax to Pickering Brothers as completed typescripts. *Frank Fairfax and the Lost City of Atlantis* and *Frank Fairfax among the Mayans* were well written and tightly plotted, if a little less original in their details than *Frank Fairfax and the Search for El Dorado*. Magda knew that neither Mr. Lipscomb nor the average reader of Pickering books would notice the difference, but she couldn't help thinking, wistfully, that she, Gene, and Tom worked better together than they did alone.

Gene, too, had written the next two books in the Alice Gold series, *Alice Gold and the Museum Mystery* and *Alice Gold and the Mysterious Visitor*, without much help from Magda and, it seemed to her, without much enthusiasm. As Lipscomb requested, Alice's activities remained fairly domestic—though she did venture into the Metropolitan Museum of Art for the title mystery of the second book. In his manuscripts—for Gene sent his books to Magda handwritten and she typed them for him—she could sense his frustration, his desire to have Alice burst the bonds of domesticity and show the world what she could really do. Magda understood Alice perhaps more deeply than Gene knew, and she suspected that Alice's success—for Buck Larson received more fan mail than either of the other two—was because American girls of 1909 felt the same way she did. They felt trapped by the roles they had been assigned, but desperate to fly.

While Tom never, to her knowledge, returned to visit New York, Magda saw Gene on occasion. They had met at Putnam's to admire each new round of books and had had a late dinner at Childs perhaps a half dozen times in the past couple of years. He worked long hours at his job, he said. He claimed to be happy, but to Magda he looked tired and pale. He had lost weight, and his clothes hung loosely on his shoulders. Magda had closed the door to the part of herself that had been in love with Gene, but she still cared for him. She worried that he pined for Tom, and while she understood the ache for a man one could never have, she had moved on; she feared Gene might never do so.

As Magda gazed skyward, waiting for Wilbur Wright to return, she wondered if Gene was watching the flight from somewhere else in Manhattan. She suddenly remembered his saying that he wanted Alice Gold to invent a flying machine, one that could take her around the world. If this many people turned out to watch a man fly ten miles up the Hudson River and back, how many, Magda wondered, would celebrate in the fictional streets if Alice Gold flew around the world? What might *that* say to the girls of America?

Of course, flying around the world would take more than just an inventor. The skills of an explorer might be useful, not to mention the courage of a daredevil. As the sound in the sky announced that Wilbur had safely turned around and was soon to fly back past the crowd that surrounded her, Magda felt a bolt of inspiration.

What if Alice Gold *did* get out of the house and build a flying machine? What if Frank Fairfax went on a journey of exploration more daring than any before? What if Dan Dawson rescued people from a stampede in Africa *and* a sandstorm in Arabia *and* a tidal wave on a Pacific island all in the same book? What if Alice and Dan and Frank teamed up in a new series, a series called the Three Adventurers, or the Wonder Team, or, better yet, the Tremendous Trio? And what if these books—for surely the market for such a grand idea would support multiple volumes—were written by a team of authors: Buck Larson, Dexter Cornwall, and Neptune B. Smythe working together?

The aeroplane flew lower on its return journey, so low Magda could almost make out the face of the pilot. But, with the wind at his back, Wilbur Wright flashed by at an unbelievable speed. The crowds cheered once more, but before the aeroplane was out of sight, Magda was rushing up Twenty-Third Street. She passed her rooming house, crossed Eighth

Avenue, and ducked into the Western Union Telegraph Office. She didn't want to take the time to send a letter, and besides, Gene, the master of electricity, would appreciate a telegram. She scribbled her message on the order form and handed it to the clerk:

Brilliant idea for Alice, Dan, and Frank. Childs 7pm. Magda

"It will never work," said Gene.

"You mean Alice can't design an aeroplane that can carry three people and travel across oceans?"

"Oh, that part's easy," said Gene. "To build a machine like that on the principles the Wrights have pioneered would only take money, and Alice has plenty of that. No, I mean you'll never lure Tom back to New York."

"I might," said Magda.

"You're not going to lie to him," said Gene.

"What, you mean tell him I love him? No. But I can tell him I forgive him."

"It might not be you he's running away from," said Gene. "Maybe he's just being kind to me."

"It's been three years," said Magda. "Don't you think we can all just be friends? After all, you and I seem to have made friendship work."

"There's not a tiny part of you that still wants me to be different?" said Gene.

Magda knew that part of her was more than tiny, that given the slightest encouragement she would be back in love with Gene in an instant, but some things, for the sake of friendship, were best left unspoken.

"No," she said firmly. "You are who you are and I would never try to change that. I can't be in love with you, so I'm happy to have you as a friend. Don't you think Tom will feel the same way?"

"Even if he does, that doesn't mean he'll come back to New York. His career is in Chicago now."

"We could do it through the mail. You and me working together here and Tom sending us his chapters."

"It wouldn't be the same," said Gene.

"I know it wouldn't be the same," said Magda testily. "I don't expect it to be the same. But it would be better than this. Tom off in Chicago and the two of us having lunch every few months."

"It was a special summer," said Gene, "but it's over."

"Forget about the summer," said Magda. "Forget about Tom being in love with me and me being in love with you and you . . ."

"It's all right," said Gene softly, "you can say it."

"You being in love with Tom," said Magda, lowering her voice. "What about the book? Do you think it's a good idea?"

"*The Tremendous Trio*?" said Gene. He took a long drink of coffee and drummed his fingers on the table for a moment. "That's the problem. I think it's a fantastic idea."

"Really?" said Magda, her anger melting away.

"But they shouldn't go around the world in the first book. Save that for volume three. Start out with some adventure closer to home. Something that uses all their skills."

"So you'll do it?" said Magda.

"Not without Tom," said Gene. "And like I said, you'll never get Tom."

"Let me get Lipscomb first," said Magda. "Then I'll worry about Tom."

⌇

Magda knew better than to suggest new ideas to Mr. Lipscomb during the Christmas season and she knew, too, that after the holidays he would be making his annual trip of a month or two to visit his family in England. Once he returned, he would be frantic to catch up on business for a few weeks. That meant there was no point in floating her idea about combining the forces of Alice Gold, Dan Dawson, and Frank Fairfax until March or April. That gave her some time to soften up Tom, and to work on an outline for volume one of *The Tremendous Trio*.

She started with a Christmas card, a picture, ringed in holly, of a family arriving at a farmhouse in a horse-drawn sleigh. On the back she wrote:

Dear Tom,

Last year you wrote that you hoped I could forgive you. It took some time, but I have, and Gene has, too. We miss you and hope to see you in 1910.

Fondly,

Magda

Tom replied with a card showing Santa sitting on a bench in his toyshop, looking over his naughty and nice list. *Hoping you have a happy holiday*, he wrote. *Give my best to Gene if you see him*. It wasn't exactly a promise that Tom would rush back from Chicago to see them, but it was a start.

While Mr. Lipscomb was gone, Magda answered correspondence, including the fan mail that always peaked in the weeks after Christmas, dealt with visitors to the office, and did whatever else Mr. Lipscomb asked of her in his near daily telegrams. One day, with the office quiet, she threaded a sheet of paper into her Hammond and typed: *The Tremendous Trio*. Gene had said to keep them closer to home in the first volume, so she needed someplace not too far from New York where they could have an adventure that combined something a daredevil might do with the potential for invention and rescue. She crept into Mr. Lipscomb's office, where he had a map of the United States on the wall with pins pressed into all the spots where bookstores carried the Pickering series. Most of the pins were clustered around New York City. She moved her eyes in concentric semicircles around the city, moving farther away until she spotted it, four hundred miles to the northwest. After the words *The Tremendous Trio* she typed *at Niagara Falls*.

About the time Lipscomb was sailing for home in March, Magda wrote Tom again, this time on a postcard of the Flatiron Building. *Mr. Lipscomb might have a writing project for the three of us. Could be fun to work together again.*

Tom did not respond for nearly a month. His postcard of the Field Museum bore the message: *Likely to be in lovely Chicago indefinitely. Apologies to Mr. Lipscomb.*

Magda did not plan to give up. In the months since she had first suggested the idea to Gene, the Tremendous Trio had taken root in her mind. They had given her a drive she hadn't felt since the summer of 1906 and that drive had twin motivations. Yes, she wanted to reunite the trio of Gene, Tom, and Magda, but she also wanted to create something wonderful. Something that would both entertain and inspire children. Isn't that what they had all set out to do in the first place? Tom's hiding in Chicago was not about to deter her.

In late April of 1910, Marcus Stone, the author of the Daring Dan Dawson books, sent Julius Lipscomb of Pickering Brothers, Publishers, a telegram saying he had come to New York from Philadelphia and would like to meet to discuss an idea. Magda would have liked Gene's help in transforming into Marcus Stone, who had been hanging in her wardrobe for the past four years untouched, but Gene had sent her a postcard three weeks earlier with the message: *Working on a project at the power plant here for a few months. I'll let you know when I'm back in NY.* While she missed seeing Gene, the coincidence of the postcard meant she had absolutely chosen the right setting for the first Tremendous Trio book. The picture on the front of the card showed Niagara Falls. Gene might not be able to help her transform into Marcus Stone, but he would soon know all about the falls. That wouldn't matter, of course, if she failed to play the role of Marcus Stone convincingly and sell Mr. Lipscomb on the idea of *The Tremendous Trio*.

The first challenge was no challenge at all. Mr. Lipscomb hardly glanced at Marcus Stone after the two "men" shook hands.

"A series that combines heroes?" said Lipscomb, when Mr. Stone had presented his idea.

"Exactly. Stratemeyer hasn't done anything like it, and you could sell books to fans of all three series."

"What sort of adventures would they have?"

Mr. Stone hesitated. He didn't want to give Mr. Lipscomb any details of his ideas, at least not yet. He certainly didn't want to intimate that Alice Gold, whom Lipscomb wanted to stay within the confines of her home or at least her neighborhood, would soon be flying around the world.

"I'd need to discuss that with the other authors, of course, but they would be consistent with the books already published."

"But I'd be paying three authors."

"You'd pay each of us a third as much. After all, we'd each only be writing a third of the book."

"Stratemeyer has three new series coming out this year," said Lipscomb, "College Sports, Motor Girls, and Tom Swift. And he's putting out breeder sets for all three."

"Breeder sets?" said Mr. Stone. Magda knew all about breeder sets, but Mr. Stone would not. Stratemeyer always started each new series with three volumes published simultaneously, so he could build interest more quickly. It involved a bigger initial outlay of expense but also a bigger potential return. Lipscomb had been loath to follow this example, not wanting to spend the money for a set of three volumes that didn't sell. One volume at a time not selling, he said, was more than enough. But now he seemed to have changed his mind.

"If I do this," he said, "I want to do three volumes at once. And I want them for the Christmas market. And I can only pay one hundred dollars per volume."

Magda had no idea if she could convince Tom to take part. She had no idea when Gene would be back in New York. She had, in short, no reason at all to believe that the three of them could write three books in the next five months. But she wasn't about to give up the advantage she had gained in the conversation with Lipscomb. "I think we could provide three volumes in time for Christmas."

"Not this Christmas," said Lipscomb. "I've already set the list for this Christmas. Did it on the ship on the way over. This will be for Christmas 1911."

Magda breathed a sigh of relief. That would give her plenty of time to convince Tom and for Gene to get back to the city. The Tremendous Trio might not see the light of day in 1910, but she could look forward to 1911.

"And will there be another Daring Dan Dawson on the list for this Christmas? Or Alice Gold or Frank Fairfax?" said Mr. Stone. Magda needed to know if they would all be writing individual volumes again this year.

"No," said Lipscomb. "More about sports this year and less about inventions and adventure. And it works out well. It means two years off from Dan Dawson and Alice Gold and Frank Fairfax; that will build anticipation for the new series. I can run advertisements in the back of all my new titles. What did you say you called it?"

"The Tremendous Trio," said Mr. Stone.

"The Tremendous Trio," said Lipscomb, trying out the sound of the words. "I like that."

⌒⌒

Two weeks later Magda had letters from both Gene and Tom responding to the news that Lipscomb wanted a triptych of Tremendous Trio books for the following Christmas. Gene wrote:

> *Magda Dear,*
>
> *Great news that "Marcus Stone" has prolonged the lives of Frank, Alice, and Dan. I may be in Pittsburgh for a few months after I finish here, but should be back in New York no later than New Year's. I think the idea of sending Dan over Niagara in a barrel, invented and built by Alice, is brilliant. And how convenient that Buck Larson is currently residing in earshot of those very falls.*
>
> *I hope your goal in all this is simply to create good books and not to try to recapture the past through a reunion of our own trio. In any case, I doubt you will convince Tom to return to town. I'm sure you could write the books on your own, if it came to that, but know that I will be glad to lend a hand.*
>
> > *Fondly,*
> > *Gene*

Tom's letter was hastily scrawled on the letterhead of the *Chicago Examiner*.

> *Magda,*
>
> *Sounds a grand idea, but I will be in Chicago indefinitely. I'm sure you and Gene will do a great job and I'm happy for you to split the share of Neptune B. Smythe.*
>
> > *Tom*

XXIX

NEW YORK PUBLIC LIBRARY,
WHEN TAFT WAS PRESIDENT

Gene's work in Pittsburgh had led to another job in Detroit and he had been out of the city, and out of touch, for nearly a year. Tom responded to Magda's occasional cards with polite curtness, never showing any interest in either writing another book or returning to New York. Magda's life felt very much as it had in the years before she had met Tom and Gene. Except it didn't. When she climbed the steps to the El, she could see Gene in front of her, reaching out his hand. When she read in the Muhlenberg Library, she could hear Tom whispering to her about Dan Dawson. When she walked in Central Park or read about a baseball game or went to a museum, she could feel them beside her. When she ate at Childs, she could hear their laughter, mingling with her own, drifting over the crowd from the table in the back. Whenever the door to the Pickering Brothers offices opened, she looked up, half expecting to see Tom in his double-breasted suit carrying his silver-handled walking stick. Tom and Gene were everywhere and nowhere. She was both comforted by their presence and saddened by their absence. But the one thing she never felt, even when she had genuinely forgiven Tom and missed him all the more for it, was alone.

Feeling their presence by her side, she had the courage to be unconventional—to wear Marcus Stone's trousers and shirt once in a while on a Saturday just because she felt like it, to go to the theater unescorted and ignore the looks

of disdain from the wives of gentlemen, to stand up to Mr. Lipscomb when
he was being unreasonable, to hail her own taxicab, to ride a bicycle, to have
a drink, and especially to scorn the advances of men whom she knew would
wrest that unconventionality from her, men whom she could tell in ten seconds
of conversation had never read a book, men who would consider her intellect a
liability, her independence a handicap. Tom and Gene had shown her that she
deserved to be more than the background decoration in some other person's
story, that she did not need a husband to feel worthwhile, or successful.

But when, late in April 1911, she received notes from both of "the
boys," as she thought of them, on the same warm spring day, she could not
contain her excitement. Tom and Gene were both returning to New York,
both wanted to see her, and would both be in town in time for a grand
event to which she had been looking forward for years.

To the delight of the fifty thousand people surrounding Magda on the
sidewalks of Fifth Avenue, the predicted rain had not materialized. The sun
shone overhead and the spring breeze wafted away the usual smell of horses
and humanity. It was May 23, 1911, and the gods and goddesses of reading
smiled on New York. Magda could remember when on this site, between
Fortieth and Forty-Second Streets, had stood the Croton Reservoir, a
massive and imposing granite structure that looked vaguely like the walls
of an ancient Egyptian city. How much more beautiful was the building
they had come to dedicate today—the new central library, with its broad
steps passing by two stone lions before leading up to the columned portico.

Neither Magda, nor anyone else in the crowd, paid much attention
when a single car drove up in front of the building and a lone man got out
and mounted the stairs. Surely the dignitaries arriving for the dedication
would not come one at a time and without escorts. This man must be a
library official or an uninteresting functionary. Then, when the man was
halfway up the stairs, someone shouted and Magda, along with the rest of
the crowd, took a closer look and realized they had been duped. There was
President Taft, waving to the crowd as he ducked into the library entrance.
A great cheer went up and Magda experienced a moment of feeling truly
American. She had laid eyes on the president of the United States.

The ceremonies took place inside, and Magda would not know what

President Taft had said until she saw the paper the next morning. She read the excerpts from his speech several times over, and especially liked the part about how the new library was "the consummation of a noteworthy plan for bringing within the grasp of the humblest and poorest citizen the opportunity for acquiring information on every subject of every kind."

But, as momentous as the dedication of the library was, and as overwhelmed as Magda felt when she had the chance to walk, with thousands of others, through its spectacular spaces, seeing the library and the president was merely the prelude to the highlight of her day. At four o'clock, she ascended the great marble staircase of the grandest monument to books New York had ever seen, to where Tom and Gene, by prior arrangement, stood waiting for her.

She embraced each of them warmly, secretly pleased to discover that she felt no lingering feelings of either anger or unrequited love, but only a great joy at seeing her two friends again at last. When Tom gave her a light kiss on the cheek and said, "Hello, old friend," she knew she had forgiven him; apparently he had forgiven her, too.

Conversation proved impossible with the throngs surging around them, and every eatery in the neighborhood overflowed, so they walked down Fifth Avenue to Twenty-Third Street toward the Childs where they had spent so many happy times. Magda felt light-headed as they made their way south. The excitement of the possibility that she might not have to write the Tremendous Trio by herself paled in comparison to the bliss of having the trio reunited.

"So, what brings you back to New York?" said Gene to Tom when they had settled at their usual table. Magda had avoided this question, afraid the answer would be *I'm just here for a few days*.

"It's my father," said Tom. "He's ill and, well, frankly, he's dying, and I thought it best, for his sake and for my mother, to spend some time at home."

"Oh, Tom, I'm so sorry," said Magda.

"It's always been a fraught relationship," he said. "My father wanted me to go to college and become a banker. He never understood why I wanted to write. And of course, all mother ever wanted was for me to marry a rich girl, as if we didn't have enough money. And now I'm back living in the same house with both of them. It will be a tense summer."

"I don't suppose you'd like to relieve some of that tension by writing some children's books," said Magda.

"Ah, now we come to it," said Gene.

"The Tremendous Trio?" said Tom.

"Exactly," said Magda.

"So, she told you about it," said Gene.

"Wrote a very impassioned letter," said Tom, smiling weakly at Magda.

"What do you say?" said Magda. "We can work in that glorious new library."

"I don't know, Magda," said Tom. "I'm not feeling very creative these days."

"It's not exactly what I had in mind for the summer," said Gene. He did not add that what he did have in mind was frequent trips to the Bowery of Coney Island. His pledge to ignore his physical desires had faded into a hazy memory and now that he was back in the city, he planned to engage in pursuits that months in Niagara and Pittsburgh had prohibited.

Magda could feel the possibility of a happy summer with Tom and Gene slipping away. She couldn't bear the thought that this dinner might be the end of their trio and that she would spend her evenings in the library working alone. But she had known the men would take some convincing, and she had come prepared.

"Let me read you something," she said, withdrawing three folded sheets of paper from her handbag. "These are just samples, but I think they make the point." Magda spread one of the papers on the table and read.

Dear Mr. Dexter Cornwall,

   Thank you for writing the Dan Dawson books. I love those books. I read them over and over and I am only six years old. They are the best books. At school some of the boys call me names and make fun of me because I like to read books instead of playing at sports. Sometimes I wonder what Dan would do if boys called him names. He is so brave. I will try to be brave, too, thanks to Dan. I don't know what I would do without Dan. Thank you for giving me my best friend.

                                Your Friend,
                                Howard

"Very touching," said Tom. "And it just proves that you are perfectly suited to write books for children."

"But I'm not the only one who gets fan mail," said Magda. "Gene, listen to this one."

Dear Mr. Buck Larson,

My name is Katie and I want to be a scientist when I grow up. Some of the boys and even some of the girls at school say that I cannot be a scientist because I am a girl. But I say they are wrong because look at Alice Gold. She is an inventor and knows more about science than any boy I ever saw. Thank you for writing about Alice and for making me believe that if I want to be a scientist I can be one.

Yours Truly,
Katie Collins

"Okay," said Gene, "I get the point, but . . ."

"Wait," said Magda. "No comments yet. There's one for Tom, too."

Dear Mr. Neptune B. Smythe,

My family and I live in one room in a tenement on the Lower East Side of New York. I hate living here because it is so crowded and dirty and noisy. More than anything I want to go somewhere else, but I was always afraid I never would. Then a friend gave me a book about Frank Fairfax. I have read that book over and over because Frank takes me away from my horrible neighborhood to amazing places. I will keep reading your book every time I need to get away and I just wanted to say thank you for writing it. Because of you and Frank, my life is not so miserable now.

Sincerely,
Jacob

Magda looked up to see tears in Tom's eyes. Gene smiled wryly and shook his head. "That wasn't playing fair," he said.

"Fine," said Tom, "when do we start?"

XXX

NEW-YORK HISTORICAL SOCIETY, 2010

Robert stared at the photos in the De Peyster album for what seemed like hours, trying to see into the eyes of Eugene and Magda and Thomas, trying to divine something of their personalities, their relationships to one another, their plans for the future—both their own futures and that of their creation, the Tremendous Trio. Of course, the Tremendous Trio books had been published in 1911, five years after the date on this photograph—July 28, 1906. But the first books by Buck Larson and Dexter Cornwall and Neptune B. Smythe were published sometime in 1906, so no wonder these three were already styling themselves the "gods and goddess of children's books."

"You can photograph that item if you like," said a voice at Robert's side.

"I beg your pardon?" said Robert, looking up to see the librarian who had brought him the album. He was a young man with bright-red hair, a neatly trimmed red beard, and blue-rimmed glasses.

"As long as you don't use a flash, you can photograph the materials in that scrapbook."

He had taken copious notes on each item, but Robert thought if he photographed everything in the scrapbook, he could mount those photos into an album of his own. Such a facsimile might keep him from wanting to return to the Historical Society every day.

Robert flipped back to the first page, took out his phone, and began carefully photographing. The Childs restaurant menu seemed closer and closer to detaching completely from its page, and he turned the leaf as delicately as he could. Within a few minutes, he was back on the page with the photos of the three authors, carefully focusing the images on his phone's screen, and imagining what he might see when he got these photos loaded onto his computer and could enlarge them.

On the next few pages he saw a dozen or so photographs of the woman identified as Magda Hertzenberger. Unlike in the photos at Bethesda Fountain, Magda did not pose in these images. In fact, she never looked at the camera, and Robert imagined they had been taken without her knowledge. Some were blurry or poorly lit, but in all of them, the photographer had captured Magda at a perfect moment. She smiled, gazing up at the light of a Broadway marquee. She looked contemplatively out the window of an elevated train. She sat at a desk typing, her brows furrowed in concentration. Robert sensed that Thomas De Peyster had been in love with Magda Hertzenberger.

The next three pages brought Robert back to the world of children's series books. Each featured the front panel of a colorful dust jacket—the original wrappers for the three Frank Fairfax books. Pop Pop's copies had long ago lost their dust jackets, and Robert had never seen these color illustrations. *Frank Fairfax and the Search for El Dorado* showed the young reporter, camera in one hand and steno pad in the other, perched at the crest of a hill with a glittering city of gold laid out in the valley below him. *Frank Fairfax and the Lost City of Atlantis* featured Frank in a yellow rain slicker, standing at the prow of a sailing ship, rain whipping past him as he looked into the distance. The jacket for *Frank Fairfax among the Mayans* pictured the boy atop a pyramid, hands cupped around his mouth, shouting. As far as Robert was concerned, this collection of dust jackets could only mean one thing: Thomas De Peyster had written the Frank Fairfax books; Thomas De Peyster was Neptune B. Smythe.

If De Peyster used the name Neptune B. Smythe, it seemed logical that Magda Hertzenberger must be Buck Larson, that the one female among the Tremendous Trio authors would have chosen to write about a female heroine, Alice Gold. That meant Eugene Pinkney must be Dexter Cornwall, author of the Daring Dan Dawson series.

But was that right? Robert turned back to the pair of photographs at the Bethesda Fountain, and reread the captions. If the pseudonyms were in the same order as the real names then Eugene Pinkney, not Magda Hertzenberger, had written the Alice Gold books. Why would a man in 1906 choose to write about a girl inventor? Robert realized that, though the album was an incredibly rich resource, it might raise more questions than it answered. But he liked those questions. How did these three come to know each other? Thomas worked as a journalist, but what about Magda and Eugene? And what was the meaning of all those other items in the album—the baseball ticket and the postcards and the playbills and the menu? What story did they tell?

Robert had lost interest in telling stories since the publication of *Looking Forward*, but now he felt what he had felt all those years ago when he began to write about his grandfather's adventures in the war. He felt a story tugging at him, insisting to be told. He didn't know if anyone would want to publish it or read it, but he remembered, at last, that that wasn't the point. He needed to *tell* the story. That was all that mattered.

He spent the rest of the afternoon immersed in the album, photographing every item and every caption. After the dust jackets came a clipped review of the first Frank Fairfax book. The reviewer wrote, "Frank Fairfax and the other new offerings from Pickering Brothers this Christmas season represent a distinct improvement over the typical fare we have come to expect from these cheap volumes for youngsters." Robert agreed, but if the Pickering books represented such an improvement, why did so few of them survive? More stories to be told, he thought.

The rest of the album contained more postcards of New York City and studio portraits of several famous New Yorkers of the period, including Stanford White and Nikola Tesla.

Between the page with the photograph of Tesla and one with three postcards of a Coney Island theme park called Dreamland, someone had inserted another postcard as a bookmark. On the back was a one-cent stamp, with a cancellation dated March 27, 1910. The address read:

Mary Stone, 316 West 23rd St., New York City. The message read simply: *Magda—Working on a project at the power plant here for a few months. I'll let you know when I'm back in NY.* The note was unsigned and the handwriting did not match that of Thomas De Peyster. Who had sent this postcard to Magda and why was her mail in Thomas's scrapbook? Why was it addressed to Mary Stone? He made a note to investigate the address then flipped the card over to see a familiar image that brought back a flood of memories. This picture of Niagara Falls could have been used as a reference for the illustration printed on the cloth cover of *The Tremendous Trio at Niagara Falls*. The angle, the placement of the boat on the water, even the building in the background were identical. The falls had not looked so very different when Robbie had stood on the Canadian side, feeling the spray on his face, and pretending to be miserable.

Robbie had, in fact, been excited about the trip to Niagara with his father to follow in the footsteps of the Tremendous Trio. He had done his best to hide that fact, knowing that a teenager shouldn't be keen to spend time with his father, but he suspected he had not been entirely successful in concealing his anticipation.

The drive, in the family's aging Oldsmobile station wagon, took seven hours, enough time for Robbie to read *The Tremendous Trio at Niagara Falls* aloud. They had left early in the morning, so by midafternoon they stood beside the falls, almost where Alice and Frank had stood as Dan's barrel plunged over the rim. Robbie had not been able to resist the joy of the moment. He felt the power of the falls in his sternum and almost laughed out loud. And then his father had ruined everything.

"This is just the beginning, kiddo," he said, slapping a hand on Robbie's shoulder. "Think of the miles we'll put on that old wagon following the Tremendous Trio, especially Dan Dawson. He went to San Francisco and Chicago and Galveston. Your mother never liked to travel, but you and me, Robbie, we're gonna see the world."

Robbie felt his stomach sink, almost as if he had been swept over the falls. He had seen this trip as an ending—the last hurrah of his childhood and a way to say goodbye to that world of series books with celebration and no regret. He had pictured turning away from the falls and never thinking about the Tremendous Trio again; putting on his earphones and listening to music on his Walkman all the way back to Rockaway Beach. But his father saw this trip as a beginning, a new chapter in their relationship built on the only thing they ever managed to have in common.

Staring at that postcard in the De Peyster album, Robert recalled the exact sentence that had formed in his head as he stood in the spray of Niagara, words that, even though he never spoke them, he could never take back: *Why won't my father just go away and leave me alone?*

He hadn't thought about Niagara in a long time, and the physical pain the memory of those words caused him reminded him why he had buried these events deep out of sight; but the immediacy of that pain also convinced him, more than ever, that he needed to tell these stories. He could almost hear the words Rebecca would say after he described the silent, miserable car ride home from Niagara:

"You shouldn't feel guilty," she would tell him. "After all, what teenage boy wants to spend all his time traveling alone with his father, talking about a bunch of kids' books?"

The final pages of the De Peyster album were empty, but a bulging envelope was pasted inside the rear cover. Robert opened this and tipped onto the table several dozen clipped newspaper articles. He carefully photographed each one—articles on the San Francisco earthquake, the Stanford White murder trial, and other major and minor stories of 1906. Robert guessed that Thomas De Peyster had written all of them.

Once he had photographed each article, he gently returned the newspaper clippings to their envelope. He held the volume upright, gave it a light tap against the table, so that the paper would slide all the way back into its container, and was dismayed to see that the Childs menu came fluttering out of the album, its century-old paste having finally released its grip. Robert opened the volume, to return the menu to its proper place, resolving to inform the librarian it had come loose. There on the front page, where the menu had hidden it, was another photograph of a woman.

This was clearly *not* Magda Hertzenberger. Even a black-and-white photograph showed that Magda had blond hair and this woman's hair was jet black. She might have been Italian or Spanish; she certainly looked Mediterranean, whereas Magda was clearly of Northern European descent. The photo had no caption, and the story it did not tell intrigued Robert as much as anything in the album. She sat on a bed among a mess of tangled sheets, one of which barely covered the swell of her breasts as she leaned toward the camera. Her smile and the look in her eyes left no doubt about her invitation to the photographer. It had taken two people to get those sheets into such a tangle, and as soon as the camera clicked she would no longer be alone in that bed. But who was she? Where was she? And why had Thomas De Peyster hidden her under a menu from Childs restaurant? Robert could think of a thousand answers. To tell a story, he only had to pick one.

⌒⌒⌒

"I wonder," said Robert, as he returned Thomas De Peyster's album to the desk, "if there's any way to find out more about the woman who donated this item? I'd love to talk with her." He had no idea if Sarah Thomas was still alive, but perhaps she had known Thomas De Peyster and might be able to answer some of Robert's questions.

The redheaded librarian took the catalogue card from Robert and peered at it through his glasses. "I'd have to check the records and see if we have any information we're allowed to give out. If you want to leave your phone number, I could call you tomorrow."

"Tomorrow morning?" said Robert, eager to pursue this lead as quickly as possible.

"Before lunch," said the redhead.

"Excellent," said Robert.

XXXI

NEW YORK CITY,
THE SUMMER OF THE GREAT HEAT WAVE

They agreed to meet in the main reading room of the new central library on Saturday afternoon. That gave Magda four days to polish up the outlines she had created over the past year for the three volumes of the Tremendous Trio. She lay in bed that night thinking about what Gene had said to her after Tom had left Childs. "Just remember, Magda, we've all got broken hearts and at best this is going to be bittersweet. It might just be bitter."

But Magda had begun to question whether she did have a broken heart. Had she ever truly loved Gene? She enjoyed having him as a friend, liked spending time with him, but that ache she had felt in the early days had faded long ago. Perhaps what she thought was love had been only a young woman's infatuation. As far as Tom was concerned, she just wanted to be his friend, to move forward rather than looking back. Why was Gene so pessimistic about that possibility? It never occurred to her that Gene had not gotten over Tom, that for all his talk about forgiveness, he felt betrayed by the man he still loved and that whatever the months ahead held for Magda, they would hold nothing but pain for Gene.

On Saturday afternoon, Magda and Gene sat at a table in the new library's massive main reading room. Table after table was crowded with readers, some deep in their books, others taking a break to enjoy the majesty of this temple to learning. Natural light from the giant arched windows flooded the room, and the elaborate paneled ceiling, with its painted insets of clouds in a blue sky, glowed overhead.

She had shown Gene the outline for *The Tremendous Trio at Niagara Falls*, a story that culminated in Dan Dawson going over the falls in a special barrel invented and built by Alice Gold. Gene told Magda about the geography of the falls while sketching ideas for Dan's barrel at the same time. Only one person had ever gone over the falls and survived, he said. That had happened in 1901, and people in Niagara still talked about it.

Tom arrived late, unshaven and looking as if he hadn't slept in two days. Nonetheless, he smiled, slapped a folded newspaper down on the table, and said, "So, what's the plan?"

Magda saw her opening. He clearly meant what was the plan for this trilogy of books they had agreed to write together, but Magda chose to interpret his question another way.

"We hadn't really talked about it," she said, "but, since tomorrow is Sunday and it's opening weekend, and, well, to get ourselves in the proper frame of mind and sort of, I don't know, exorcise the past, I thought we might go to Dreamland."

Tom and Gene looked at Magda aghast, as if she had made some horribly rude comment in a loud voice.

"What?" said Magda, trying to keep the pleading tone from her voice. "Is it such a terrible idea?"

"She hasn't heard," said Gene.

"Heard what?" said Magda.

"Maybe you'd like to read my article in this morning's paper," said Tom, spreading out the paper in front of Magda. "It's not the lead, but it does provide some color."

Magda stared at the almost incomprehensible words that stretched across the top of the front page: DREAMLAND IN ASHES; FIRE DESTROYS

PARK. She could not even breathe for a moment, but she finally managed to gasp the word, "How?"

"Does it matter how?" said Gene.

"Here's my piece," said Tom, pointing to a smaller headline farther down the page. Magda leaned over the paper and read, her tears making splotches on the newsprint.

Dreamland Fire Destroys More Than Park

Brooklyn, May 27, 1911

Dreamland is a land of dreams no more, and the many blissful memories of halcyon summer days in that magical land by the sea are now no more than wisps of smoke rising from the smoldering remains of the once great park. Who knows what dreams, as yet unfulfilled, may rest forgotten on the shores of Coney Island, buried forever in the rubble that is all that remains of this happy spot.

While the widely reported fire, which began in the Hell Gate attraction and eventually consumed the entire park, took no human lives, the scene was heartbreaking to many who counted themselves as regulars at the park, and especially those lovers of animals who returned again and again to Bostock's menagerie. On this night they came from all corners of Brooklyn to watch the flames, but encountered a more horrible scene than they could imagine. The shrieks of lions, pumas, tigers, deer, antelope, llamas, and even little Hip the baby elephant being burned alive in their enclosure was more than many bystanders could take. Captain Jack Bonavita and others did their best to rescue these animals, or at least to humanely end their suffering with a gunshot, but the flames moved too quickly to admit mercy to those suffering innocents.

Black Prince, a widely advertised Barbary lion, escaped from his enclosure, but the fire had caught his mane and the thicker coatings of his bristly hide. He burst through the passageway leading to Surf Avenue and headed east without apparent thought of the hundreds of human beings who started a wild scramble to escape him. In the short but exciting chase which followed, Black Prince seemed to pay far less attention to the shower of leaden bullets from the policemen's revolvers that struck him than he did to the terrible growing blaze on his body from which he could not escape. At the top of an incline, he halted, but even then he scorned to notice the advancing policemen, who were blazing away at him as swiftly as they could discharge their revolvers. Patrolman Joe Haynes had picked up a fireman's axe as he joined the chase, and with that he smashed two fierce blows on the lion's skull. The Barbary dropped at the first and if that did not finish him the second blow did, but even then the policemen made sure of their ground by firing a dozen more bullets into the prostrate body. Many onlookers, terrified for their lives only a moment before, then defiled the memory of the poor beast by extracting teeth and other body parts as gruesome souvenirs.

"Oh, it's too awful," said Magda, who could hardly bear to think of the pain and indignity the poor animal had suffered. "I can't read any more."

"Just skip to the end," said Tom. "The last paragraph. You'll appreciate that bit."

When the great Beacon Tower, the symbol of Dreamland, visible from far out at sea, collapsed, the roar was heard across the island, and the queen of the Coney Island skyline disappeared in an instant. The many special moments shared by the romantics of New York on the observation deck of this tower while gazing out on a sea lit by the glow of a million electric bulbs are now only memories, destined to fade to nothingness, just as Dreamland's lights are now only darkness.

The destruction of Dreamland on the very day they began work on the Tremendous Trio books set the tone for the summer. Where writing the first three books five years earlier had seemed so easy and natural, this collaboration on the Tremendous Trio was labored and awkward. They argued over details of the story and criticized one another's writing—more than once at such volume as to attract a scolding librarian, for they continued to meet in the cavernous reading room in the central library. Tom often arrived late for their writing sessions. One day Gene did not come at all, and when he showed up the next day with a bruised face and a split lip, Tom only said, "You should stop stepping out in front of taxis."

The Saturday afternoon excursions they had enjoyed during that wonderful summer of 1906 never materialized. Tom claimed he needed to stay with his father and Gene usually sneaked out to the Coney Island dives, leaving Magda alone to spend the day reading at the Muhlenberg Library. As much as she loved the central library, she couldn't pass through those doors without keenly feeling the absence of the others.

Tom said he had no interest in baseball games since the Polo Grounds had burned in April. Even though other amusement areas like Luna Park and Steeplechase Park still operated, Gene discouraged the idea of a Coney Island trip. In early July, a heat wave struck that made the simplest of activities miserable. Magda tried walking in the park, where men slept on the grass in the shade, desperate for the rest that would not come in the stifling indoors, but the heat left her wilted. The next day, Tom informed her glumly that the death toll in New York from the heat wave was over a hundred and still climbing.

As the summer progressed, Tom became more and more distant. Concerned for his father's health, instead of relying on the others for help and support, he pushed them away. He contributed less and less to the writing and limited his conversation to the day's newspapers. On July 26, he showed them a headline on the previous evening's paper:

Over Niagara in Steel Barrel; Escapes Death

Bobby Leach went over the Horseshoe Falls at 3.13 o'clock this afternoon in a steel barrel. Flashing over the brink the barrel shot downward with the roaring tons of water and disappeared in the spray and spume 158 feet below.

"Looks like he stole Dan Dawson's thunder," said Tom.

"Maybe it will make children more interested in Niagara Falls," said Magda. "Besides, Leach broke his leg. In Alice Gold's barrel, Dan didn't even get bruised."

By this time, they had completed *The Tremendous Trio at Niagara Falls* and more than half of *The Tremendous Trio and the Secrets of the Amazon*. Magda had written many of the non-technical chapters of *The Tremendous Trio around the World* on those lonely Saturdays. The work would be done by the end of August. Mr. Lipscomb would have his books in plenty of time for the Christmas season, and Magda could put a hot, miserable summer behind her.

"Are we done?" said Tom as they sat in the library on the last day of August, three clean typescripts on the table in front of them.

"We're done," said Magda quietly. "I think people, I mean children, will like them." The books had turned out well, certainly much better than what Stratemeyer was churning out, but the toil of the past months had felt nothing like the magical summer of 1906. This time they were simply hired hands, working against a deadline and hoping someone would enjoy the stories into which they had poured so much effort. They sat in silence for a minute, Magda not knowing what to say. She presumed she would never see Gene and Tom again, and, after the way the summer had played out, with Tom's distance and Gene's refusal to talk about anything but work, she wasn't sure she would miss them. She desperately wished she could take one good memory from the summer for which she had had such high hopes.

"Let's celebrate," said Tom, sounding more cheerful than he had all summer.

"What do you mean?" said Gene.

"I mean it's been a lousy summer, we all know that. Gene with his taxicab accidents, and me unable to look either one of you in the face even after five years, my father on his deathbed. But we did something good here. These books are good, and maybe some more children will write letters like the ones Magda read to us. So before we say goodbye, let's celebrate. I'll get us tickets for the *Ziegfeld Follies* on Saturday night. It's the last performance and we can have dinner afterward someplace nice. Make a night of it."

"It sounds lovely," said Magda, trying to smile at Tom in such a way as to say, *I really do forgive you, honestly.*

And so they spent an enchanting final night together. Magda had never seen the *Ziegfeld Follies*, a lavish revue mounted in a new version every year since it began in 1907 and performed in the Jardin de Paris, a rooftop theater above the New York Theatre at Broadway and Forty-Fourth Street. The show, with its seventy-five chorus girls, was more glamorous than anything Magda had imagined, with an audience dressed almost as lavishly as the performers. This year's follies included satires of *The Pink Lady* and *H.M.S.* Pinafore, as well as a cabaret entertainment depicting life in the slums of San Francisco. "There's no escaping San Francisco," Tom said quietly to himself when they reached this portion of the evening.

When the chorus girls first appeared, shimmering in dresses that revealed almost more of their underlying figures than no dress at all would have done, Tom said, "The sense of sight was caressed in every scene with the sight of beautiful women dressed and undressed with exquisite taste moving in spirited and graceful dances to the lovely music."

"Did you just come up with that?" said Gene.

"From my review back in June," said Tom.

"I thought you said you hadn't seen it," said Magda.

"I hadn't," said Tom. "But Mr. Hearst doesn't stand on such formalities. Besides, I saw last year's version in Chicago."

Magda particularly enjoyed the comic sketches of Leon Errol and Bert Williams. In her limited experience of theatergoing, she had never seen a black man onstage before, and Williams left the entire audience howling with laughter and cheering his comedy. He then earned even more well-deserved applause with his singing. Fanny Brice singing a

Yiddish song provided another highlight. The *Follies*, thought Magda, reflected the sort of America she had wanted to be a part of since child-hood—perhaps a little overly interested in beautiful girls, but with plenty of room for women and blacks and Jews and people from around the world to work side by side and bring their unique talents to bear. She knew the *Ziegfeld Follies* was more fantasy than reality, but she enjoyed the fantasy nonetheless. After all, she sat snugly between a rich man from uptown who had grown up haunting the slums and a man raised in those slums who made good through his own natural genius. And they were, for that night at least, all friends. Surely that could only happen in America.

Even though the show did not end until nearly midnight, Tom insisted they go out for a late dinner. "Tomorrow is Sunday," he said. "You can sleep in. Besides, Delmonico's is only two blocks away and dinner is my treat." Neither Gene nor Magda could resist.

"How are you?" said Magda to Gene as they followed Tom down Forty-Fourth Street. She detected a note of wistfulness in his expression.

"It still hurts," he said. "I think it will always hurt."

"I'm sorry," said Magda, linking her arm through his. The intimacy of the gesture would once have thrilled Magda, but now she felt only warmth and compassion for a man who had become, after all, a dear friend.

"I've been with a lot of men," said Gene, looking down at the side-walk. "But I never fell in love with any of them."

"You still love him?" said Magda softly.

"Achingly," said Gene.

"It must have been a hard summer for you."

"Yes," said Gene, "but I'm glad you made us do it."

At the restaurant, Tom ordered champagne and when the waiter had filled the glasses, he raised his. "I know it may not seem like it," he said, "but working with the two of you again, seeing you in the library every night . . ."

"Almost every night," said Magda.

"True. Almost every night. It's been, well, it's been a great relief from the rest of my life at the moment. Father seems to get worse by the day, and only has the energy to complain of what a disappointment I am; Mother only pesters me about marriage. So, I apologize for my ill humor, but I want you to know that disappearing into the Tremendous Trio for a few hours *almost* every night and spending time with you two fine people has provided the only happiness in my life at the moment. I will miss this."

For a split second, Magda thought of interrupting Tom, of telling him he didn't have to miss it, that even if they weren't working on a book the three of them could remain friends, could still see one another. But then she thought of Gene and of how crushing it must be to be near someone he loved so desperately but could never have. She settled back in her chair without speaking. Tom's glass still hung in the air and he clearly had more to say.

"Tomorrow I leave for Asheville where my father is being sent for the weather and the clean air. And if he lives until winter it will be Florida next. So I may not see you again for a long time. But here's wishing all success to the Tremendous Trio—may they change the lives of boys and girls everywhere. And to the gods and goddess of children's books, may we meet again someday."

They clinked their glasses, and Magda did her best not to cry as she took a gulp of the champagne. At least, she thought, she might still see Gene.

"I have some news myself," said Gene. "I've just taken a job with an electric company in Philadelphia. I leave on Monday."

"So Magda will have to look after New York for us," said Tom.

"It couldn't be in better hands," said Gene. He smiled at her, but Magda could not see. The tears had clouded everything. She took another sip of champagne.

XXXII

On the walk home from the Historical Society, Robert detoured by an art supply store and bought a glue stick and a scrapbook that was the closest thing to Thomas De Peyster's photo album he could find. He spent the rest of the evening printing out photographs of every item from the original album and pasting them into his new scrapbook. The facsimile of the Childs menu he attached only at the top, so he could lift it up to see the uncaptioned photograph of the mysterious woman. He even glued a manila envelope inside the back cover and filled it with the copies of the newspaper articles. In as close an imitation of Thomas De Peyster's handwriting as he could manage, he copied out all the captions onto the pages of the modern scrapbook. Rebecca would have done a better job of this. She had taken a class in calligraphy last year.

On his computer he enlarged the photographs to get a closer look at the faces. Only then did he see that the man captioned "Marcus Stone" was not a man, but a woman—the same woman in all those candid photographs, Magda Hertzenberger. But why had she dressed as a man? He loved questions like this. When he wrote, he began with questions. Not just prompts to the imagination, but questions he desperately wanted to answer. Recently, he hadn't known what questions to ask, but now the questions exploded out of everything on his desk.

The first issue of *Tales of Excitement for Boys and Girls*, for instance. Was there ever a second issue? And if not, why? Had something dramatic happened to bring the entire enterprise crashing to the ground? And if there was no second issue, was there any way he could keep his promise to his father to find out what had happened to the Tremendous Trio? Robert hadn't found any books published by Pickering later than 1912. Maybe the first issue of *Tales of Excitement* had been Pickering's final publication. But why?

One item on his desk did not relate directly to his search for answers, but was more important to him than all the rest—a framed picture of Rebecca standing on Bow Bridge in Central Park. She wore a blue-and-yellow sundress and a perfect smile. It had been a Sunday afternoon in early summer. They had gone to a matinee at Lincoln Center Theater and decided to walk in the park afterward, gravitating, as always, to the Ramble. When they emerged onto the usually crowded bridge it had been empty, and Robert insisted that Rebecca pose for a picture. The late afternoon sun glimmered off the water behind her, reflecting the lush greenery and the taller buildings of the Upper West Side. Robert didn't remember the play, but he remembered that instant. He was an unsuccessful novelist. She was a successful interior decorator. They had never been happier.

During their walk in the Ramble, Rebecca had said to Robert, "What do you think about children?"

"In general or belonging to us?" he said, suddenly panicked.

"Belonging to us."

"The idea scares me to death," said Robert.

"Okay," said Rebecca, laying a hand on his arm. "I just wondered."

"What do you think?" said Robert.

"Maybe one day," she said. "But only when it doesn't scare you to death. Only when it scares you just a little bit."

But in the moment that he snapped that picture, Robert suddenly thought it might not be such a bad thing to make a child with this woman, that he might someday be able to reach the point of only being scared a little bit.

Then Rebecca had run off the bridge and he had chased after her and they had laughed all the way home and made love in his apartment and eaten delivery in their bathrobes while watching *North by Northwest* on TNT. The next morning the phone rang and Robert's novel sold and everything changed.

He set the picture down, longing for Saturday morning, for the chance to finally share his stories—all his stories—with Rebecca. And maybe after that, he would have a new story to tell—a story of three writers and the book they never finished. He took out a sheet of paper. Although he composed at his computer, he liked to take notes and brainstorm with old-fashioned pencil and paper. At the top of the page he wrote: *The Last Adventure of the Tremendous Trio*. Below that he wrote the word *Questions*. And then he began to ask.

The batteries on Robbie's Walkman had given out a couple of hours after they had left Niagara Falls, but he had pretended it still worked, leaving the headphones on and hoping his father wouldn't notice that the sound of the tape turning had stopped. Robbie had stared out the window at the blur of passing trees, never turning to even look at his father. When they finally arrived home he had gone straight to his room, feigning exhaustion. But he had heard the conversation between his parents through the thin walls.

"He's a teenager," said his mother. "He likes to listen to music."

"His music gave out before we got to Syracuse," said his father. "I'm afraid I'm losing him." Robbie had never known until that moment that resentment and guilt could be so intermingled.

The phone woke Robert the morning after his visit to the New-York Historical Society, perhaps because he had been up until nearly three taking notes and writing questions about the Tremendous Trio and its creators.

"This is Edward at the New-York Historical Society. I hope I didn't wake you."

Robert glanced at the bedside clock and winced to see it was 10:35.

Doing his best to sound caffeinated, he replied. "Not at all, thank you for getting back to me so quickly."

"I found the donation file for that scrapbook, and there was a note in it that said . . . let me read it to you. 'If anyone shows an interest in this item, please contact the donor, Mrs. Sarah Thomas.' And there's a phone number."

Robert scrambled out of bed and dashed toward his study to get something to write with. "Can you give me the number?" he said.

"No," said Edward.

"She's dead," said Robert, sinking into his desk chair. "I knew she would be dead."

"She's not dead, it's just that the note specifically said *we* are to notify her."

"Well, notify her," cried Robert. "Let her know that I'd very much like to speak to her."

"I did," said Edward. "I've just gotten off the phone with her, and she said to ask you if you can come to her apartment at two o'clock this afternoon."

"Yes, yes, of course I can. Do you have the address?"

Edward gave Robert an address on the Upper East Side, only a few blocks from where Sherwood Whitmore lived with his collection of children's series books. As he dressed and swallowed a cup of coffee and two slices of toast, Robert wondered if New York was about to reveal another of its secrets.

XXXIII

NEW YORK CITY, ON THE DAY OF A FUNERAL

"We've had a nice response to the Tremendous Trio," said Mr. Lipscomb to Marcus Stone as they sat in his office on a January morning in 1912. He had dictated a letter to "Mr. Stone" a few days earlier asking for a meeting and obliging Magda to resurrect the Philadelphia writer. Lipscomb had dictated similar letters to Thomas De Peyster and Eugene Pinkney, but Magda knew those would go unanswered. She had sent three letters each to Gene and Tom over the past few months and received no response. She tried to believe that Tom's had not been forwarded from his New York address to Florida and that Gene's were waiting at his rooms on Carmine Street for his eventual return to the city. But, as the days and weeks and months had gone by, she had become more resigned to the possibility that she would never see or hear from either of them again. If the summer of 1911 had proved anything it was that, no matter how much everyone had forgiven everyone else, they could never really escape Dreamland. Yet Magda also found, as time passed, that she thought less and less about Tom's betrayal and Gene's unrequited love and remembered them as they had been for most of that summer of 1906—friends. And it was her friends that she missed, though their absence became easier to bear with each passing day.

"When I say nice response," said Lipscomb, "I mean in comparison with some of our other titles. It's tough going up against Stratemeyer, which is why I wanted to try something new."

"And what does that have to do with me?" said Mr. Stone.

"You're the only one of the Trio authors who would even answer a letter," said Lipscomb. "So you get the offer. I want to launch a monthly magazine for children. Nice color cover, cheap printing inside, lots of adventure stories and serials, and as many advertisements as I can sell—that's where the money comes from."

Magda had seen such cheap magazines on the newsstands and in Putnam's and Dutton's—magazines like *Argosy* and *Adventure* that sold for ten cents an issue. She had actually bought a copy of one of these magazines a week ago—a publication called *All-Story*, in which she had read the intriguing opening chapter of the serial *Under the Moons of Mars* by a writer named Edgar Rice Burroughs. She could understand why Lipscomb would want to launch a similar venture. Most children could more easily spend ten cents than fifty, and once you got readers hooked on a serial, they would buy a new magazine every month.

"So you'd like me to write something for this magazine?" said Mr. Stone.

"I'd like you and your partners to write a Tremendous Trio serial. I even have a title for you. *The Last Adventure of the Tremendous Trio.*"

"Does that mean you won't want any more after this one?" said Mr. Stone.

"Don't be ridiculous," said Mr. Lipscomb. "Haven't you ever heard of Sherlock Holmes? He dies falling over a waterfall in 1893, ten years later he's back, tells Watson he faked his death, and on he goes. But if we tell the readers this is the final adventure—well, that's intriguing, isn't it? And that much more exciting when we bring them back in a year or two."

"And what if my partners are not interested?"

"Then write it yourself," said Lipscomb. "I don't care. I'll put all three names on it either way. It's easy money for you—short chapters, fifteen of them. Five dollars a chapter. I need the first one in two weeks."

"But in two weeks . . ." Magda had been about to say, *you will be sailing for Europe*, but she caught herself just in time, remembering she was not Mary Stone, personal secretary to Julius Lipscomb, who had booked his passage on the *Olympic*, but Marcus Stone, who knew nothing of the publisher's movements.

"In two weeks I am to be married," said Mr. Stone. It was the first thing Magda could think of.

"You can always send it sooner," said Mr. Lipscomb. "Are we in agreement then?"

"Can I let you know tomorrow?" said Mr. Stone.

"No later than midday," said Mr. Lipscomb. "If you don't write the Tremendous Trio, I'll find someone else to do it. Our first issue will be dated April, but I'll need your first installment by the end of February. I shall be out of the country, but I'll have my secretary send everything directly to the production office."

Even if the pain of Tom's and Gene's absences had eased, Magda hated the thought of writing a Tremendous Trio story by herself. However, the idea of a total stranger writing about the characters she and Tom and Gene had invented was even worse. She decided that Mr. Stone would accept the commission, which he did later that day by telegram. She would make one last effort to contact Tom and Gene, hoping they would be willing to have at least a little input into the serial—there wouldn't be time for a lot of exchange of letters in only two weeks, but still, they might have ideas she could use in future installments.

After work she put on her very best clothes and rode the Sixth Avenue El to Fifty-Eighth Street. She would present herself at the De Peyster home on Fifth Avenue, a house she had never been inside, but which Tom had pointed out one time when the trio were heading into Central Park. With luck, she could convince someone there to give her an address where Tom could receive a telegram.

The house, though not as imposing as some of the palaces in nearby blocks, intimidated Magda with its wrought iron fence and its heavy stone portico. She stood on the doorstep for a full minute before she mustered the courage to lift the heavy knocker and strike it against the door three times. It took no more than a few seconds for the door to open and for Magda to find herself looking into the face of Tom De Peyster.

"Magda," said Tom soberly. "It's so kind of you to come."

"There just wasn't time to wire everyone," said Tom, "but of course Gene saw the notice in the paper. He wired that he's on the way up on the train from Philadelphia. I knew you would see it, too."

It had taken Magda only a few seconds, after being led into a vast reception room full of people dressed in black, to realize that Tom's father had died. She had been so busy transforming into and out of Marcus Stone that she had not read the papers that day; otherwise she might have seen the obituary and the announcement that the funeral would take place that afternoon at four o'clock at St. Nicholas Church on the corner of Fifth Avenue and Forty-Eighth Street. Magda had missed the funeral but arrived at the house during the exact time that the family had announced they would receive visitors.

Magda did not admit to Tom that her arrival had been a matter of coincidence. It seemed in poor taste to bring up the Tremendous Trio, and anyway, before she had a chance to even consider doing so, Tom had rushed back to the door to welcome newly arriving guests, leaving her alone in a room full of people she didn't know and who, she assumed, must be looking down on her. She, after all, was the one person not wearing black—thank goodness it wasn't summer, or she might have shown up in white. Still, her deep-burgundy dress must have marked her as a misfit. She spent the next two hours creeping from room to room, listening to snippets of conversations without ever joining in. Tom remained too busy to pay her the least notice and Gene had not yet arrived. She felt awkward and miserable and yet she knew she had no right to be despondent—it wasn't her father who had just died. The clock in the hall was just striking eight and Magda had narrowly escaped a face-to-face encounter with Mrs. De Peyster, when Gene finally appeared.

Once Tom had greeted Gene with a firm handshake and ushered him into the largest of the several rooms in which the "receiving" was taking place, Magda sidled up to him.

"Do you feel as out of place as I do?" she whispered.

"Magda!" Gene said, grabbing her hand. "How good to see you. I was hoping you'd be here."

"Because you don't know anyone else in the room?"

"Actually," whispered Gene, "do you see that man next to the silver punch bowl?"

"The bowl that's big enough to go bathing in?"

"As it happens, I do know that gentleman. Though I wouldn't describe him as gentle."

"You mean?" said Magda, blushing deeply.

"Does that shock you?"

"I am a bit surprised that someone so . . ."

"A bank balance with many zeros does not dictate one's desires," said Gene. "It only means, as I learned years ago from Stanford White, that those thirsts are more easily slaked."

"I wrote you," said Magda, "at Carmine Street. But you never wrote back."

"I don't keep the rooms in New York anymore. I'm staying at the Astor tonight and in the morning I'm off to San Francisco."

"Is there a job there?" said Magda.

"I'll find out when I get there. I decided I've had enough of the East Coast. I thought I'd start over out West. Do me good to be as far as possible from you-know-who," said Gene, nodding toward Tom.

"So you're moving. For good."

"That's the plan," said Gene.

Magda digested this bit of information for a moment. Even though she hadn't seen Gene in many months, she still believed he would always be a part of her life. Now he was moving across a continent.

"Oh my god, is that Tom?" said Gene, grabbing Magda's arm.

"Well, yes," she said. "He's still greeting—"

"No, not Tom. I mean, not the real Tom. That painting of the miserable-looking little boy surrounded by silk and satin." He pointed to a large canvas in a gold frame hanging above the fireplace. A grown woman and four girls sprawled across an expanse of divan, surrounding a boy dressed in black.

"Oh my," said Magda, stifling a giggle. "That *is* Tom."

"All those silky dresses," said Gene. "Lucky boy."

"Only you would think that," said Magda, giving Gene a good-natured jab in the ribs with her elbow.

"I beg you to admire any other work of art in the house, my literary friends," said Tom from behind them as he slapped a hand on each of their shoulders. "Now, the wolves are retreating, the punch is running low, and Mother is starting to ask if the beautiful woman in the burgundy dress is available to marry her stubborn son. What say we adjourn upstairs where we can have a proper reunion?"

Magda got the impression that Tom had had more than his fair share of punch, but she didn't care. If she could have a few minutes alone with him and Gene, what did it matter if he was a bit tipsy? She and Gene followed Tom through a series of gradually narrowing hallways until they arrived at a small winding staircase.

"Servants' stairs," said Tom. "No chance of Mother running into us here." He took them up two flights and into a long, carpeted corridor with doors on either side. "Guest bedroom," he said, opening the third door on the left. "One of many." The room was small by the standards of this house, but still dwarfed any bedroom Magda had slept in. A fire burned in the fireplace and a bottle of brandy and three glasses stood on the mantel. Three upholstered armchairs sat in front of the fire.

"Three chairs in a guest room?" said Gene.

"And three glasses?" said Magda.

"I was hoping you'd both come," said Tom. "One last evening before . . ."

"Before what?" said Magda.

"Before Gene goes to San Francisco, if what he said in his telegram is true. Though if he does go, it will be against my better advice. And before I go to London."

"You're going to London?" said Magda.

"As soon as my father's estate is settled," said Tom. "I need to get as far away from Mother as possible, and luckily she hates ocean journeys."

"So this is it, then," said Magda.

"The last adventure of the Tremendous Trio," said Tom, handing them each a glass of brandy.

"It's funny you should use those words," said Magda, smiling.

꩜

"Look," said Tom, after Magda had explained Mr. Lipscomb's commission, "if we are going to write another story, we have to do it tonight. Gene leaves tomorrow, and I'll be with lawyers round the clock until I sail."

"This is really the last time we're going to see each other?" said Magda.

"Probably so," said Tom.

"Well, I'm not going to write any more Tremendous Trio books or stories without you," said Magda, "so if there are any adventures after this one, someone else will have to write them."

"What's your point?" said Gene.

"My point is," said Magda, "if this is really the end, let's go out with a bang. Let's write something that's never been written before. Let's show the world the way it really is, or at least the way it should be. Let's show characters who have problems and are confused and frightened just like real children. Let's write a story that might convince a girl she doesn't have to be defined by whether or not she gets a husband, a story that tells a boy . . . a boy like Gene that he is not alone."

"Do you really think Lipscomb would publish something like that?" said Tom.

"Of course not," said Magda, "but that's the beauty of it. Lipscomb is leaving the country. He'll be gone for a couple of months at least. I'm sure the April issue will be published before he gets back, and probably the May issue will have gone to press. He won't be able to read what we've written until it's too late."

"Yes, but what about the rest of the chapters?" said Gene. "When he gets back, he'll shut it down for sure."

"Not if the magazine is selling. If he gets heaps of fan letters from readers who want more Tremendous Trio he'll have to keep publishing. If there's one thing Lipscomb can't resist, it's money."

"But we can't write fifteen chapters in one night," said Tom.

"If we write two chapters together, I'll write the rest, and we can still share the money."

"You keep the money," said Tom. "I'll be right back."

"Where are you going?" said Magda.

"To my father's study. We need a typewriter and some pens and a lot of paper. And I'll get some hot coffee sent up. It's going to be a long night."

"It's not exactly a chapter," said Tom, when Magda had read aloud their edited version of the first installment of *The Last Adventure of the Tremendous Trio*. "It's more of an introduction."

"Yes, but what an introduction," said Gene. "What kid is going to read that and not be desperate for more?"

"So, what is the more?" said Tom. "Where do we go from here?"

The coffee urn stood empty and discarded notes littered the floor. Magda sat at a small table by the window where Tom had placed his father's typewriter. They had been so focused on their work that she had hardly had time to breathe in the loveliness of spending these last few hours with Tom and Gene. She looked out on a streetlight illuminating a circle of sidewalk somewhere in the mid-Fifties. She couldn't even remember the side street. A sole pedestrian scurried through the light and disappeared around the corner onto Fifth Avenue. Magda wondered what business he had out at this time of night. What secrets was he keeping from the rest of the world?

"Secrets," she said, turning around in her chair to face the other two.

"I beg your pardon," said Tom.

"We begin with secrets," said Magda.

"What do you mean?" said Gene.

"Everyone has secrets, right?" said Magda. "So, what secrets do Dan Dawson and Alice Gold and Frank Fairfax keep from the world and from one another? How can we show them as completely different people from the heroes we thought they were after the first three books, just by revealing their secrets?"

"Everyone has secrets," said Tom. "But do you really believe the Tremendous Trio would have secrets from each other after all they've been through together?"

"The three of us have been through plenty together, and we have huge secrets from each other, don't we?"

Quiet shrouded the room for the first time since they had started working. Magda could hear the clock on the mantel ticking and the sound of Tom's breathing. Gene seemed to sink lower in his chair and would not meet Magda's eyes. After a long minute she looked at Tom. "You have secrets, don't you?"

"Is it enough to say yes," said Tom, "or do I need to tell them?"

Magda swallowed hard. She was not any more excited about sharing her darkest secrets than Tom or Gene appeared to be, but if they were going to cut to the bone in this story, didn't they need to do the same thing in real life? Besides . . .

"We'll never see each other again," she said. "And if we all share our secrets, then there's no reason for any one of us to be embarrassed."

"It seems a faulty logic," said Tom.

"She's right," said Gene. "This book shouldn't be about some made-up heroes doing things no child would ever do. It shouldn't be about Dan and Alice and Frank, not really. It should be about Magda and Gene and Tom. We *are* a tremendous trio, but with all the secrets and lies and weaknesses and fears that any other three people in the world have. Put that in the story. Put *us* in the story. Then you'll really have something. Who wants to go first?"

"There's a reason I didn't want Gene to go to San Francisco," said Tom. "I've been there myself. It was the most horrible experience of my life, and the most wonderful. I met a girl named Isabella, and she died in my arms." And he told his secrets.

"After the *Slocum* burned," said Magda, "I did something terrible." Her hand rose to her chest and felt the absence of the necklace her mother had given her, the necklace she had placed on a horribly burned body in that makeshift morgue on the pier. "I killed myself, and no one ever knew." And she told her secrets.

"There was a fairy resort on the Bowery we used to call Paresis Hall," said Gene. "And there was a girl named Dame Pinky who made a lot of money there. And it was the happiest time of her life." And he told his secrets.

Just before dawn the trio made their way down the servants' stairs and through the kitchen to the back door through which Tom had sneaked so many times in his youth. They stopped just inside the door in a bleak, narrow passageway.

"Do you have everything?" said Tom to Magda, who carried a large envelope bulging with the drafts of the first two chapters as well as many pages of notes about what might happen next.

"Everything I'm allowed to take with me," she said, smiling wryly at the two men.

"What would your mother say if she knew you'd had a woman here all night?" said Gene.

"If she thought it meant imminent marriage," said Tom, "she'd probably be thrilled."

Away from prying eyes, it seemed preposterous to Magda to abide by the rules of society. She threw her arms around Tom and held him close, whispering in his ear, "Forget me."

"Never," he said.

A tiny flame in her heart wondered if, with a mother so eager for him to marry, he might once again propose, but she knew he wouldn't. And if he did, she knew she would say no. It had been a wonderful night, yes, but last summer had taught her what life would be like with a man she did not love. Besides, she had come to value her own independence over the last few years. She had built a successful life for herself and she was proud of that. Like Alice Gold, she had no intention of judging her life by her ability to land a husband.

Magda kissed Tom on the cheek and released her hold on him.

"Take care of yourself," she said to Gene, now wrapping him in an embrace. "And don't walk in front of any taxis."

"Tell the story," said Gene, looking into Magda's eyes. "And make the gods proud."

XXXIV

NEW YORK CITY, UPPER EAST SIDE, 2010

Sarah Thomas lived in a plain-looking seven-story brick apartment building on East Eighty-First Street almost to East End Avenue. It was a bit of a hike crosstown for Robert, and he thought about taking a taxi, but he was eager to go nearly an hour before their appointment and the best way to pass the time was to walk. So he headed out across the park toward the long blocks of Eighty-First Street.

Crossing the park, just north of the Ramble, he thought about meeting Rebecca there in just two days. Somewhere in those trees, assuming she showed up, he would begin to tell her his story. She had quoted his own adage about storytelling back at him during their fight. He did believe that storytelling was what set mankind apart from other creatures. Now, by telling Rebecca his whole story, he felt he had a chance to become fully human himself.

But the stories suggested by Thomas De Peyster's scrapbook were welling up inside him, too. He knew which story he needed to tell Rebecca, but what story did he want to tell the world? Did he want to tell a story of Thomas and Eugene and Magda? Or did he want to finish the story of the Tremendous Trio? Or, could those two stories be one? Maybe, he thought as he crossed Fifth Avenue a few blocks north of Alice Gold's fictional home, Thomas and Eugene and Magda *were* the Tremendous Trio.

The woman who greeted Robert at the door walked with a cane and a slight stoop, but also with a bounce in her step that belied her eighty-six years.

"Mr. Parrish, I presume," she said, a wide smile playing across her face. "It's not often I get such a distinguished visitor. In fact, short of my daughter and my friends from Zion-St. Mark's, it's not often I have visitors at all. I barely had time to go around to the library and check out a copy of your book before you arrived. Will you come in?"

"Thank you," said Robert, stepping into the small living room. The walls were lined with shelves crammed with books and photographs, and the room was furnished with mid-century modern pieces that looked worn enough to have been bought at the actual mid-century. Light poured in from the street window, however, and the room felt alive and cheerful, loved and lived in. Robert had feared that the apartment of an old woman might smell or feel like impending death, but this room, like Sarah herself, was still very much a going concern.

"I'll get us some coffee," said Sarah.

"Can I help you?" said Robert.

"Don't be silly," she said. "Cream and sugar?"

"Please."

With Sarah out of the room, Robert began to examine the books and photos that cluttered the shelves. He scanned the cases quickly, then stopped short when he spotted, on a bottom shelf almost hidden behind the sofa, a row of six familiar-looking spines—Daring Dan Dawson and the Tremendous Trio.

Seeing them among the rest of Sarah's books reminded him of the den in his childhood home, where, after the Niagara Falls trip, the Tremendous Trio books had taken up residence. The day after he and his father had returned, Robbie had walked down to the liquor store around the corner from his house and asked for some boxes. Back home, he had packed up all of Pop Pop's books and, without comment to his father, carried the boxes up to the attic and shoved them in among the Christmas ornaments. An hour later, he heard the creak of his father pulling down the attic steps and, while most of the books remained out of sight where Robbie had put them, the Tremendous Trio trilogy reappeared on the shelves of the den, between an old set of World Book Encyclopedias and last year's phone book.

In Sarah Thomas's sitting room, the books had less ignominious company. They stood surrounded by classics of children's literature from *Anne of Green Gables* to *Alice in Wonderland*.

Most of Sarah's photographs were in color and showed weddings and family gatherings, but next to the Pickering books stood a black-and-white photograph in a silver frame of a woman standing at the edge of the East River, the lighthouse of what was then called Blackwell's Island in the background. Robert recognized the face. She was older and more care-worn than she had been in Central Park in 1906, but the picture clearly showed Magda Hertzenberger. Sarah Thomas was somehow connected to both Magda and Thomas. Robert had come to the right place.

Robert continued his examination of the room until he heard the tinkling of china behind him and he turned to see Sarah, sans cane, carrying a tray with two coffee cups.

"Please, let me get that," said Robert, taking the tray from Sarah and setting it on the coffee table.

"So," she said when they were settled with their coffee, "what is a famous novelist doing poking around in Thomas De Peyster's scrapbook?"

"Did you know him? Thomas De Peyster?"

"I never met him," said Sarah. "That album was from long before my time."

"It's from 1906," said Robert.

"And I was born in 1924," said Sarah.

"So how did you come to have . . ."

"It belonged to my aunt. It was one of the few things she had with her when she . . . reappeared. That was just before I was born."

"What do you mean 'reappeared'?" said Robert.

"Have you heard of the *General Slocum* disaster?" said Sarah.

"Vaguely," said Robert. "Was it some sort of boat fire?"

"A steamboat that caught fire in the East River at Hell Gate not far from here. Killed over a thousand people, including my uncle and my grandmother.

Everyone thought my aunt died, too. That was in 1904. In 1922, she showed up at my parents' apartment just a few blocks from here. She had no idea that her little sister, my mother, had survived the *Slocum* as well."

"Where had she been?" said Robert.

"I never knew the details," said Sarah. "I would catch bits and pieces every now and then from something she said to my mother, nothing more. But she came to live with us and for me it was like having a third parent. She took me on long walks around the city, and played games with me, and oh, the books. She was always bringing me books. When I was in grade school we went to the library every Saturday and on the way home we would go down to the river and sit on a bench and talk about what we read, and if the weather was nice, she would tell me a story. She told the most marvelous stories. They all had the same three heroes. Oh, I wish I could remember them. They would have these wonderful, interminable adventures. I remember flashes—a desert island, a wild lion, a terrible fire—but no more. It's been so long now that her stories are just a few grainy photographs fading and curling in the back of my memory."

"But what does all this have to do with the scrapbook?" said Robert. He was sitting forward in his chair and had nearly slipped off the edge when she spoke of her aunt telling stories about a trio of heroes having adventures.

"I'm getting to that," said Sarah. "I've waited thirty-four years for you; you can wait a few minutes for me."

"Thirty-four years?"

"Shh," said Sarah. "I married an ex-GI in 1946. Gregory Thomas. A medic. Such a handsome man. We lived out on Long Island for a few years, but when my father died in the early 1950s and then my mother a few years later, we moved back to the city to live with Aunt Magda. By then we had our own children, and she told them stories, but these were different. She had moved on from adventure stories to fairy tales. When my children grew up and left home, we decided to move to a smaller apartment. We were sorting through things trying to decide what to take and what to get rid of, when I saw the scrapbook for the first time. At first, Aunt Magda didn't even want to look at it. She told me to give it away or throw it out. But I left it on her dresser, and a few days later I found her sitting on her bed, with the scrapbook on her lap and tears on her cheeks. She told me to come and sit next to her and we went through every page of that book together. And that's when I found out who she was."

"Who was she?"

"You already know," said Sarah, "or you wouldn't be here. I saw you looking at her picture."

"She was Magda Hertzenberger," said Robert.

"Magdalena," said Sarah. "But that wasn't her only name."

"Dexter Cornwall," said Robert.

"Author of Daring Dan Dawson and the Tremendous Trio. It took me years to track down all six volumes, mostly in bookstores on Fourth Avenue, but when I did, I recognized snippets of the adventures she had told me when I was a child. Aunt Magda would never read them, but I loved them."

"My grandfather introduced me to them," said Robert. "He sent a fan letter to Dexter Cornwall and somebody wrote him back."

"Probably Aunt Magda," said Sarah. "She worked for the publisher, Pickering Brothers, and the only thing she told me about her job was that she answered the fan mail. After we moved, I would take the scrapbook out every now and then and look at those pictures and read all those newspaper articles in the envelope in the back."

"I've read them all, too," said Robert.

"The whole thing seemed so mysterious to me. By then my aunt was in her late seventies, and it was hard to imagine her a girl in her twenties in 1906, going out with these two men in the pictures and writing children's books. I always thought there must be a great story behind it all, but she never would tell me more than the basics. She had worked for the publisher, had briefly known Gene and Tom, that's what she called them, and the three of them had written a few books together. Tom gave her the scrapbook."

"Did she ever marry?" said Robert. "From those candid pictures of her in the album, I got the impression Tom was in love with her."

"She never mentioned a husband," said Sarah. "But I think she kept a lot of secrets."

"What about the woman under the menu?" said Robert. "Did your aunt ever talk about her?"

"I'm afraid I don't know what you mean," said Sarah.

Robert reached into the Zabar's canvas bag he had brought with him and retrieved his re-creation of Thomas De Peyster's album. He opened it to the first page and set it on the coffee table in front of Magda.

"I sort of made my own version of the scrapbook," he said.

"Oh, how delightful," said Sarah. "I haven't seen this in so long. I always thought it was odd that the first thing in it was something as ordinary as a menu from Childs. Aunt Magda wouldn't tell me about that. All she said was, 'Sometimes the most ordinary days are the ones you cherish the most.'"

Robert gently lifted up his facsimile of the menu to reveal the woman underneath. "When I was working with the scrapbook at the Historical Society, the menu came loose and I found this photograph underneath."

"Goodness," said Sarah, leaning over to examine the picture closely. "There can't be much doubt about what she has in mind."

"My thoughts exactly."

"But I've never seen her before. I wonder if Aunt Magda knew."

"I don't think so," said Robert. "That menu had been glued down on all four sides. I think she must have been Tom's secret."

"Or one of them, anyway," said Sarah. "I got the impression from Aunt Magda that all three of them had secrets."

"Did she ever tell you why she dressed up like a man?"

"As I said, she had secrets. But I don't want you to get the idea that she was a sad old woman living in her secret past. She was an inspiration to me and to my daughter. She was independent and free-spirited and creative and compassionate. She knew every street of New York and she used to take my two children and me on long walks around the city on Saturdays and tell us what each neighborhood was like at the turn of the century. She could paint a picture of old New York so clearly you could practically hear the elevated train rumbling overhead and the horse-drawn wagons rattling down the street. And nothing scared her. When she was in her sixties she slapped a mugger so hard across his face that he just stood there dumbfounded while she walked on. And when they told her she had cancer, she didn't even flinch. Death didn't frighten her any more than anything else."

"And after she died, you gave the scrapbook to the Historical Society?"

"We were cleaning out her things," said Sarah, "and I thought they might like all those old photographs."

"I think what you said before is right," said Robert. "I think there is a great story in this scrapbook, but I'm almost glad we don't know all the details."

"Why?"

"Because I want to write a novel about it. About your aunt Magda and Thomas De Peyster and Eugene Pinkney and Dan Dawson and Frank Fairfax and Alice Gold and the Tremendous Trio—all of it." As he and Sarah had spoken, Robert had begun to see more and more clearly the story he wanted to tell. "I want to tell their story, even if I don't know what it is. That's what I do—I tell stories. I want to write about the day they had lunch at Childs and about the days those photographs were taken and I want to imagine the stories of all the places on those postcards—the Flatiron Building and the old Madison Square Garden and Coney Island."

"Oh, she did used to talk about Coney Island," said Sarah. "She claimed she had only been there once, but she could describe it in such detail that sometimes I wondered if she was making it all up."

"There's something else I want to do," said Robert, thinking of the children in the library, wide-eyed and ready for a tale. "You might not know this, but there was a fourth Tremendous Trio story. As far as I know they only ever wrote the introductory chapter, but for 1912 it was a bombshell of a chapter."

"*The Last Adventure of the Tremendous Trio*," said Sarah.

"You've heard of it."

"I have."

"Do you know if they ever finished it?" said Robert, taken by the idea of writing the book himself, of fulfilling his promise to his father in the most personal way.

"They never did," said Sarah with a smile.

"That's a shame," said Robert, though his heart leapt with excitement.

"I thought the day would never come, but it has," said Sarah, breaking into a laugh as musical as the tinkling of the coffee cups. "You are the one."

XXXV

On April 16, 1912, Magda sat at her desk staring at three items and pondering the power of ink and paper. The first was issue number one of *Tales of Excitement for Boys and Girls*, containing the first installment of *The Last Adventure of the Tremendous Trio*. Mr. Lipscomb had never seen the typescript she had sent to the production office, and the introductory chapter appeared exactly as she, Gene, and Tom had written it. The printing had taken longer than anticipated, and the magazine had not been ready for distribution until the previous day. As it happened, only a few copies would ever make it into the hands of readers, those sold by a newsstand in Madison Square to whom an errand boy working in the production office had delivered a bundle that morning. The rest of the press run sat in a warehouse in New Jersey.

The second item was a telegram that the Pickering office had received six days earlier. Magda had paid it no mind until yesterday. It read simply: SAIL TODAY FROM SOUTHAMPTON ABOARD RMS TITANIC. LIPSCOMB.

The third item was the morning paper, with the grim headline: 1340 PERISH AS TITANIC SINKS.

The death of Pickering Brothers, Publishers, was not quite as rapid or dramatic as the death of its founder and sole proprietor, Julius Lipscomb, aboard the *Titanic*, nor did much of anyone take notice. The company's

demise went unrecorded by the papers and even the book industry publications made no note of the occasion.

The survivors of the *Titanic* disaster arrived in New York on the evening
of April 18. But even then, there was no confirmation that Mr. Lipscomb
had been among those lost. That word came four days later, when the
White Star Line released the official list of casualties. But all this made no
difference. From the moment the word of the sinking arrived in New York,
the vultures began circling Pickering Brothers. Magda would discover,
in her final few days of employment, that Pickering had been deeply in
debt; that, despite the map in his office, Lipscomb had never succeeded
in placing his publications in more than a few bookstores, all of them
in New York City. Magda suspected that Mr. Lipscomb might have even
written some of the Pickering "fan letters" himself. He had, apparently,
lived under the delusion that someday his books would be discovered and
his warehouse emptied under a deluge of orders. In fact, almost 90 percent
of the books ever printed by Pickering Brothers still sat in storage. Before
the end of the month, creditors would sell them, along with almost all the
copies of *Tales of Excitement for Boys and Girls*, for pulp. The end came for
Magda on April 23, when she left Pickering Brothers with a copy of *Tales
of Excitement for Boys and Girls*, the three fan letters she had removed from
the files to show Gene and Tom, and the typescript of the second chapter
of *The Last Adventure*, which she had retrieved from the production office,
claiming she wished to return it to Mr. Marcus Stone.

She allowed herself to grieve—for Pickering Brothers and for the fact
that she could seek no comfort in the friendship of Gene and Tom—for
the length of the elevator ride to the ground floor. Then she stepped out
onto Fifth Avenue and got on with her life.

◦◦◦

YPRES, BELGIUM, 1915

On a spring night, in a field in northwestern Belgium, Thomas De Peyster finally had the opportunity to rescue someone. His flight to London

had come none too soon. During the weeks it took to settle his father's estate, his meddling mother had been more insistent than ever that he, with all haste, marry some Vanderbilt or Carnegie or Roosevelt. The time he had spent with Magda, working on the Tremendous Trio books, had convinced him of two things—he would never marry anyone else and he would never marry her. Stepping off the ship at Southampton, he welcomed the promise of a new country, new friends, and a life far from the world of American children's adventures and Mrs. De Peyster.

He filed the occasional story for Mr. Hearst, but, as he had inherited a substantial fortune from his father, he had no real need to work. He spent much of his time exploring England and traveling on the continent. Except when using his passport, he lived as Thomas Poster. There were enough aristocrats in England with small bank balances and single daughters that if word got out that the unmarried heir to the De Peyster fortune was roaming the English countryside, he would never have a moment's peace. So, instead of drinks parties at posh London clubs and hunting weekends at country estates, he lived a modest life, never quite settling in one place long enough for people to ask too many questions about his past. Then the war had come and the recruiters in rural Oxfordshire to whom he had presented himself did not show any concern about his slightly odd accent or his lack of proper identification. At thirty-two he was obviously old enough to enlist. He became a private in the British Second Army. By the time he arrived in Belgium, the Western Front had stabilized and trench warfare had begun.

On that night in early April 1915, low clouds hung in the sky, and the German guns had been silent for several hours. An officer in a trench not far from Tom's decided to send a dozen men creeping into no-man's-land, in hopes of reaching the German line and inflicting some damage before the enemy noticed them in the darkness. Two minutes after they climbed out of their trench, the sky lit up with artillery shells and machine guns began blazing from German positions. Tom peeked over the edge of his trench to see man after man falling to the onslaught.

In the near daylight of exploding shells, Tom saw not a ravaged Belgian field, covered with barbed wire and strewn with the bodies of soldiers. He saw a hotel room in San Francisco and a woman who could be saved simply by pulling her back from the window a split-second sooner. He saw a man trapped in the rubble of a collapsed house, who needed only a savior of stupendous strength to free him before the fire reached his prison. He saw a woman in the third-story window of a burning hotel, with nothing below her but cobblestones. He saw the faces of all those he could not save that day in San Francisco, and he leapt out of the trench.

The incessant roar of guns and artillery faded from Tom's consciousness and he believed he could hear the cries of agony from the injured. He raced through the mud, paying no more attention to the barbed wire that tore at his clothes and flesh than to the sound of the battle. Two British soldiers, pale with fear, ran past him the other way, diving back into the trenches. A moment later, four more did the same. Tom had counted a dozen men entering no-man's-land a minute before; that meant six were still there. Through smoke and fog he found his way to the fallen men, one by one. Whether he had ever seen their faces before, he didn't know. Men came and went from the trenches with sickening speed—arriving grim and erect, convinced they could make a difference for God and country; departing on stretchers, too often with their faces covered.

The first two men he dragged back to the trench were so splattered with mud and blood that he would not have recognized them if they had been his own brothers. But he did know this—they were alive. The next two he found almost on top of each other. One was uninjured, save for a twisted ankle. But he was frozen with fear, and Tom wasted precious seconds prizing him from the mud and shouting at him to run low and fast for the trench. Tom ran behind, carrying the body of a man who screamed in either pain or fear. Either one meant life, thought Tom.

The last two proved harder to find. One was nearly buried in the mud, his shape almost unrecognizable as human. But in a lull in the gunfire, Tom heard a moan next to him, and found the soldier, limp but breathing, and easy to carry to the trench. He was only a boy.

That left one. Tom had operated on adrenaline and memory for the past several minutes, thinking not about the battle, but about Isabella. A sudden sharp pain in his right shoulder brought him back to the reality of the moment. He was not walking through the streets of San Francisco observing death from a safe distance; he was grabbing death by the hand and daring him to squeeze. He did not stop to examine what he assumed was a bullet wound in his shoulder, but rushed back onto the field, scanning that scene of horror for one more man. The artillery shells stopped, and the darkness rapidly returned. The flash of the machine guns gave little light, but Tom thought if he could not see the field, then the Germans could not see him. For five, ten, fifteen minutes he crawled back and forth in the muck, occasionally stumbling over a body that was cold with a death that had come long before tonight. Then he heard it, the faint sound of a man at prayer. "Please, God," the voice said. "Please."

Tom summoned a last bit of strength and dove under a burst of machine gun fire in the direction where he had heard the voice. The soldier was entangled in the barbed wire and, as best as Tom could tell, had a badly wounded left leg. Tom pulled out his knife and slashed at the uniform, freeing the man from the wire. He heaved him over his shoulder and ran for the trench.

From within that trench, men watched this act of heroism; they saw Tom rushing toward them, saw him fling the injured soldier toward the trench. They grabbed that man by the hands and pulled him in, and watched as Tom, two steps away from safety, fell forward lifeless, a bullet in the back of his head.

"Thomas Poster" was buried in a nearby church cemetery and after the war reinterred in Tyne Cot Cemetery in Flanders. He was posthumously awarded the Victoria Cross. However, as the address and other information on his enlistment papers proved to be false, the medal was never presented to any family member.

In trying to trace his family, an officer searched the pockets of Tom's uniform, but found only two black-and-white photographs. One showed the head of a sleeping woman, her hair cascading across a tangle of sheets, the other a different young woman, sitting on a park bench, her head thrown back in laughter.

◌⌒◌

SAN FRANCISCO, 1918

Gene did not die the way Tom always feared he would. He was not brutally beaten by a man he had asked into his bed. But a visitor to his bed did kill him—a young man, probably too young for a thirty-six-year-old to seduce, but a man so beautiful that Gene could not resist. He called himself Reginald and he did not raise a finger to harm Gene.

For the previous six years, Gene had been working at Pacific Gas and Electric, helping to modernize their systems. He liked San Francisco. There were no memories here for him. The first day he arrived in the city, he had made it a point to stay at the rebuilt Palace Hotel. He walked the halls of the hotel, trying to feel the presence of Tom, whose tryst with Isabella had taken place there six years earlier, but he felt no sense of connection. He liked that. He had come to San Francisco to forget Tom and it was already working.

Gene met men less often than he had in New York, but, as in that city, he found places in San Francisco where one might encounter men who shared his desires, and when Gene did find a willing partner, he always returned to the Palace—not out of any reverence for Tom, but because, while he had no need to live in luxury, he loved sharing it with others. Reginald had been properly impressed by the soft bed and the crisp sheets and the fireplace in the sitting room. They had spent a Saturday afternoon together in room 719 and then Reginald had left, giving Gene a gentle kiss on the cheek before he did so. Gene saw no reason not to spend the night in the room he had paid for, so, exhausted by the afternoon's activities, he rolled over and fell asleep. It was October 7, 1918.

The next morning Gene felt feverish and achy. He told the chambermaid he would stay another night and resolved to sleep off whatever illness was plaguing him. He woke again around midday, gasping for breath and coughing up a frothy, bloody mucus. Three hours later, he was dead.

The chambermaid found his body the following morning. Eugene Pinkney was one of the first residents of San Francisco to die in the great influenza pandemic of 1918; more than three thousand residents of that city would eventually follow him. Because he had registered at the Palace under a false name, the hotel management was unable to locate any friends or family. To prevent panic and fear among the other hotel guests, the management quietly arranged for a burial, with a simple stone bearing only the name Gene had given: Buck Larson.

XXXVI

NEW YORK CITY, UPPER EAST SIDE, 2010

"What do you mean I'm the one?" said Robert.

"I've been waiting for you all these years," said Sarah. "That's why I told the people at the Historical Society if anyone ever comes looking at that scrapbook, you be sure to call me. I knew anyone who wanted to see the scrapbook might be the one."

"Who is the one?" said Robert. "I'm not some sort of prophet. I'm just a writer on the trail of a good story."

"Oh, you're more than that, Mr. Parrish," said Sarah, pulling herself up. "You wait here. I'll be right back. Oh, to think the day has come at last." She laughed again as she left the room, leaving Robert alone and perplexed.

From deep within the apartment he heard sounds like moving furniture and falling boxes, but when he called out, "Are you sure I can't help you?" Sarah replied in a voice strong enough to be heard in the living room, "Not a bit. I'll be there in a minute."

Robert returned to the shelf where Magda's picture stood and picked up the tarnished silver frame. What had happened to her between 1906 and 1922? What, besides the simple passage of time, had turned Magda from Thomas De Peyster's youthful object of adoration into a middle-aged woman, alone by the river, looking out—he supposed she was looking out toward Hell Gate, the spot where the *General Slocum* had caught fire. As he looked at Magda's face, trying to guess what it hid, he felt excited about imagining her story.

"Here we are," said Sarah, stepping back into the room. She stood more erect than before and looked ten years younger. Robert had the feeling this would not be his last visit to this apartment and he thought how much Rebecca would enjoy getting to know Sarah. She had a talent for engaging with older people. Robert had seen it in casual encounters in shops and restaurants, and in the way Rebecca would pal around with her mother's friends.

Sarah carried a rectangular cardboard box covered in peeling paper. Robert could just make out the word *Siegel's* on a bit of paper still adhered to the side. Sarah sat down and clutched the box in her lap.

"It will be such a weight off my shoulders to give this to you," she said. "I was beginning to worry about what I should do with it since no one ever came."

"What is it?" said Robert.

"Aunt Magda called me into her room the night she got her cancer diagnosis and gave me this box. She didn't show me what was in it, and she made me promise not to look even after she died, though I admit I broke that promise a few years later. That night she explained to me that someday, someone might turn up asking about *The Last Adventure of the Tremendous Trio*, and if that happened, I should give them this box. I supposed at the time that she thought Gene or Tom might still be alive and might come looking for her. But that was thirty-four years ago. Magda was born in 1882. I gave up on any of her friends still being alive a long time ago. But I kept waiting, and finally you came. You're the one she meant."

"But she can't possibly have known that I would come knocking on your door trying to find out about the Tremendous Trio," said Robert.

"No," said Sarah, "but I think she hoped that sooner or later *somebody* would. So now I can give you this and stop worrying about it." She held the box out to Robert reverently and he took it in both hands. It was heavier than he expected and he felt his breathing and pulse quicken as his hands touched the worn corners. Magda Hertzenberger, also known as Dexter Cornwall, had reached out across nearly a century to send him a message.

What would Robert's teenage self think if he knew that the secret treasures of one of the authors of the Tremendous Trio lay hidden in a box just a few miles from his home? In the months that followed the ill-fated Niagara trip, months during which Robbie rarely initiated a conversation with his father, he often sneaked into the den late at night when his parents had fallen asleep. He sometimes read a chapter or two of the Tremendous Trio, but more often he pulled out those mysterious pages that began *The Last Adventure* and read them over and over. He felt guilty that he had lost interest in sharing the books with his father. But reading those pages always made him feel better. Knowing that he was not the only person with dark thoughts and anxieties and confusion lightened his load ever so slightly. And every time he finished reading those pages, he longed for even a hint of what might happen next.

"Do you mind," said Robert, setting the box on the coffee table, "if I open it here?"

"Not at all," said Sarah.

Robert gently lifted the lid and set it aside. On top of the contents lay a yellowing piece of letterhead Robert recognized—the same letterhead his grandfather had carried with him in Alsace bearing a letter from "Dexter Cornwall." This sheet of Pickering Brothers stationery was blank and Robert removed it to see what treasures it hid.

First was a near pristine copy of *Alice Gold, Girl Inventor* in its original dust jacket. He lifted the book out, smiling to see, in the bright colors of the jacket art, Alice just as he had always imagined her—boyish, a bit grimy, clad in greasy blue coveralls, and holding a wrench. He opened the front cover of the book and read the inscription: *To Dexter Cornwall from Buck Larson, in memory of a summer day. Christmas 1906.*

The next item had been carefully wrapped in brown paper, and Robert unwrapped it to discover a copy of *Tales of Excitement for Boys and Girls*, issue number one, identical to the borrowed copy he had at home. Now he could return that copy to Tony Esposito. Again, it looked as bright and crisp as the day it was published.

Robert peered into the box and saw a mass of papers, yellowing and furled at the corners. "Is there somewhere I could spread this out?" he asked.

"Of course," said Sarah. "You can use the dining table. Why don't you empty it out there and we can see what you've got. Even when I did look into that box years ago, I didn't understand most of what I saw, but I'm sure you'll explain it all to me eventually."

At the dining table, Robert reached into the box and pulled out the stack of papers. Over the next two hours he and Sarah paged through each sheet. Some of them astounded him, some confounded him, but they all seemed to be fragments of a story longing to be made whole.

Most of the material clearly related to *The Last Adventure of the Tremendous Trio*. There was a typescript, headed Chapter One, of the chapter that had been published in *Tales of Excitement for Boys and Girls*, marked up with notes and emendations clearly written by three different people. Clipped to this document with a rusty paperclip were several pages of cryptic notes in the same three hands. If Robert was looking for questions, these notes would provide hundreds of them. Hardly a single line in these pages made any sense, and he did not read them all there with Sarah, but they did take turns, for a while, deciphering some of the fragments.

Dan like Gene. What are secrets of G, T, M? Inventions—War? Explosives from aeroplane. Truth about parents. Alice suicide? Poverty in Lower ES. Children on streets. Enslavement of locals? Triangle fire? DL fire? Love triangle.

There was much more like this, giving Robert the sense that *The Last Adventure of the Tremendous Trio*, had it ever been completed, might have been a very dark book, especially by the standards of children's books in 1912. What sort of scandal would have ensued in the pages of *The Outlook* if Pickering had published a book for children that dealt with suicide and weaponry and death and slavery and sex?

The next item in the box was, perhaps, the most exciting and the easiest to understand. It was another typescript, this one without any stray markings on it. At the top it read merely, Chapter Two.

XXXVII

LOWER EAST SIDE, AS THE TWENTIES BEGAN TO ROAR

On a warm June afternoon in 1922, Magda Hertzenberger stood in Tompkins Square Park looking, for the first time, at the memorial to those lost on the *General Slocum*, dedicated in the autumn of 1906. It was a slab of pinkish marble, with a bas-relief of two children, the younger of whom could have easily been her sister, Rosie. An inscription above them read, THEY WERE EARTH'S PUREST CHILDREN, YOUNG AND FAIR.

Magda had not thought about Henry and Rosie for a long time. She had not been back to Kleindeutschland since the days following the disaster, and as she had walked to Tompkins Square from the Eighth Street El station, she no longer heard German spoken in the streets of her old neighborhood. A few days ago, she had noticed a small item in the *Herald*:

> The seventeenth annual memorial service for the unidentified dead of the steamship General Slocum, which burned in the East River on June 15, 1904, with the loss of nearly a thousand lives, was held yesterday afternoon in the Lutheran Cemetery at Middle Village, Queens. More than a thousand persons attended.

Magda did not often think of the past—yes, she cherished her memories of Tom and Gene and of the work they had done together, occasionally

letting her mind wander back to Dreamland and the summer that had led
there; but she almost never thought about the *Slocum*. Life was too short,
she thought, to dwell on tragedy. She was proud of the work she had done
and the life she had led since the demise of Pickering Brothers. But that
notice in the newspaper telling her that nearly a thousand people had
attended a memorial service for the twins—both of whom fell into the
category of "unidentified dead"—while she had never paid a visit to the
mass grave and memorial on Long Island, awakened a guilt Magda had
not felt for many years. She wasn't sure she could face the trip to Middle
Village, so she resolved to return to Tompkins Square Park and visit the
memorial there. She found it a quiet, peaceful spot—not the sort of place
to remind her of the rambunctious Henry and Rosie in the slightest. She
had brought a rose with her and she quietly laid it at the base of the
memorial, but she felt no connection to her departed siblings. Magda saw
no point to wallowing in painful memories.

She rationed her happy memories, but allowed them in moderation.
After Mr. Lipscomb died, Magda had packed away all the remnants of the
Tremendous Trio in a box and promised herself not to open it until either
Gene or Tom returned. She did not keep that promise. Every year, on
the anniversary of their Dreamland trip, Magda opened the box and read
Chapter Two of *The Last Adventure*.

Once upon a time there were three children who had
secrets. You might know them as Alice, Dan, and Frank,
but the secrets began right there, because their real
names were Gene, Tom, and Magda. No one knew Magda was
named Magda, everyone thought she was named Mary. Most
people thought Tom's last name was Poster, though it was
really De Peyster. A few people thought Gene was a girl,
even though he was actually a boy. And some people knew
this trio as Buck, Neptune, and Dexter. Confused? Well,
life is confusing, so you may as well get used to it.

For the purposes of this story, we will call these
children Alice, Dan, and Frank, and we will say that they

were fourteen or fifteen or sixteen. But just remember, no one is exactly who they say they are. Everyone has secrets. Everyone has desires. And everyone has secret desires. Alice and Dan and Frank were no exception.

Our story begins on what should have been the happiest day in the lives of these three heroes. They had just returned to New York City from a trip around the world in an aeroplane of Alice's own invention. On a sunny afternoon in May, they sat together in the back of a fancy automobile, driving up Broadway and waving at the hundreds of thousands of people who cheered for them. Ticker tape streamed down on them from the windows of tall office buildings. Preceding them was a marching band playing a new tune by John Philip Sousa which he had composed in their honor. From the moment Alice's aeroplane had left Governor's Island in New York Harbor four months earlier, they had dreamed of this moment. They all should have been deliriously happy. None of them were.

They smiled and waved at the crowds and looked as cheerful as any three children had ever looked. No one knew what they were really feeling. Not one of them knew what the other two were feeling.

Alice, who gritted her teeth behind her smile, seethed with anger. She could not believe that Dan would say to her what he had said. She did not believe it was true and if it wasn't true then the only reason for him to say it was to hurt her—and he had hurt her. Alice hated that she could be blood-boilingly angry at the same time she was soppy in love, that she could want so achingly to throw her arms around him and also to slap him as hard as she could across the face. It just wasn't fair.

Frank, who waved enthusiastically at the crowds and shouted greetings to every pretty girl who waved back, had never felt so sad in his life. How could he be so close

to what he wanted, what he desperately desired, and yet
be unable to get it, unable to even ask for it? The world
was a cruel place and he could feel it turning him into
a cruel person. What was the point in being kind when
the world would never repay you? Better to be callous,
to build up the calluses he would need to protect himself
from the pain of reality.

Dan shook his hat in the air with one hand and
swept away cascades of ticker tape with the other. He
looked bravest of the three, and everyone who lined the
streets knew about his acts of heroism. They had read
in the newspapers how he had saved Frank and Alice in
the desert and how he had saved those children in the
jungle and that man in the sea. But, of course, Frank had
written those articles and no one in New York had been
there to see the truth. Dan was so filled with fear that
he wanted to hide away from the adoration of that crowd
and never show himself again. Dan was afraid they would
discover who he really was—not a hero but a coward. In
his nightmares Dan saw not the faces of those few people
he had saved, but of the many he had not.

And so, they rode up Broadway, smiling and waving,
and each thinking he was the only one in abject misery.
But that's the thing about misery, isn't it? One of the
things that makes it so miserable is that you keep it to
yourself. If Alice and Dan and Frank had each admitted
to the others what they were feeling, they would not
have felt quite so bad. But of course, that was not going
to happen.

As the parade crossed Twenty-Third Street and
into Madison Square, the children noticed a commotion
in front of the Flatiron Building. A horse pulling a
wagonload of produce, spooked by the noise of the parade,
had ignored his driver and was galloping at full speed

down Broadway where the crowd spilled across the street. In that instant Alice and Dan and Frank felt that, if they were true heroes, they would know what to do to prevent what looked like certain disaster. But none of them made the slightest move to do anything. They looked away, pretending they hadn't seen the horse or the wagon rattling dangerously behind it.

As it turned out, the crowd drew aside, the driver slowed the horse, and no one was hurt. No one noticed that the children had ignored the incident. The cheering crowds assumed the heroes simply hadn't seen, in all the noise and excitement. But the three children in the car knew better. When the parade had ended, when the mayor had presented them with the key to the city and a prominent inventor had treated them to dinner at his club, they found themselves alone at last in the drawing room of Alice's house.

Only then did they speak of what they had seen and at that moment they all agreed—they were not heroes. They were not even particularly good people. They had taken unnecessary risks, disobeyed their parents, and put the lives of both friends and strangers at risk. And for what? For adventure? For a ticker tape parade? Or just to prove to themselves that, as long as they didn't mind what harm they did to others, they could do whatever they liked?

"So we're agreed," said Dan, doing his best to push away his fear. "We are thoughtless, self-centered, ill-behaved, reckless gadabouts."

"Indeed," said Alice, trying to forget her anger. "With a heartless disregard for the safety of others or the consequences of our actions."

"And," said Frank, swallowing his sadness, "a complete lack of sympathy for our fellow human beings."

"We should be locked up," said Alice.

"We should be thrashed," said Dan.

"We should on no account be given a parade of any sort," said Frank.

"Good," said Alice. "Now, since we are all in agreement, the question is, what do we do now?"

"Where do we go?" said Frank.

"I'm glad you asked that," said Dan, unfolding a map on the table. He pointed to a big X he had made on the map in red ink. "I thought we could go here."

"Brilliant," said Alice.

"Brilliant," said Frank.

They sat down and began to plan.

XXXVIII

Under the Chapter Two manuscript Robert found a set of bizarre-looking schematics and technical drawings he assumed represented some of the inventions of Alice Gold.

"Now these I recognize," said Sarah, after Robert had removed the drawings from the stack of papers. She picked up three postcards of the Dreamland amusement park on Coney Island.

"They're the same cards that were in the scrapbook," said Robert.

"Yes," said Sarah.

On the back of each of the postcards was a date written in ink: *September 22, 1906.* "And that's the same date as in the captions Thomas De Peyster put under these cards. Maybe they both went to Dreamland that day."

"Maybe so," said Sarah. "I don't think she would have kept these if they didn't mean something."

"But she did keep them," said Robert.

"Yes," said Sarah, "and this."

The next item in the pile was a clipped newspaper article with the headline DREAMLAND FIRE DESTROYS MORE THAN PARK.

"There was a fire?" said Robert.

"Read," said Sarah.

The last items in the box were three folded letters and three envelopes. The letters were pieces of fan mail, clearly written by young children, one to Buck Larson, one to Neptune B. Smythe, and one to Dexter Cornwall. Robert read them through quickly and was just about to set them aside when he noticed the signature on the letter to Dexter Cornwall. The letter was from a boy named Howard, a boy who feared his own lack of bravery in the face of bullies. Robert's grandfather had been named Howard. Could this possibly be the letter Howard Parrish had sent to Dexter Cornwall? The letter to which Magda, as Cornwall, replied, writing the words his grandfather would carry with him in Alsace? The text seemed to fit with Cornwall's reply. Trembling, Robert set the letter aside, now convinced that, as Sarah had said, he was the one.

Two of the envelopes from the packet were still sealed and bore the names *Eugene Pinkney* and *Tom De Peyster*.

"I never opened those two," said Sarah. "Not even when I looked in the box before. Only you should open those."

Robert picked up the third envelope, which had been mailed, and opened by its recipient. It was addressed: *Mary Stone, 316 W. 23rd St., New York*. The paper that Robert withdrew was a thick creamy stock, engraved at the top with the initials *TDP*.

June 11, 1912

Dearest Magda,

    After some delay in settling my father's estate, I sail for London tomorrow on the Mauretania. I am sending under separate cover an album of photographs and other scraps that I think it best for me to leave behind. It will hold meaning only for you and Eugene, and mostly for you. Perhaps someday, when all else is forgotten, you will peruse its pages and remember that there was once a summer when the sun was always warm and the breeze was always cool and when anything could happen.

                        Yours,

                        Tom

"That one made me cry," said Sarah, as Robert read the letter aloud.

"So that's why she had the album," said Robert. "Do you know what happened to him?"

"As I said, she never spoke about Tom or Gene except that one day when we looked through the album. 'Don't live in the past' was like a mantra to her. I loved her for that, though. It meant she was always truly present."

"Should I open these now?" said Robert, indicating the sealed letters.

"Wait just a minute," said Sarah. She disappeared and was back a moment later with a silver letter opener. "This was a wedding gift to me and Gregory from Aunt Magda. She said she planned on writing me letters from all over the world and she wanted to think of me opening them in style."

She handed the letter opener to Robert, who carefully slit the first envelope, addressed *To Eugene Pinkney.*

May 8, 1945

Dear Gene,

I could never bear to finish The Last Adventure *on my own, but I hope if you are reading this it means you came to find me and discovered this box. It's all I still have of our notes and ideas, and if you only found it and not me, then I am just a memory now. Do with this what you will, but it makes me happy to think that someday you might finish what we began together all those years ago.*

As for all the rest, no words are needed. You know how I feel.

Yours,
Magda

The letter to Tom was identical, except for the last sentence: "You know how sorry I am about all the rest, but I have found, as I hope you have, that the present offers joys and the past only memories."

"May 8, 1945," said Robert. "That was VE Day."

"As good a time as any to put one's affairs in order," said Sarah. "Though she lived for another thirty-two years."

"So, all that time she thought Tom or Gene might come back, that they might finish the story."

"But they never did," said Sarah.

Robert looked wistfully at the two letters in his lap. Though he had discovered Magda, it felt as if Tom and Gene had slipped through his fingers. If Magda never knew what happened to them, what hope was there that he could discover their stories? He, and not Tom or Gene, had been the one to open Magda's letters, so perhaps the best way to know these two forgotten men was to step into their shoes and do what Magda had wanted *them* to do and what, he now realized, he had promised his father to do so many years ago.

"If you'll allow me," said Robert, "I'd like to write *The Last Adventure*. I've been reading one of the Tremendous Trio books to the children at my local library and the kids love it. And I think the final adventure could be something that . . . I don't know, that really speaks to kids, older kids who are going through, you know, the things you go through when you're a teenager. And I have . . . well, I have a personal reason for wanting to write it. It would help me keep a promise I made a long time ago—a promise I'd like to tell you about sometime, but I have to tell someone else first. So, if I have your blessing—"

Sarah smiled, patted him on the arm, and said, "Why do you think I kept the box?"

♾

Robert looked at the bookcase he had crammed with what he now knew were Stratemeyer books—Tom Swift, the Great Marvel series, the Hardy Boys, and many others. He didn't need these anymore, he thought. These formed no part of the story of Magda and Tom and Gene, not really. An hour later he had boxed them all up and put them in the storage room in the basement. Only the Pickering books remained lined up neatly on the shelf. Rebecca liked neatness.

He had been trying not to think about Rebecca, knowing that the excitement of possibly seeing her tomorrow, his nervousness about the story he wanted to tell her, would pour so much adrenaline into his veins that sleep would prove impossible. But, with a little more than twelve hours until their scheduled rendezvous, and with the Tremendous Trio all arranged on his desk and waiting to inhabit his writing, he could think of nothing but her smile—the smile he hoped would be playing across her face the next day in the Ramble.

Robert spent the night scrubbing every surface in the apartment, doing laundry, cleaning out the refrigerator and restocking it with all her favorites from the twenty-four-hour bodega on the corner. He bought flowers for the kitchen island, flowers for the dining table, flowers for the living room, and flowers to take to her in the park. He washed the towels and sheets and made the bed. At five a.m., knowing her phone would be turned off, he called and left her a voicemail.

"I just want you to know that I'm so excited to see you I haven't slept at all tonight. There is so much I have to tell you, but for now I'll just say, I love you."

He lay in bed for an hour or two, staring at the ceiling. For a while he tried rehearsing the story he would tell Rebecca, but he quickly realized that the truth didn't require rehearsal, only courage. And so he only pictured an ideal summer day on Long Island—a day when the sun shimmered across the rooftops, a haze of laziness hung in the air, and, sitting in his room with the window open, Robbie could hear occasional screams of delight drifting in from the beach a half mile away. He wanted to bottle that moment, that last perfect, innocent second before his father knocked on the door and began the final chapter in the story that had returned to haunt him.

⌒〜〉

The crowd at story time at the St. Agnes Library was bigger than the previous Saturday.

"Apparently word got out someone was reading an exciting story," said Elaine.

Trying his best to focus on the narrative, when all he could think about was whether or not Rebecca would show up in the park, he gave a quick summary of the previous week's reading before launching into the second installment of his revised version of *The Tremendous Trio around the World*.

The children, who crowded every square foot of the room, sat silent and entranced, only occasionally trying to scoot closer to the storyteller as he read. Robert felt like a magician and when, at the cliff-hanging end of each chapter, he peered into the eager eyes of his listeners, he felt a sudden and unexpected pull, almost as strong as the force tugging him toward the Ramble. It was a yearning he couldn't wait to confess to Rebecca.

By the end of the hour, he had read another third of the book. "Would it be all right if I came back next week and read the end?" he said, meaning to address the question to Elaine, but her answer was drowned out in cries of "Yes!" from the children.

As much as he wanted to stay and chat with his listeners, answering their questions and accepting their thanks, Robert stuffed his manuscript into his messenger bag, grabbed the flowers he had brought for Rebecca, and dashed for the park. He would arrive a good thirty minutes early at their favorite spot in the Ramble, but he didn't care. He would wait.

XXXIX

NEW YORK CITY,
AFTER THE GERMANS MOVED TO YORKVILLE

A few weeks after the *Titanic* and Pickering Brothers both sank, Magda had taken a job with another firm in the Flatiron Building—a publisher of magazines and periodicals. She worked mostly on a publication called *Matrimonial Times*, which, in addition to a variety of general-interest articles, carried advertisements from readers, mostly men, seeking spouses. Magda watched as the other female employees of the magazine eventually succumbed to the enticement of these advertisements. She could not imagine stepping off a train somewhere in the Midwest to be greeted by a total stranger about to become her husband. So Magda worked on as the other girls in the office came and went.

When war came to Europe, she spent all her spare time volunteering for the Red Cross. She had seen a poster in Times Square proclaiming "You Can Help," and showing a woman about her age knitting, and so she knitted socks, sweaters, mufflers, helmets, and wristlets—anything to keep the boys warm in the miserable trenches of France and Belgium. She rolled bandages and even helped out in a Red Cross hospital, preparing meals for soldiers who had returned lacking limbs or large swatches of skin and, judging by the vacant look in their eyes, lacking something else as well. Whenever she spoke words of comfort to one of these broken boys, she always thought of Tom and Gene, wondering if they were in the war and saying a prayer for their safety.

As hard as she had tried to think of herself as nothing but an American, she felt the burden of her German heritage during the war. Whenever someone in the street or even at the Red Cross said something awful about Germans, or called them filthy Huns, she thought of the kindness of her mother, the wisdom of her father, and the sweetness of so many of their neighbors back on St. Mark's Place—qualities so incongruous with what so many people now said about Germans. The invectives hurt, but whenever anyone asked where "Mary Stone" was from, she answered only, "Twenty-Third Street."

War made the business of working at a marriage magazine seem frivolous, and so Magda had returned to Grace Institute where she had received her secretarial training. She took up a position teaching typing and related skills, mostly to poor immigrant women. It seemed a good way to repay New York for all it had given her.

Four years after the war ended, Magda began thinking about looking for a job back in publishing. So, she passed her job at Grace Institute on to one of her former pupils and was now flush with the promise of a new start.

On Magda's way to Tompkins Square Park to visit the *Slocum* memorial, she had walked past the Flatiron Building and glanced up at the window where her Pickering office had been. As she walked through Union Square Park and across town through what had once been Kleindeutschland, she thought about how awful Mr. Lipscomb's attitude toward women had been. Even so, she missed him. Walking past that building and then through the old neighborhood had put her in a rare nostalgic mood. In spite of her efforts to forget the worst parts of her past, memorials, like the one to the dead of the *General Slocum*, were designed to remind people of what might have been. How could Magda, standing here alone, not spare a thought for Mr. Lipscomb and Gene and Tom, as well as her mother and the twins.

"Good afternoon, miss," said a deep voice behind her. Magda started out of her reverie and turned to see a well-dressed middle-aged man standing behind her. "I couldn't help seeing you at the memorial. Did you lose someone on the *Slocum*?" His voice had the faintest trace of a German accent.

"Yes," said Magda. "My mother, my brother, and my sister."

"It was a dark day," said the man. "I myself was lucky. Though I lost many friends, my wife was at work that day at the Freie Bibliothek."

"I went there often," said Magda, smiling. "In fact, I went there that day. Mrs. Heidekamp gave me a copy of *The War of the Worlds*."

"My wife!" said the man. "Frederick Heidekamp, at your service." The man doffed his hat and gave Magda a slight bow.

"And is your wife . . ."

"We live now in Yorkville, where so many of us Germans moved after . . . after that day. She works in the public library there. You must come to see her."

"I would like that," said Magda. "I think I would like that very much."

"If you are not busy," said Mr. Heidekamp, "I am on my way home now. Perhaps you could join us for dinner."

Magda had not come to the *Slocum* memorial with the intention of reconnecting with her old community. And yet, one way to start the next chapter of her life would certainly be to return to the beginning and perhaps atone for the way she had denied her heritage. "As it happens," she said, "I am not busy at all."

"Excellent. Now, you must tell me your name."

Magda hesitated. For the last eighteen years she had been Mary Stone to everyone but Tom and Gene—and those few readers who knew her as Dexter Cornwall. And yet, if she really intended to make a fresh start, why not be honest? "I'm Magda," she said. "Magda Hertzenberger."

ꞈꞈ

Mrs. Heidekamp had aged over the eighteen years since Magda had seen her, but she would have recognized the librarian even if Mr. Heidekamp hadn't introduced her.

"My dear, this lady says she knows you from the days at the Freie Bibliothek. This is Magda Hertzenberger."

Mrs. Heidekamp's pale face turned even paler. "Magdalena?" she said in a trembling voice.

"That's right," said Magda.

"*Mein Gott*," said Mrs. Heidekamp, "but Magdalena Hertzenberger died eighteen years ago on the *General Slocum*."

"That was a mistake," said Magda, not willing to confess to Mrs. Heidekamp what she had confessed to Tom and Gene.

"*Oh, mein Gott!*" said Mrs. Heidekamp again, pulling a scarf over her hair. "You must come with me. Come now."

"What is it, *meine leibste?*" said Mr. Heidekamp.

"Come, come!" said Mrs. Heidekamp excitedly.

"I suppose we should follow," said Mr. Heidekamp to Magda with a shrug.

Ten minutes later, they stood on the landing outside a third-story walk-up apartment on Eighty-First Street. Mrs. Heidekamp pounded on the door and shouted, "Mrs. Müller, Mrs. Müller! Open up!"

The door opened to reveal a woman holding a large spoon in one hand and a dishtowel in the other. Her apron did not disguise the fact that she would be a mother sometime very soon.

"Yes, yes, what is it, Mrs. Heidekamp? Why all the shouting?"

"Mrs. Müller, you know this woman?"

"I do not think so," said Mrs. Müller, looking at Magda.

"You do not understand," said Mrs. Heidekamp, turning to Magda. "Before she was Mrs. Müller, this fine lady was Rosie Hertzenberger. Rosie, this is your sister, Magdalena! She has come home!"

NEW YORK CITY, UPPER EAST SIDE,
NINE DAYS AFTER D-DAY

The East River flowed steel gray and solid under a cloudy sky forty years to the day after it had taken Magda's mother and brother into its depths. Rosie liked to come to this bench, looking out across the water, every year on the anniversary. Magda, who owed so much to her sister, saw no harm in humoring her. And so they sat, silent and sober, gazing north toward Hell Gate, that particularly turbulent section of the river where the *General Slocum* had taken fire.

Rosie had not perished when she plunged into the fire with her twin brother, Henry. She had little memory of exactly what had happened, but somehow she had made it into the water and floated free of the wreckage. Someone—she never knew who—pulled her from the river onto one of the many craft that had come nearby to attempt rescues. Rosie's left shoulder and arm had been badly burned, a disfigurement she still bore.

She had been taken in by the Müller family, who had lost two daughters on the *Slocum*. Like so many of the survivors, the Müllers had eventually moved to Yorkville on the Upper East Side. For the Germans who had not perished on the *Slocum*, Kleindeutschland held too many memories. Willie Müller, four years older than Rosie, had helped nurse her back to health. Later he would tell her he had loved her from the first day she came to the Müller house, at eight years old; he waited ten years before he proposed marriage.

Like Magda, Rosie had learned not to let the past control her life, but on this one day a year, she came to the river to say a prayer for her mother and Henry.

"I used to pray for *you*," she said, squeezing Magda's hand, "and look how God has blessed me."

The two sisters watched as a group of young boys ran along the edge of the river, doubtless looking for U-boats. Since D-Day, a little over a week ago, there had been a surge of interest among the youngsters in the neighborhood in anything war-related. Magda could not know, of course, that at that very moment an officer in the Allied forces was taking courage from a letter she had written to him when he was a child.

It was a cool day for mid-June, and Rosie shivered when a breeze blew up across the river, carrying with it the smell of diesel fuel and the slightest hint of the sea.

"Sarah will be here in a few minutes," said Rosie. It hardly seemed possible that Magda's niece was now twenty-one years old and in her final year at Barnard College. Sarah had just taken a part-time summer job at the local public library. "I went to see her at work and she said she wanted to talk to you." Magda often had talks with her niece on the bench by the river. She loved Sarah as she imagined she would have loved a daughter, and had taken great joy, in years past, in using her skills as a storyteller to entertain the child. Now Sarah was a woman, and stories had become conversations and confessionals and advice. But Magda cherished the time no less.

"You go in," said Magda, patting Rosie gently on the knee. "I'll wait for her here."

Magda's miraculous sister, who had, so it seemed, come back from the dead, stood and took one last look at the river. Then, squeezing Magda's hand, she turned toward home. A few minutes later, Magda smiled at Sarah, who slid onto the bench beside her aunt.

"I love your smile, Aunt Magda," said Sarah. "It always makes me feel good after a bad day."

"Tell me about it," said Magda.

"The bad day? There's not much to tell," said Sarah with a sigh. "Just another boy gone that I knew when we were kids. A boy I used to play with in the park."

Magda reached out for her niece's hand and squeezed hard. War was cruel to everyone, but especially the young.

"How do you do it?" said Sarah. "How do you smile when there is so much . . . so much bad news in the world?"

Magda considered this carefully. It was true, she did find a way to smile even though boys she had known as children, boys she had taught to read in her classroom after she became a schoolteacher, died in Europe and Africa and on Pacific islands she had never heard of before. It wasn't that Magda didn't grieve for them, but that she had learned early that life was as full of loss as it was of wonder. She chose to focus her thoughts on the latter.

"When I need to smile," said Magda, "I just go to a place that always makes me happy."

"Where is that?"

"A place called Dreamland," said Magda.

"Will you take me there?" said Sarah, brushing away a tear.

"Of course," said Magda. "Close your eyes, take a deep breath, and smell the popcorn and the sea air and the sweet aroma of adventure."

XL

Robert saw Rebecca before she saw him. She too had come early. Rebecca had her back to him, and the low winter sun glowed in her hair. Beneath her overcoat she wore a sweater Robert had bought her at the Columbus Circle Christmas market before . . . everything. He longed to run up to her from behind and throw his arms around her, but he didn't dare. Robert couldn't see Rebecca's face; couldn't guess if her eyes and jaw were set like steel for confrontation, or soft with the promise of forgiveness. When she turned and saw him, he still couldn't tell.

"I brought you flowers," he said quietly. He was afraid to even touch her as he held out the bouquet.

"Thank you," said Rebecca, not yet meeting his eye.

"I'm glad you came."

"I almost didn't," said Rebecca. "I almost decided this is too hard. But I wanted to give you one more chance. I'm not saying you *deserve* it, but I wanted to give it to you."

"Could we find someplace warm to talk?" said Robert.

"We can talk here," said Rebecca.

"I have a story to tell you," said Robert. "A long story."

"I knew we were in trouble when you stopped telling me stories."

"That was because I needed to tell you this one and I didn't have the courage to do it."

"What changed?" said Rebecca, turning to walk down the path.

Robert followed, falling into step beside her, uncertain if he should reach for her hand. "Thanks to you, I finally took a long look at the stories that made me who I am. I've kept them hidden for so long that I'd almost forgotten what they meant to me. But all that's happened in the past week is a story for tomorrow—and it's a good one, I promise. Today I need to tell you an older story."

"I'm listening," said Rebecca, wrapping her arms around herself.

"Remember the day we met, when I told you about the first time I came to Central Park?"

"That story you made up to try to impress me," said Rebecca, with just the hint of a smile behind her words.

"You knew that was made up?"

"Of course," said Rebecca. "I mean, chasing the bus down Fifth Avenue? Come on."

"Well, my real first visit to Central Park was part of a long, complicated story," said Robert, and as they walked he told her everything—how he had nothing in common with his father until they found Pop Pop's books, how the Great Marvel books and Tom Swift and the Hardy Boys changed all that. He told her about the Tremendous Trio and the mysterious pages and the promise he had made to his father to find *The Last Adventure*. He told her how much he had loved reading with his father and how they had followed in the footsteps of the Tremendous Trio characters in their own adventures around Manhattan. He told her how he had begun to lose interest as a teenager and how his father had planned the trip to Niagara Falls to try to maintain a relationship with his son. He talked for an hour or more and Rebecca listened as they wandered through the Ramble, covering the same ground over and over until they emerged onto Bow Bridge.

"Can we stop here?" said Robert. "Can I tell you the rest here?"

"Your favorite spot," said Rebecca.

"Because of you," he said. "Because of the picture on my desk."

"It's still there?"

"Of course it's still there."

Rebecca turned to lean on the railing, looking out across the lake. Ice had crept across the surface from the shore, but the central part remained unfrozen, sparkling in the early afternoon sun. "Tell me," she said.

"Do you ever have one of those days you can play over and over again like a film and it never goes fuzzy? July 23, 1990, was that day for me. For a long time I kept that film from playing, but when people started asking me about my childhood and the books I read, it started back up again. I was fourteen and I was lying on the bed in my room doing absolutely nothing—not listening to music or reading or talking to friends on the phone. I remember the delicious nothingness of the morning. And then my dad knocked on the door and told me he had a surprise for me. And I can remember thinking, Great, he's ruining my whole day. I can still feel the weight of that thought."

"You were a teenager," said Rebecca.

"That's no excuse," said Robert. He clenched and unclenched his hands, willing himself to go on.

"Dad said we had to drive to wherever this surprise was, so we got in the car, but he wouldn't tell me where we were going. I kept the window down—partly to enjoy the fresh air but mostly because I thought the noise of the wind would keep my father from trying to talk to me. But he was so excited that day, he just talked louder.

"He said, 'You've probably wondered why I haven't been around a lot lately.' I ignored him but he just said it again. So I said, 'I hadn't noticed.' But of course I had noticed. God, I was so good at being an ass."

"You don't have to judge yourself," said Rebecca. "You said what you said. Most adolescents would have done the same."

"Anyway, Dad just plowed right on. He told me there was a good reason he had been gone and that I was going to love it and then he called me Robbie, so of course I said, 'My name is Robert.' I hate that I can remember with such clarity the ways I disrespected him.

"But he ignored my attitude and kept talking. He told me when we got back from Niagara that he realized I thought I was too old for the Tremendous Trio and all the others. So, he asked himself: What do fourteen-year-old boys think is cool? 'Not their dads, that's for sure,' he said. I didn't even give him the satisfaction of an eye roll. He started talking about how *The Tremendous Trio around the World* was always my favorite and how he knew that I still read it sometimes. 'If you're going to sneak around in the middle of the night reading a book, you have to put it back on the same spot on the shelf when you're finished or someone will notice,' he said. I remember blushing at having been so easily caught out, but I didn't say anything.

"And then he said he wanted to do something with me, something *for* me, that would remind us both of *The Tremendous Trio around the World* and all the fun we had reading it over the years. He said he wanted to find something that would be cool for a fourteen-year-old.

"And how did I respond? I said, 'Nobody says *cool* anymore, Dad.' Why did I have to act like that?"

"You're judging again," said Rebecca.

"Anyway, he just let that comment slide. I hadn't seen him so excited since the morning he walked into the kitchen and announced we were going to Niagara Falls. He spent the next hour recapping *The Tremendous Trio around the World*, and in spite of my teenage contrariness I got caught up in the story. I almost didn't notice when the car came to a stop in front of a green cinder-block building. This man in a black T-shirt and mirrored sunglasses stood by the glass doors, waving at my father, and I remember thinking, How does my boring dad know a guy with mirrored sunglasses?"

"You thought *that* was cool?" said Rebecca.

"Hey, it was 1990," said Robert.

"We got out of the car and I saw the words on the building and for a minute I stopped feeling like a teenager. First I thought, *How could my father even afford this?* And then I thought, *Is he going to take me with him?*

"The next thing I know, I'm walking with sunglasses man—who turned out to be named Jason—and Dad across a strip of tarmac, toward a Cessna 152 single-engine airplane. I know the make and model because Jason wouldn't stop talking about what a great little plane it was and how my father had been taking lessons with him for six months now.

"I remember exactly what my father said as we walked around the plane. 'I can't fly you around the world, son, but I can fly you around Long Island and maybe even a little farther.'"

Robert paused, fighting back the tears he knew would come anyway.

"And he did it," said Robert, sniffling. "He broke through to me, and I looked at him with this big grin on my face and said, 'Dad, this is so cool.'"

Robert took a deep breath and felt the emotion that had pushed him to the edge subsiding just enough that he could go on without his voice cracking.

"Dad knew from years of my insisting that we return to *The Tremendous Trio around the World* that I loved the idea of flying. I had never been in an airplane, and now he could fly me anywhere we wanted to go.

"I tried to play cool, like I hung out around airplanes all the time. I literally kicked the tires on the Cessna before I asked when I could go up, but I couldn't hide how excited I was."

"I like it when you don't hide your emotions," said Rebecca.

"Jason told me Dad was supposed to make his first solo flight that day. He said a solo was a pretty big deal."

Robert swallowed hard and stopped talking, hearing Rebecca's breathing next to him. He tried to focus on the far side of the lake. He didn't dare look at her. He had come this far. He had to finish.

"My dad wanted me to see him solo," said Robert. "He was so proud. He said he wanted me to watch him and then the two of us would fly up the coast fifty miles or so. Like that was a typical Saturday afternoon outing."

"Sounds wonderful," said Rebecca.

"That's what I thought. I mean, if my dad thought he could win me back by becoming a pilot, he was right. When that little plane bobbled up off the runway with my dad at the controls, my heart soared with it. I was with Dad, deep in the world of Dan and Alice and Frank, circling over the mountains of Borneo or gliding to a landing on the beaches of Polynesia. And then I heard Jason say, 'Shit.'"

Robert felt Rebecca's hand encircling his own and squeezing hard. He could feel strength radiating even through their gloves. Now he didn't even try to keep from crying.

"I don't know what Jason saw. Everything looked fine to me. Dad circled the little plane around and headed back toward the runway, but Jason was running toward the building, yelling 'Shit!' over and over. I found out later he was going to call emergency services, but he left me alone on the tarmac, watching that little Cessna and gradually realizing that with the nose that far down, the front of the plane would hit the runway before the wheels did. And so I watched my father die."

They stood in silence for a long minute, Rebecca still holding his hand.

"My god," said Rebecca, almost in a whisper. Robert finally turned to look at her and saw that she was crying, too. "Robert, why didn't you tell me?"

"That I killed my father?"

"You didn't kill him. It was an accident."

Robert couldn't speak for a long minute. He felt warm tears on his cheeks, he felt that familiar guilt, but he also felt an overwhelming sense of relief. He had told Rebecca and the world hadn't ended.

"My mother blamed me from the very beginning," he said. "She hardly spoke to me through my high school years and as soon as I left for college, she left for Florida. Our next-door neighbor called me one morning and said my mom was dumping boxes of my stuff out on the curb with the trash. Most of it I didn't care about, but I asked him if he would rescue the books for me. I'm surprised Mom didn't burn them. She hated those books with a fiery passion. She blamed them for Dad's death almost as much as she blamed me."

"It wasn't your fault," said Rebecca. "Oh God, I wish you had told me, and not just hidden yourself away from me."

"I know," said Robert. "But that's over now. This is who I am, Rebecca. I'm a damaged man who drove his own father to an act that took his life. And for a long time I buried all the pain and guilt that went with that. But everything I know about telling stories and about writing is so connected to my dad and the books we read together that when the novel took off and people started asking me about my influences and my past—the door to that horror burst open again and I was so distracted by trying to shove it closed, that I shut you out of my life."

"Jesus, Robert, you need some therapy. We can get you some help."

"I've tried it before but I never could manage to tell them anything . . . important. Turns out I'm supremely talented at denial."

"Obviously."

"But now that I've told you, it's no longer this . . . this monster in the closet that I'm afraid to let out. Now I think I *could* tell a therapist. The idea still scares me, but I think I could do it."

"It's not just someone to tell; it's someone who can help you figure out how to . . . how to live with that door open."

"Do you think maybe, at least the first time, you might come with me?"

Rebecca dropped his hand and stood silent for a moment. It was the first time in the conversation Robert had asked her for anything.

"I'm not going to lie, Robert, this has been hard for me. There have been times this past week when I've been ready to end this."

"God," said Robert, leaning back against the railing. He felt like he might be sick as he saw what a thread everything hung from. Rebecca was *everything*—he could live without his success, without the Tremendous Trio, without all the adventures and discoveries of the past week, but he wasn't at all sure he could live without her.

"I'm not saying I want to leave you," said Rebecca, laying a hand on his arm, "I'm just saying it's more complicated than you telling me what was wrong and me waltzing back into your life like nothing ever happened."

"I know," said Robert. "And I don't expect you to come back as if nothing has changed. So much has changed. For starters, I'm going to stop keeping secrets. I'll tell my story and share my pain. Even though that's no bargain, I'd like for you to be the one I share it with. I want to tell you *all* my stories."

"I just felt like I didn't know you anymore," said Rebecca.

"That's fair," said Robert. "But I want you to know me. Even if I have this giant scar, I'm still your Robert. The man who likes to drop everything to take a walk in the park with you and who goes out in the middle of the movie to get you extra popcorn and leaves notes for you in the steam on the bathroom mirror. And I'm the Robert who's scared to death this is the last time I will ever see you."

"If it makes you feel any better, there were also times this week when

I wanted to come running back to you. To be honest, I was a little tired of listening to Bradley bash on you."

"That does make me feel better," said Robert with a smile. He felt as if the blood had started to flow in his veins again.

They stood in silence for a minute, both leaning against the concrete railing of the bridge. A cloud glided across the sun and a gust of wind blew off the lake. Robert wondered if any of the passing walkers and joggers had the slightest idea that a momentous conversation was taking place. A young man zipped by on a bicycle, and he suddenly thought of the opening scene of the first Alice Gold book, which had happened on this very bridge.

"Maybe you're right," said Rebecca.

"Right about what?" said Robert.

"Maybe we should get some therapy together."

"I'm willing," said Robert. "If it means I have even the slightest chance of getting you back, I'm more than willing; I'm eager."

Rebecca smiled and reached once more for his hand. "You do."

"I do what?"

"You do have the slightest chance of getting me back."

"I want you to know that I'm sorry," said Robert, feeling tears welling up again. "I'm so sorry. I was acting like a child, and the irony is, I've grown up a lot this past week by becoming a child again—or at least by appreciating what it means to be a child. But I want you to know, if you do come back, whether it's for an hour or a day or the rest of our lives, I will try every minute to be the new and improved Robert—you know, all the features of the original plus some extra added bonuses."

"Bonuses like not being an ass?" said Rebecca, nudging him in the ribs with her elbow.

"How did you know?" said Robert. "That's the first improvement on the list."

"So, where do we go from here?" said Rebecca. "I'm not sure we can find a therapist open on a Saturday."

"Come home," said Robert. "At least for the afternoon. All I'm asking is that you be willing to take it one step at a time, and in return I promise to show you the real Robert Parrish, warts and all."

"Oh, I've seen the warts," said Rebecca with the faintest hint of a laugh accompanying her tears.

"We have fresh bagels," said Robert. "Sesame seed from Barney Greengrass, your favorite."

"Well," said Rebecca, sniffing and wiping a sleeve across her eyes, "if you went to all the trouble to get bagels." She took Robert's outstretched hand in hers, squeezing him tightly. Robert wanted to laugh out loud with relief, but he simply squeezed back. There would be time for laughter.

They walked in silence across the Bow Bridge and along the shore of the lake toward Strawberry Fields. When they had left the park and were standing at the corner of Seventy-Fourth Street waiting for the light to change, Robert turned to look at Rebecca and saw the steely set of her jaw, the look of resolution in her eyes. She was giving him a chance, and that was all he could ask, but he knew he had a lot of work ahead—not the work of his new novel or even the work of writing about Magda and Gene and Tom and the Tremendous Trio, but the important work. The work of daily trying to be the sort of man who, in some small way, deserved the love of the woman about to cross Central Park West. He decided to tell her at that moment, not in some attempt to score points or curry favor, but because he couldn't hold it in for another minute.

"So, here's a funny story," he said. He thought of the joy he had felt when reading to the children at the library, the life he had seen in their eyes. "But I'll start with the ending of this one. You remember how you're always saying you think you might want to have children and I'm always changing the subject?" The light turned green and they crossed into their future.

 C ᴑⳋ

It had been an exhausting day—at times wonderful, at times awkward, at times painful. One moment it felt like a first date and the next like Robert and Rebecca had been married for ten years. They had eaten bagels and talked about children and that had been lovely. He had told her more about his father and that had been tough. She had told him about places she had visited around the city while trying to "give Bradley some privacy"—from Grant's Tomb in Morningside Heights to Castle Clinton in Battery Park. During Rebecca's entire narrative Robert had wanted to throw his arms around her, but they stayed on opposite ends of the sofa, not quite ready for intimacy yet. Robert had told her about his adventures of the past week, about Sarah Thomas and the way he had discovered to keep his promise to his father. They had ordered delivery from a Turkish restaurant around the corner, and he had read her a few chapters of his revised version of *The Tremendous Trio around the World*. Then, with no emotional energy left for talking, they watched *His Girl Friday* on TCM. At times, they even laughed.

Robert had told her if she would stay the night he would sleep on the sofa. They both thought it best for the time being.

"Just for now," said Rebecca. "I hope."

He gave her a chaste kiss good night and quietly closed the door to the bedroom, but instead of curling up in the living room, he turned on the light in his office. He wouldn't write for long, he told himself, but today was a day for beginnings. He flicked on his computer and opened a new file. Starting a new book was both exciting and intimidating, but Robert was ready. He would begin work on the *Last Adventure of the Tremendous Trio* soon, but tonight he wanted to start the novel about Magda and Tom and Gene. He wanted to imagine what had happened to Magda on the *Slocum* and why she and Gene and Tom had stopped writing together. He wanted to imagine the stories of the mysterious woman under the Childs menu and the picture of Magda dressed as a man. If he couldn't find out what had happened to Tom and Gene, then he wanted to imagine that, too. He wanted to imagine how three young people had created the world of the Tremendous Trio, and why *The Last Adventure* had never been finished, and why an amusement park called Dreamland had seemed so important to them. He wanted to imagine it all.

There were so many ways he could begin—with a baseball game or a day in Central Park; with the Flatiron Building or Niagara Falls; even with a young boy and his father sitting on the porch in Rockaway Beach, sharing a story. For now, though, he would begin with the ending.

On those rare occasions when Magda thought of the past, she didn't recall the flames and the screams and the rows of bodies; she came here—to these mementos gathered in an old shoebox, souvenirs not of tragedy but of happiness.

XLI

GAZING SOUTH, ACROSS THE YEARS

After Rosie left, Magda shifted her body so that she looked not north toward the real Hell Gate, but toward another Hell Gate—the whirlpool ride at Dreamland that had given her the opportunity to hold on so tightly to Tom and Gene, the same ride where the fire that destroyed Dreamland had begun. Unlike her sister, she had no interest in dredging up memories of the *Slocum*, not even once a year. But Magda did allow herself this indulgence as she waited for Sarah; she did sit for a few minutes and remember that night at Coney Island.

She closed her eyes and saw the lights of Dreamland as crisp and clear as though they were still spread out below her. She imagined a scene that had flitted into her girlish head all those years ago on the night before Dreamland, the night before her dream of a happy life with Gene ended.

On a pier, jutting out over the black water from Dreamland, stood the largest ballroom in America. In her daydream, Magda felt the cool of the evening as Gene escorted her across the main courtyard. Seeing her shiver, he slipped an arm around her and pulled her close and in another moment, they stepped into the warmth of the ballroom where hundreds of couples spun around the floor to the tune of a waltz played by an orchestra on a balcony at the far end of the massive space. The dance floor was lined with decorative arches below and overlooked by balconies above. On the ceiling, a thousand tiny light bulbs glittered, shining off the slicked-back hair of the men as they glided their partners around the floor. The song ended, and Magda stepped into Gene's arms as the band began their signature tune, "The Dreamland Waltz."

Gene did not dance like a scientist; he danced like an artist, like a man who had attended the swankiest clubs with men like Stanford White. With a grace Magda had always suspected lay beneath his guarded exterior, he swept her across the floor, weaving through the other couples as if there weren't even there. Magda did her best to keep up, feeling she was on yet another thrill ride as they swirled around the floor and darted through openings in the crowd. She laughed with the delight of it all and Gene laughed back. In that moment, Magda felt so giddy with happiness that she thought she might faint. This was the dream she allowed herself once a year—not the nightmare that her sister remembered on this day, but the joy of what never happened.

Gene and Tom would always be with her. They had given her the strength to do so much; they had given her the courage to be an independent woman and the wisdom to cherish every moment of life. Though Magda had gone home alone on that night so many years ago, in her daydream she stood flanked by her best friends, holding hands and watching the magical glow of Dreamland and all the rest of Coney Island from the vantage point of the sea as the ferry pulled away. They stood at the rail and as the sounds of music and shouts of glee and the splashing of Shoot the Chutes faded slowly into the night, they watched the unnatural beauty of those shining lights until the boat rounded Norton Point and Dreamland became nothing more than an aura in the east, wiping all trace of stars from the sky.

THE END

AUTHOR'S NOTE

Most of the historical events in this novel actually happened and are depicted as first reported at the time, including the arrival of the SS *Hammonia* in New York Harbor on October 29, 1886, the 1899 newsboys' strike, the celebration of New Year's Eve 1899, the 1906 San Francisco earthquake, the *General Slocum* disaster, the murder of Stanford White, Camille Saint-Saëns's performance at Carnegie Hall, the flight of Wilbur Wright up the Hudson, the opening of the New York Public Library, the Dreamland fire and the death of Black Prince, the 1911 *Ziegfeld Follies*, the 1911 heat wave, the sinking of the *Titanic*, and the homemade American flag flying over Turckheim in 1945. The stories that Robert finds published during the first week of October 1906 all appeared in the New York papers that week. The 1906 Christmas window displays at Siegel's showed a panorama of Coney Island, just as described in the text.

While in some cases fictional dialogue has been attributed to them, the locations and actions of the following historical figures was, in broad terms, as depicted in the text: Grover Cleveland, John Singer Sargent, Edwin Booth, Enrico Caruso (whose spat with Olive Fremstad was as recorded here), Stanford White, Evelyn Nesbit, Harry Thaw, Nikola Tesla, Samuel Clemens, Mademoiselle de Tiers, the Florenz Troupe, Murray Hall, George M. Cohan, Tiny Tim the newsboy, Kid Blink (whose speech rendered by Tom is exactly as reported in the papers), Emma Stebbins, Maude Raymond, DeWolf Hopper, Eltinge, Cy Seymour (whose eleventh-inning home run beat the Pirates on August 11, 1906), Marie Dressler, Camille Saint-Saëns, and William Howard Taft. I have, perhaps, been a bit more liberal with William Randolph Hearst, but I do not believe he, in the pages of this book, acts wholly out of character.

Edward Stratemeyer and his syndicate remain one of the great success stories in American publishing. All the books and magazines mentioned in the text (except those published by the fictional Pickering Brothers and the novel *Looking Forward*) are real.

Many of the buildings and sites mentioned in the historical portions of the text can still be found in New York City. Among my favorites are the statue of Liberty Enlightening the World, Castle Garden (later the New York Aquarium and now Castle Clinton National Monument), the Freie Bibliothek (the city's first free library and now the Ottendorfer branch of the New York Public Library), the *General Slocum* memorial, the Astor Library (now the Public Theatre), Trinity Church, the Flatiron Building, the New Amsterdam Theatre (though the Roof Garden is long gone), Brentano's bookstore on Fifth Avenue (no longer a bookstore but still there), Carnegie Hall, Bethesda Terrace and Fountain, the Metropolitan Museum of Art, the American Museum of Natural History, the St. Agnes and Muhlenberg Branches of New York Public Library, and, of course, the main branch of that library. You can still eat at Delmonico's, though not at the midtown location.

Other New York sites and institutions have vanished long ago, and we can only dream of the second Madison Square Garden with its Moorish tower and rooftop theater, St. Nicholas Church at Forty-Ninth Street and Fifth Avenue, Tesla's lab at Wardenclyffe, Columbia Hall (a.k.a. Paresis Hall), Childs Restaurant (of which there were several in the city), the bookstores of Twenty-Third Street including Dutton's and Putnam's, the Polo Grounds, Tony Pastor's vaudeville theater, the Jardin du Paris (atop the New York Theatre) at Broadway and Forty-Fourth Street, and the Iron Steamboat Company. North Brother Island is now a wildlife sanctuary and generally off-limits to visitors, but the ruins of its hospital buildings remain. The Dreamland amusement park was completely destroyed in the fire of 1911. It was never rebuilt.

Both the surnames and given names of all the German characters in this novel are taken from the list of those lost in the *Slocum* disaster. May they rest in peace.

ACKNOWLEDGMENTS

I am indebted to scores, if not hundreds, of sources, but in particular to the New York newspapers archived by the Library of Congress on the website Chronicling America. These papers provided not only detailed firsthand accounts (and in some cases the only accounts) of events in New York City, but sometimes bits of the actual prose I used in my own descriptions. Details such as the little boy climbing the flagpole of the *General Slocum*, President Taft sneaking up the front stairs of the library, or the death of Black Prince rarely make it into the history books, but newspaper accounts are filled with such details and provide the novelist and historian alike a unique look into the past. Digitized materials from the New York Public Library and New-York Historical Society, including menus, photographs, maps, and city directories, also proved invaluable.

I could not have created Gene without the help of George Chauncey's *Gay New York: Gender, Urban Culture, and the Making of the Gay Male World, 1890–1940*. Other books that proved especially useful included *A Crack in the Edge of the World: America and the Great California Earthquake of 1906* by Simon Winchester, *New York, Year by Year: A Chronology of the Great Metropolis* by Jeffrey A. Kroessler, and *The Gilded Age in New York, 1870–1910* by Esther Crain. The excerpt from *The Outlook* magazine is reprinted verbatim.

I grew up on the 1960s versions of the Hardy Boys books, and so I, like so many others, must thank Edward Stratemeyer for producing the books that first got me excited about reading. In researching this book, I read, or reread, many of the books mentioned in the text, particularly the Great Marvel series by Roy Rockwood (a.k.a. Howard Garis) and works by Jules Verne and H. G. Wells.

Descriptions of Dreamland, its various attractions, and the fire that spelled its doom came from newspaper accounts and from *Coney Island: Visions of an American Dreamland, 1861–2008* by Robin Jaffee Frank, et al; the Heart of Coney Island website; and from a careful examination of postcards and photographs of Dreamland.

Special thanks are due to Anna Worrall who believed in this novel from the beginning and shepherded it through many rewrites with patience and kindness. Thanks to Madeline Hopkins for her expert and careful editing, to Josh Gross for his meticulous copy editing, to Sean Thomas for his beautiful design, to all the rest of the team at Blackstone, to my early readers Janice Lovett and Stephanie Lovett, and to Jimmy Lovett, who offered judicious advice especially for the binding scene. The aforementioned Lovetts and Jordan Xu provide the love and support without which the life of a writer is impossible.

To the many readers, book clubs, librarians, and booksellers who have supported my work over the years, and especially to the staff and volunteers of Bookmarks, thank you for waiting for this book. I hope you enjoy it.